WHAT HAPPENED
THAT
NIGHT

A NOVEL

SANDRA BLOCK

sourcebooks
landmark

Published by Sourcebooks Landmark, an imprint of Sourcebooks, Inc.
P.O. Box 4410, Naperville, Illinois 60567-4410
(630) 961-3900
Fax: (630) 961-2168
sourcebooks.com

Library of Congress Cataloging-in-Publication Data

Names: Block, Sandra, author.
Title: What happened that night / Sandra Block.
Description: Naperville, Illinois : Sourcebooks Landmark, [2018]
Identifiers: LCCN 2017041155 | (trade pbk. : alk. paper)
Subjects: | GSAFD: Suspense fiction.
Classification: LCC PS3602.L64285 W48 2018 | DDC 813/.6--dc23 LC record
available at https://lccn.loc.gov/2017041155

Printed and bound in Canada.
MBP 10 9 8 7 6 5 4 3 2 1

PRAISE FOR
WHAT HAPPENED THAT NIGHT

"Sandra Block's *What Happened That Night* is an unflinching exploration of the fine line between justice and revenge. Block expertly compels readers to examine a diverse number of issues through the eyes of Dahlia and James, who are bound together by personal tragedy, heartache, and the search for justice. *What Happened That Night* is a visceral thrill that will keep you reading late into the night. Perfect for book clubs."

—Heather Gudenkauf, *New York Times* bestselling author
of *The Weight of Silence* and *Not a Sound*

"I will read anything Block writes. You should too."

—Lisa Scottoline, *New York Times* bestselling author

"Block expertly navigates the emotional landscape of trauma survivors in this deeply satisfying thriller. What begins as a quest for revenge becomes so much more as Dahlia fights to uncover the truth and reclaim her life after a brutal attack. Block handles the weighty subject matter with a deftness I've come to expect from her work—she never disappoints."

—Laura McHugh, award-winning author
of *The Weight of Blood* and *Arrowood*

ALSO BY SANDRA BLOCK

Little Black Lies

The Secret Room

The Girl Without a Name

To my roommates,
Who have always been there for me.

PROLOGUE

I t sucks me in.

It is a freak of nature. An undertow, a vortex, a tornado, all in one.

I can't fight it. The pull is too strong and my limbs bend to it. Like a rag doll, I fall down backward. My elbow hits the floor, and I start shaking. I can't stop. My leg bangs against a table. My head is turning side to side, my neck wrenched, aching.

Oh my God, I think she's having a seizure.

Hey…hey…are you okay?

My watch is hitting against the tile in time with my head. Last time I broke my watch, and I can't afford a new one. But I can't stop my arm from smacking the floor.

Should I get a spoon or something?

No, you're not supposed to do that. Just get her away from anything sharp.

Hands pull me away from the table. The hem of my shirt gets caught under someone's shoe and rips. Now my back is lifting up. My pelvis, rising and falling like my body has been possessed. I am possessed. My eyes are clenched shut, and someone tries to pry them open.

What should we do?

I'm calling 911.

I can hear myself yelling no. It comes out as a moan. My head is shaking back and forth, hard, as if it might rip off my neck. I don't want to go to the hospital. Needles, doctors, questions. EEGs, EKGs, MRIs.

Pills, fake sleep. Questions.

They call 911. Burly EMTs barge into the room, clipboards in hand. A gurney is sprung up beside me.

Does she have a history of seizures?

Is she on any medications?

Ma'am, can you hear us? Ma'am.

Questions, more questions. I have no answers. I cannot speak.

Dahlia.

The voice breaks through the fog, strong and commanding. I recognize the voice with utter relief. It's Eli's voice.

Thank God, Eli is here.

He bends down, his body shadowing the overhead light. My knee bounces against the floor a few more times, then stops. Like magic, I feel the spell lifting.

The vortex unwinding.

A deathly silence fills the room. People standing around me, their breathing audible. My sore body, ripped shirt, bruised elbows, Eli holding my hand. The stillness after the tornado.

I open my eyes.

CHAPTER ONE

DAHLIA

As with any other support group, the cookies are stale.
I should know. I've been to my share.

In this particular one, the coyly named S.O.S., for Survivors of Suicide, the punch is also overly sweet. You might wonder who would come to such a group, since the most successful members are inherently absent. But here, *survivors* stands for the people they left behind, or the lucky ones who tried but didn't hit the six-foot-under mark.

People like me.

Or my best friend, Eli, who is sitting beside me. I haven't been to S.O.S. for a while, which is a good thing, of course. I haven't felt the need.

But today is my anniversary, so I'm here. And Eli is here for moral support.

Fred is the leader of the group. He favors bulky madras shirts and torn khakis, a scruffy almost-beard and thick glasses that are always smudged. I haven't figured out if he's a millionaire or near the poverty line. Fred formed S.O.S. twenty-five years ago after his brother's suicide. His brother never left a note, and Fred never found out why. This is his life's mystery, which is why he comes back every week. To make the not knowing a little easier.

I know why I tried. Eli knows why he tried. No mysteries there. Just life's boringly familiar tragedies, nearly claiming another soul.

"Would you like to go next?" Fred asks the young man across from me. He looks a tad younger than me, a couple years out of college. Muscular, strong cheekbones, mixed something.

Japanese or Korean, maybe. He probably graduated from somewhere around here, pick a college...MIT, Northeastern, Boston University. Or Harvard, like me. If I had bothered to graduate.

The young man clears his throat. "I'm James."

The room says "Hi, James," a response stolen right out of the AA handbook. (Yes, I've been to that one too, but not for me.) I can see Eli perk up. James doesn't let off any gay vibe that I can tell, though Eli's gaydar is better than mine.

"I'm here for my sister, Ramona. She killed herself a year ago." His hands are laced together and he is looking at them. Long, tapering fingers. "Jumped off a bridge," he went on, as if someone had asked him. And he was probably used to that. Bystanders are ghoulish that way; they always want to know the how.

There is a long pause, which the group waits out.

"Do you want to say any more?" Fred asks.

James shakes his head. His face gets flushed, but his eyes do not fill. I've become almost scientific at determining when people are about to cry. There are so many tells. The lip tremble, the jaw clench, the eyes reddening. And for James, the blush. Hang around S.O.S. long enough, and it becomes an art.

"Thank you, James," Fred says, and like robots, the group members repeat this. Then they move on to the next member. I've already said my piece, as has Eli, and I'm getting ready to call it a night. But the circle hasn't finished its tale. We have three more members to go.

Luckily, the last of the bunch turn out to be taciturn as well. Sometimes you get someone who goes on and on. Not the new ones; they're too stunned to say much. Usually it's the borderline personalities, who are always leaning over the edge, literally and figuratively. Then, a week comes around when they don't show up, followed by murmurs about how something was in the paper, etc. And I feel guilty as hell for wishing they would just shut up already during their turn when twenty minutes had gone by. But at the same time, I have to admit, I feel an odd sense of relief for them. I would never voice this in the group, of course; it's anathema to S.O.S. But it's a tough world out there. Some people just aren't cut out for it.

Fred calls the meeting to a close with a spiritual quote that doesn't mention any particular God, and metal chairs squeak as the circle stands up.

"You want to go for a drink or something?" Eli asks. Drink means soda for me, something stronger for him. I don't drink; Eli drinks too much. "We could hit a club."

"Nah. Not tonight. I've got a date with a book."

"Lame."

"'Tis," I agree.

"All right," he says. "Let me run to the bathroom, then we'll go."

He lives two floors above me, so we came together and we'll leave together. As he walks off, a few women turn their heads, though they know from his spiel that it's not in the cards. Still, it's hard not to turn your head. Eli is soap-opera-star cute. Perfectly sculptured blond hair, blue eyes, and a gym-built body. The kind of guy where you say "He's got to be gay" because he's so good-looking, and it turns out you're right. I wander toward the stale-cookie table for something to do.

James walks over as well and reaches for a peanut butter cookie. Biting into it, he makes a face.

"Stale," I confirm.

He nods, then quickly swallows and surveys the tray again. "How about the oatmeal?"

"Not any better."

"Huh," he says, then adjusts his napkin. "I know you, by the way."

"You do?" I search my memory, but I've never been good with faces.

"Miller and Stein?"

"Yeah," I say, still trying to place him. Not a secretary. Maybe a new lawyer?

"I'm in IT. I debugged your computer last year."

"Oh." I have a vague recollection of this. I would ask how he remembers me, but I've got purple hair (or was it pink then?), three nose rings, and an arm full of tattoos. So I'm memorable, for a paralegal anyway. We stand awkwardly for a moment, the cookies too stale to munch on as an excuse. "Sorry about your sister," I say.

He nods. "Sorry about you." His dark eyes meet mine just a second, then they fall away.

Out of the corner of my eye, I see Eli coming over. "Hey," he says, wiping his just-washed hands on his red Bermudas.

"Hey," I answer back and make introductions, though James has already been introduced in the meeting. Eli assesses him, likely judging him as a potential suitor for me—not for him. I'm sure he will come up wanting, somehow. Eli finds something wrong with most of my potential suitors, for whatever reason. Protective, he would say. Overprotective, I would say.

"Ready to go?" Eli asks.

Eli is waiting behind me in the doorway, whistling. I twist open the third bolt lock, then yank open the door, which sticks as usual. I always tell him he doesn't need to stop at my doorway. He always does anyway. It's our thing, I guess.

"You sure you don't want to come out?" he asks. "Shakers. You could meet a nice gay man."

"I already have a nice gay man," I say, patting his shoulder.

He smiles, then takes a buzzing phone out of his pocket. "What's up?" He gives me a head bob goodbye, heading to the stairwell. "I don't know. I figured I'll probably take the T," he says, his voice fading as the door closes behind him.

As I walk in, Simone skulks out from behind my bedroom door. She patiently accepts a head rub, then skulks off again. The apartment is small and feels even smaller on these hot and sticky nights, especially when the A/C is on the fritz. I venture into my room, which is essentially a smaller box inside of a box, kick off my flip-flops, and lie down on the bed. Glancing through my phone, I find nothing new. No urgent emails or notifications. No likes or loves on my social media pleas for self-validation.

The phone screen throws a faint glow into the room, the date beaming at the top of the screen. September 30.

My unhappy anniversary.

Jumping up off the bed, I open the window to an anemic breeze. The cicadas are a wall of buzzing. It's fall, but it doesn't feel like it. I used to love the autumn. A season of promise, new beginnings. My mom would take me to buy a new dress for Rosh Hashanah, the Jewish New Year, which always felt like the *real* new year to me. Not the one dolled up with fireworks, glittering balls, and morning television show best-of lists. A day with cold days behind and ahead of it.

Fall is literal change, signaled by the breakdown of chlorophyll and a bite in the air. Though that was in Chicago, where I'm from. In Boston, September is more an extension of summer. The days are long and muggy. Back in college, the days would turn into muggy nights full of revelers, in clusters outside of the dorms, afraid of missing something cosmically important at 3:00 a.m. Groups of students would buzz around Harvard Yard like some kind of sociological experiment, the smell of pollen, beer, and sweat in the air.

Turning away from the window, I open the bureau drawer, which squeaks, and throw on a nightshirt. My cell phone rings on my bed, and I glance at the screen. My mom again. Last time I let it go to voicemail, so this time I answer.

"Hi, Mom."

"Oh, Dahlia." Her voice registers relief, and I feel guilty that I didn't pick up before. "How are you?"

"Okay," I answer. As I lean out the window, an ambulance flashes down the street.

"How was your day?"

"Fine," I say. "I ended up taking off from work."

There is a pause. "Are you sick?"

"No, just…" I don't finish the statement. "Hey, guess what? Sylvia's getting married," I say with forced enthusiasm. Sylvia is my "friend" from work. It's a spot of normalcy I know my mom would appreciate.

"Oh, that's wonderful. Good for her." She pauses. "And how's Eli?"

"Fine. Same old, same old."

"Did you do anything fun tonight?" she asks, likely hoping I had a date lined up.

"Not really." I sit back down on the bed. "I went to S.O.S."

"Oh." The word is charged with unease. "Are you feeling... I mean... You're not..."

"No, I'm not. Sometimes I just like going anyway." On my anniversary, I don't say. Since we're both dancing around the subject.

"That's good," she says with warmth. "You should go, when you feel that way."

We wade through some more stilted conversation until I finally beg off, yawning, and she lets me go. I lie down on the bed again, the springs creaking. My book sits beside me on the nightstand. But I don't have the energy to open the pages, let alone allow the words inside my head. So I just lie there, listening to the grinding vibration of the cicadas.

Maybe I should have gone to Shakers after all, sat there like a bump on a log sipping Dr Pepper while Eli got sloppily sentimental and ended up leaving with some guy.

So maybe I shouldn't have gone to Shakers.

The phone rings again, and I see it's Shoshana, my sister. Another phone call for my anniversary, which she won't mention. Though I suppose I should answer, if only to ask about her baby-to-be. The only one who hasn't called me yet is Daisy. But she will, eventually. I turn the ringer off, and the phone eventually stops buzzing. Simone jumps onto the bed and sits, gray and regal as a small statue. Lying down next to her, I stare at the calendar on the wall.

The square date stands out like a bruise.

I close my eyes. Soon enough, I will be asleep. Finally, this dreadful day will be over. Simone meows at something, then settles herself in the crook of my knees. My hand snakes under my pillow until I feel it. I hold on to it, like a lover's hand.

The cool, textured grip of my Beretta.

And I finally allow myself to relax.

CHAPTER TWO

JAMES

Sitting on the comfy Starbucks chair, I think about her.

The air-conditioning hums beside me, a soothing white noise that is calming and, at the same time, incredibly productive, shooting the air through a compressor and then a condenser and then right back out again.

I didn't expect to see her, but there she was.

I wasn't even going to go. My therapist recommended it. I hate saying the word *therapist* because it sounds like I'm crazy or weak, and I'm not either. But Jamal is nice. He doesn't judge me. He says I see things too black-and-white, and he's probably right. Part of my disorder, though he doesn't like to call it that. *Differentness* is what he calls it. When I told him that's not really a word, he said he knew that. I guess that's just me being black-and-white again. But I don't need a made-up word for it. I'd rather just call it what it is.

Asperger's syndrome.

My father doesn't believe in it though. He called it the flavor-of-the-month diagnosis. My mom just wants me to be happy, however I am. (Which is what she wanted for Ramona, unlike my father. My father only ever cared about Rob anyway.)

Asperger's doesn't explain everything, but it does explain a lot.

Like why they used to call me Robot Man in high school. And why girls don't like me. Why I don't like sarcastic jokes that everyone else thinks are funny but are actually just mean, and why I get along with the IT guys who don't make those jokes. Why I suck at English but am good at math and programming. It explains me, pretty much.

A fly buzzes by my ear for a second, then darts up to the ceiling light. I hate flies, though I know that's not logical. We've learned a ton from the drosophila and they don't mean to upset me, but still they're dirty and loud. I grab a crumpled newspaper from the next table and the fly zooms away to hide. I hate flies, but that doesn't mean they're dumb.

Sitting back down, I take a sip of my drink. It's pumpkin latte something, which I like because it doesn't taste like coffee. I hate coffee. But I like Starbucks, because it's quiet and calm, and no matter which location you go to, they all look the same. And I couldn't stand going home right away. I was buzzing too much, after seeing her.

I usually don't go to these things, but Jamal said it might help me to see other people dealing with this. *This* being suicide. He said there are lots of people like me, grieving over the death of someone we loved but who didn't love themselves. He gave me a flyer for the group last time I was there. S.O.S.

Jamal has given me flyers before. I have a stack of them for Asperger's support groups and autism this and that, but I've never gone. But for whatever reason, I went to S.O.S. I came in late and everyone looked at me. The room was poorly air-conditioned and smelled bad. Then there were the fold-up metal chairs, which I hate.

The leader was nice enough. His glasses were dirty, which kept distracting me. But everyone told their stories. And Jamal was right—it did help. Other people were feeling just as shitty as I do, which made me feel better, in a weird, probably-not-very-nice way.

When it came to me, I clammed up. I always do that. Everyone was looking at me, and I said what I had to say. I told them about Ramona, how she jumped off the bridge. In my opinion, they should just shut that damn bridge down, but I know that's not logical. Things need transport.

I didn't expect much from the meeting, but then, I saw her.

I don't believe in fate, except maybe some computer god up there writing out the world with code. Code that is full of glitches but also so amazing that no one understands it. So when these things happen, people just call it fate.

Either way, she was there.

Dahlia, the girl from my work. The one I've always wondered about, with the purple hair and tattoos. Who's smart and doesn't take shit from anyone, but manages to be polite about it so she never gets in trouble or called into meetings or anything. She reminds me of Ramona, in a weird way. There is something raw but gentle about her too.

I remember the day I worked on her computer. She smelled like freesia. I thought it was weird, that a dahlia should smell like freesia. I know it was freesia, because I had a friend in college who always wore Bath & Body Works's freesia and I'm good with smells. I always get them right in those science museum thingies, where you smell the boxes. Sometimes it's not such a good thing though. For instance, it annoys everyone how I won't go to a particular restaurant or the zoo because of the smell. I have a strong sense of smell, also part of Asperger's, so it's not my fault. But the point is she smelled really good, and I noticed her. I started watching out for her without meaning to. She would go to the break room with her friend Sylvia, who's loud and obnoxious and not at all like Dahlia. I started noticing what Dahlia was wearing (usually black or dark purple), the sound of her voice, and how carefully she spoke, with long words but not trying to sound smart. I was nervous around her, like my cortisol levels were jacked up. I noticed her. And I saw how Connor, the lawyer guy whose wife died, noticed her too.

Dahlia never seemed to notice us back though. Me or Connor.

The fly zaps right by my ear this time, then starts scaling the wall, and I roll up the newspaper, reach out for a lightning quick swipe, and nail it. I scoop the crushed body into the tube and get up to toss the whole thing in the garbage, feeling bad about killing the poor thing and not recycling at the same time. I don't like to kill things, of course. But as I said, I hate flies.

The air conditioner revs up again as I sit back down. Crossing my arms in the cold air, I see her face in my mind. Dahlia always looked right through me, like everyone else does. It's not her fault, necessarily. I don't know if it's the half-Japanese thing or the Asperger's thing, or maybe neither. No one seems to notice me.

But this time, she looked right at me, so hard that it hurt and I had to look away. She saw me. She said she was sorry about Ramona.

I don't know why Dahlia tried to kill herself, and I'm sorry for whatever happened to her, but it doesn't matter. I like her. She probably doesn't like me, but it seemed like maybe she did, the way she was looking at me. I've gotten this type of thing wrong, very wrong, before.

But I like her, that's all.

And the way she looked at me, I think maybe she might like me too.

CHAPTER THREE

Five Years Ago

*D*aisy hands me the trippy, pink plastic bong, which bubbles pleasantly in my hands. The sweet taste expands in my mouth and lungs. When I feel the softness trickle into my brain, I let my breath out.

"*Good, huh?*" Daisy asks.

I nod, still savoring the taste. I am sprawled out on the pink papasan in the common room. My eyes are bombarded with shades of pink. Daisy decorated the room, and she likes pink. Bubble-gum, hot, pastel, and yes, even Dahlia pink.

Daisy and I have been inseparable since we were roommates in freshman year. Dahlia and Daisy, D and D, the flower girls…we have quite a few nicknames. Hard to believe it's September of our senior year already.

"*How about this?*" *Daisy holds up a pair of white pants in one hand and red in another.*

"*Red.*"

"*That's what I thought.*" *She takes the bong.* "*Another hit?*"

I shake my head. I don't know what mix she has, but it's heavy. The red pants are swirling.

"*Okay, let's do you now,*" *she says.*

"*I'm not going,*" *I say, which is what I always say.*

"*You are too going, introvert-girl.*"

"*There's nothing wrong with being an introvert. I like being an introvert.*"

Daisy is beautiful, in an innocent, blond way. Boys swarm around her. I am her counterpoint. Black hair, pale-white skin, black eyes. I'm the

Disney princess's sidekick, but not the princess. Only the hearty, intrepid boys stick around for me.

"Come on," she says, and I feel myself being dragged from the calm peace of my papasan.

"Okay, okay," I say. The words come out echoey.

She holds up a low-cut, white cotton shirt and a frilly one. "Slutty Girl or Pretty Girl?"

"Pretty Girl," I say. I don't mention there's a coffee stain on Slutty Girl anyway.

"Fine," she says. "But you need the black mini, then."

"Done," I say, grabbing the skirt from her.

I go to my room, which has no pink whatsoever, to put on my clothes, my high mellowing out to a blurry, fuzzy, happy feeling. I check myself in the full-length mirror on the door and decide on a short, black heel. I smooth out the skirt, straighten the frill on the neck.

Pretty Girl, *I think, admiring myself.*

CHAPTER FOUR

DAHLIA

The next day is better. It always is.

Everything goes smoothly. No paper jams in the printer. No asshole clients on the phone. Sylvia's in a good mood. The coffee is perfect. One of those excellently boring days.

"Hey, where were you last night?" Sylvia asks. "I called you."

"Yeah, I went out."

"Where?"

"Shakers," I lie. She's never heard of it anyway, so it doesn't register as a gay bar.

"I wanted to introduce you to Travis, remember? Beau thinks you guys would be great together." Sylvia has a thick Maine accent. The first time I heard it, I thought she was putting it on as a joke. She wasn't. "Anyway," she says, then goes on about Travis, her fiancé's brother.

Her fiancé is nice enough but dumb as nails, and I got a glimpse of Travis with that same thick-necked, square-jawed look. They're both into professional wrestling, which tells me I don't need to suffer through a first date to know we're not a match made in heaven. Sylvia prattles on, and I start highlighting a document for Connor, my boss. I pick purple for Connor today. He doesn't care what color highlighter I use, whereas his associate, Tabitha, favors orange. So I highlight hers in orange. I am nothing but eager to please.

"He said he's not usually into the goth type, but he thought you were cute."

"Who?" I ask.

"Travis," she says, a touch annoyed.

"Oh yeah, right." The goth type. I guess that was supposed to be a compliment. "Eli was going through a tough time. So I was hanging out with him."

Sylvia sniffs at this. "You're never going to find someone if you just hang out with Eli all the time."

As if that's my ultimate goal in life, finding someone. A princess waiting to be rescued. Though I admit, I don't even know what my goal in life is. So I suppose that's as good a one as any. "I'm getting some coffee, you want any?" I ask.

"No, but get me a jelly donut if they have any." She stabs the dial pad on her phone with long, cherry-red nails. "Not that I should have one, if I'm gonna fit into my freaking dress."

I take a deep breath, as I have already heard about her *freaking* dress three times so far this morning. I grab my mug that says COFFEE, which I got at last year's white elephant office party exchange. I thought it was hilarious; no one else got it. Except Eli, who tried to steal it from my pantry.

Once in the break room, I pour myself half a mug before wandering over to the table in the center where there is indeed a lone jelly donut.

"They might be stale," a voice says.

I turn around to see James in the doorway. He is wearing gray pants and a blue button-down, the picture of nondescript, which is probably why I never noticed him before. But he is staring at me with dark, quizzical dark eyes. And those cheekbones. I notice him now.

"It's not for me anyway," I say.

"You're not into donuts?" He wanders over and surveys the table, eyeing a couple misshapen powder Dunkin' holes but doesn't appear tempted.

"Not jelly. Glazed. I'm a purist." I grab a napkin. "You?"

"I don't like any donuts."

"Oh." I notice he doesn't have a coffee mug either, and there's nothing else in the break room in the morning.

"I just saw you come in," he says in answer to my unasked

question, "and I wanted to get your number." He whips out his phone. "So?"

I'm trying to figure out if his social ineptitude is intentional or not. I'm thinking not. I pause. If this is his game, I don't really get it. He's a couple years younger than me and not my usual type. But there's something about the way he is staring at me. And as Sylvia so nicely reminded me, I'll never find someone if I just hang out with Eli all the time. Hell, it's not like men are pounding down my door.

Maybe he's a little weird. But the truth is, I'm a little weird too.

"Okay," I say and give him my number.

Sylvia brays on about her freaking dress for the entire rest of the workday. She is just starting about V-neck versus the lacy jewel neck when five o'clock hits and I am finally released. I race off to see Rae-Ann for my monthly appointment. This month, I could really use it.

Stepping off the train at Harvard Square, sweat runs down my back. I take the shortcut through Harvard Yard on the way to the office. I started seeing Rae-Ann while still in college, and though it's totally out of my way to go to Cambridge at this point, I still make the trek. We click, as they say in the parlance. She gets me, and there's no way I'd ever go through the trial of explaining my past to someone else.

The Yard is gorgeous in its usual, standoffish way. The majestic gray-and-red buildings, laced with non-proverbial ivy, line the grass in the center. Sugar maples tower above, their leaves turning tangerine. I walked under this canopy of trees my freshman year, the breeze whistling through them, feeling full of wonder and awe. I trudged the same path as a senior, the trees brooding and smothering now, blocking all the sunlight. The Yard is stunning, but haunting at the same time.

Because something very ugly happened here, in this beautiful place.

As I pass the science center, the fountain shoots water into arcs that scatter onto the rocks below. I turn onto a well-worn but charming side street lined with compact cars, grand old trees, and not-so-grand old apartments, one being Rae-Ann's duplex. The rickety wooden stairs could use a coat of paint.

Two other people sit in the small waiting room, one I recognize from other visits. We share a brief smile and I sit in the same brown chair I always sit in. The air is stale, and I am giving myself a quick sniff check as Rae-Ann comes out to get me. As we enter her office, a soft peach scent fills the room, and I notice the tea steeping on her desk. After a little chat about the hot weather, she breaks right in. "How was yesterday?"

I twist my earring. "As good as can be expected, I guess."

Rae-Ann smiles, her chunky teal-blue beads clacking as she leans back in her chair. Rae-Ann is all earth mother. She is rather obese, with matching hemp tops and bottoms and always a long strand of beads to accessorize. She exudes calm. You would meet her at a cocktail party and immediately start pouring out your soul. "Any seizures this time?" she asks.

"No. Not this time."

Another gift from my anniversary. Sometimes, it throws me into seizures. Well, not *real* seizures, I am told. Fake seizures, sort of. The neurologist explained this to me, after removing the electrodes from my head, with glue that would stick in my hair for days to remind me of this particular humiliation in my testing. They used to call them "pseudo-seizures," but this fell away as a term of art. Too demeaning, I suppose. Now, they are called "stress-related seizures." Eli calls them glorified panic attacks. He's probably right. I don't know. All is know is what happens when I have them. I fall down, and I can't stop shaking. It may go on for minutes; it may take an hour. There's no medication for it, because these aren't real seizures. "Not caused by electricity in the brain," the neurologist explained to me. "But talking with someone could help."

So I talk with Rae-Ann. It does help. I used to get them all the time, after it happened. Now thankfully, not so much.

"Any nightmares?" she asks.

"No." I used to be plagued by those too. Frustrating snippets of memory. A stale mattress. Twisting pain. Laughter. The odd sound of birds, which I've puzzled over again and again. *Birds at night, in the middle of a room?* "No, not this time. No nightmares."

"Good," she says.

"I don't know. It just seems so…" I struggle for the word. "Unfair in a way."

"Of course it's unfair," she says.

"No, I mean. Not the fact that it happened. I know that's unfair. That's pretty obvious." My hand is twisting my earring again, and I consciously bring it down, squeezing my palms together. I already had one earlobe split and sewn up from all this twisting. "The fact that I can't even remember it. But I have to live through it anyway."

Rae-Ann shrugs helplessly for me. "It sucks."

For a while, this fact obsessed me. I wanted to remember. Even if remembering would hurt, at least it would make me whole again. Instead of this fractured being, with a piece of my life ripped out. I pored over books about recovering memories. I replayed the night over and over, pestering friends who may have been there. Like a reporter digging out the truth of my own life. But I never got anywhere. Just sad looks, pats on the arm, and soft suggestions that "maybe I should let it go." The same thing my parents said, that Shoshana said. But they don't understand. No one does. Of course I'd love to let it go.

But it won't let *me* go.

"If I could just remember something," I mutter, for the millionth time.

She nods sadly. "At some point, you may have to accept that there is some time missing from your life that you can't account for. Time that was taken from you and that you can't get back. And try to be okay with that."

I don't answer, but I know she's right. And the truth is, I do understand that, and I do accept it. Someone stole some time from my life. Time that changed me.

But no, I can't be okay with it.

CHAPTER FIVE

JAMES

When I get back to the cubicle, Cooper looks up at me with a questioning expression.

"Got it," I say with a smile that takes over my face.

"Dude!" He high-fives me, and although I don't like high-fiving because it's totally stupid and basically a vehicle for spreading germs, I high-five him back anyway. Jamal told me it's an easy way to be sociable, and he's right.

I'm not sure why Dahlia gave me her number, to be honest.

Earlier this morning, I told Cooper about seeing Dahlia. I didn't tell him about S.O.S., just said I saw her at a meeting and he said, "You should ask her out."

I explained that she's two years older and much cooler than me, and she'll probably say no. He said I was probably right, but sometimes guys can get girls way out of their league. We both understood that she's way out of my league. "You never know," he said. Then he got on the phone with one of the lawyers. The team usually lets Cooper deal directly with the lawyers because everyone else was getting bad reviews. The last lawyer, this asshole named Corbyn who's since moved to Portland, complained that I was arrogant. But actually, he was the arrogant one, while I was trying to keep calm with his frustratingly stupid, unhelpful suggestions about what was wrong with his computer when obviously it was a simple problem with his ad-blocking software.

Anyway, Cooper said I should ask her out so I started thinking of ways to run into her. I could come up to her station, saying we were doing computer checks, but I didn't think I could pull it off.

I'm not good at lying. I have her address from the directory, but not her cell number. It wouldn't be that hard to figure out, but I don't want her thinking I'm stalking her.

Then, it happened. My chance came. Like I said, I don't believe in fate exactly, but I was walking to the bathroom and she was right there. I didn't have to make up any excuse or anything. She went into the break room, and I never go in there because it's just people making small talk, and I hate coffee anyway, but I went in there. And I got her number.

"James," my boss barks out.

"Yup?"

"Where are we on the system 508 update?" Grayson asks.

I look down at the mini window at the bottom of the screen. "Sixty-three percent done."

He loops his fingers through his belt loops. Grayson has a big belly and a gray mustache that curves up. He reminds me of a walrus, and he's not that intelligent, but he's nice enough. A monkey could do a systems 508 update, but they give me complex things to do sometimes. Quasi-complex things, at least.

"Let me know when it's finished," he says, then walks away. I go back to the scan I'm running on Tabitha Jackson's computer, which has already come up with three viruses.

I put my phone down on my desk, thinking about Dahlia's number stored in there now.

It seems incomprehensible. She actually gave me her number. I could tell by the way she looked at me that I did it wrong. I don't know exactly what I did wrong, but it wasn't exactly smooth, because I'm never exactly smooth. Still, the important thing is, she gave me her number. Maybe it's the wrong one. I hope not, but girls do that sometimes. To me, anyway. But I'll know soon enough.

Because I'm calling her tonight, and I don't care if it's smooth or not.

CHAPTER SIX

Five Years Ago

Wu-wu!" *I am screaming.*

My voice is hoarse. I am drinking a grape-flavored, cloying drink, laced with grain alcohol. Wu-wus are what they're called—wicked drinks—and I have had quite a few of them. Daisy loops her arms around my neck. She smells like cigarettes.

"Yo, girlie! What's up?"

"Wu-wu," *I say to her, somberly.*

She checks me over. "You are seriously fucked up."

"This is correct."

"Want to go to the Phoenix?" *she asks.*

"I don't know," *I say, looking around the room.* "Where are we right now?"

This question elicits peals of laughter, though only drunk people would find it funny. "The Fly," *she answers, which is a final club. Final clubs are men's clubs that make up a limited but undeniably significant portion of Harvard's social life. I rarely go to these parties. Daisy always does. This time, she convinced Introvert Girl to come.*

"Or we can stay here if you want," *she says.*

"No. We could go to the Phoenix." *My speech sounds slurry.* "That's fine."

She leans into me. "Should I hook up with Jay?"

"Who's Jay?"

"The guy from Eastern Studies. I told you about him."

"I don't remember." *I hold her shoulder, as the room takes a spin when I move my head.* "Is he cute?"

"Totally adorable."

A guy comes over in a porkpie hat and a bow tie. Daisy sees him and squeals. "Jay, I was just talking about you! This is my best friend ever, Dahlia."

"Daisy and Dahlia?"

"Yeah, yeah, yeah," I say. "We've heard it all before."

He tips his hat in a mock formal way. "Pleasure to make your acquaintance."

"She thinks you're hot," I inform him, to a strong elbow to my ribs.

"The feeling is mutual," he says, looking at her with enthrallment at his apparent luck.

"Maybe we should stay here," she says.

"Either way." I am handed another purple drink, but put it down. The room is spinning, and the sweetish smell is making me sick. "I'm going to step out for a second," I say, but Daisy doesn't answer, cooing at something Jay is saying. The walls are stumbling toward me and I lurch my way onto the front steps. The pounding of the base rattles the iron railing as I stand there, gripping it. The night is hot, heavy. The sky looks smoky gray, like rain is coming.

I sit down, my skirt sticky against my thighs, and my head hangs down. I might have closed my eyes.

"Hey, Dahlia!" It's a girl from Winthrop House, my dorm. I think her name is Leah, but I'm not sure.

"Hey," I answer weakly.

She sidles up to me. "You okay? You don't look so good."

"A little drunk. I'm fine."

"Cool." She pulls a crinkled cigarette packet out and offers me one, and I shake my head. "You want to walk around a bit? See if anything's going on? I heard there's a party at Adam's."

I consider Daisy for a minute, who has Jay and won't miss me. I could use an escape from the blaring music anyway. "Sure," I say and stand up.

My head is steadier this time. We walk together while she chatters about the party she just came from and the strap from my left shoe bites into my heel.

And that's the last thing I remember.

CHAPTER SEVEN

DAHLIA

Y ou sure you don't want a glass of wine?" Daisy asks.

"No, I'm good." I take a long sip of my water. San Pellegrino, because tap is too pedestrian for Daisy. She's working at an investment-banking firm doing something that I will never understand. Which is to say, she can afford San Pellegrino.

I try to avoid seeing Daisy, but she's persistent and lives in Boston, so we end up doing lunch biannually at least. It's not that I don't like her. It's just that we're in very different places right now. She's got a perfect life, and I've got an imperfect one. Sometimes, it's hard to see that in such stark relief.

"How's the paralegal thing going?"

"It's going." I rip into a piece of bread. Daisy has pushed her bread plate away, which is probably how she maintains a size 0. I don't bother with such niceties. And it's not a calling card that I want to put out there anyway. Wispy, feminine.

Prey.

"How's Jordan doing?" I ask, proud of myself for remembering his name.

"Awesome." She grins. "I think he's going to ask."

It takes me a second. "To get married?"

She nods, her eyebrows raised in victory. "Yup."

"Oh, wow." I met him once. Handsome, thin, preppy, very much the male mold of Daisy. Just like every other guy she used to date. I wouldn't have said he was or wasn't marriage material. But then, I don't know. I hardly know Daisy anymore. The marriage thing seems to be catching: first Sylvia, now Daisy. Though they are like an entirely different genus. "Aren't we a little young for that?"

Daisy shrugs, her bra showing through the cream-white flounce. Between her flounce and her gray herringbone pants, her wardrobe probably costs more than what I made last month. "I'm twenty-six. He's thirty. When you know, you know, right?"

"Sure, I guess." But maybe I will never know. I drink more water; she, more wine.

"Have you heard from Quinn?" she asks.

"Not lately." Quinn was our other roommate, not counting Trish, who hung out at her boyfriend's apartment all the time but kept a toothbrush in our dorm for convenience's sake. Quinn is artsy and cool. Lives in LA cool. "Last I heard she was living with Marta."

Daisy shakes her head. "They broke up. Marta was sleeping with some girl from her yoga class."

"Oh. That's too bad." The plates are brought to the table. Salad for her, risotto for me. "The heart wants what it wants, I suppose."

"I suppose," she says. "But it doesn't seem very *namaste* to me."

I laugh, and in that instant, I remember why I like Daisy. Or used to, anyway. It's like a smell that calls up a long-lost memory, shooting past your cortex and straight to your limbic system. An instant that lurches me back in time in a way that is almost melancholic.

"How's Eli?" She spears some lettuce.

"He's good. Still bartending."

"Good," she replies, carefully. She doesn't like Eli, never "got my infatuation with him," in her words. Once over dinner, she told me we were stopping each other from "progressing." I told her she didn't know what the fuck she was talking about. After that, we stuck to lunch.

I spoon some risotto, which is just the right creaminess and easily the most delicious thing I've eaten all year.

"So, are you going to the reunion?" she asks.

I just got a postcard for it. Fifth year. "I don't know. I didn't even graduate yet." I don't mention that I felt physically ill when I saw the postcard in the mailbox.

"Yeah, but who cares? You're, what, two semesters away?"

"Actually, I've only got the one class left at this point. Going tonight, in fact."

"Oh yeah? What are you taking?"

"Feminism in the Law."

She shakes her head and smiles. "You were always so smart."

"Yeah, well," I say. I've never been great at accepting compliments, and Daisy was always very free with handing them out. "It's not as easy as it was back in college. Working full-time takes its toll."

"Oh, I can't even imagine," she says, which comes out sounding patronizing, though I'm sure she doesn't mean it that way. "Well, come to the reunion anyway," she continues, "I'm on the committee. Quinn said she's coming."

"Maybe," I say. "We'll see." Though I might as well just say no.

There is silence, then Daisy says, "There were good memories too, you know. Before it happened. Years of good memories."

"Uh-huh," I say and drink my San Pellegrino.

The professor has spoken the last of her lecture, and farewell noises ring around me. Bags being zipped, books snapped shut. I throw my stuff into my army-green satchel. Some of my fellow students, who are all women incidentally, except for one man with a "yes, I am a socialist" button on his backpack, are talking about getting together, hitting a bar or a coffee shop. They've asked me to go a few of times, and I've politely refused. There was one especially persistent woman named Whitney, who's a pseudo-celebrity in here. She's beautiful in a Nordic sense, with the light-blue eyes of a Husky and flaxen-blond hair. She reminds me of Daisy, but in a crunchier, I-don't-shave-my-legs way. Even she stopped asking, which is both a relief and a disappointment. I don't know what I want from them. To beg, maybe.

The pavement is shiny from the earlier rain, which emptied the humidity from the air. A streetlight glows a fuzzy line through a puddle. I adjust the straps of the satchel, then notice a form against the brick wall near the Harvard station stop. She's got a cardboard sign in black, fuzzy marker that reads PREGNANT AND HUNGRY. PLEASE HELP.

"Spare some change?" she asks as I read the sign.

"Oh, yeah. Wait a sec." I scrounge around my satchel for a dollar.

"Dahlia?" she asks.

Taken aback, I take a closer look at her. "Natasha?"

"Hey!" She jumps up like a jack-in-the-box. "How are you, girl?" She reaches over for a hug, and I smell smoke and grime in her faded-green-dyed hair.

"Liking the color," I say. Though she's a chubby, busty girl who is barely five feet, fully standing now, the green calls to mind a leprechaun.

"Yours too," she returns, signaling my purple. "So what's up with you?" Her voice is animated. She's always been bubbly, but this is overboard, like she's jacked up on something. Meth probably. When she smiles, she is missing a front tooth. "Anything new?"

"This and that," I say.

"Still a lawyer?"

"Paralegal," I correct, downplaying it.

"That's good," she says. "Real good."

"And you're...?" I point down to the sign.

"Oh, no. That's just for the money." She laughs raucously, which is uncomfortable. "It really works though. My profits are up, like, twenty percent."

"Huh. Well, that's good, I guess." I have an odd vision of her handing a P&L sheet to Daisy. *See, I really think this new sales pitch is working.* As we stand there, some people pass by, looking at us, then away. "Well," I say, "I'd better..." I motion to the Harvard subway station to finish my sentence.

"Yeah, yeah, of course," she says and hugs me again. "It was good to see you."

As we awkwardly disengage from the hug, I hand her two twenties. "Here," I say. It's all I have. Hopefully, Eli can lend me some money this week. "Don't be a stranger, okay?"

"Yeah, sure, thanks," she says, fingering the bills with real pleasure. "You know where to find me, right?" she asks with her lopsided smile and plops back down to her spot. We both wave, and walking away, I reflexively reach into my bag for my wallet and gun. I find both. With Natasha, that isn't a given.

I saw her boost off various girls in our support group. This one was S.O.R., not S.O.S., if I remember correctly. Survivors of Rape, following the S.O. theme. The logo has an eagle, as the founders meant it to sound inspirational, like *soar*. Though, to me, it always brought *sore* to mind instead. Natasha never stole from me, but I wouldn't put it past her. I wasn't surprised when she was asked to leave the group, and I haven't seen her since.

The roar of the subway rises up the stairs, along with a faint whiff of urine. As I hit the last stair, a red train rumbles past, so I'll have to wait for the next one. I stand up straight, making sure I give off a don't-fuck-with-me air, but there's just a woman texting in a cheap, blue business suit and an older, wizened-looking African American man whistling.

When my phone rings, I jump anyway.

I don't recognize the number. "Hello?"

There is a brief pause. "Hi," the voice says. "It's James."

CHAPTER EIGHT

Five Years Ago

*T*he rest comes in a jagged puzzle.

The smell of a stale carpet. Brush burns all over my face. My cheek red and swollen, the tip of my nose bleeding. I don't remember the color of the carpet. Blue? Gray? An old mattress in the corner. Rust stains on it, or maybe blood.

The room is empty, and it takes me a while to stand up.

My legs are leaden. I have to concentrate to walk. My ankles keep collapsing. I get out of the room. I don't remember how I get out of the room.

Then somehow, I am in my dorm room. I don't remember how I got there. It takes a long time; I remember that. Shadows on cobblestone, people whispering as I pass. I remember raindrops glistening on the ridges of a leaf. My vision veers between telescopic and microscopic. Somehow, I get to my dorm room. And I must have fallen into bed, though I don't remember this either.

I remember waking up.

Crackers in my hair. Bruises everywhere. My tongue is swollen. I must have bitten it, or someone else did. Unconsciously, I am cataloging it all.

My underwear is missing. My white shirt is stained with beer. Dried semen and blood on my thighs. (It will hurt to sit for days. It will hurt to urinate, like pissing through razors.) Holes in my sweater. Holes in my memory.

Holes.

I have been raped.

I can't get around the word. I realize at once that I have to go to the hospital, because that's what you do when you get raped. But the idea seems overwhelming. I need to shower. But I know from movies that I'm not supposed to shower.

Movies tell you what to do when you are raped. They do not tell you how you will feel.

I sit up in my bed, and my head spins. Aches. Pounds. I want to vomit and begin shivering uncontrollably. Carefully, I stand up. My legs are shaking too. Every joint hurts, every bone hurts. My hips hurt, like they had been wrenched. Fingernail scratches on my breasts, my back, my ass. Like animals had clawed me. I am cataloging it all, but I cannot name everything that hurts. I walk over to the mirror, an effort that takes time. I am short of breath by the time I get there. And when I look at me, I feel like I am seeing a stranger. There is a rap on the door.

Bum-bum-bum-bum. Daisy's knock. "Hey, are you okay in there?"

I don't answer.

"I didn't hear you come back last night. Can I come in?"

I still don't answer and hear her feet shuffling, then the door slowly creak open. She gasps. Her beautiful face transforms. Horrified, like she is looking at a monster.

"Oh my God, Dahlia," she says, her lips trembling.

But I don't feel like Dahlia. I look in the mirror again and realize that I'm looking for someone, but I'm not sure who. Then I realize who it is.

Pretty Girl. I am looking for Pretty Girl.

But she is nowhere to be found. And I understand that she won't be coming back.

Pretty Girl is dead.

CHAPTER NINE

DAHLIA

James is late.

It took me an embarrassingly long time to come up with my outfit: strategically torn jeans and a black, V-neck T-shirt. I sit in the moody coffeehouse, having fended off multiple order requests by a moody waitress. Maybe I should have gone to the movies with Eli. When I turned him down, he was not only shocked that I had an actual date, but more shocked that it was with James. *The IT guy? With the sister?* Eli didn't explain his qualms, just that he thought James was "different." And when asked if "different" was code for not white, he rolled his eyes. He's right. Eli doesn't discriminate on skin color. Or personality. Or anything else I can think of. But for me, he discriminates against everything. No one is right for me. I assume for James it's that he's too quiet or awkward or shy. Or something.

Eli made me promise to text on my way home, in case *different* means ax murderer, or more likely, rapist. Eli always asks me to text him when I go out, which I never do. I put my phone down, my stomach grumbling. This is why I don't date. So I don't end up in this situation, sitting, waiting, and feeling like a loser. I'm about to leave when the door opens, and I see him.

Framed by the doorway, haloed by the outside light, James catches my eye and shyly waves. Rain falls in a mist around him. I wave back, but I don't smile. He's forty-five fucking minutes late.

"Sorry," he says, approaching the table and peeling off a soaked raincoat. Water is beaded on his brush cut. "There was some delay on the T. Engine problem."

"It's fine."

"No, it's not fine. I'm never late."

"Okay, coffee?" I try to catch the moody waitress's eye.

"Sure," he says, though at this point I'm hungry enough that I want actual food. The waitress comes over, we order coffee, then we sit there.

It's as awkward as I'd feared. We talk about work, which is boring on both ends. We talk about the weather, which is pathetic. Finally, we get our little drinks of overly strong coffee in white teacups. They don't do decaf at this place.

"You weren't at S.O.S. this week," he says.

I tear open three sugar packets and dump them in to mitigate the bitter taste. "No. I don't go very often anymore."

"I suppose that's good." He downs his coffee like it's a shot, then makes a hilariously awful face. It's as if he's new to the planet. *What is this thing you humans call coffee?*

"Yeah, it is." I fiddle with my napkin square. "But it's good to have S.O.S. out there anyway. I could go with you some time, if you need it." Which would probably be even lamer than this date.

"Thanks."

A woman coughs to our left, a heavy, gurgly, tubercular cough. James plays with his teacup, his legs splayed out like he's too big for the table. A giraffe in a china shop. "I didn't want it to be like this," he says.

I stop spinning my napkin. "Like what?"

"Weird."

I smile. "It is kind of, isn't it?"

"Yeah. So, what should we do about that?" He asks this like it's a fascinating problem to be solved. He's so matter-of-fact about the awfulness of this date, it's almost intriguing.

"I know a great pizza place?" I offer.

"All right," he says, apparently satisfied with my solution. "Let's get out of here."

We are both sopping wet by the time we get to the next restaurant, and the mood has lightened considerably. My mouth is watering from the smell of real food.

The waitress places a beer down on the plastic, red-checkered tablecloth for James, and I squeeze the lemon wedge in my non–San Pellegrino water. We order a large pizza from an un-moody waitress and hand her back our plastic menus.

James's face is turning a bit ruddy, though he's only taken a few sips of beer. He leans back in his chair and crosses his legs. His large, black Birkenstock dangles on his foot, his leg tapering up to smooth, pear-shaped calf. A swimmer's calf. I have an urge to touch it.

"Can I ask you a question?" he asks.

"Sure," I say. But a little piece of me shrivels up in the usual disappointment. In the end, he's just like everyone else. *Why did you try to kill yourself?* He needs to know the why.

"How did you end up as a paralegal?" he asks.

"Oh," I say, pleasantly surprised. "I don't know. I wanted to be a lawyer. That wasn't in the cards. Miller and Stein were hiring." I reach over for my water. "Eli found the job for me, in fact. We were both paralegals for a while. Then he got bored." I take a quick sip and swallow. "Eli gets bored easily."

He nods, taking another sip of beer.

"How did you end up working there?" I ask.

"Job fair." He plays with the paper on the neck of the bottle. "In fact, it was the first booth I went up to."

"Meant to be, I guess."

"Maybe." He puts his elbows on the table. "So, are you happy?"

The question irks me some. *No, I'm not happy. I got raped, quit school, and ended up in a job I don't love. What do you think?* But, of course, he doesn't know any of this, so I can't exactly blame him. "I don't know," I say.

"Because you don't seem very happy."

"Why?" I ask, definitely irked now. "Don't I smile enough?" I offer a ferociously fake smile, and he gives a sincerely uncomfortable one in return. "What about you?" I ask, turning the tables.

"Are you happy? Are you entirely fulfilled with your existence, James Gardner?"

He thinks about it, his eyebrows torquing downward. "No. Not really."

His honesty shames me. The pizza arrives, leading to an uncomfortable silence while the waitress takes her time separating and serving our slices. I'm mad at myself for acting so rude. Though rudeness is one of the many tricks in my bag, as Rae-Ann has pointed out. I have a crop of them: acting out, turning stone silent, or mounting the guy after five minutes, all self-sabotaging ploys against a true relationship. Some sauce squirts onto my plate, as James wrestles with a long string of cheese. "Sorry," I say. "I didn't mean to be a jerk about it."

"No, it was a stupid thing to ask," he answers, then sips his beer again. "I don't have the right to demand that people be happy. Ramona would have been all over me for that."

I nod, but I don't have a satisfactory response. If Ramona were happy, maybe she would still be here.

"You remind me of her sometimes," he says.

"Oh yeah?" I grab another napkin from the stack at the middle of the table. "Do you have a picture or anything?"

He reaches into his wallet and pulls out a little creased square. She looks like James but thinner, smaller. A bit boyish but with perfect, slick black eyebrows and red lipstick. Same cheekbones. "She's pretty," I say.

"Yeah," he says and puts the photo away. I scoop off another piece of pizza, and he flicks the beer bottle's neck with his fingers, making a *ponging* sound.

"I might still do it," I say, thinking about what he said. Being happy.

He squints at me. "Do what?"

"Become a lawyer."

"Oh yeah?" he asks.

"Yeah." I mix the ice cubes with my straw. "Of course, it would help if I graduated college first."

James gazes down at the table, appearing uncomfortable with

my open admission of failure. After a bit, he looks up again. "So, how did you meet Eli?" he asks, obviously changing the subject.

The music changes to another Italian song, with loud, clangy accordions. "I guess you could say we were the original S.O.S. I met him in the psych ward. He was in for wrists, me for pills. Fall of my senior year, sophomore of his."

"You were both at Harvard?"

"No." I take a drink. "He went to BU."

As he leans forward on the table, his face is deep red, the flush spreading to his neck. "Were you ever dating?"

"No. He's always been gay. Since I knew him anyway." I shake my ice cubes in the plastic cup. "That's what he was on the psych floor for. He came out to his parents. Didn't go so well."

James frowns, looking down at the table. "That's too bad."

"But they're all good now. Amazing how nearly killing yourself can make your parents love you again."

He puts his beer bottle on the table. "Are you speaking from experience?"

"No. Mine never stopped loving me. They just don't understand me."

"Yeah," he says. "Mine too."

I pause while he drinks his beer. "Can I ask you a question now?"

"Sure," he says with a smile. "I guess it's your turn."

"Why are you so red?"

"Oh." He feels his face as if to confirm this. "I am, aren't I?" He examines his arms. "Asian flush." The waitress refills my water, and James waves off another drink.

"What's that?" I ask. "Sounds like a card hand or something."

"It's an enzyme thing," he explains. "Some Asians don't process alcohol correctly, so we turn red." He shrugs. "From my mom's side, obviously."

"Oh."

"Yeah, my dad's white. My mom's Japanese." He pushes his beer bottle to the side. "Which is why I don't usually drink." He *pongs* the bottle's neck again. "Do you drink?"

"No," I say. This has been a deal breaker for some, but not for

James, I would imagine. "I mean, I never had a problem with it or anything. I just don't like to… I don't know. A control thing, I guess." It's quiet for a moment. Then, out of nowhere, he reaches out, touching my arm, and I jump involuntarily.

"Sorry," he says.

"No, it's okay. I just…didn't expect it."

He pauses and points to my arm this time but doesn't touch. "What does it say?"

I realize he's referring to my tattoo and twist my arm to show him the black, cursive writing—SURVIVOR. It flows into the other designs. Black and gray screaming monsters that morph into forest-green and deep-purple victorious nymphs. Good triumphing over evil and so on. Much like Rae-Ann, my tattoo artist gets me.

"Nice," he says. "Any others?"

"One on my back," I say. "Hard to describe." A goddess emerging from smoke—same theme. It's the kind that you wear with a strapless dress and everyone stares. Which is, I suppose, the point. "How about you?"

"I've got one," he says.

"Oh, yeah?" I ask, fairly flummoxed. He seems too straight-laced for that. "Where?"

He swallows. "On my chest."

I move my chair in closer. "Can I see it?"

He looks hesitant, but then undoes a few buttons on his blue button-down, with clumsy fingers. The rain has dotted his shirt with dark drip marks, like teardrops. The top of his chest is flushed too, like his neck. On the skin is a black thunderbolt, made up of Japanese characters. It's beautiful.

"What does it say?" I reach over slowly and trace the characters with my fingers.

"It says…" He looks down at my hand. "Revenge."

———

I don't expect to see Eli when I walk into my kitchen. He has a key and comes and goes as he likes, as I do in his place. But not usually after he's been out. Then, he usually ends up sleeping somewhere else. He is standing in my tiny galley kitchen, drinking orange juice from the carton. I glance over to see he's filled Simone's food bowl.

"There are actual cups in the pantry, you know," I say, pointing.

"Waste of time." He wipes off his upper lip.

"Cups are what separate us from orangutans."

"I thought it was the red butt," he says.

"That's baboons."

He laughs and takes one last sip before putting the carton back on the shelf and shutting the door. "Dahlia and her useless knowledge."

"From one non–college graduate to another," I say. It's low. I don't always fight fair with Eli. He's like a kid brother; you can only take so much of him.

"You didn't text me," he says.

"And yet I survived." I yawn. "Did you end up going out?"

"Yeah. Didn't hook up though."

"Wow. That must be a first."

He ignores my jibe. "I Googled your boyfriend. Wanna know what I found out?"

"Not really." I sit down in a kitchen chair, and he jumps up to sit on top of the table, next to me. Looking closer, I can see he's a bit wild-eyed, with dried crust on his nose. "Were you with Kevin?" I ask. Kevin the asshole who always has blow.

"No," he says. "He hates me, remember?"

"Yeah, I know. Just checking." Kevin was Eli's first "true love," who broke his heart after Eli finally opened up to him. "He was weird anyway," I say.

"True," he allows, his knee bouncing up and down like a wind-up toy.

"What about Brandon with the AC/DC tattoo?" I ask. "Weren't you guys dating?"

Eli shrugs. "He's never at the bars."

"I like Brandon," I say. And I do. He's a cute, normal guy who works in IT. Worlds better than Kevin the asshole with blow.

"Anyway. We were talking about James."

"Actually," I say. "*You* were talking about James. I was not."

"First off," he says, "Gardner. What kind of name is that?"

Simone slinks over to me for a pet. "His dad's white. So I suppose it's a white name."

"He's a total geek-head, by the way," he says.

"As am I."

"I'm talking Dungeons & Dragons–member geek-head."

I could say so fucking what, but then I'd be inviting a fight. Eli is like this when he gets high sometimes, oddly possessive. *I'm your best friend. Me, me, me.*

I stand up from the table, and Simone follows me. "I'm going to bed."

Eli springs up too. "I'm kind of wired. I was thinking of going out again. You want to come?"

"No. Don't go out, Eli. You'll feel like crap tomorrow. Go to bed."

"But I'll never fall asleep," he whines. "Come on. Come out with me, one drink."

But it's never one drink. "Eli, I'm tired. I'm going to bed. You should too."

He sighs, suddenly deflated. "All right, fine. Maybe you're right." Then he grabs my shoulders and stares into my face. "You know I love you, right?"

"Yes. I know."

"And you love me too?" His questioning look is almost pitiful.

"Yes, Eli. I love you too," I say, wondering what the hell kind of drugs he took tonight. He nods though, apparently satisfied with the response. "You're sure?"

"Positive."

He nods again and finally leaves. As the door shuts, I lock up the three locks, then head to my bedroom with Simone in tow. I peel off my black shirt, which is damp from the soft sprinkle outside, and throw on a T-shirt. Lying down, I think back to the date.

After finishing the pizza, we sat a little longer in the restaurant. A group of college kids was leaving as another gaggle came in, and I started yawning. James yawned too and asked if I wanted to get going. He looked at the side of my face as he asked. I noticed that sometimes, how he doesn't look straight at me. I agreed, and we walked to the T together, then he went his way, and I went mine.

All the way to the subway, I wondered if he would ask me to his place, but he didn't. Which is just as well. I don't know if I would have said yes or no. Probably yes.

I turn on my fan, which starts at a low moan before building up to a steady pace. Lying on my bed, I pick up my book from the nightstand. The pages flutter in the breeze every time the fan spins toward me. Simone keeps trying to lick the air. I read until my eyes go blurry. Then I flick off the light and slide my hand under the pillow to cradle my Beretta.

My own little teddy bear.

When I close my eyes, I can see the thunderbolt tattoo.

As I drift off, the Japanese characters float in front of me, worming onto a stark-white sheet of paper, then floating off the page again. I keep trying to grab them, but they slip away like wisps of smoke. The question pierces me as I am falling asleep.

Why does he want revenge?

CHAPTER TEN

JAMES

On the last leg of the subway ride, I Google her again.

There's not much out there. Tons of awards from high school, including valedictorian. It looks like she was really good at field hockey. Some article about a legal aid club at Harvard, a picture from a picnic at Miller and Stein, then her Instagram. That's not too revealing either, because she's too smart for that. A couple pretty pictures of her with all her tattoos, one with her cat, some quotes. I don't do Instagram, because it seems like a waste of time.

The subway isn't too bad right now. Quiet, only a few people in my car. Usually, I hate the T. So sweaty and loud, people bumping against me, and all those exhaust fumes. I never take the subway if I can help it. But my car is still at the shop so I don't have a choice.

Earlier, the subway was delayed, which nearly killed the date.

Some sort of electrical problem, and it went on forever. I sat there in the smelly car with people groaning and ranting all around me, and I wanted to explode. Just rip the metal pole right out of the floor. I was trying to calm down and deep breathe like Jamal taught me, but I could feel people staring at me. So I sat there, sweating and looking at my phone, watching the minutes go by and thinking how she'll probably leave. I hate it when people are late. It tells me that they don't respect me or my time. If it were me, I would have left.

She didn't leave.

But she didn't look happy to see me either. The coffee place was small and dark, and I was too nervous to admit that I hated coffee when she suggested it. I burned my tongue drinking it too fast, but then we went to the pizza place, which was perfect. She showed me her tattoos, the sleeve going up her arm. I've always wanted to see it up close. Ramona had a tattoo on her chest, in Japanese characters that read *Reborn*. My father hated it, of course, but my mother smiled when she saw it. Because she understood it, like a code. My father didn't even bother to ask what it meant.

So after what happened, I got my tattoo there too, in Japanese characters on my chest. But mine doesn't say reborn. It says revenge. And my mom read that too and looked troubled.

Dahlia liked it though, I could tell. And I could have told her, what happened to Ramona, what it meant. I could have told her how the tattoo shamed me now, when I saw it in the mirror every morning. Because I never did anything. I never got my revenge.

But I couldn't tell her. Not yet. She put her face up so close, I could feel her breath against my neck. And when she touched my chest, I wanted to hold her hand there forever. Her soft fingerprints on my skin.

I think she'll see me again. I really do. But even if she doesn't, I'll always remember that moment. Jamal said I focus too much on the bad things that happen and forget about all the good things. He said a negative viewpoint can mold your brain that way. Something about neural pathways, which sort of makes sense, and Jamal's smart about those things. He said I should save room for the good things in life. I thought that wasn't a bad idea, so I freed up some RAM in my brain and put a file folder in there called *good things*. It isn't very full yet, but that moment will go in there, definitely.

Her fingers on my chest. My skin tingling.

That moment goes in there and can never be erased.

CHAPTER ELEVEN

Five Years Ago

We take a taxi to the hospital.

A piece of electrical tape sticks against my thigh from the seat. The road is bumpy, and everything hurts. The windows are open, and students are rushing by, laughing with their backpacks on. Like everything's okay. Like it's just another day.

The driver keeps checking back on me with a worried face and gives Daisy his card to bring us back when we're done.

I ask the hospital not to call the police. They call the police anyway.

We don't wait long. Not like freshman year, when they thought I had the flu but ended up getting my appendix out. We are ushered right into a room. Soft voices. My dirty, torn clothes in a thick, blue plastic bag on the chair. The doctor says he's from Puerto Rico; I never catch his name. His face is embarrassed. He doesn't meet my eyes.

A nurse rips open a packet officiously, as if she's done this too many times before. She doesn't baby me, but she's not mean either. She treats me like a person. She talks me through the exam.

Cold stirrups. Swabs. Speculum.

Daisy's warm hand holding mine behind a curtain and my eyes keep crying. I don't feel like I'm crying, just my eyes. Someone gives me a tissue. I touch my cheek and there is gauze on the brush burn. I don't remember anyone putting it there. Time is flipping. Jagged pieces of time. Memories of men laughing. Men clutching me. Pain. Someone else's mind. Somebody else's body.

A soft voice breaks into my head.

"Do you want to talk about it?" The social worker asks me. I don't remember her name either. Light-skinned black woman, or maybe Hispanic. Big purple glasses and kind eyes. Daisy repeats the question, because I must have forgotten to answer.

"No," I say finally, then realize this might sound rude. "No, thank you." It's like I am reading a handbook on how you are supposed to act. Talk to people. Don't shower. Try not to cry too much. Let them touch you. And above all, be polite. Remember: just by being there, you are making them uncomfortable.

"Here's my card," she says. "Is your mom here, or anyone?"

I haven't called my mom. I have to call my mom.

"Just me," Daisy answers. "I'll take it."

"Do you need anything for pain, honey?" A nurse asks. A different nurse. I nod.

"Where do you have pain?"

But I just shake my head. I don't know where I have pain. Everywhere. It hurts to breathe. It hurts to cry. It hurts to sit. It hurts to pee. It hurts to move.

It hurts to be.

"Give her ten of morphine," the doctor says.

"She's little," the nurse says.

"Five, then." His rolling chair squeaks. "Wait a second. Did they already get a tox screen?"

"Yes."

"Her roommate thought she'd been drugged," the doctor says.

Daisy nods in response. "Definitely. She was definitely drugged."

"The tox was already done," the nurse repeats, annoyed at the doctor for not trusting her. "I drew it myself."

"Okay, five milligrams."

I am swimming in and out of the conversation. In and out of the room. The only anchor is my hand, clenched to Daisy's hand. I have to tell my mom. I have to tell my sister. I don't want to tell them. I don't want to tell anyone.

The nurse finds a spot on my ass that isn't bruised or scratched and plunges her needle in. A bee sting. A flare of pain then the soft, soft wooziness. The blaze of hurt everywhere that is my body recedes. My brain unclamps. My body is my body again. But then, I remember, it's not.

A flash of a vision. Men in a line. Laughing.

Is this real? I try to cling to this pseudomemory, follow it to its source. But the image tunnels away as soon as I chase it.

And finally, I give into the warm, lovely rush of medicine, and I sleep.

CHAPTER TWELVE

DAHLIA

So did you sleep with him?" Sylvia asks.

"No," I say, coldly. "I didn't."

"Yeah, he is kind of weird," she says, misunderstanding.

I grip my pen, so I don't grip her neck. "Why do you say that?"

"I don't know." She scans her computer screen. "He doesn't really look you in the eye. And he talks kind of weird. Like a robot or something."

I shrug. "I think he's cute."

She uncaps the Wite-Out, and the scent fills the cubicle. "He's not bad looking, I guess, if you're into that."

I don't ask her what *that* is.

"Anyway, I wouldn't have slept with him either. I always went with the three-date rule." She applies dots of Wite-Out onto a document with precision, then waves her hand over it to dry it. "Sometimes I couldn't hold out though," she says, then laughs. Sylvia has a donkey-like laugh that you can hear for miles. "Lucky, I won't have to worry about that anymore." She gives me a conspiratorial grin. "Beau's an animal. He can go for hours."

Fortunately, Tabitha walks over to the cubicle and saves me from further details. Tabitha is a first-year associate. She's a mousy little thing, afraid of her own shadow. And she has an odd habit of giggling after everything she says. "Dahlia?" (Giggle, giggle.)

"Yes?"

"Do you mind if maybe you could make a medical chronology on the Stevens case?" (Giggle, giggle.)

"Sure, no problem." I grab the towering stack of paper from her with two hands.

"And are you almost done on the Rizzo closing?" (Giggle, giggle.)

"Finished this morning."

"Great." (Giggle). She scoots out of the room. I have a feeling she won't be partner track. Not in litigation, anyway, unless the jury can overlook a giggle after every phrase in a murder case. I stare down at the stack of papers. The top one is an orthopedics office note, dated 1993. I highlight the date and put it to the side, because you have to start somewhere, then tackle the next one in the pile. Cardiology, 2010. It strikes me that this is going to take hours, and I need sustenance.

So I grab my COFFEE mug and make my way to the break room.

Some lawyers are gathered in a cluster, glued to some video on a cell phone. It's odd to see them in the break room, since they rarely hang out there. Usually, this is the province of the lowlier types, the secretaries or the paralegals. The lawyers are behind a divider in the corner and can't see me, which is just as well. Someone might come up with a project for me or something. After pouring out the last dregs from the pot, I rip open a new bag, being a good Miller and Stein citizen who always refills the coffee maker when I've finished the last cup.

"Holy shit," one of the guys barks out. Steve, from tax. He's an asshole. Unlike Tabitha, he probably *will* make partner.

"You think that's her?" another voice asks. "It looks like her."

"Holy shit," Steve repeats. "That's got to be her."

"Guys, this isn't cool. Turn that crap off," another lawyer says. It sounds like Connor, my boss. Moaning sounds are emanating from the corner. Not really sexual, more like a hurt animal. Laughter erupts on the phone's speaker, and the lawyers turn silent. So silent, they might be holding their breath.

I stride over, because now I'm curious. "What are you all looking at?" I ask.

Steve's eyes widen, like he's seen an actual ghost, and Connor turns a fierce red.

Now I've *got* to know what they're looking at. "What is it, you guys?" I grab the phone from him. Connor reaches over to stop me, but I hold it up like a game of keep-away and duck over to the corner so I can see what they're looking at.

And then I see it.

A girl, barely awake and moaning. Her face is slack, drugged. A young man with his shorts fallen around his ankles. Raping her. He emerges from the bed, laughing, sweaty, and drunk and beckons another young man, who starts undoing his belt. Her white shirt is torn. Her black skirt is pushed up.

Pretty Girl.

The last thing I hear is the phone dropping out of my hand. The screen shattering.

And then I feel the tunnel sucking me in.

CHAPTER THIRTEEN

DAHLIA

I t was on some video site," I say. "At work."

My speech is heavy and a bit garbled, since they gave me about ten shots of Ativan in the ER. I tried to tell them it wouldn't work. Fake seizures, I said, stress seizures. But I don't think it came out right, and my body finally stopped shaking, so maybe it did work in the end.

"What did you say?" Eli asks.

"They were watching it in the break room. On their phone."

Eli looks horrified. "The rape? Someone put the rape online?"

I nod.

He shoots up from his chair and starts pacing. "Jesus. That's awful."

I nod again. All I can do is nod. The drugs have slowed down my brain. Eli reaches in for a hug. I am sweaty, hungry, and exhausted, but the hug feels good anyway. I am not crying though. I have no tears in me right now, but when he releases me from the embrace, his eyes are wet. Maybe he is crying for me. "I want to fucking kill them," he hisses.

My nurse walks in, and Eli quickly wipes off his eyes. Matthew is my nurse—a bit paunchy, ever-cheerful, and, as Eli confirmed, most assuredly gay. Even my gaydar picked up that one. "Lunch time," Matthew says brightly, dropping off the tray.

"Let's see," I say, feigning interest as I lift up the lid. "Oh, chicken." My stomach burbles.

"She's vegetarian," Eli says.

"No she's not," Matthew answers.

"Actually," I say, though it comes out with an extra syllable, "she is."

"Oh." Matthew looks peeved. "It didn't say that on the sheet."

"It's okay," I say. "Could you take it back though, please?"

"Okay, hon. Of course," Matthew says, as if suddenly remembering his role. "I'll get you the frittata."

The idea of a hospital frittata makes me want to retch. "No. No frittata." I can barely say the word with my frozen lips. "I'm fine."

Eli stands up. "Hummus wrap from downstairs?"

I answer with a thumbs-up sign, and Matthew clears the tray with a smile to show we're all friends again. I lie in silence a while, my back hurting from the awkward angle of the hospital bed. My head is killing me too, but I don't want to ask the nurse for Tylenol, or I'll probably end up with a spinal tap. I've been here enough times to know you shut up, put up, and get the hell out as soon as you can.

Rearranging myself in the bed, I hear my roommate through the curtain. She's berating someone about her son's birthday party, from what I can gather. *Didn't he call the clown people? Didn't he pick up the cake?* A knock interrupts my unintentional eavesdropping.

"Hello?" a voice calls out.

I pull my covers up, feeling a sudden chill, as James ventures into the room with flowers in a crinkly bag. Mixed carnations, with a strong, not altogether pleasant scent. He lays them by the window. "How are you feeling?" His voice is soft, a bit unsure.

I smile, weakly. My lips feel tight. "I've been better." My speech sounds a bit clearer though.

"What happened?" He glances around the room then takes a seat next to me. "Do you mind my asking?"

"Yeah, sure, it's fine." I rub my arms. "I had sort of a seizure, but not really."

His eyebrows raise in question.

"Pseudo-seizures, they call them," I say with some embarrassment, as I'm not even accomplished enough to have real seizures. "They're stress-related," I add, but realize how lame that sounds. "But, not like, a little stress. A big stress."

"A big stress," he repeats.

"Yes. Big stress. The sort of things that make people join S.O.S. That kind of stress."

"Oh, I see." But his unsettled look tells me he doesn't really.

I decide that it's time. Time to tell him the why. "There was a reason I tried to kill myself, you know."

"Yes. I assumed so." This is followed by an uncomfortable pause. "Is this about the video?"

My stomach turns. "You heard about it?"

He nods, ashamed.

"Bad news travels fast, huh," I say, venom rushing through my veins.

"Like a virus," he says.

I lay my pounding head back on the thin, mushy pillow. "Did you see it?"

"No."

"Me neither." I rub my forehead. "Which is the worst part. That everyone else knows. And I didn't even get to see it."

He nods a moment, then appears to think about something. I close my eyes, which doesn't help the pounding, and I hear him scoot his chair in closer. When I open my eyes, his dark-brown eyes are staring right at me. I look for pity in them, or revulsion, but find nothing of the kind. His gaze is without any pretense. His dark eyes, which often swim away from mine, hold steady.

"Do you want me to help you find it?" he asks.

It doesn't take him long.

James heard the video was hosted by some men's rights website, with a mission statement of "reasserting the natural order of white male primacy." Reportedly, Steve, the asshole, was researching the site for a sexual harassment case and came across my video. And as per the natural order of white male primacy, he decided to show his friends instead of telling me about it.

"You sure you want to do this?" he asks.

"Yes," I answer. And he hands my phone back to me.

The phone trembles in my hands. As the picture pops into motion, I have an odd sense of being above myself in the hospital bed, watching me watching myself on the phone. The same feeling I used to have right after I was raped. Sometimes, my brain would slyly and unpredictably leave my body, slipping away and floating up to the ceiling. And I am there again now, both in myself and hovering over myself.

The video goes on for eight minutes.

It is grainy and shadowy, taken off a phone probably. I assume the attack went on longer, but I don't know for sure. It is an odd scene, grisly in a strangely, anodyne way. Students mill about in the corner, like it's no big deal that someone is getting repeatedly raped on a mattress in the corner of the room. Another kid is doing a bong in a recliner. There is some laughter and high-fives, as you might expect, but also an animated discussion about a math problem somewhere in the background. A brief but loud debate about the hockey team in minute three.

And lying on a mattress is a girl being raped, repeatedly. She is twisted in odd ways, like a rag doll. She is spun over several times. Her head hits the floor once, with a maneuvering. The girl is silent at times, moaning at others. Sometimes she cries.

And I can't get my head around the idea that the girl is me.

Three people rape her, on camera at least. I recognize only one of the perpetrators. Terry, from my Civ Ed class. I can't remember his last name. He asked me out once, and I turned him down. Nicely, I thought. But I guess not nicely enough. Terry is the first, then two others, then the third rapist says, "Dude, quit filming. It's your turn."

The scene sways and then goes black.

I assume he raped the girl too, the cameraman. But I can't see him.

I put the phone down on the bed. I hear James's ragged breath next to me. I hear my roommate arguing with her boyfriend again, about balloons this time.

And then I come down. The hazy, gauzy feeling is stripped off and I am me, in the bed again, the cell phone askew on the blanket with only the baseball cap of the fourth rapist showing. I am her. I am the girl in the video. The girl who woke up with brush burns on her face and time ripped out of her life.

A hand reaches over and holds on to my elbow. An anchoring hand, that keeps me from disappearing into the ceiling again.

"I'm sorry," he says.

And I nod. And I try not to, but I can't help it. I lie back in the bed and I cry.

———

At some point, I must have fallen asleep.

A brisk knock wakes me up, and when I glance at the clock, I can't believe it's only been fifteen minutes. James is still sitting next to me when Eli saunters in.

"A hummus wrap, m'lady?" He sees James, then my puffy face. "Is everything okay here?"

"Yeah," I say and sit up a bit. "James is keeping me company."

Eli takes in the flowers and nods. He walks in to place the hummus wrap on the table, along with some perfume-y magazines. He walks toward me, then stands there a second, appearing to be debating something. Then abruptly, he says, "Well, I better be off. You seem like you're in good hands here." He zips up his leather coat.

"You don't have to…" James says. "Because of me."

"No, no. I have to get some stuff done before work anyway." He leans over and kisses me on the forehead, in a way that declares friendship, not ownership. "Call me when you get home," he whispers, then straightens back up and waves goodbye to James.

After Eli leaves, we don't talk for a while, the air charged between us.

"Sodium oxybate," James says out of nowhere. "I would bet my life on it."

"What's that?"

"Date rape drug. Potent enough to erase your memory. Kill

you even." He swallows. "That's what they would have used. You didn't stand a chance."

"Yeah, well, they screwed up the tox screen so…guess we'll never know." I shift in the bed, tugging on my IV. "And I was drunk. And pretty fucking high."

"All the better for them," he says. "They knew exactly what they were doing."

This gives me pause. I'd never thought of it that way before. Of course they knew what they were doing. Plausible deniability. She was drunk and high—the get-out-of-jail-free card. And oh, we might have just drugged her to seal the deal.

"Who would do that?" I ask with a certain disbelief. "What kind of human being does that?"

He shakes his head. "Monsters."

"No. That's the thing. It's not monsters," I stress. "Just normal guys at a party, having a good time. It meant nothing to them. Plowing some drunk girl like she's some piece of…meat. Like she's just part of the entertainment." The tape around my IV itches, and I scratch fiercely at it. "Who would do that?" I repeat. My heart races, triggering an alarm on the monitor. I find myself gritting my teeth, my jaw clenching so hard that it aches.

"I want to fucking kill them," I say. "Each and every one of them."

His lips tighten into a line. "I'm sorry, Dahlia."

"To make them hurt, you know?"

"I know."

"Hurt. Like they hurt me."

James is bent over in the chair, his elbows on his knees, his long fingers interlaced. "I wish I could solve this."

"You can't," I say, shaking my head. "There is no solution. It's done. It's over."

He frowns. "It isn't over for you though. Just like it isn't over for me. With Ramona." He looks glumly at my blanket. "It will never be."

I don't have an answer to this. And there doesn't seem to be a reason to pursue this line of reasoning, which will do nothing but depress us further. James sits there silently brooding, and I lick my chapped lips. I'm getting tired and trying to think of a nice way to ask him to leave.

But he looks up at me. "We could do something, you know."

I shift in the bed. "What?"

"Hurt them," he says. When I don't answer, his face flashes doubt, but he does not look away.

"What do you mean?" I ask.

"Hurt them," he repeats.

I stare at him, to make sure he is serious. "What, you mean…"

"We have the tape now. We've seen them all. We could—"

"I'm not going to the police," I say, before he goes any further.

"I didn't say anything about the police," he answers, carefully. "Just…however. We could come up with something. To hurt them back." He swallows. "The way they hurt you."

I don't say anything for a minute, just stare at the clock on the wall, the seconds ticking by.

Hurt them. My jaw loosens for an instant. Could I do that?

"I mean," he hedges. "We don't have to." He slumps an inch in the chair. "It's probably a stupid idea."

I am still staring at the wall, when I realize that I don't have the energy to think about this right now. I am so, so tired. And the truth is, I want to be left alone. My eyes start to close again.

"Hey," he whispers, and my eyelids flutter open. "I'm going to get going, okay?"

"Thanks for coming, James." I slur the words out, almost asleep.

And as I hear his footsteps tap out of the room, the idea worms its way into my mind, half dreaming already. *Hurt them.*

Hurt them, like they hurt you.

And I feel something flitting around the corners of my mind. Not quite getting in, but trying to worm its way through. Something unfamiliar.

Something like hope, maybe.

CHAPTER FOURTEEN

JAMES

I hate hospitals.

Walking outside of the automatic doors, I take in a cold breath that hurts my lungs. I've only been to a hospital twice. Once when I broke my arm and the other time for Ramona. When I came to see Dahlia, I had a sick feeling on the elevator, not just because of the cologne from the man in the business suit. Just being there brought it all back. The chime of the elevator, the squeak of the floors, the ammonia. Ramona was lying in the bed, her face swollen to twice its size, lip split, nose pushed to the side. She looked like a cartoon character of herself. My father paced around the room while my mother stared straight ahead, like she couldn't see anything.

But when I got to see Dahlia, she looked okay. She looked like Dahlia.

She told me about her seizures, and I know all about seizures because a kid from my high school had them. He was the closest I had to a friend—probably because he got shunned by everyone else. *I don't know what they're all so afraid of,* I told him. *It's an electrical problem with your brain. Just faulty wiring is all.* But he looked like someone else when he was having them, drooling and his body in spasm. I could see why the other kids were scared.

Dahlia looked like herself, but tired. And we watched the video.

A car honks at me as I cross the street, and I notice that the signal has turned. That happens to me sometimes. My thoughts get so strong that they take over the real world, and I don't see things right in front of me. Walking down the street, I count my steps. When I get to seventeen, my nerves start to settle down. The counting thing is weird, but it works. Another thing Jamal taught me.

But then, I think about the video and start counting again.

The video. There's no word for it. If there were a *bad things* file in my head, it would be locked away in there. I would cordon it off like the worst virus ever made and kill it dead.

Sitting with Dahlia on the hospital bed, I had a flashback to Ramona that night.

What can I do? I asked my sister. I remember feeling guilty, like I should have helped her, protected her. *Let me help,* I said. But Ramona didn't want my help. She said, *Don't worry about it. It's not worth it. They're just a bunch of stupid townies.* Tears ran down her purple-blue, swollen cheeks. I couldn't help but wonder if that's what Rob would have said. But Rob wasn't there. So I asked her again to be sure, and she said, *Forget about it, James. That's what I want you to do. Forget about it.* For the first time in her entire life, she looked tired of me.

I was going to do it too, anyway. I was going to hunt every one of them down, even if I had to go to jail. But then, she died. And it wasn't worth it anymore. There was no point. So I tried to do what Ramona asked me to do, forget about it. But I couldn't.

And maybe Dahlia wants the same thing, just to forget about it. But I don't think so. I could tell by the way she was looking at the wall. Thinking about it. And maybe I shouldn't have said anything. But I wanted to help somehow. I remember having nightmares after Ramona died. That somehow I was programming the video game she was in. And I couldn't stop building the bridge that she jumped off. I kept trying to make it lower, or create a trampoline underneath her, but I wouldn't stop coding the damn bridge. It was awful.

But this is different. We actually have a chance. We could work on the code together this time and change the game. So Dahlia wins. Dahlia stands victorious with her purple hair and all her tattoos, and the villains in the video lose. They lose badly.

We make them hurt.

I've stopped counting my footsteps by the time I get to the T station. As I'm walking down the stairs, someone bumps into me. I feel in my pocket for my wallet, which is still there. That happened on the subway once when I first went to MIT, and they took everything. My parents had to help me get my driver's license and credit cards back. Another reason I hate the T.

Soon, my car will be fixed, and I won't have to worry about all this, standing there in the gray, damp tunnel, waiting for the train and calculating how many minutes I'm wasting. But I hardly even think about that now.

I couldn't help my sister, but maybe I can help Dahlia.

CHAPTER FIFTEEN

HAWK CLUB CHAT ROOM

Bruinsblow: Okay, guys. Vihaan and I called the meeting because we got a situation here.

Joe225: Wait. Before we go any further, no one can hack into here, right?

Holts: Yeah, Vihaan. We're using names etc. You sure this is secure?

Desiforever: Yes, for the hundredth time. It's secure. It's got like 10 firewalls. This isn't a fucking Facebook group.

Holts: Fine. Chill. I just want to be sure.

PorscheD: What's up?

Bruinsblow: Someone posted a video of one of the parties.

Taxman: WHAT??

Bruinsblow: Stevie-O saw it. On some dumb-ass men's rights website.

Mollysdad: Vaguely remember Stevie-O. He was outgoing President when I punched.

Joe225: Yeah, he's a solid guy.

Bruinsblow: He's at a law firm in Boston. Researching some case and he found it.

Taxman: Which party was it?

Bruinsblow: I didn't remember but Stevie-O said her name was Dahlia.

Mollysdad: No recollection. But we were pretty wasted.

PorscheD: I remember a Daisy? Never got partied though.

Creoletransplant: No. Daisy was the hot one. Blond.

Joe225: I remember Dahlia. She was in Civ Ed with me and Cary Graham. Total stuck-up bitch.

Holts: I do too. She was pretty smart though, bro.

PorscheD: Not that smart, lol

Bruinsblow: Here's the problem, some of us are on that clip, and she saw it.

Creoletransplant: She SAW it???

Taxman: Who's on there?

Desiforever: Don't know. The link Stevie-O sent didn't work. He's trying again, but Graham called me totally freaking out. Guess he's on it front and center.

Mollysdad: Oooh snap. Not good.

Holts: Who cares? She was so messed up. She probably doesn't remember a thing. It's not like she was putting up a fight or something.

Bruinsblow: Yeah, but what if she goes to the police?

Desiforever: Supposedly she had some kind of seizure after she saw it. Doubt she's going to the police.

Holts: No way. She'd get crucified.

Mollysdad: Who put it on the website though?

PorscheD: *crickets*

Mollysdad: No one on here obviously

Desiforever: I think it's good we all know about it. Don't think it requires action though.

Taxman: Agreed.

Bruinsblow: You sure about that?

Desiforever: Absolutely. Just wanted to let people know.

Bruinsblow: Fine. All in favor then? Do nothing?

Creoletransplant: Aye, aye.

Holts: Second.

Bruinsblow: Okay then. Agreed. We watch and wait.

Desiforever: For now.

CHAPTER SIXTEEN

Five Years Ago

For some reason, I keep staring at his hood.

The thick, gray faux fur stitched onto the hood of the campus policeman's coat. I never really paid attention to them at all before, much less their hoods. They were just "security guys" who were neither here nor there.

Right now, Security Guy is standing next to the "real" police, in a starchy blue uniform that pouches at the belly. Officer Morris, his name tag says. He is in his thirties with oily skin and ginger, balding hair.

"So you claim you were raped?" he asks.

Daisy answers for me. "She doesn't claim *anything*. Look at her."

He does, then looks back at his notebook. "And when did you say this occurred?"

"I don't know."

Now he looks my way again, eyebrows raised. "You don't know?"

"I was pretty out of it. Last night sometime."

"Uh-huh." The phrase is fairly dripping with disdain.

"Jesus," Daisy breaks in. "She was obviously drugged or something. She barely remembers anything."

"Did you have anything to drink last night?" he asks me.

I nod.

"How much?"

There is a pause, while Security Guy slurps coffee.

"How much?" Officer Morris repeats, with less patience.

"I don't know. Four...five."

"Aren't you going to take pictures or anything?" Daisy asks.

"How about drugs?" Morris asks, ignoring her. "Did you have any of those? Uppers? Pot?"

I avoid Daisy's eyes. Even I'm not stupid enough to fall for this one. "No," I lie.

"So you were at a party," Morris says, pronouncing it in the Boston way, "pah-ty." He scratches an incipient mustache. "And what, you were kissing and things got a little rough?"

"Pick a scenario," Daisy mutters. "Any scenario."

"No," I say. "I was raped." I look down at my hands, more scratch marks. "I don't remember how I got there. But there was a mattress. More than one guy."

Security Guy starts writing. "Where was this?" Morris asks.

"I don't know."

"Not the actual address," Morris explains. "Just the place."

"I don't know," I repeat, feeling like an idiot.

He shrugs at Security Guy. "That's not much to go on, hon."

I don't answer. I want them to go away. I need them to go away.

"This may be kind of tough," Morris says, using a fake, caring tone that he probably learned in a sensitivity class. "But you say you were raped. Can you tell me exactly what they did to you?"

I have a flash of a face looming over me. Two boys trying something. Pain. I have a flash of being pushed off a mattress. Repositioned, tugged. Pain. A line of men, laughing.

"I don't remember."

Morris snaps his notebook shut. "Listen, dear, we can't help you if you won't help us."

Daisy rolls her eyes. "And you were being ever so very helpful."

"I'm sorry," I say. From the handbook. Always be polite, always apologize.

"Well," Morris says. "You've been through a lot."

I nod and start crying. I am pathetic. Just a tincture of kindness will do it.

"Okay," Morris says. "We'll talk more later, when you're not in shock."

Is that what this is, I wonder. Shock?

"We're going to have to take some quick pictures now, like your friend wanted."

So I let them. The flashes blinding me. Documenting scrapes, bruises, my privates. Like some kind of weird forensic centerfold. I am seeing red spots. Daisy is holding my sweaty hand and I think I can't possibly get through this. There is no way, but then I realize that it's going to be okay. Of course it will be okay.

I won't have to apologize, or be polite, or be helpful, or anything. It'll all be better soon. Because I have a brilliant, infallible idea.

I'm going to kill myself.

CHAPTER SEVENTEEN

DAHLIA

A t work, people tiptoe around me.

And why wouldn't they? Not only did I perform my extravagant fish-flop routine in the break room, but now I'll also be forever known as the "girl in the video." Not that I'm ashamed of what happened. If Rae-Ann has taught me anything, it's that I'm not responsible for the behavior of violent assholes. But, be that as it may, people still treat you differently. They shouldn't, but they do. And it sucks. For instance, no one has asked me to do any extra projects today, and Connor didn't meet my eyes in the hallway.

At least Sylvia doesn't tiptoe around it. "I heard about what happened," she says the moment I sit down.

I yank a file drawer open. "Uh-huh." I'm hoping my tone conveys my desired reticence on the subject right now.

"If you ever want to talk about it…" She lets the sentiment trail off, which is probably for the best. Sylvia is many things, but a social worker is not one of them.

"Thanks," I say and put on a smile. "It was such a long time ago."

She uncaps a pen and starts crossing out paragraphs with a flourish. "My cousin got raped by some jerk in college too."

"Oh…yeah?" I don't have a pat answer for that one.

"Never reported it though." She recaps the pen, then looks back up. "I wouldn't either. Cops are such assholes."

"Uh-huh." It's a generalization, but I can't say my experience belies this.

"Hey, did you see that IT guy again?" She is apparently ready to move on to safer conversation topics. Men. Men who don't rape, anyway.

"James," I answer. "Sort of." I'm not sure if a hospital visit counts.

"He seems really…intense or something," she says. "Reserved. I mean, what do you guys talk about? Still waters and all."

"I don't know," I say. "You don't always need words to communicate."

She shoots me a knowing grin, misunderstanding this, and I decide to let her. "Okay, now I gotcha." She lets out a lurid giggle, then crosses off more paragraphs. "He does have nice shoulders," she admits. And when I think about it, it's true. "You do your thing, honey. I totally got you now."

What she doesn't know is that I've been thinking about James, a lot.

I took two days off work after my seizure. Maybe they're not real, but they're still exhausting and I needed to recover. But instead of the deadening self-care that I usually do after them, I couldn't stop thinking about what he said.

We could hurt them, like they hurt you.

I didn't focus on acceptance and understanding, things I've been taught to do like a trained monkey. I didn't lie on the couch while Eli cheered me up with goofy stories, or take hour-long baths.

I felt angry. Deeply, deeply angry.

And the idea kept coming back to me, like a boomerang that will always fly back no matter how far it's thrown.

Hurt them. Make them pay.

And I kept asking myself. Could I do that? Could I do that to them? And I've decided the answer is yes. I could. I want to do that. I want to act finally, not just react. I don't want to understand and accept. Not anymore.

I want to make them hurt. I want my revenge.

My text sound dings and I turn the volume down. We're not supposed to be checking our phones at work. But I doubt anyone would challenge me on it today. I would just give them puppy dog eyes and say it was "my family checking up on me." I can work the system when I have to. It's James.

Hi. Wanted to see how you were doing?

Better, thanks. I pause, and before I can second-guess myself, I keep writing. Were you serious about what you said in the hospital? About revenge?
The response is quick. Yes.

Then I want to do it.

After a pause, another text bubble appears. When?
Do you have any plans tonight? I ask.

No.

Wanna come over?

Sure.

Good. 7 pm? I type in my address.
He texts, Okay. Bye.
So I write okay, bye too.
Grabbing my eponymous mug, I decide to head to the break room. Two of the senior lawyers skitter away when I enter. But Connor stays behind.
"Hey, Dahlia," he says.
"Hi, Connor." I head over to the coffee maker.
He trails me, then leaves a foot between us. "I'm really sorry about the other day. Those guys shouldn't have been watching that. Actually, no one should have been watching that."
"Oh yeah, I know," I mutter. "It's okay." It's not okay, of course, on so many levels. But there's nothing else to say. And if he's worried about me suing for sexual harassment or something, he doesn't have to.

He pauses, and I can see his cheeks are flushed. "If you ever want to prosecute those…people," he says, as if he'd like to call them something else. "I'd be happy to help you. Just so you know."

"Thanks." I toy with the handle on my mug. "Not right now, but…thanks." I look up at him, and he nods, then leaves the room.

After work, I run to see Rae-Ann before my date with James.

She agreed to an early session when I called her from the hospital. Now sitting next to her on the musty couch, watching the video again, my resolve has not weakened. Hearing their glib comments while raping me, the pained moaning noises I'm making in the video, I am filled with the same feeling. The feeling that simmered in me in the hospital bed, that I've beaten down and held back for such a long time now, I can barely remember it.

Rage. Burning hot rage.

Rae-Ann holds my phone with a death grip until the video ends, then she sighs. "This is awful, Dahlia." It's the right thing to say, though the obvious thing. She stands up from the couch and goes over to her desk, and as she rips open her packet of tea, her hands are shaky. The scent of peach ripples through the room. "Are you going to the police?"

I shake my head.

The top of the flowery china teapot clinks as she removes it. "It might be different this time."

"Or," I say softly, "it might not be."

She leans back in her chair with a frown. "You're right. The awful thing is you're right." Staring in the distance, she lifts and dunks the tea bag. "I can't promise you it'll be worth it in good conscience. I just can't." She replaces the lid, and sinks back into her chair. "Have you gone back to S.O.R.?"

"No. Not yet." Survivors of Rape, the one I met Natasha in.

I always hated the survivor thing, to be honest. Surviving. What kind of life is that? It's not like we chose it. The Unlucky Club would be more appropriate.

"You might want to go back," she says.

"Yeah, maybe," I say, though I'm not sure. I may have finally reached support group saturation point. At some time, you have to act, not just keep talking.

"At the risk of sounding like Pollyanna," she says, "there may be a positive in this."

I stare at the vanilla candle flickering on the side table, which sends off a scent that competes with the peach. "What would that be?"

"You got some of the time back." The tea gurgles into her mug as she pours. "Maybe that will help bring some more memories back."

I shift on the couch, playing with a loose brown thread. "I know it's what I always wanted. But in the end, it's kind of a watch-what-you-wish-for situation."

Her smile is sad. "We've talked about integration, right? Closure?"

"Yes," I say, holding back a yawn. It's been a long couple of days.

"Having that gap of time seemed to be preventing that. Maybe this will help you close it."

"Maybe." It makes sense. Patching a piece into my life's quilt to make it complete. But to extend the metaphor to absurdity, it's a terrible square of fabric.

We talk a bit more and then I leave, back through beautiful-ugly Harvard Yard, back to the brick T station that will carry me to a job that I don't love. My body is exhausted, bone-tired. Spying the station up ahead, I realize that for the first time ever, I didn't tell Rae-Ann the truth. I didn't tell her about my date with James tonight. I didn't tell her about my dreams last night, of people holding me down. Laughter over me. Pain in my stomach. But weaved in there was the vision of James's tattoo, like a beacon.

Revenge.

Rae-Ann is not about revenge. The concept is antithetical

to her. She is about accepting, integrating, moving on, with a cup of tea and a vanilla candle by her side. But right now, I'm ready to take a different path. Right now, there is no closure, no moving on.

Pretty Girl is dead.

And I'm ready to hurt them, like they hurt me.

CHAPTER EIGHTEEN

DAHLIA

While waiting for James, I try to ward off pangs of guilt.
Because I know in my heart, I shouldn't get him involved in all this. Just because he gave me the idea doesn't mean he needs to be ensnared in it. I have the video. I can track down the rapists on my own. I don't need to risk getting James in trouble. And if he comes tonight, we're crossing the Rubicon. We're doing this thing.

But I can't forget the feel of his hand on my elbow. The determined look in his eyes. His tattoo. I guess the fact is, I'm selfish. I want to get him involved. And if I'm honest, I'm afraid to do it alone.

My stomach growls. Simone lifts her triangular head off my lap and stares at me with some disdain. "Sorry. I'm hungry." I glance at the clock. 6:40 p.m. James will be here soon, with food.

Crouching on the couch, I turn on the video on my iPad. James helped me save it in case the site goes down, which was rather resourceful in my opinion.

I don't want to watch it.

It goes against every fiber in my being and every basic instinct. I literally fight the urge to throw up to do so. But I have to. If I'm going to take revenge, I need to be scientific about it. I need to figure out who these people are and where the attack took place. And this is my only horrible, despicable clue.

So I keep watching. Then at minute 3:10, I notice something. An odd noise.

I rewind the video a bit and replay it. Simone pricks up her ears.

I play it once again, focusing on the sound. A tinny, metallic noise, followed by a high-pitched, two-tone whistle. Like a birdcall. With a shock, I realize it's the sound from my nightmares. Birds. But where would there be birds in the room?

It takes a couple of times replaying the ten-second clip, when I realize it's a mechanical sound. Then I see it in the corner of the screen. A little bird emerging from a clock, tweeting.

"A cuckoo clock," I say with the satisfaction of solving one vital chunk of a jigsaw puzzle. I rewind it one more time, staring at the screen, when a memory jars me. A party, freshman year. Daisy is drunk and yelling above the music, *Why do you guys have a cuckoo clock? You guys should have a Hawk Clock, get it? Hawk Clock?* It was a stupid, barely memorable joke. But I remember it. I think I remember it anyway, or maybe I just want to remember it? It is a hazy, dreamy fragment of memory. Grabbing my phone, I text Daisy.

Did the Hawk Club have a cuckoo clock?

I play the sound from the video one more time while waiting for her response, which comes back immediately.

So that's completely random. But yes, I think so. Why?

Did you know any of the guys in that club?

A few of them. What's up?

That's where the rape occurred.

My phone rings in my hand while I'm still texting.

"How do you know?" she asks, her voice breathless. "Are you sure?"

"I think so. I remembered the cuckoo clock." A faint squeaking noise comes through the wall of the apartment next door, followed by the hum of a vacuum. "And if they had a cuckoo clock, it has to be them."

"But... I mean... So you started getting some memories back?"

"Not exactly." I pause a minute, deciding whether I should tell her. The vacuum noise blares, then retreats. "Someone put up a video of it on this psycho anti-woman site. It's a long story, but I saw it. At work."

"What?" Her voice is panicky, which is why I didn't want to tell her. Daisy veers toward the dramatic side at times. "It's on the internet? You saw it?"

"Yes, they did. And yes, I saw it." I try to sound nonchalant, though it could throw me into a seizure. A fake seizure.

"Oh my God," she says in a shocked whisper. "Did you recognize anyone?"

"Just one guy. Terry, I think his name was? From Civ Ed. But I can't remember his last name."

"Terry," she repeats, as if trying to place him. "I don't remember any Terry in our class. Though I wasn't in Civ Ed. Was Quinn? She remembers everyone."

"I'm not sure. Did you know anyone else from that club?" The vacuum suddenly stops, leaving utter silence. Then, the bumping sound of it being put away.

"Jeez, I'm not sure... Tom Lashmore?"

"Yeah, I know him. Wasn't in there. Well, he could have been, but not in the video."

"Justin Heller... He was the one who drove a Porsche everywhere."

"He sounds kind of familiar," I say.

"Taylor Dewey, he was their token black guy."

"Not there."

She exhales. "I'd have to think, Dahlia. But no one else comes to mind."

After debating a moment, I decide to plunge ahead and ask. "Would you be willing to watch it? Just to see if you recognize anyone?" There is a long, painful pause on the other end. "Forget it. You don't have to—"

"No, no," she jumps in. "Of course I will. You lived through it. The least I can do is watch it."

"I know it's not exactly pleasant. But I would appreciate it."
I pet Simone, who yawns extravagantly. "I'll email you the link,
okay?" I ask and realize how odd that sounds. Like I'm sending
her a funny puppy GIF or something.

"I'll watch it later when I get home," she says. "And, Dahlia…"
Her voice gets thick. "I'm sorry that you're going through this."

"It's not your fault," I say and hang up. As I do, another text
comes in from James.

I'm here.

⸻

"This is nice," James says.

He's referring to the Coltrane playing from my cheap wireless
speakers. I dig into my rice container. "You play an instrument?"

He tears open a packet of soy sauce. "I played cello for a while.
But I sucked."

"Really? That surprises me."

"Yeah, I know. An Asian kid who can't play an instrument."
His tone is only half-joking.

"Actually, I meant…" I scoop out more rice. "It just seems like
you're really good at everything."

He shrugs, looking embarrassed, but not displeased. "Not
cello," he says and puts his water bottle down, crinkling the
plastic. "Total disappointment to my parents. They're both good
musicians." He twirls the lo mein with his fork. "Rob was a great
musician too. Violin."

"Who's Rob?" I ask, grabbing another napkin.

"Oh," he says, his gaze dropping. "No one, forget it." He takes
a long drink of water, maybe to hide his expression. "How about
you?" he asks then. "You play anything?"

I wipe my mouth with the napkin. "I played guitar for a little
bit. Pretty much to be cool. Didn't get past the calluses though,"
I say, examining my fingers.

We don't talk for a bit as the music plays and we finish our meals. The evening has darkened to black outside, as the soft base line rumbles through the room. James tosses his Chinese food containers in the trash, then goes to the couch while I rinse off the plates and put them in the tiny dishwasher. Simone rubs by my leg, then perches on her favorite seat, and I go sit next to James, bringing a plate of Rice Krispie Treats. Brandon with the AC/DC tattoo made them for Eli, who was too polite to say he wasn't a fan. I am a fan. I'm hoping Brandon makes lots of Rice Krispies Treats.

"So," he says, putting his hands on his knees. "Where should we start?"

For a bizarre second, I think he's referring to the protocol for making out. "With what?"

He tilts his head at the question. "The revenge plan."

"Ah," I say with some relief. "The revenge plan, right." I smooth the armrest of the fake brown leather. Then I stand up, walking over to the windowsill. "Here's the thing. I've been thinking about that…"

He leans back in the couch. "You don't want to do it?"

"No, it's not that. I do want to do it. It's just…" I turn toward the window, the rows of gray streetlights below. A car zooms by. "I don't want to drag you into all this. This is my fight. You are under no obligation here."

"I know," he says, seemingly undeterred. "It's not about obligation. I want to."

"Yeah, but I don't even know what's going to be involved. It could be dangerous. We could get in trouble." I throw up my hands. "All sorts of things."

"I'm fine with that."

"Right. But I'm not sure if *I'm* fine with that."

James sucks in his lower lip, then stares down at the coffee table. His face is blurrily reflected on the veneer. "I couldn't help my sister," he says in a deep voice. "She got hurt, and she jumped. And I have to live with that." He looks up at me. "But I *can* help you."

"James," I say, softly. "This isn't about Ramona."

"No. I know that. But…" He puts his hands on his knees. "It's just… I like you. And I want to help you."

"I like you too," I admit. "But we hardly know each other."

"True. And you have no reason to trust me." He squares his body to me. "But I promise that you can. I'm…" He pauses, searching for the right phrase. "I'm like…a QWERTY keyboard."

I stare at him in confusion.

"No, that's not quite right…" He drums his fingers on his thigh, thinking. "I'm…WYSIWYG," he says with a decisive nod. "That's it. I'm WYSIWYG."

I stare at him another second. "I'm sorry. I really don't understand."

"WYSIWYG," he says, as if it's obvious. "'What you see is what you get.' It's a type of programming. Lets you program without even knowing code. That's me. Easy. What you see is what you get. No surprises."

Smiling at this, I sit back down. "You're WYSIWYG."

"A hundred percent."

I consider this. I don't trust many people, for obvious reasons. I trust Eli. That's about it. Not Shoshana, not Daisy, not even my parents really. But James is WYSIWYG. And a little piece of me wonders if I could trust him too.

"Okay," I say. "Let's do it."

James reaches over to pet Simone, who purrs in delight.

"First off," I say. "We need to have rules."

"Uh-huh. Rules are good." He glances at his laptop on the coffee table. "Should I write this down?"

"Oh, no. I don't think we need to. It's really just one basic rule, as I see it," I say. "We can do whatever we have to do to get justice. But we can't physically hurt anyone."

He scratches his chin, which I notice has the tiniest cleft. "That makes sense. I'd rather not hurt anyone either." He takes his hand away from his chin and starts stroking Simone again, his biceps rippling with the motion. "So what exactly do you mean by justice?"

"Good question," I say and reach over to the plate of Rice Krispies Treats on the coffee table. "Prison."

"Prison," he repeats.

"Do you want one?" I ask, between chews.

He shakes his head. "I hate Rice Krispies Treats."

This almost makes me chuckle. WYSIWYG. He would have told Brandon he wasn't a fan.

"Anyway," I say, "prison. That's it, quite simply. I just want to put each and every one of them in jail where they belong. Where they should have gone for what they did to me in the first place."

He uncrosses his arms, and Simone takes the opportunity to mold her body against him. "How do we get them there?" he asks.

I brush some Krispies off my jeans. "Obviously not for the rape. Because no one ever goes to jail for that. And I'm not dealing with the police."

"Right."

"So, we frame them for something else. Anything else that works."

He squints, thinking. "And if we have to lie and cheat to do it?"

"So be it."

"That's not against the rules, then?"

"Not at all."

He crosses his arms, "Good then. We have rules. So, who should we nail first?"

I smile at him, quite taken with his enthusiasm, and swallow the last of my Rice Krispies Treat. "Okay. Let's be methodical here."

"Methodical. Yes. Good."

"We have four men in all," I say. "Three should be easy to identify. The guy filming will be harder."

"Agreed," he says.

"We know the first guy, rapist number one. Terry Somebody, from my Civ Ed class."

James starts typing into the laptop.

Rapist #1—Terry BLANK.
Rapist #2—unknown.
Rapist #3—unknown. Redhead.
Rapist #4—unknown. Filming.

We both stare at the computer screen, acutely aware of how little we actually know.

"Not looking promising," I say, voicing our predicament.

James stares at the screen another moment, then nods his head, as if he's reached a decision. "We need a funnel."

I turn to him. "A funnel?"

"Yes."

"I...I don't know." I glance around the apartment. "I probably have one in the kitchen somewhere."

"No, not that. An informational funnel. Cloudlock. EverString. That sort of the thing."

I shake my head. "Different language, James."

"A data funnel. So we can find these guys. We need to start with the correct data, then funnel it."

I'm still staring at him blankly, which he registers. "Here, let me show you." He starts typing. "What's it called again, the Hawk Place?"

"Hawk Club," I correct him. "It's a final club."

James moves in toward the screen. "Which is...?"

"Kind of like a fraternity. Only snobbier."

He moves farther in toward the screen, while Simone takes the opportunity to crawl onto his lap. "So that's our first data set. The names of all the members."

"Yeah, but how do we get that?"

He shrugs. "We hack into it."

"Ah," I say with approval. "Of course we do." I chuck him on the shoulder. "You are so smart, James Gardner." He smiles, self-consciously. I feel a bit foolish, like a kid playing detective or something. But there's no script for this. No Revenging-Your-Rape-for-Dummies out there.

"So step one, we identify them," he says. "Step two, we frame them."

"And step three," I say, "we watch them wriggle on the hook."

He smiles. "I think that's my favorite step."

"Me too," I agree. I stare at his computer screen, a Wikipedia page on Harvard final clubs. "Step two is going to be the hardest one though. Framing them for something."

Again, we pause, considering this. "It might help to do some field research," James says.

"Go on."

"It wasn't really my thing. But my friend Allison did it. She watched meerkats for an entire summer. This could be kind of like that."

"Interesting," I say, warming to the idea. "Only hawks instead of meerkats." I push the plate of Rice Krispies to the side. "I like it. We examine them in their natural habitat to plumb out any weak areas. Come up with something plausible but illegal and then…"

"Step three," he says, and we both grin. As I shift on the couch, my knee touches his. Not a light touch, more of a smack. Bone on bone. We stare at each other for a second. Then a loud knock rings out, and we both turn to the door as it squeaks open.

"Hey," Eli says, cradling a six-pack of beer.

Eli surveys us both.

"I didn't know you had company," he says, but he doesn't motion to leave. James stares at him, and there's an awkward pause while we wait for him to suggest he come back another time, and he doesn't.

"That's okay. Come on in," I say.

Simone jumps off James and struts over to rub against Eli. She is a fickle one, my cat. Eli wanders over to the coffee table and leans over to peer at the screen.

"What's that?" he asks with a startled glance at the Hawk Club web search.

James closes the program out. "Nothing."

Eli straightens back up. "Didn't look like nothing." His beer bottles clink in the carrier while he sits down on the opposite couch.

"It's a project we're doing," I say.

"For work?" he asks, dubious.

"Kind of," I answer, then exchange a look with James.

"What, is it top secret or something?" Eli asks. He uncaps a beer bottle, then pulls one out to offer James, who shakes his head.

"I'll tell you," I say, "only if you promise not to get mad."

"Right." Simone leaps up onto his lap, and he takes a long sip of beer. "Because you always listen to what I think."

"We're planning something," I say.

"Okay...I'll play. What are you planning?"

"Revenge," I answer.

"Revenge," he says, then stares at me. Simone taps at the beer bottle with her paw, and he pulls it away. "Revenge for what, may I ask?"

I fold my arms across my chest. "Revenge for raping me."

A heavy, uncomfortable silence follows my statement. "What do you mean?" A tremor ripples in his voice.

"I mean that I'm taking revenge on everyone who raped me. And James is helping."

Eli keeps staring at me. He doesn't blink. "You're not serious."

"As the plague," I answer.

"Wow." Eli stands up from the couch as Simone leaps off him. "Wow," he repeats and starts walking back and forth, shaking his head. "Can I just say that this seems like an extremely bad idea?"

"Why is that?" James asks. His tone is level, not belligerent, but not exactly friendly either.

"Well, let's see." Eli keeps pacing, not even looking at him. "Pissing off a bunch of rapists. Ripping open a nearly healed wound. I mean, really. What could possibly go wrong?"

"Maybe this will help to heal the wound," I say.

"And maybe it won't." Eli stops and turns to me, purposefully ignoring James. "You don't even know these people. You could be poking a bear here."

"Yeah, well, some bears deserve to be poked."

He shakes his head. "There are always consequences with these things," Eli says. "Unintended consequences."

"You're right," I say. "I will be giving them consequences. That they surely did not intend."

Eli sits down again, putting his hands in a prayer position under his chin. "This is not a good idea. You don't want to go back there, Dahl. Remember what it was like? What you were like?"

I don't answer him, and he sits on the couch, staring at the floor for a little while, before he nods, probably realizing there's no point in continuing that argument. He inhales sharply and stands up from the couch. Simone turns her head to watch him leave. When he gets to the door, he puts his hand on the knob and turns back to me. "Promise me you'll think about this, okay?"

I nod. It's not a lie. I'll be thinking about it a lot.

"Because I don't want to see you get hurt," he says, his jaw clenching. "And maybe you don't care about that, Dahlia. But I do."

CHAPTER NINETEEN

JAMES

I look around my empty apartment.

Maybe I should get a cat. I never really liked cats, but I wasn't ever close to one before tonight. And Simone was nice and soft. When she purred, the sensation was surprisingly calming. Perfect sine waves of vibration.

Ramona always loved cats. I think she would have liked Dahlia too.

But here we go, back to Ramona. Circular thinking, Jamal calls it, where I'm constantly going back to what I could have done, what I should have done. Like an if-then statement that loops around endlessly.

So I won't think of Ramona.

I'll think of Dahlia and how close we were in the kitchen. How I leaned into her, her warm skin, her soapy clean smell, and her smile that is like sunshine. How our knees touched each other.

My cell phone vibrates on the table and I see on the screen that it's my mom. I haven't called her back in two weeks, which makes me feel guilty, so I answer.

"Hi, Mom."

"Hi, James. You okay?"

"Yeah, sure, Mom. I'm okay."

She speaks English with a heavy accent and imperfect grammar. But I only speak a tiny bit of Japanese, so I shouldn't talk. She says the problem with English is "the rules don't make sense." My mom is a math professor at a little college in Maine, my father a physics professor—they're both big on rules. Which is probably why it hurt so much, when Ramona broke them.

"How is work?" she asks.

"Okay," I answer. My mom knows I don't talk much, but she doesn't take it personally. Dad doesn't talk much either.

"No problems?"

"No," I say. She knows about the bad review when I first got hired and the few meetings with Grayson. "Things are good now."

"How is...Jamal?" I can tell by her voice that the question makes her uncomfortable, but she asks it anyway.

"Fine."

"You coming for Christmas? Your father wants you to."

I pause a second. "Um...okay." I doubt Dad actually wants me to, but I can't think of an excuse not to. After all, they live only four hours away. And I will hopefully have my car back by then. Otherwise, they would have to face the holiday alone. The first Christmas without Rob. And Ramona.

"Good," she says with relief. "Your father is so happy then."

"Okay," I say, though I'm not so sure about that. "I gotta go. I'll call soon, okay?"

"Okay," she answers, and we hang up.

I sit down on the couch, listening to the clock ticking, and think of sitting next to her. So close that our knees bumped. Another one to stow away in the good things file.

Jamal suggested I write them down in a journal so when I'm feeling sad, I can look through the pages and remember all the good things in my life. Part of the remolding my brain thing. I once kept a journal in high school for English class. I wrote a poem in there for this girl Sarah Gibbons and gave it to her. She said it was creepy though, and I never wrote anyone a poem again. But if I wrote a poem to Dahlia, it would go like this:

> *I like you.*
> *I like everything about you.*
> *I like your black eyebrows. I like the notch in your clavicle. I*
> *like the way your voice is soft and brave at the same time. You*

smile a lot but when no one is looking, you always seemed sad, and now I understand why. They say I can't read faces but sometimes I can.

And I could read your face all day.

CHAPTER TWENTY

Five Years Ago

*I*t isn't so easy to kill yourself.

I don't have a gun. I don't take any medication, except Motrin once in a while, and any Google search will tell you that won't do it. I could try hanging, but I'd probably fuck it up and end up as a vegetable. I could go the carbon monoxide route, but I don't own a car or a garage. I don't have the nerve to jump in front of a car (and again, run the risk of ending up paraplegic, but not quite dead). And I hate the sight of blood too much to cut my wrists.

It isn't easy to kill yourself. But then again, it isn't easy to live either.

I spend three days holed up in my room with Daisy and Quinn bringing me food from the dining hall, whispering in the hallway outside.

Should we call someone?

I don't know. Would she be mad at us?

Maybe we should just give her some time. She's been through a lot.

I lie in my bed all day. Sleep is bliss when it comes. Usually it doesn't. My body hurts. My face hurts. My head hurts. I hold my pee until my bladder is bursting because even with the antibiotics, it hurts too much to go. I think of them touching me under the heat of the lamp, the doctor debating whether he should stitch me or not. But I don't want to think about that.

Thinking is dangerous. Closing my eyes is dangerous. I could fall into a panicky swirl of darkness and grabbing and distorted laughter and pain. But I don't even know what's real right now. I don't remember anything.

My memories feel like a pastiche of rape scenes from movies or news shows. And that is the utterly worst part of the whole thing: I don't remember. Only brief flashes. Birds chirping. Men in a line. I don't know what's real and what isn't, and I can't even trust my brain.

On the fourth day, there is a knock on the door.

I don't answer. I don't open it.

But the door opens anyway, and in walks my mom and my younger sister, Shoshana.

My mom's face tells me everything. "Oh, Dahlia." She hones right in on me, hugging me with blankets and all, while Shoshana stands awkwardly at the foot of the bed.

I start crying. I haven't cried since the rape. I haven't had any tears left.

"It's okay," she coos. She is rubbing my back. Nothing has ever felt so good. The bed rocks as Shoshana sits down at my feet. "You want to come home?" my mom asks.

I shake my head. "I have to go to classes."

"Take the semester off, honey. You can do that. I can talk to them."

I shake my head again. I am still crying. "I can't."

She pats my back. "It's all right. We'll figure it out."

I sniff, catching my hiccupping breath, and she kisses my face, my tears. I feel worse somehow, with all this love. Not deserving of it.

"Do you want to tell me about it?" she asks.

I don't really, but I tell her. And it feels good to let it out. To tell the whole story to a fully loving audience. Not a doctor who won't meet my eyes. Not the police who are muttering behind my back. My mom still has her arm around me, and when I'm done, I can see that she is crying too. She digs a tissue from her purse and rubs her nose. There is a long, painful silence before she speaks.

"I don't blame you, honey, of course I don't," she says, her chin wobbling.

I can't tell if she's angry or sad. Maybe both. A sick feeling creeps into my stomach.

"But I warned you about this, didn't I? Drinking too much? What could happen?" She lets out something between a sob and a sigh.

I feel time stop, slow down. My arms go heavy and fall from the hug. My mom sits there, shaking her head, noiselessly crying, while Shoshana stares at her knees.

CHAPTER TWENTY-ONE

DAHLIA

Daisy gets back to me the next day. Saw the video. This is followed by a sad face emoji. It seems trite for the situation, but then again, there's really no appropriate emoji for this situation.

Do you remember Blake Roberts?

Doesn't ring a bell. Is he in there?

I don't want to say for sure, in case I'm wrong. But I think it might be him.

I plug the name into my Google search box.

He's a gazillionaire, Daisy texts. But maybe it's not him? Face a little shaded on video.

I click on images and get plenty of head shots. She's right. It looks a lot like one of the guys in the video from what I remember, but it's hard to say for sure. He was mostly in shadow, though I do recall a beak-like profile in one part of the shot.

Not sure, I answer back.

Had an unpleasant run-in with him after college. And he was in WSJ a few days ago. So he might just be on my brain.

WSJ? I am typing, but don't send, as I figure it out. Thanks, I type, then put my phone away. "Have you seen the *Wall Street Journal* this week?" I ask Sylvia, who looks at me like I've lost my mind.

"Yeah, right. You know me. I'm always perusing the *Wall Street Journal*."

"I need it," I say, trying to control the urgency in my voice. "For a case."

She puts a red pencil in her teeth and lisps, "It's probably in the conference room." Then she adds, "Or online," before taking the pencil out of her mouth.

"I'll check the conference room," I say, launching out of my chair. We probably have an online subscription, but I don't know the password or anything. Connor is sitting cross-legged in a chair, his dark-gray socks showing. And of course, he is flipping through the *Wall Street Journal*.

"Hi," I say.

He peeks his face over the paper and looks surprised to see me. I'm not a regular in the conference room. "Hi," he says back. "Just waiting on a client. Did you need something?"

"Nothing major." I readjust my barrette, as a piece of purple hair slips out. "I was actually looking for the *Wall Street Journal* too."

"Today's?"

"No, last week's." I wander over to the table, to the neat outlay of newspapers, all from today.

"Might have been recycled already." He heads over to the bin with me, watching me with a mixture of concern and curiosity.

I start sorting through the bin, flipping through soft, loose pages.

"Do you know the exact date?" he asks.

"No…" Then I see it. The paper is folded over to that page, with his face. "I'm just going to…" I say, motioning toward the back of the room.

"Oh, sure," Connor says and returns to his chair.

I steal off to the back corner, by the window. Traffic flows by on the street, oddly silent all those floors below. Like I'm in a bubble up here, hermetically sealed off from the world that plods on below me, like any other ordinary day.

I turn on the video and put it on silent. At minute 2:15, he pops up, and I get one solid glimpse of his face. It's definitely him, the same face from the article.

It's hard to miss it. The article features a huge picture of him. *Blake Roberts: Hedge Wunderkind.* His face is enormous. His smile, ghastly. And a smaller picture is included, with his beak-nosed profile smiling at his lovely wife. The same face that in minute 2:19 of the video announced, "This is getting boring. I'm going to do her in the ass." I notice a crinkling noise and realize the paper is shaking in my hands. After folding the paper back up, I walk back to the front of the room.

Connor looks up at me from his own paper. "You okay?"

"Yeah," I answer, my voice scratchy.

"You look like you've seen the proverbial ghost."

"Yeah, sort of," I answer in a daze. I motion to the paper. "I just need to make a copy of this…because…" My voice trails off.

"I think you can have it." He shrugs. "It was just going in recycling." There are footsteps in the doorway, and a smile brightens his face. "Chuck," he calls out and strides over to his client, his arm outstretched. I walk out of the room, the paper tight underneath my arm. And I text Daisy.

It's him.

"Did you get what you were looking for?" Sylvia asks, sliding open an overhead shelf and pulling out a hefty binder.

"Yup." The article is splayed out on my desk, and I don't even look up to answer.

"I never read that one. I just get all my info on Facebook."

"Uh-huh," I answer, still poring over every word. She seems to sense my myopic viewpoint and stops talking, flipping open her notebook.

Blake Roberts is a billionaire. Not a millionaire, like a number of my classmates who also immediately became hedge fund managers directly after graduation. He bet big on some particular wheat product, of all things, as well as other unlikely money magnets, and is now a billionaire. His ugly face is handsome, his expression pure confidence. Zipping over to his profile in his company website, I learn that he is happily married and a Big Brother for less fortunate kids in Cambridge because he "just wants to give back to the community."

I feel physically ill.

"Is that something for work?" she asks, probably noting my sour expression.

I take a deep breath. "Yeah. We're getting this guy for tax evasion."

"Good," she says, glancing at her computer screen. "Rich pricks. They deserve it."

She has no idea the truth she speaks. My phone rings, and I figure it'll be James, informing me of a hundred things he's already found on Blake Roberts (a.k.a. Rapist #2) since I texted him the name a few minutes ago. But it's not him. It's Daisy. "So, you're sure then?" she asks. "It's him?"

"Yeah."

There is a pause. "I wanted to make sure before I called." She coughs. "I saw him a couple years ago at a conference in New York."

"Uh-huh?" I turn the paper over, to stop staring at that disgusting smile.

"He had just gotten married. And he totally made a pass at me. Made ridiculous hints the entire time about visiting his hotel room." She chokes out a laugh. "Not even hints. He slipped his fucking hotel card into my pocket with a note about what a great night we could have."

"Ew."

"Exactly. I wouldn't have gone in there for a million dollars."

"Well," I say, "he certainly had a few million to give you."

"Yeah," she grumbles. "The whole conference was sort of gross. Caviar freaking everywhere."

"I'll bet," I say, thinking how he'll have to do some adjusting though.

Because they don't serve caviar in prison.

I can barely concentrate all class.

My mind keeps drifting away, dreaming up all sorts of vengeance plots for Blake Roberts, each with serious pitfalls. Finally, the professor wraps up, and I file out with the others. Dodging past some students glued to their screens, I walk through the Yard, then see a familiar form waiting by the front gate.

"Hey, stranger," I say.

"Hey." James is standing in front of me, casting a shadow in the streetlight. A bite of fall is in the air, but he's still in Birkenstocks. He happened to have an appointment out this way, so we decided to meet after class to take the T home together. As we walk out past the gates, the noise of the cars swells, the tires rumbling over the streets.

"How was your appointment?" I ask.

"Good." He shoves some papers in the front of his hoodie, maybe from the appointment. He doesn't offer what it was for. "How was your class?"

"Good," I say. A car races by us, spraying a light sheen of water from a puddle. "I thought you hated the T."

"I do," he says. "Car's not quite ready."

We race-jaywalk together across the street to Harvard Station. "So, any thoughts on Blake Roberts?" I ask. The squeaking of trains rises up the stairs at the mouth of the station. "I've come up with a few million ways to kill him. Unfortunately, it goes against the code."

"What do you mean?" he asks, his voice bobbing with each step. "We're coding this?" We get to the bottom of the steps. "I suppose we could," he says. "Java would be simple enough. Or Ruby maybe, but then again—"

"James," I interrupt him. "What are you talking about?"

"Computer code," he says.

"Oh," I say. "Not that kind of code. I meant a code of conduct. Our rules. Not hurting anyone."

"Oh right. *That* code." The train emerges, drowning him out. As it screeches to a stop, we step on. The train is nearly empty, and we easily find two seats together. We settle into the red plastic seats as the train lurches away, announcing the next station.

"Maybe we could hack into his computer?" James asks.

"Maybe," I say, realizing that hacking appears to be James's answer for everything. I sway back and forth with the movement of the train. "What will that do for us though?"

"I don't know." His eyes wander up to the subway map. "Won't be easy anyway. I've already looked into BR Funds. Super good firewalls."

The train veers to another track, and we rock forward then back in our seats. A wall rumbles by us then floats off, leaving us in blackness. I remember when I first rode the subway. It reminded me of some sort of dystopian Disney ride. I'm used to it by now, but sometimes it still leaves me feeling disjointed and displaced. "This is me," I say, as the train announces my stop.

"Yeah," he says. "I'll change over here too." We step off together onto a crowded platform. The shuffle of the passengers shoves us together and we push our way toward a steel pillar, away from the crush of people.

"Oh, hey," he says, reaching into the front pocket of his hoodie. "I almost forgot." He hands me a folded-up stack of papers. The paper crackles as I unfold it, straightening out the creases. It appears to be a list of names. "It's the Hawk Club members," he says, "starting from five years before your attack."

My mouth falls open. "You got it? Already?"

He looks down at his Birkenstocks. "Yeah. I tracked down an old reunion invitation that made it onto the web. They've changed servers since, but they didn't deactivate the old one so I got into their membership database."

"Uh-huh."

"It wasn't that hard," he explains.

A wave of passengers files onto the train, running past us. I am gripping the paper in my hands. My treasure map. "James," I say with appreciation.

He blushes, then gives me something between a wave and a salute, before disappearing into the crowd.

CHAPTER TWENTY-TWO

DAHLIA

H ow are you doing?" Connor asks, touching his beard, which is rustier than his blond hair.

"Good," I answer.

He rakes his fingers through his hair, and I worry that he is going to bring up the video again. "Good, good." He clears his throat. "So, where are we with the Davenport file?"

The simplicity of his work-related question fills me with relief, rapidly followed by total panic. The Davenport file. *Shit.* I'd completely forgotten about it. "Um, still working on it. Just got to make a few more changes."

"Great. End of day then?" he asks.

"Definitely," I say with false certainty. The file is seventy-five pages. End of day will be a stretch.

"Okay, perfect. Thanks." He walks away.

I start searching my pile for the Davenport file. "Crap, I'm dead," I say once Connor's out of earshot.

"Need some help?" Sylvia asks.

"Oh my God, could you?"

"No problem." She scoots out her chair from her desk. "I know you've had a lot going on lately."

Translation: *I know the entire law firm just watched you get raped.* But what the hell, I could definitely use the pity-help right now. I peel out the last twenty-five pages from my ream. "I'll email you what he wants."

"Sounds good," she says, taking the stack. She peers over toward his office and lowers her voice. "He's cute, isn't he?"

"Connor?" I ask, pretending I never noticed. "I suppose, for a boss."

"Yeah," she agrees. "I wouldn't date my boss either but still…" Sylvia tosses something in the recycling bin, then spins back to the desk. "So sad, about his wife. I had a cousin who died of breast cancer."

"Yeah. It's too bad." Uncharitably, I wonder if she is making up some of these cousins.

My phone rings, and it's Daisy. I don't have time to chat right now, but she never calls during work, so I figure it might be some news. "Hey, what's up?"

"Nothing much," she says. Then she pauses. "I have a question for you."

"Okay," I say, disquieted by her weighty tone.

"Do you remember Sean Gowers, from our class? Works for his father's law firm?"

"No." It doesn't surprise me not to remember him. Daisy knows everyone and I know no one. "Was he from Hawk Club?"

"No. Phoenix Club."

"Okay." Phoenix is one of the "good" final clubs, one that started accepting women early on. "What about him?"

"Well, he's doing some work for us. And I asked him about the Hawk Club. He said he knew some of the guys there. Turns out he was punching for Hawk Club and dropped out. Said he heard some scary shit about them."

"Oh?" My interest is piqued.

"He might recognize some of those guys. You mind if I show him the video?"

The question makes me wince, but it's a solid lead. "Sure. Of course."

"Great," she says. "I gave him your number. If he knows anything, he'll call you."

It's past seven by the time I'm done with the Davenport file, and the office is empty. But the file is complete, scanned, and emailed. I'll have to bring Sylvia a Starbucks tomorrow as a thank-you.

My stomach is complaining as I clean up my desk. On the way out, I stop by the vending machine, staring at the dull light. Pretzels might do the trick, if the machine will take my crinkly dollar. I am pulling out my wallet when I get a text from Eli.

Got extra from the kitchen tonight. Pumpkin ravioli.

Getting free food is one of the few perks of his bartending job. I put my wallet back. Pumpkin ravioli definitely trumps pretzels.

My apartment at 8?

See you there, he texts back.

A half hour later, I'm off the subway and a block away from the apartment. I pull out my phone to see if any more comments were added to the video. It was off-line for a while, but someone put it back up. Eli told me I was sick, watching it all the time. He's probably right, but I can't help it. It's like an itch that I need to scratch, even if it draws blood, even if I tear the scab off. Because now it's out there, that night. Part of my life that I could never account for was finally given back to me. Like a gift, spiked with poison.

I scroll through all the old comments, many suggesting Photoshopping, rape apologists explaining about what the girl might have been wearing or how much alcohol she might have had or how she shouldn't go to parties anyway and how I would never let my daughter get in that situation, etc., along with the usual bitch-whore-cunt type of stuff. But there is one new comment, at the bottom.

I stop in my tracks, staring at the screen. People jostle by me on the street; someone bumps my shoulder. A car whizzes past me, and I'm still staring. A sick feeling in my stomach boils over into fury.

It wasn't rape. That cunt was begging for it all night.

—Cary G.

———

When I get to my apartment, Eli is already in the kitchen, dumping the ravioli into a strainer. Steam twirls above the pasta hissing in the sink. My brain is racing through all the people I know named Cary, which is no one.

"Yo," I say.

"Yo back," he answers, then peers over at me. "What's wrong? You're scowling."

"I'm not scowling."

"Fine," he says, putting a loaf of bread on the table. "You're not scowling. You always look like someone just killed your dog."

"I don't have a dog."

"Not the point," he says.

I wasn't going to say anything because he's so touchy about the revenge thing, but he's too good at reading me. Always has been. As I am at him. So, as he turns the burner off the sauce, I show him the comment on the screen. His expression sours. "Jesus." Handing me the phone back, he starts ladling ravioli onto our plates.

"Did you know him?" he asks as we sit at the table.

"No." I rip off a piece of the bread. "For the life of me, I cannot remember anyone named Cary." But as I say the name, a chill passes through me. A flash of a memory from senior year. The guy from Civ Ed, whom I politely turned down. Quinn and I were walking out of Sanders Hall the next week, and as he passed me, he said something under his breath but loud enough so I could hear it: *Cunt.*

"Cary," I say. "Not Terry." I pick up my phone again to look at the screen.

"Who's Cary not Terry?" Eli asks, his mouth full.

"The guy from Civ Ed class," I answer. "Rapist number one." But then I remember Eli's never watched the video, so he doesn't know what I'm talking about. I tap my finger against my forehead. "What the hell was his last name? Cary, Cary, Cary," I repeat, trying to stir it from my memory. Then it hits me. "Of course. I'm such an idiot!" I jump out of my seat.

"What?" Eli asks, stabbing a piece of ravioli.

"Face book," I say, heading over to the other room.

"Why would he be on your Facebook?"

"No, not Facebook. The freshman yearbook thing," I call back from the storage closet. "The original face book." I'm referring to the book sent out to all incoming Harvard freshman with wallet-sized photos of the whole class. Folks call it the "face book," after which Zuckerberg famously titled his website. Rifling through a box of stuff, I'm wondering why I didn't think of it before. Probably because even looking at the book made me nauseated. I had thrown it out when I left college and came home, and my mom snuck it out of the garbage. The musty box is full of stuff I haven't looked at in years: knickknacks, old textbooks, a gray sweater I notice has a moth hole. "If he's in my year, he could be in there." My voice echoes in the closet. "Maybe the other guys too," I mumble, not relishing the idea of scouring the faces in there for my other rapists. I shove aside the box and tear the tape off another. More crap. An old field hockey trophy. An out-of-style jeans jacket that smells like pot. More books, tanned at the edges. I'm about to tackle the last box when I see the corner poking out of a stack on the floor. Dark, maroon (crimson, really) with a wrinkled, faded binding. With some effort, I yank it out, slam the closet door shut and sit back down. "Got it."

"Oh joy." Eli spoons some more ravioli on his plate. My plate is still half-full.

I start flipping through the black-and-white pages of the face book, unsticking a few. "Cary…Cary… Where are you, my friend?" I start through the grainy photos, scanning through the Gs when his picture leaps out at me. The same face in the video. But this time he's not closing his eyes, frowning while coming and thrusting. He's not pushing my legs as far open as they will go.

I stab my index finger into his stupid, smiling face.

I found you, Cary Graham. And I'm going to wipe that smile off your face.

CHAPTER TWENTY-THREE

JAMES

There is a point when it happens every time.

The rhythm melds my body into a machine, my bones, tendons, muscles all working together. Not a perfect machine, but close, with batteries that get recharged daily and a heart muscle that lasts for eighty years or more, notwithstanding a coding mal-function (e.g., cancer) or a disruptive outside force (e.g., slamming into a wall of water at a hundred miles an hour).

The swimming was Jamal's idea too. For stress-relief, he said. But it's more than that for me. In the pool, I am at peace. I don't have to worry about how other people see me, or if I'm offending someone or acting weird. It's easy to be normal in the pool.

I do freestyle only. I learned the other strokes when I was a kid. But it was torture back then, I remember. My father looming above me like some D&D ogre, yelling at the side of the pool. The cold water, the echoing noise, the shimmer of the waves on the ceiling in a bewildering array of values you could never draw a vector through.

But at some point, it changed.

I don't know how, but it did. That happens sometimes, and I don't even notice it. Jamal calls it acclimatization, which makes sense from a neuronal standpoint. But I think it could be just growing up.

The other good thing about swimming is how people look at me differently now. Cooper told me that. "Dude, you been lifting weights?" he asked about six months after I started. My shoulders got bigger, my leg muscles more defined. My perfect machine became mine. I can't tell if Dahlia sees me that way or not though. I think she might. I thought so, when we were sitting together on the subway. But I could be wrong.

I thought about her idea of a code for the project and decided she's right.

We should have a code. And I need a code too. If I'm helping her so she'll be my girlfriend, that's not right. And it probably won't work. And if I'm doing it for Ramona, it won't bring her back. It won't erase that night, my mother calling me in college with tears in her voice. It won't change the fact that my father won't even say her name.

And there's my circular thinking again.

So I focus on swimming, letting my mind go empty, my arm arching through the air, my hand slicing the water at the right angle. The right amount of water slipping through my fingers. I touch the rough concrete wall and take a deep breath. Thirty-eight.

Plunging into the water again, I shoot my arm out and swim mindlessly, in a dream state, for laps and laps and laps.

When I get out of the pool, my muscles are soft and relaxed. The hot shower feels great, washing off the chlorine smell (though I don't mind the smell anymore). After these swims, I know sleep will be no problem, that I won't be up for hours trying to solve problems that are unsolvable.

A guy smiles at me from across the bench. "Hey."

"Hey," I say back, then busy myself with my locker. I'm not trying to be mean, but the last time a guy struck up a conversation in here and said he liked my tattoo, I thought we were trying to be friends, but it turns out he wanted to kiss me. I'm fine with biological diversity and different people being attracted to different people, but I happen to be heterosexual, and he was a little put off when I explained all that to him.

I get dressed quickly, and the guy finally leaves.

Reaching for my phone in my hoodie pocket, I see a text on the screen. Automatically I smile when I see it's from Dahlia.

Found rapist #1. Not Terry BLANK. Cary Graham.
#1—Graham
#2—Roberts

I text her back. Two down. Two to go.

CHAPTER TWENTY-FOUR

DAHLIA

I'm so slammed at work the next day, I barely have time to think about Cary Graham at all. The first couple of hours, I'm rounding up medical records from various hospitals for different clients—one hip surgery gone awry, one cataract surgery gone awry, and one canine surgery gone awry. No idea why Connor accepted that one, but he said it's a friend of a friend who's torn up about the whole thing and he's going for emotional suffering.

Sylvia runs in late from an appointment, and I hold up her Starbucks venti triple triple. Her eyes widen in delight. "What's this for?"

"Davenport. You saved my ass."

"Aw," she says, taking it from my hand. "That was sweet." She peels off her coat and starts straightening out her desk.

Turning back to my computer, I look up Paul Snyder's number. He's our PI, our go-to guy for sniffing out disability fakers, and I need him for another medical case, this one a back surgery gone awry.

"Hey there, gorgeous," he says, answering the phone.

"Hey, Snyder." I have no idea why I let him get away with calling me that. But he's sixty and sees me as a daughter, I think. And he does good work.

"Okay, gimme the story," he says.

"The name is Terence Malone," I say and explain how Terence is on worker's comp for back pain but as per the ex–Mrs. Malone (who isn't exactly a disinterested party) still manages to attend his weekly bowling league.

"Got it." I hear him cap his pen. "Just him? Any others?"

An idea hits me then. Probably not a good idea, but one that lingers in my head for a couple extra seconds nonetheless. "Maybe one more person."

"Maybe?" he asks with a note of intrigue.

I tinker with the corner of a sheet of paper, flicking it back and forth, deciding. "It's more of a personal thing you know, versus a work thing."

A long pause follows this. "Go on." Though his tone is more hesitant now.

"Forget it," I mutter. "You know what? It's not a big deal. Let's just hit our stealth bowler."

But he doesn't hang up. "Why don't you tell me about it, gorgeous? I might not be able to help. But maybe I can."

I flick the paper faster, so much that Sylvia glances over at me. "It's like this." I turn to the corner, lowering my voice. "There's a guy who did something to me. Something bad. A while ago."

"Yeah."

"I'm trying to get some information on him."

I hear scribbling on the other end of the phone. "Something bad?" he asks. "Are we talking broke up with you or something?"

"No," I say. "Bad bad." I pause. "The worst you could do to a woman and not kill her." My finger is madly flicking the paper and I stop it. "Do you understand me?"

His breath is heavy in the phone. "Yes, I understand you, gorgeous. Give me the name."

By the end of the workday, I've found out a bit about Cary Graham.

Like any other monstrous sociopath, he lives among us. A Google search spilled out all his vital information in about 0.8 seconds. Though he's nowhere near Blake Roberts's stratus, he's doing just fine. After graduation, he joined Dunbolt Investment Banking and is currently enrolled in Harvard Business School at night. So, we're both night students, he's just making twenty-fold what I do.

He's not in the White Pages though, so I don't get a home address. It's a start, anyway, though James probably turned up more information in 0.6 seconds. So we've got two out of four. The last two rapists weren't in the face book, unfortunately. And I've just started making my way through the Hawk Club list that James discovered.

I have faith we'll get Rapist #3, but I'm not so sure about #4, the guy filming. He's the only dark horse out there. All the video shows is a glimpse of his forehead with a Red Sox cap with some kind of stain on the bill. And a stained Red Sox cap in Boston is not much of a clue.

The sound of whistling emerges down the hall, some jaunty show tune, and I turn around to see Snyder bebopping my way. He looks like an old mobster of sorts, had he decided to join the other side of the law, with greased-back gray hair and a bit of a potbelly. But his ratty button-down and a lop-sided tie announces him as one of us. He drops a beat-up briefcase on the floor. "Hey there, gorgeous." He nods over to Sylvia too. "Sylvia, my dear."

"Hey, Snyder," she returns, not looking up from her screen.

He perches himself on the corner of my desk, folding his arms over his gut. "You want the goods or what?"

"I do." I rifle through my satchel and yank out a notebook from my night class. "Give it to me."

"The kid's got a pretty good gig," Snyder says, flipping open his own little notebook. "Makes a lot of money from this Dunbolt thing. Investment banking."

"Uh-huh."

"He's got a girlfriend. Tina Delgado. Hispanic girl. Very pretty. Don't know what she's doing with that schmuck."

"Okay." I write this down, though it doesn't seem terribly pertinent.

"Nice little apartment on Chase Avenue—49 Chase Avenue, to be exact. Key code 8-8-8-8. Which is plain stupid, if you ask me."

"Wait," I say. "Key code to what?"

"The apartment," he says. "The garage box."

"Oh." This tidbit, I am definitely writing down. "How'd you figure that out?"

"She keyed it in," he says. "The Delgado girl."

"And you could see her?"

He raises an eyebrow. "Ever hear of binoculars, gorgeous?"

"Right," I say, drawing the word out with recognition at my own dim-wittedness.

"Anyway," he says, adjusting himself on the edge of the desk. "They seem pretty serious. Window-shopping for wedding rings on Thursday night."

I cross my arms. "You can find out a lot with binoculars."

"Actually, that one was Instagram," he says with a chuckle. "I do have the internet, you know." He leans a hand on my desk. "Oh, and another thing. She's pregnant."

"How'd you…?" I ask, but answer myself. "Instagram."

"Oh yeah," he says. "About a million pictures of the smallest baby bump ever."

Sylvia picks up her purse and heads off with a little wave. "Girl's room," she mouths. I nod back at her, then put my pen on the desk. "Sounds like he's got the perfect little life then."

"Perhaps. But with one tiny little wrinkle," Snyder says, leaning toward me with a grin.

"Oh yeah?" My pen is alight again.

He lowers his voice. "He's a cokehead."

I lean back in my chair, a smile growing on my face. "A coke-head. That is a serious wrinkle."

"It certainly is."

"You didn't get that one off Instagram."

"No, I did not," he concurs. "But I did see him leave work to snort in his car three times this afternoon."

"Cokehead," I muse, with pleasure. Field research at its finest. We certainly found a weak spot for this particular hawk. I can't wait to tell James.

"I still gotta figure out his dealer, but that shouldn't be too hard. I'll trail him tomorrow." He stands up from the desk and performs a loud, groaning stretch. "I just wanted to give you the good news."

I stand up too. "Thank you, Snyder. So much."

"My pleasure." He drops his notebook into his briefcase and picks it up.

"So, what do I owe you?" I ask, reaching for my purse.

"On the house, gorgeous."

"No, really. You...you don't need to do that."

"Next time, I'll charge you. This time, it was my pleasure." He gives me his old mobster grin. "Helping to nail some bastard is just a perk of the job."

———

"Coke?" Eli asks over the phone. "How very old-school of him."

"Yeah, he's pretty behind the times on that one. Anyone who's anyone knows fentanyl is where it's at." Walking to the subway station from work, I pull my hat over my ears against the chill.

"So what are you gonna do with that little nugget?" he asks.

"Not sure." Stale heat rises up from a sidewalk grate. "I have to think about it." As I walk on, I hear laughter and yelling sound out over the phone.

"Hey, gotta go," he says. "Bunch of people just walked in."

"See ya." Hanging up, I get to the stairs of the station, my mind looping through all possible modes of revenge. As I walk down, a text rings in my purse, and I grab my phone next to my Beretta.

Send anonymous tip to the police text line? It's James. I have to chuckle that he's obsessing over this too.

Police might fall for it. But wouldn't go to prison, I answer.

No?

No. He's white. Would end up in rehab.

The dot-waiting message stays on my phone while I wait for the train. What if we make him a dealer?

I think about this one. That might actually work. He would have to get some time for that.

I'm about to answer, when a voice interrupts me.

"Dahlia?"

I look over to see a figure with green, stringy hair coming my way from the bench by the wall. "Natasha," I say, as we give a mini-hug. "This isn't your usual spot." This may not be entirely coincidental. I did give her forty bucks last time.

"Changing things up a bit," she says. She's still got her pregnant sign. And with her pudgy belly, she could pass. She clears her throat, possibly a cue for me to give her money, and we wait awkwardly for the train that never comes when you want it to. I reach into my purse for a ten this time, when suddenly the train is barreling down the tunnel, the light soaring toward us. I'm about to hand her the money, when an idea strikes.

"Hey." I pull her over by the elbow to the bench. "I have an odd question for you."

"Yeah?" she asks, sitting down, peering into my purse.

I wait for the stragglers to board the train, then look around to make sure no one else is around. "Would you be able to get me cocaine?"

For an instant, she looks at me like I've gone mad, then quickly assembles her professional face. "Maybe," she says. "For the right price."

CHAPTER TWENTY-FIVE

Five Years Ago

I decide.

Pills.

That would be the easiest.

It's amazing how much one can think about this, especially when one stops doing homework or much of anything else.

Sometimes Daisy or Quinn manages to drag me out of bed for class. When my mom left, they convinced me to come to English class. It's a required class, and we're all taking it. I don't want to fail.

It was a labor. I had to get out of bed. I had to shower. I had to put on clothes. I had to do my best not to cry. They helped me with every step. We walked slowly to the class. My book bag was too heavy and they carried my books. It's usually a pleasant, fifteen-minute walk. It took us forty-five minutes and I rested on a couple of benches. By the time we finally got to class, we were late.

When we opened the door, the room turned to look. A hundred eyes staring at me in absolute, deathly silence. Daisy cleared her throat as Quinn made her way down the aisle to find us seats. And all I could think, with my face burning hot with shame is:

They know.

They absolutely have to know. So now I don't go to class. Sometimes I try to get up for lunch, but I can't eat. The smell is nauseating. My clothes are hanging off me and people keep asking me if I'm sick.

The flu, I tell them. It's easier than saying "Yes, I'm sick. I got drunk and high and people took me in a room and raped me and I don't remember anything, but I can't stand to be talking to you. You with your cheerful voice and sparkly headband and plate full of food that makes me want to retch."

It's hard to tell someone, yes, I'm sick. When I wake up in the morning, I don't want to be awake. I can't bear to think about all of the minutes looming ahead of me. The day is a gaping hole of hours. The day is quicksand, waiting to suck me under.

And I want out.

I don't blame myself for what happened, but I do blame myself for what happened. My mom blames me for what happened. I'm afraid to sleep at night because I dream of hands holding me down, but I can't stand to be awake. There is no place for me to be. It was not like this a month ago, but a month ago is a lifetime ago.

Daisy brings me hot chocolate, but it smells rank.

Quinn leaves me sticky notes with the social worker's number in a heart that says "We love you," but I can't call the person. I don't have the right to call her. People with real problems should call her. I just did something stupid that wasn't my fault.

Pills. I've been reading up on the best ones. Tylenol will take out your liver, but it's not fast. Aspirin might or might not do it. Motrin will just give you an ulcer. Antidepressants, ironically enough, might be my best bet. So, I'm thinking of going to the UHS and getting me some. But I won't mention the S word. No one's asked me anyway. Not sweet-talking Daisy or uncharacteristically careful Quinn. I suppose they're afraid that they'll give me the idea, which is hilarious. It's the only idea that I have nowadays.

I can't tell anyone the truth, because they wouldn't understand. Suicide sounds so big, so dramatic and final. I guess that's because it is.

But it's also the only thing that gives me a shred of hope these days.

CHAPTER TWENTY-SIX

DAHLIA

James unwraps his silver energy bar. "Five thousand dollars?"

"That's what she said."

The wrapper crinkles. "Sounds pretty steep to me."

"Probably." I flick a crumb off the table. "I suppose we could negotiate it. But I am the one asking for the coke."

"True," he acknowledges. "Do you have that much?"

"No," I scoff, amused at the thought. "Do you?"

"No," he admits. He unfolds another inch of the bar. "We could get a loan maybe."

With a chuckle, I put on an official sounding voice. "Yes, we'd like to borrow five thousand dollars for a promising business venture. We're investing in an extremely large amount of cocaine."

James purses his lips. "And I suppose robbing a bank might go against our code."

I stare at him, and he offers a little grin. "Attention," I announce. "James Gardner is making a joke."

He smiles again and pops the remainder of the bar in his mouth. Then he straightens himself in his chair, all business. "Okay, so let's just say we get five thousand dollars and your friend actually gives us the cocaine."

I nod. "Both huge ifs."

"Correct," he confirms. "Then what would we do?"

"Frame him," I say.

"Right," he answers. "I got that. But how do we do that exactly?" He drums his fingers on his thigh, something I've noticed he does when he's thinking. "We need to make him a credible dealer."

"Agreed."

"So if we can get the cocaine, somehow we need to tie him to it."

I take a sip of coffee. "We need to plant it in his house."

"Which means we have to get into the house," he says.

"Snyder got us the key code," I remind him.

"Alarm?"

I pause, taking another sip from my mug. "Don't know." I put the coffee down on the table. "If so, we're screwed." We both pause, flummoxed by this roadblock. "All right. Let's just say we get in there," I proffer.

"Okay." He opens another protein bar and offers it to me, but I shake my head.

"First off, we'll need to be sure we don't get our DNA all over."

He shrugs. "Glove, booties, scrub hats. So, hospital supply store."

"And I'm envisioning little baggies," I say. "With bright-green BIG G labels on them."

James lets out a hearty laugh, then assesses me when I don't laugh back. "Wait, were you serious?"

"Of course." I peer into my now-empty coffee mug. "Hand it to the police on a silver platter."

He pauses. "'Silver platter' means 'easy,' right?"

"Right," I say, wondering how he can hack into a computer and not know what a silver platter means. "Anyway," I say. "Plant some bags in his place. Give some to Natasha to spread around." I yawn into my hand. "That would be the basic gist."

"If we can get a hold of five thousand dollars," he adds.

"Yes. There's always that."

He crumples up his wrapper. "I don't know. I could ask my parents but..."

"No. Don't do that. Maybe we could—" But then I stop. Because he gave me an idea. Not an enticing, or even promising idea, perhaps. But an idea nonetheless.

"I think I know someone I can ask," I say.

"Five thousand?" Shoshana asks with obvious surprise.

"Um, yeah. That's, um…that's right." I want to bury my head under the desk. She should be spending the money on baby stuff anyway, not giving it to her ne'er-do-well sister. And if she asks what it's for, I'm not sure how I'd answer. *What's it for? Oh, nothing. I just have to pay my homeless friend for a large stash of cocaine.* I am holding my breath in the pause before her answer.

"Okay," she says.

"Okay?" I repeat with disbelief.

"Yeah," she says. "Noah and I did really well this year. That should be no problem."

Noah is her husband, whom she married right out of college. Noah is essentially perfect. Jewish, good-looking, kind. I even like him. And now they are making perfect progeny together.

"I just took on a new client too," she continues, like she might be convincing herself. "Yeah, no problem. Five thousand should be completely doable."

"Great!" I sit up in my chair as Sylvia rounds back to her seat, and at once, the telltale scent of Wite-Out fills the cubicle.

"You want me to wire it or something?" Shoshana asks.

"Oh, well, that would be perfect, if you could," I say, scrounging around my drawer for my checkbook. I give her the routing number, etc. in a low voice, then stash my checkbook away again. "I'll pay you back," I say, hoping this is true, eventually.

"Don't worry about it."

"No, I will."

"Should be there EOD," she says, ignoring my protests.

"Great," I answer, thinking how no one actually *says* EOD. Lawyers write it in emails all the time, but they don't say it, because it's just as fast to say *end of day*. But she is giving me five thousand dollars, so I shouldn't be churlish.

"Who was that?" Sylvia asks.

"My sister, Shoshana."

"Oh yeah?" She starts collating a file into stacks. "I didn't know you had a sister."

"Yeah," I say. "Three years younger. A lawyer."

"What firm?" Sylvia asks.

"Greenberg and Fein. Out in California." I open up my email, then remember my manners. "You have a sister, right?" I vaguely remember hearing about her bitching about the bridesmaid dresses.

"Four of them."

I turn from my computer screen. "Seriously?"

"And two brothers. Typical Catholics, you know." She purses her lips to blow over some Wite-Out. "You're Jewish, right?"

"Sort of."

She lets out an abridged donkey laugh. "What's that mean?"

It means I don't believe in God anymore. "Lapsed, I guess."

"Yeah, right. Beau's the same. Catholic though."

"Uh-huh."

"Lots of Jewish people in the firm," she comments. "Not that it's bad or anything."

"No, I didn't think you meant that."

Sylvia is right. There are lots of us in the firm. So much so that my last name gives them pause. *Edelman... Wait, you're one of us!* This is followed by a puzzled look, then unasked questions: *How come you didn't go to law school? What are you doing slumming with the paralegals? How can you even live on what you're making? You got into Harvard, for God's sake. Why didn't you graduate?* Questions, if I'm honest, I sometimes ask myself.

They're more used to a Shoshana, who will definitely be making partner in her firm. Like my dad did before her. Shoshana is the white sheep of the family, who did all the right things. Went to Yale. Graduated. Married a perfect Jewish man. Became a lawyer. No tattoos. Two right-size diamond earrings only. And of course—the kicker—she never went and got herself gang-raped. Which is the real reason she's wiring me five thousand dollars, no questions asked.

Not that it's her fault, it isn't. But at the same time, it never happened to her. She wasn't a member of the Unlucky Club.

And when Mom said I shouldn't have drunk so much, when Dad turned bright red and said he never wanted to hear another word about "the incident" again, Shoshana didn't say a word. She just sat there and stared.

We had been close before "the incident." We weren't afterward.

I don't know if she blamed me too, for getting raped, for fucking up the family. I don't know because I couldn't bear to ask her.

Just in case the answer was yes.

———

"Protestant," James says in response to my question.

We are playing chess outside Au Bon Pain in the cooling, cloudy afternoon while waiting for Natasha. Well, he's trying to teach me, and I'm trying to feign interest in the game. I keep glancing over at the brick wall at the corner, her usual spot. So far, nothing. I have five thousand dollars in cash, fresh from the bank across the street, flaming a hole in my purse.

"I'm Jewish."

"Yeah, I know." He moves his pawn.

"How do you know?" I ask, mirroring his move.

"It's a Jewish name," he says, shifting his pawn again. "You don't want to do that."

"I don't?"

"No, use the other pawn, or go with the other side. You're opening yourself up."

"I thought the pawns were pretty much disposable."

"Kinda," he says unhelpfully.

Feeling a phantom vibration on my thigh, I check my text for the hundredth time in case she got back to me. "I really don't get this game."

"It takes practice." He moves his pawn again, encroaching onto my board.

"Do you care that I'm Jewish?" I ask.

He shrugs. "Do you care that I'm Protestant?"

"No." I move my pawn again.

He smiles. "Good move." His queen clicks on the board. "Religion is basically just different programming languages, in my opinion."

"How's that?" I ask, as he consumes yet another one of my pawns.

"Everyone's trying to figure out the universe, right?" He lines up my purloined chess pieces on his side. "So God is the array programmer, and people try to translate into assembly languages. Analytica, Octave, etc."

"Hmph," I say, surveying the board. "I don't understand a thing you just said, but somehow I think you're exactly right." I make another move, and he smiles again.

"Oh," he says. "I had an idea for your seizures."

"My seizures?" I ask, rubbing my cold hands together. "Were we talking about my seizures?"

"No, sorry." He glances up at me. "I do that sometimes. Go off on a tangent."

"That's okay." I puzzle over my next move. "What about my seizures?"

"I had an idea how you could stop them. Since they're not electrical and it's more a mind-set thing." Finally, he reaches over to make a move for me.

"Okay, what is it?" I lean back, more than happy to let him play against himself.

"My friend from D&D used to have this spell when she played. She stole it from the Wiccans, I think, but it was pretty cool. It's to ward off evil."

"Wiccans," I say, definitely interested now. "How does it go?"

James stops, puts his palms up, and closes his eyes. In a deep voice, he says, "'Go back from whence you came. Go back from whence you came. Go home.'" He pauses and opens his eyes. "And you keep repeating it."

Someone races by me on a skateboard, clacking the cobblestone. "And that's it?"

"That's it," he says.

I nod, leaning back in the stiff chair and putting my palms up as well. "Go back whence you came. Go back whence you came. Go home." I feel silly. "Then you keep saying it?"

"Until the evil goes away." He moves his king. "And you have to close your eyes."

I move my queen. "And do you think this actually wards off evil?"

"No," he says carefully, examining the board for his next move. "But if your mind holds on to that, then you might not have the seizure."

I shrug. "Worth a try. Better than meds anyway." I turn back to the board, but thankfully, my text buzzes for real this time.

I CAN GET IT.

"Natasha?" he asks.

"Yup." My knee is jiggling in excitement.

Great! We're at Au Bon Pain by Harvard.

Okay. Be there soon.

I groan, showing him the text. "'Soon' has many meanings to Natasha."

He smiles at this while plowing farther into my board. "You give her that money, you think you'll ever see her again?"

Glumly, I push my bishop the wrong way, and James corrects it. "Doubt it," I answer.

CHAPTER TWENTY-SEVEN

DAHLIA

*S*oon is two hours later. It's dark out, and we've played about ten games, all of which I lost, even though James somewhat patiently talked me through every move. I am rubbing my arms through my thin jacket when Natasha finally deigns to appear.

"Hey." She adjusts her ragged backpack on her shoulder. "You guys playing chess? I love chess." She sits down, cradling her backpack between her feet.

"No, we don't have time," I say before James can agree, which, by the way he glanced at the chess table again, I can tell he might have. "So what's the word?"

"Hey," she scolds me. "Aren't you going to introduce us?"

"Oh, sorry. Natasha, James. James, Natasha."

She looks him up and down and smiles her toothy grin. "Tall, dark, and handsome, huh?" she states in approval, and James blushes. "Filipino?" she asks him.

"Japanese," he answers. "Half."

"I had a Filipino boyfriend once," she says, nodding. "Crazy good sex."

James blushes some more.

"Okay, Natasha. What's happening?" I ask to rescue James from further lewd comments.

"Yeah, okay." She peels her eyes away from him with reluctance. "I talked to a few different dealers. I can get you guys enough. But it's going to take some time. I can't look like I'm trying to deal myself or it'll be a shit storm out there."

"Okay, makes sense." I shiver with cold. A couple college kids walk by us, smelling of alcohol.

"Do you have the money?"

"Yeah," I say. "Two thousand now. And two thousand when you give it to us."

Natasha shakes her head. "That's not what we agreed to. Five K."

"It's what I have. Take it or leave it."

She pauses. "Twenty-five hundred now."

James and I look at each other, and he shrugs at me.

"Okay," I say. "Deal."

We shake on it, and she stands back up.

"Okay, so when do we do the pickup?" I ask.

Natasha glances at the cracked screen of her phone. "I'll text you. Probably sometime next week."

"Next week?"

"I told you. It's going to take time." She boosts her backpack higher on her back and gives me a vibrant grin. "Why? Don't you trust me?"

I don't bother to answer, but peel off twenty-five hundred dollars and hand it to her. She stuffs the money in one of the front pockets of her dirty jeans, then practically bounces away. As she turns the corner, we both stand up from the chairs. My butt is stiff and cold.

James stuffs his hands in his hoodie pockets. "You wanna ride home?"

———

As he slows down, we both search around the road in front of my apartment for a parking spot, not a given at this time of night. "Oh, there," I call out, and he spots the space and executes a perfectly smooth parallel park. As the car idles, I pause a second, not looking forward to leaving the warmth of the car.

James turns off the car and unhooks his seat belt. "Here, I'll walk you in."

In silence, we walk through the chilly night to the vestibule. The heater hums in the silence, and then the door squeaks open, cold air shooting in again. Alethia, a woman from the apartment, gives me a wave and a shy smile.

"Hey," I say.

"Hey," she answers. Alethia practically lives at the gym, so this is how I always see her, in a tracksuit and her hair slicked back, like she just got out of the shower. She usually wears a bleached-out boy cut, but it looks more pinkish today. She's my height with a tattoo sleeve and facial jewelry, so people mix us up sometimes, but I don't see it. Eli calls her Wonder Woman. She's some kind of extreme judo fighter and is pure muscle. After the rape, I took self-defense classes. I have my Beretta and like to think I'm pretty tough, but she'd kick my ever-loving ass in like three seconds.

Alethia grabs her mail and runs to the stairwell, leaving James and me standing there, his hands in his pockets again. "Do you… want to come up?" I ask.

It takes him a long moment to answer, as he looks at the door to the apartment with something like longing. "I probably shouldn't."

"You could," I say, hoping I sound polite and not pathetic. "It would be fine with me."

"No, that's all right," he mutters to the floor. "Maybe next time."

"Okay, no problem," I answer, trying to keep the disappointment, and perhaps tinge of annoyance, out of my voice. "Well," I say, "thanks for tonight. The chess and all that."

"Oh, sure. You're pretty good," he says. He's a terrible liar.

There is a pause, and for some reason, maybe because he is tall, dark, and handsome as Natasha observed, I reach up to hug him goodbye. He hugs me back. His back muscles expand under my fingers, and he pulls me in closer, my chest pressing against his. The hug goes on too long. I can feel his breath rising and falling. He looks down at me, and I catch a peek of his chin, the little cleft, and think he's about to kiss me, but he backs away.

He is staring at the dark marble floor, his arms draped by his sides. "Bye," he says almost in a whisper, and the door buzzes as he leaves.

CHAPTER TWENTY-EIGHT

Five Years Ago

*H*er name is Vrushka. She's a family physician, she tells me, not a psychiatrist. And I hate to admit it, but she's nice.

"Can you tell me why you want an antidepressant?" she asks.

I guess my opening line may have been a bit suspicious. Not Hi, how are you? *Or even* You know, I've been feeling a bit down these days. *Just* Hi, my name is Dahlia, and I want some antidepressants.

"I heard they could help," I say, figuring simplicity beats all.

She nods, a kind smile on her face. "And what do you need help with?"

I bite my lip. "Feeling better."

"Okay." *She scoots her wheely chair closer to me, and I fight the urge to scoot mine away. Personal space has been an issue with me lately. Go figure.*

"Have you been feeling sad?" *she asks.*

I start crying, which both pisses me off and makes me cry more. I had promised myself I wasn't going to cry. I rehearsed before I got in the room. Keep it together. Say you felt a little down and thought this might help. *I wanted to keep things as painless and professional as possible. But my heart isn't listening to me.*

"I can see that's a yes," *she says with warmth.*

I nod at the obvious. She hands me a tissue box, and I rip a few out. I've barely cried since it happened. It's odd. I haven't felt like crying or laughing or anything. It's like someone gave me a shot of novocaine for my feelings. But it appears they might be coming back.

"Sometimes people are embarrassed by this question, but I want you to answer me honestly," she says. "Are you feeling suicidal? Or thinking about harming yourself in any way?"

I shake my head forcefully. I am not falling for that one right now. Whatever happens, I am not screwing up this plan.

"Okay." She sits back in the chair, appearing relieved. "Let's backtrack a little here. Did something happen that started all this?"

I nod.

"Do you want to tell me about that?"

I pause, then give her an honest answer. "No," I say.

She purses her lips. "You don't have to," she says carefully, "but I do think talking about it could help." She scoots in again, squeaking the tile. "Maybe even more than the pills."

"Maybe," I say, the tears dried up now, the numbness seeping back in. "But I can't do that right now."

Vrushka flips through a manila folder, my chart. "I can see that you were in the hospital recently."

"Uh-huh."

"It looks like you were hurt, Dahlia."

Tears threaten again, but I hold them back this time. We are not doing this right now. I need the pills. That's all. So I can move on to step two and get the fuck out of this place. "I don't really want to talk about that."

She puts her hand on my knee, and I jump back. I don't mean to; I just do.

"Sorry," she says.

"No, it's okay," I say. "I'm just...a little jumpy."

"Yes, I should have realized that." She looks back down at the folder, flipping through the pages with an unconscious frown. Then she puts the stack down on the table and smiles at me again. "I'm going to give you some antidepressants."

I can feel myself perk up. Lighten. I am smiling, for the first time in weeks. The smile feels funny on my face.

Vrushka is feeling my joy, probably misinterpreting it, and smiles even wider. "I've faxed it to the pharmacy. But a one-month supply. No refills."

I nod, pretending to ponder this disappointing caveat. But all I'm feeling is relief. I don't need any refills.

"I'm going to give you a name of a social worker. She's wonderful."
She hands me a business card with a sunset on it and the name Rae-Ann
Rhimes. *A weird part of me, the old part of me, pictures telling Daisy
about this.* I wonder if she really rhymes? Like, does she sit in her
apartment all day and say, "Bored, ford, chord?" *It strikes me that
the world is a happier place when you know you won't have to be in it
much longer.*

"Okay?"

"Okay," I agree and slip the card in my backpack.

"And I'd like to see you again in one month."

"Okay," I repeat, but with a weird realization that I am lying. I won't
actually be here. If I go through with it. And I'm going to go through with
it. We set up an appointment, which she plugs into her computer and me
into my phone.

*Then as I stand up, the sinking feeling returns. I don't know why. I
had almost fooled myself into thinking it might be okay. Doable. If I had
the promise of the pills, the escape hatch, then things could get better. But
as I stand up, the grayness stealthily seeps back in, and I know that's a
lie. It won't get better. Today is like every other day. I will have to go
outside and walk all the way back to our dorm. Maybe see friends along
the way and pretend I'm okay. Make conversation. Smile.*

I'm so fucking tired of smiling.

*"But before you go, I have to ask you one more time. Are you feeling
suicidal?"* Her gaze meets mine, revealing no misgivings at the question.
*"Do you have any plans to commit suicide, or any thoughts about it
at all?"*

I answer with a sturdy, convincing headshake. *"No,"* I say. *"Not
at all."*

CHAPTER TWENTY-NINE

DAHLIA

W hat time is it?" I ask.

James consults his iPhone watch. "Ten after twelve," he says, then goes back to sweeping. Simone watches him warily as he eliminates every speck of gray hair in the place. "You should get a hand vacuum thingy. It's much faster."

"I had one. Gave it to Eli."

"Why?"

"It scared Simone."

"Oh." He dumps a mound of dust and hair into my garbage. "That makes sense."

I have to titter. James will forgive Simone everything. He loves that cat. James reaches the broom under a cranny near the sink. "You should do something to distract yourself."

"I know." I stand up and start pacing. "It's just really annoying. She's never on time." Natasha is supposedly on her way over to my apartment any minute with a boatload of cocaine. But as with *soon*, *any minute* is also wide open to interpretation.

"By the way," he says, tapping the pan to settle the dust. "I reached out to a friend from D&D about Blake Roberts."

"What do you mean?" I don't love the idea of my video being spread around to his D&D friends for shits and giggles.

"Hacking into his site." He dumps the dustpan again. Then he meets my eyes. "I mean, I didn't say anything about…why…just to look into it for me."

"Oh." I stop pacing and sit on the couch again. "Did he think he could help?"

"She's going to check it out." He leans on the broom. "I trust her. Solid hacker."

"Oh, good," I say, trying to ignore the unmistakable stab of jealousy from the unexpected *she* pronoun. I take James's advice to distract myself, grabbing the Hawk Club list to Google some more people on it. The crumpled stack of paper is on the coffee table, full of cross-outs and highlights.

Gregory Tambor
Terence Maxwell
Mark Monkarsh
Matthew Sanderson
Vihaan Patel

It reads like a list of Mayflower members, except for a few standouts like Vihaan Patel. James surveys the room and, apparently satisfied, puts the broom back in the closet. Then he sits down next to me on the couch as Simone struts up next to him.

"I did think of something else on the video though," James says. "About the guy filming."

"Oh yeah?" I put the papers down. "What?"

James pulls out his phone and cues it up right at the end. We glimpse an inch of forehead and the flash of his baseball cap before the screen goes blank. "See that?"

I hold the phone. "Yeah, I saw that. It's a Red Sox hat. But that doesn't really get us anywhere. Everyone has a Red Sox hat around here. Par for the course."

"Meaning?" he asks.

I shoot him a look. "Par for the course. Common. Usual."

"Oh, okay," he stammers. "Anyway, but look at the brim."

I peer in closer. "I thought it was a stain?" I ask.

"I thought so too at first, but if you look really hard." He shows me a screen shot that he has somehow zoomed in. "It looks like it might be an autograph." We both lean in closer to look, and I can feel his ribs move, a puff of his breath against my hair. "Maybe we could—"

But I don't let him finish. The fine line of his lips is too close. The woodsy scent of aftershave. I put my hand on his knee, on the worn fabric of his jeans. His eyes close, and we lean in even closer.

His lips are soft with just a tickle of bristle on his upper lip. My hand tightens its grip on his knee. His long arm reaches around me, and then a buzz blares through the apartment. We both freeze. Simone is asleep on the couch, her body expanding with every breath.

Buzz.

"Damn it," I say. "It's Natasha."

———

"Hey," Natasha says. "If it isn't Bonnie and Clyde." She enters the doorway, gazing around the room. "Not bad. Kind of a shoe box, but I suppose I shouldn't judge."

"Do you have it?" I whisper, then wonder why I'm whispering in my own apartment.

"Do you happen to have any beer?" she asks, seemingly ignoring my question, which is not a good sign.

James and I share a worried glance.

"Sure," I say. "Have a seat."

"Thanks." She jostles her backpack onto the floor, smearing it with dirt, then sits down as I hand her a cold, uncapped beer. She downs half the bottle with one sip, then burps.

"Do you have it?" I repeat.

She gazes around the place again. "Sit down, you two. You're making me nervous." So we sit as commanded. "You look like you were up to something," she observes, and James blushes to his roots. "Were you up to something?" she teases.

"Natasha, it's late," I say. "Do you have the stuff or not?"

She plunks the beer down on the table with some irritation. "Fine. Yes, I have it. I was just being sociable, okay? Jeez." She makes a *tsk-tsk* noise to get Simone's attention, who wanders away after one haughty, investigative sniff. "You think I could take a shower before I go?" Natasha asks. "It's been forever."

"Sure. That's fine," I say, trying to keep the impatience out of my voice. "Just...let's see what you got, okay?"

Natasha leans down, the black roots showing through her green, stringy hair. She unzips a side pocket of her backpack with a jerk and pulls out three bags of white powder, each the size of a fist.

"That's it?" I ask, fingering a bag. "All of it?"

"Yes, and that's a lot," she says. "I told you: too much and people would start talking. It may not be much of a life, but I like having it just the same." As I reach over to my purse and open my wallet, Natasha licks her lips. "And I had to go to three different zip codes to get this much."

I hand her the rest of the money. "Well, I do appreciate it."

"Uh-huh," she says, not hiding her skepticism. She tucks the bills in another side pocket, revealing more of my money squirreled away in there. Then she stands up, stretching and rotating her body.

"We good, then?" I ask, hopefully.

"Yeah. Just..." She looks over toward the hallway. "That shower?"

"Oh, yeah, right." I lead her in, quickly assessing whether there's anything worth stealing in there. Not really. Soap. Tampons. She lugs in her backpack and gazes around the tiny room like it's a museum. "I won't be long," she says and shuts the door.

"So," James says.

I laugh. "So."

He yawns, and I pray to God she'll hurry up in there. This is the perfect opportunity for him to stay, and he hasn't made any excuse against it yet.

She doesn't hurry though. She takes forever. The water runs and runs, the soft echoey voice of her singing coming through the wall.

James leans back on the couch, his long legs crossed at the ankles, looking at something on his phone, and I start perusing the list of Hawk Club names again. Time passes, and then finally, the shower stops, and we smile at each other.

More singing. Drawers rattling, which means she is taking everything I own. And finally, she emerges, warm air flooding out of the room. Her hair smells sweet and is now a clean lime green. She looks positively beatific. She has on wrinkled but different clothes, a pair of camouflage pants that strain at her belly. I wonder if she actually is pregnant.

"Thank you," she says with near reverence. She takes a deep breath, then throws her grimy backpack on. "So," she says, looking right at James. "You going to walk me to the station?"

His head pops up from his phone. "The station?"

"I usually wouldn't care," she says. "But I do have a lot of money in here."

"Oh, right, sure." He gives me a rueful half smile. "Of course."

CHAPTER THIRTY

Five Years Ago

I go back and forth all day.

I can't pay attention to a word in my Civ Ed class. Flipping through the pages, my cursive-filled notebook has gone blank, except for little doodles here and there. My brain is as blank as my notebooks. I don't think I'll pass this class.

Walking out, Cary Graham winked at me. I'm sure he meant nothing by it, just being his "hey, dude" friendly self even after I turned him down, but it still filled me with dread for some reason. Men fill me with dread.

Life fills me with dread.

I got home, lay in the pink papasan, and cried for hours. Quinn and Daisy tried to ask what was wrong, but there are only so many times you can ask and be rebuffed, and finally, they stopped asking and just tiptoed around me.

I get a long email from my mom, telling me she is sending me cupcakes and do I want to come home for a "little break"? She doesn't mention the word.

No one says the word. It is an ugly word.

Rape.

But the word is my whole world right now.

I go in my room, which smells. I listen to music, which helps a little.

I took one pill this morning and it made me dizzy and more nauseous. I had the stupid, unrealistic idea that it would make me feel better. The pill could be all I needed. I put a lot of hope in that dumb yellow hexagon. It didn't work. I feel worse.

And the worst part is that other people don't understand. Truthfully, I don't need them to understand. I just wish they would stop giving me their advice.

Have you tried meditation? Have you tried running? Have you read "fill-in-the-blank" book? Have you tried "fill-in-the-blank" pill?

They say this with a certain frustration at my obtuseness, my perverse refusal to just go and get better. To fix myself already. That I'm too slow or lazy to try and just be happy. They take it personally, and I can't explain without frustrating them further. It's not that I don't want to. It's that I can't. I'm incapable of it. I don't know why. But I can't stop the pain in my head, my heart, my bones, my veins. My brain is just plain worn out. And it hurts. It hurts to even live. And I can see now, what I need to do. The sad truth is this—I am something that cannot be fixed.

When night comes, with the tawny streetlight below my window and students laughing and milling about, I make the decision. There is one way I can fix it. The only way.

So I pour out a mound of twenty-nine hexagonal little pills in my hand, throw them back in my mouth, and swallow a few glasses of water. I don't feel it immediately. But I start to feel a bit dizzy and realize with a start that I didn't leave a note. So I open a notebook and dash off one word.

"Sorry."

Then I crawl into bed, feeling the tug of sluggishness pull me in.

It is a relief, an exquisite relief.

I sleep.

CHAPTER THIRTY-ONE

JAMES

I let out another eye-watering yawn.

"Dude," Cooper says. "What's with all the yawning? Didn't you get any sleep last night?"

I shrug, feeling another yawn coming, probably because it's contagious and he said the word. "Some."

But he's right. I didn't sleep much. But for once, it wasn't because I was too stressed out or sad. It wasn't because I was thinking about Ramona or Rob. I was just too happy.

Last night was odd.

First off, her friend made a move on me, so she must not be much of a friend. It wasn't even questionable, so I know it wasn't just me misinterpreting things. We were walking to the station, and about ten feet away, she grabbed my hand and pulled me in to her and started kissing me. That's two times in one night, which is definitely an anomaly. But I didn't want to be kissing her, so I pulled away. Maybe not gently enough.

She said "What?" and looked hurt.

I was so shocked that I just said "Dahlia," which must have been the right thing to say, because she said "Oh, right" and gave me this smile, which was kind of pathetic with her missing teeth. Then she said "I had to try," which made no sense so I didn't answer, but she didn't seem to expect an answer anyway. "You're the bee's knees, James. You know that, right?" she asked.

Again, I didn't answer, and she gave me this weird, toothless grin and left.

I looked up *bee's knees* when I got home. It's an old saying, which is probably why I didn't get it. Still, I definitely have to brush up on my idioms. Never heard of *bee's knees* or *par for the course*. It's an Asperger's thing—the idiom problem. But luckily, I pretty much took care of that one back in seventh grade. I kept taking everything too literally when finally my teacher took mercy on me and got me a book of idioms. I memorized them, which helped, because people say idioms all the time, and they usually make no sense.

But enough about idioms. And Natasha. That wasn't what made me happy, so happy that I didn't sleep all night and didn't even mind.

What made me happy was the other kiss, with Dahlia.

It was perfect, which sounds kind of cliché, but really isn't in this case. It was actually literally perfect. It wasn't like any of the three previous kisses (four if you count Natasha, which was unwanted so doesn't really count). The kiss with Dahlia was different. It was right. When we kissed, I felt lit up inside.

"Dude," Cooper says. "What's so funny?"

I turn away from my screen. "What?"

"You're smiling like a mad man."

"Oh," I say, surprised. Usually no one can tell what I'm thinking. "I am?"

He shrugs. "Whatever. You got up to *something* last night. But I won't ask what."

I don't answer, because I really like Cooper, but it's not his business.

I reset Taylor Hale's LexisNexis password, which she seems to forget every other day after swearing "I'll write it down this time" and then not doing so. I glance at my watch once more when I get a text.

Coffee??

CHAPTER THIRTY-TWO

DAHLIA

W hat's going on?" he asks in a low voice as soon as the break room is empty. He pulls his chair closer to mine.

"Nothing." I play with the long strap of my purse. "I guess I'm a little nervous now that we're actually doing this."

"Next week though," he says, verifying. "Right?"

"Yes. Just soon, I mean."

"Okay." He nods, with a thoughtful frown. "Let's think about it. We have a plan."

"Yes," I agree, "we do."

"Next Tuesday, at lunch hour. Tina Delgado doesn't get back until four. Which leaves us plenty of time." His tone is purposefully calm. "Did you find out the layout?"

James cleverly suggested we get the specs of the condo before we get there, to save time planting the cocaine. "Yes." I zip open my purse, searching for the folded paper. "She faxed it to me."

"Who faxed it?"

"The real estate agent." I unfold the paper, smoothing it out on the table between us. "I called her about the condo, pretended I was interested in Cary's unit. She said it was taken, but she could give me one with the same layout."

Worry flashes over his face. "Did you give her your real name?"

"Of course not," I say, pseudo-offended, and he gives an apologetic grin. "Plus, I sent it to the fax for closings. No one would blink twice at it showing up there."

"Good thought," he says.

I point to the upstairs on the paper. "Master bedroom closet. I figured that would be a good place to stash the briefcase." I sit up straight. "Did you get the briefcase?"

James nods. "Paid in cash." He stretches out his legs, crossing them at the ankles. "I set the lock to 8-8-8-8."

"Same as the keypad."

"Yup. Just in case it has some special significance. It'll be hard to explain that away."

"Smart," I say with appreciation, tapping on my temple. He allows a smile. "Burner phones?" I ask.

"Yup. I even sent a text off one of them already."

"Good. We should space the rest out then." I inch closer to him. "What did it say?"

He reaches for his phone. "Here, I wrote it down." He reads from his notes screen in a stiff voice. "Great stuff, Big G. Can I re-up for another couple ounces?" He looks up at me. "But I spelled that *O–Z*."

I nod, pursing my lips. "Well. That's not…terrible."

"Yeah, it's not the best," he agrees. "I went on Urban Dictionary."

"Okay." I clap my hands together. "Let's do the rest of the list. Scrub hats, booties, and gloves?"

"Check," he answers.

"And I have the baggies, with perfectly ridiculous Big G stickers."

James chuckles.

"So, we have one little issue left," I say. One of the lawyers walks in, and we stop talking while she fills her coffee cup and puts all the fixings in. There's an awkward silence as we wait for her to leave and she finally does.

"What's that?" he asks.

"The alarm. There may be an alarm."

He pauses. "Did the real estate person say—"

"She said every apartment has one. But it costs extra to arm it." I tap my fingers rapidly on the table. "And he does have the money to do it."

"Uh-huh." Again, he pauses, then purses his lips. He leans forward closer to me. "I can offer only a few bad solutions to this one."

"All right. Hit me."

James pauses, then cocks his head.

I stare at him a second, then can't help but giggle. "It's an expression, James. I don't really want you to hit me."

After a long moment, James looks up at me. "I'm not that good at idioms." His expression is so raw and vulnerable that it shames me. It cost him something to tell me this.

"Then I'll try not to use them," I say.

He bites his lip. "It's just…one more thing to decode."

I touch his shoulder, which feels as solid as it looks. "It's fine. Really." I take my hand off, still aware of the warmth of his shoulder, the feel of his shirt against my palm. My hand wants to touch it again. "So, go on. Tell me your bad solutions."

"Okay," he says, leaning toward me. "Number one, we could ask Snyder to verify the question of the alarm, but I don't think we want him suspecting we're trying to break in."

"Agreed."

"Two, we could pay Natasha to go in and plant the drugs." We meet eyes just a second and simultaneously shake our heads. "Three. We take our chances."

I bite my lip. "And if the police come, we're standing there with a briefcase full of cocaine."

"Which leads us to number four, we try to get the hell out of there before the police come."

I sigh, putting my elbows on the table. "Those are four very bad solutions."

"I don't disagree," he says. Then he looks up at me. "So what do you say?"

I shrug. "Number three. We take our chances. And if it goes bad, number four."

After work, I'm still on edge, so I decide to head over to Crawley's and surprise Eli.

The evening is gray, cold, and depressing. Huddling into my

coat, I walk past the Thanksgiving displays and the mini-marts, as well as handful of Thai restaurants, boutiques, and mobile phone stores. The smell of a wood fireplace floats over the air from somewhere.

As I get closer to Eli's bar, the streets turn seedier. Rent-to-own shops and Western Unions, where gentrification is running into some turbulence. I'm not afraid though, however run-down the streets might be. My Beretta is safely in my purse, waiting for trouble. And when a man walks by me, grinning at me like I owe him something, I glare right back at him. Because I don't.

Finally, I turn the corner, spying Crawley's blinking neon light ahead, with the *W* grayed out. The place is dead as usual, and I saunter up to the bar.

"Hey," I say.

"Hey," he answers, with genuine pleasure. "You must be here for our award-winning chili."

I roll my eyes. They do have a vegetarian chili, but it wouldn't win any awards unless ravenous dogs were voting. I put my purse down with a *thunk*, and he hands me my usual Dr Pepper. "So, how's mission impossible going? Killed anyone yet?"

"Not yet," I say.

Eli shakes his head again, but doesn't answer, just glances up and down the bar for anyone wanting a drink, but there are no takers. "What's with this place?" I ask.

"I don't mind the break to be honest." He pulls out some glasses and starts cleaning them with a white rag. "Double Dutch is fucking crazy." Double Dutch being his other bartending gig.

"What's up with you?" I ask. "Any new job leads?"

"Nah." He waves off the question with his rag.

"The development thing?" He was looking into something at Boston University.

"Decided against it. Hours weren't great." He spritzes cleaner on the counter. Hours weren't great likely means nine to five, which makes it harder to party all night and sleep all morning. "I'm meeting up with Brandon later," he offers, as a positive slant to his life.

"Brandon? With the AC/DC tattoo?"

"Youthful mistake," he counters.

"Yeah." I jiggle my ice cubes. "We're allowed a few."

A guy in his fifties in a business suit strolls near me with a questioning gaze, and I give him an icy smile in return. He settles on a chair three chairs away. "Stoli," he says, and Eli turns to take care of him.

"So," I say, in a low voice. "We're taking care of the Cary G situation on Tuesday."

His expression turns wary. "How's that?"

"Planting coke on him."

"On him?" he questions. "How are you going to do that?"

"Not on his person," I say. "In his condo. In the street. In his name."

He spritzes more cleaner on the already-clean counter, the bitter scent filling the air. "So you're trying to frame him? Like..."

"Yes. Like framing him. Like framing him as a cocaine dealer."

He keeps wiping in circles, robotically. A soccer game blares on the television in the corner.

"What?" I ask him.

"What do you mean, 'what?'" he asks back.

"You've gone silent here."

He stops wiping then. "Yeah, Dahlia. I've gone silent. I never said I approved of this fucking revenge thing. In fact, I told you not to do it, if I remember correctly."

"Jeez," I say, taken aback at his words. "And if I remember correctly, I never said I needed your approval."

"Well, don't get me involved, then," he mutters.

"Fine," I say, sipping my Dr Pepper, swallowing back my hurt at his reaction. "I won't."

Eli straightens himself up. "I'm sorry. I didn't mean to..." He glances around the bar quickly, and no one is listening. "All I'm trying to say is...okay...it's terrible what happened to you. Of course it is. But, you know, these are real lives here. Real people. This isn't a game. This guy's about to get married. He's gonna have a kid and you're trying to send him to jail." His hand clenches the rag. "For real time."

"Wow," I say. "You sure have a lot of empathy for the rapist."

He swallows, then looks ashamed. "It's not that. It's just… I don't know. Maybe you're right." Eli shakes his head. "I don't even know what to think anymore."

A bit shaken by his response, I consider what we are going to do for a minute, our revenge on Cary Graham. I let in a sliver of conscience, an ounce of guilt. If we get away with this, it could mean years in prison for Cary Graham. Years and years. His fiancée would probably meet someone else. He would never watch his son grow up.

But all I see is his face in minute 5:11 of the video, as he called out with glee: "Dude, I think I popped her cherry!" He lifted up three blood-tinged fingers in victory, when another voice in the video chided him. "Dude, you're a fucking idiot. She's not a cherry. You're getting sloppy thirds here." Cary shrugged, grabbing my hips and thrusting away. "I must be so big that I stretched her out, man." This got a few laughs, and then his face got serious and scrunched up as he gave his final few thrusts and came inside me.

"You know what," I say to Eli.

Eli leans on an elbow, staring up at me. "What?"

Stoli-Man looks over at us, then back at his drink.

I don't bother to lower my voice. "He deserves some real fucking time."

CHAPTER THIRTY-THREE

DAHLIA

It takes an agonizingly long time for Tuesday to come.

Smoothly, James drives us down the leafy, handsome street and we park at the curb across from Cary Graham's place. Parking isn't a problem here in the suburbs. As we approach his condo, a car pulls out of a garage a few doors down, and the driver gives us a smile and a little wave through the window. James and I do the same motion, as if it's choreographed. When I drop my wave, I feel my heart jackknifing in my chest.

Glancing around quickly, we see no one else, and James slips on latex gloves and punches 8-8-8-8 into the keypad. We hold our breath for one second, but then slowly, the garage door groans open. Stepping inside, James hits the Enter button to close it, and we wait as the door folds the sunlight out, and we are left in a quiet, musty garage.

"You ready?"

"Yup."

We throw on the rest of the surgical wear, booties, hats, and gloves. Swinging the door open, I realize I am bracing myself for the buzz of an alarm system. We stand in the doorway, staring at the little alarm box, which is, quite mystifyingly, not turned on.

The small mudroom leads right into the kitchen, which is blindingly white. White-painted wooden floors and cabinets with stainless steel everything else. I feel like I've walked into the set of a futuristic sci-fi movie. I don't have much time to ponder this, however, because just then, a flash of brown fur tears out of the family room.

I fall against the wall. "Jesus."

The Rottweiler stands right in front of us, silver-link collar rattling. His pink jowls are wobbling, as he lowers himself slowly. His growl vibrates his entire body.

"Shit," James whispers in panic. "What should we do?"

I am frozen to the spot, speechless.

"Give him a baggy?" he asks.

"No, we can't. That might kill him."

His growl grows more insistent. "Yeah, but—"

"Code," I remind him.

But the dog lowers even further, his eyes trained on James. He is drooling now. "I get the code and all," James says, his calm voice belied by the briefcase trembling in his hand. "But I'm pretty sure this dog wants to kill me." The Rottweiler rears back farther, quivering with excitement and jingling the collar. He does appear to want to kill James. "Maybe just a teaspoon of cocaine?" he asks.

"Teaspoon," I repeat, the word giving me a sudden idea. I dash off to the pantry, which is also blazingly white and looks like it's been organized by someone with OCD. I spot the red-and-yellow jar right away, with Peter Pan taking flight. Unscrewing the lid takes the dog's attention off James for a second, and I lay the jar on the kitchen floor. The dog takes a quick investigative sniff. "You hide the stuff," I say. "I'll watch Cujo."

"You sure?"

"Yeah, but hurry."

So he does, tearing up the stairs with the suitcase swinging in his gloved hand. The Rottweiler takes one lick, tongue snaking into the jar, then glances up at me. The look is not a question, but a statement. *This is mine.* After a few minutes, the dog is clearly not going anywhere, so I shoot up the stairs and meet James on the landing of the plush, almond carpet, coming out of the master bedroom. He has the one large *Cary G* bag in hand but no briefcase.

"Where'd you put it?" I ask.

"Between some sweaters, with a corner sticking out a little. How's the dog?" he asks, sounding short of breath from nerves.

"Occupied." I point at the bag he's holding like a newly won goldfish from a fair. "What are you going to do with that one?"

"Had an idea." James pulls a small roll of packing tape from his hoodie pocket and heads to the bathroom. "I saw this in a movie once," he says, removing the toilet lid from the back of the toilet.

"Ooh, like *The Godfather*."

"Never saw that one," he says, taping the bag up against the lid, then replacing it with a soft clink.

"You never saw *The Godfather*?" I whisper, as we tiptoe back down the stairs. "Leave the gun, take the cannoli? Seriously?"

He shakes his head.

"Wow. I can't believe that," I say, as we descend back to the kitchen, where the dog is fully engaged in mastication, the jar stuck on his nose. He still manages to growl, in case we're thinking of taking it back.

"Aw," James says. "He actually looks kind of cute."

"Peanut butter," I say, "works every time."

James gives me a look that rightly questions how often I actually do this, when suddenly we hear the garage door. Footsteps. His eyes flash open.

Madly, I glance around the room. "Come on," I shout-whisper, motioning toward the back of the house. A doorknob is turned, someone whistling. I spy a guest bathroom, and we both tumble in. I softly shut the door. The tiny rectangle of a room has a huge, gold basin sink with a gold-gilded mirror and smells like a lemon exploded. I unlock the window latch.

"What on earth?" a feminine woman's voice scolds. "Dipsy, did you get into the peanut butter?" It must be Tina Delgado, the fiancée. "Your father," she goes on, still scolding, "forgets to put on the alarm. Never puts anything away." Her voice disappears into their pantry.

I keep yanking at the window. "Shit. It's stuck." My hands are sweating through the gloves, slipping on the wood.

"Here." James reaches over me and gives it a massive shove. The window opens but with a loud bang. We stare at each other in endless, utter silence, finally broken by crazed barking.

"Hey," the woman calls out. "Cary, is that you?" Footsteps march around the kitchen, creaking the floor.

I leap through the window and James tries to follow, but his torso gets stuck, folding him in half like the assistant in a magic show. I grab his shoulder and yank as hard as I can, and he finally grunts and falls onto me as our magic show has turned into a slapstick routine. We race to the car without a word.

In seconds, we are in the car, seat belts on and halfway down the street. James makes a sharp turn. The neck of his T-shirt is dark with sweat, and his scrub hat is askew, like some kind of deranged surgeon.

"Holy fucking shit," he says.

And out of nowhere, I start giggling. After a sidelong look at me, he starts giggling too. "Dipsy?" he asks incredulously as he races through a yellow light. "Who names a Rottweiler Dipsy?"

"Oh my God," I gasp through laughter. I put on her scolding, high-pitched voice. "Dipsy, did you get into the peanut butter?"

This sends us into another round of giggling. James wipes his eyes, and I roll around in the seat, laughing so much that my stomach aches.

In fact, I don't think I've ever laughed so hard in my entire life.

CHAPTER THIRTY-FOUR

Five Years Ago

When I wake up, I am gagging, a disgusting taste in my mouth. I try to open my eyes, but they are crusted shut. For a moment, I have a flash. Fingernails digging into my scalp. The smell of a mattress. I moan, and a hand appears in mine.

"Dahlia?"

My throat is burning. I am being choked, struggling to breathe.

"I think she's waking up," someone says. I recognize the voice. My mom? My eyelids are stuck together; I am fighting to open them and manage to see a glimpse between gluey eyelashes. A face is hanging over me. My mom.

"Dahlia?" she repeats in question. I nod and try to say something, but my lips are taped to something.

She grips my hand. "Don't worry, honey. It's a tube, to help you breathe. They'll take it out soon."

I nod but gag again, my eyes watering. Tears sting the cracked creases on the side of my eyes. My mom is smoothing my forehead, and I try to relax, then hear footsteps thudding over. Kind faces hover over me—nurses. An Indian woman joins them, with a pudgy face and dark eyeliner. "Are you ready, Dahlia? We're going to take out the tube."

She is speaking loudly, over the beeps. I love the way she says my name. Drawn out, exotic. Daah-la-ya. I have never loved my name before today. I am nodding, but they are already removing it. I feel my stomach lurching, retching, and then I can breathe.

My mother hugs my entire arm.

"*Mom.*" *It comes out raspy, barely a whisper.*

"*I'm here, honey.*" *She rubs my fingers. They feel tingly.*

Alive. I am alive. Thank God I am alive.

"*Mom,*" *I repeat, croaking louder.*

"*Shh…*" *She combs my hair off my forehead. Her touch, a warm feather.*

"*I'm sorry,*" *I say.*

She shakes her head again. "*No, honey. I'm sorry. It's not your fault.*" *She leans her head against mine, and I can smell her makeup.* "*It was never your fault.*"

My eyes close again, exhaustion hitting me. I feel her hand smoothing my blanket, and I let my guard down, which has been ratcheted up high since the day I woke up in a strange room on a mattress. I let my guard down and allow myself be pulled into her care, her warmth. I don't need to be sorry anymore. She doesn't blame me now.

Trying to kill myself was apology enough.

CHAPTER THIRTY-FIVE

DAHLIA

D id you have a good lunch?" Sylvia asks as I trot back to my desk a couple minutes late. My mouth is still dry from the shock of our escapade.

"Oh, sure." I sit in the chair, practically collapsing.

"Where'd you go?"

"This little sushi place. James took me." Rubbing my cheek, I feel the line from the elastic of the scrub hat.

"Huh." She undoes the ring of a binder with a bang. "You guys getting serious?"

I shrug in answer and log on to the computer. My hands are still trembling, my nerves jittery. As the computer loads, I take a deep breath to slow down the adrenaline coursing through me. But when a text comes, I still jump.

I expect to see James, inquiring whether Snyder called it in yet. He said he'd reach out to one of his friends in the department; we just have to say the word. But I haven't had a chance to call him yet. It isn't James though.

Hi. This is Sean Gowers, Daisy's friend. She said I could get in touch with you.

It takes me a second to remember. The one from the Phoenix Club. Yes, thanks.

Can I call?

I debate. I'm already over on lunch. But I suppose I could take a quick trip to the bathroom. I'll call you in a minute, I text back. As I walk out of my chair, Sylvia watches with open curiosity. Luckily, the women's bathroom is empty, and I sit on a surprisingly comfortable sofa chair in the corner. I make the call.

"Hello?"

"Hi. It's Dahlia."

"Sean," he says, then there is a pause. "First of all, I'm sorry about what happened to you."

"Oh, thanks." This is followed by an awkward pause. It's like making small talk at a funeral.

"But anyway," he says with an air of relief at getting that over with, "unfortunately, I don't recognize anyone from the video. The one does look a little like Blake Roberts, like Daisy said."

"Yeah, agreed." Someone walks in to put on lipstick with a comical fish lip in the mirror, then leaves, her heels clacking like nails. I don't recognize her. "There are actually only two guys left to identify," I say. "The one with the reddish hair isn't in our class, but I think I can find him eventually. But I don't know about the guy filming. It's basically a flash of his forehead."

"Right, yeah." There is a sound as if he's dropped something, then a muffling of the phone. "Sorry about that," he says. "So, here's the thing. I didn't recognize them, but I do know a possible way you could find out."

The automatic paper towel dispenser goes off against the wall, without anyone there. I jump at the buzzing sound and stand up to be sure. No one. A ghost in the machine. "Okay?"

"I heard rumors about that place. Hawk Club. Daisy might have told you. That's actually why I left."

Prickles run along my neck. "What kind of rumors?"

"Well…" This is followed by a long pause. "The gang rape thing…"

I bite back bile rising up. I detest that term. *Gang rape*. So casual and chummy. *Hey, gang. Let's all go a-raping tonight and ruin some girl's life!*

"That wasn't just a spontaneous thing," he continues, "that happened to you. Not that that makes it any better. But they do this thing, every year."

"What thing?"

"This...gang rape," he says, sounding uncomfortable. "And they record it, like they did to you. Rumor is that it's a party they have every year around punch time. They call it the rape party."

His voice goes tinny. I feel it start. A whirlwind, a vortex. "The rape party?" I squeak out. "Every year?"

"Yeah. They randomly pick someone. Roofie her drink. That year, it just happened to be you."

A rape party. My body is going loose. I can feel it sucking me in and I remember what James said then. The incantation. In my head, I say the words in my head. *Go back from whence you came. Go back from whence you came. Go home.* I stand up, and slowly, I feel the pull of the undertow receding.

"You okay?" he asks, and I wonder how much time has elapsed.

"Fine," I answer. I shake my head to slough off any remaining wooziness.

"Right. Okay. So here's the thing. This is what I thought could help you."

"I'm listening."

"When I was punching, a guy told me about it and where they keep the tapes. In a cigar box somewhere."

"A cigar box?" I search my memory for any such thing and come up blank. I'll have to look over the video again, but I didn't see it. "In the club?"

"I assume so. I didn't see it. I dropped out as soon as I heard that shit."

"Uh-huh." It sounds like he wants a medal for this. For selflessly deciding not to join a club that holds rape parties. "But you didn't tell anyone," I note, not letting him off so easy.

"No, I didn't." A guilty pause follows this. "I should have. I know that."

"Uh-huh," I say, but don't push it. I've made my point.

"But, if you can find that cigar box, or have someone else find it for you, you'll probably be able to see the whole thing. Not... that you want to or anything...but I'm sure there's more footage of the guy who was filming. Or maybe in other parties."

Other parties. The thought makes me want to vomit. "Yeah, maybe."

After a pause, he says, "I can show the video around a bit more... if you want."

"No," I bark out. "You don't have to." Someone walks in and smiles at me, then enters a stall. I lower my voice. "I mean, I know it's out there. I just don't need to spread it around anymore."

"All right," he says.

I hear the toilet paper roller squeaking. "Listen, I've got to go," I say, and we end with a quick and awkward goodbye. As I put the phone in my purse, my knees feel a touch wobbly. I push open the door and walk back down the hallway, in a daze.

Rape party. Pick a girl. Cigar box. Roofie.

Every year. Which means it happened already this year. And will happen next year, and the year after that.

I sit back in my chair at my desk and stare at my computer screen.

Sylvia spins in her chair to look at me. "Everything okay?"

"Sure," I answer. But it's not. It's not okay at all. The Hawk Club is gang-raping a woman every single year.

And I have no idea what to do about that.

CHAPTER THIRTY-SIX

Five Years Ago

I'm not in the ICU for long.

As soon as I can breathe on my own, they ship me off to McLean. I might have gone home, but when the psychiatrist came and asked if I would try to kill myself again, I said I doubted it. I have no idea why I said "doubt." I should have said "hell no," but she caught me in a contemplative moment, and so now I'm here, at the psych hospital.

Which sucks. But hopefully not for long.

My roommate is nice enough though. She's bipolar with a possible borderline personality, she told me, and trying to get her meds right. It's her third suicide attempt, and she's only twenty-five. Jeri is her name, "with an I." She's overweight from her meds and a bit doped up from them, and her wrists are wince-provoking. Angry red slices, puffy and sutured. To be honest, I'm shocked they didn't do her in.

So, I'm in the psych ward—not exactly what I planned to do when I grew up.

Six months ago, I would have told you I'd be applying to law school. Quinn and Daisy would have told you I'd be applying to law school. Ditto my family. In fact, anyone who had met me for ten seconds would have told you that. In fact, I have a stack of law school flyers on my desk at school. But looking at them filled me with such a despairing sense of ineptitude and exhaustion that I finally threw a sweatshirt over the pile to spare myself the self-loathing at each glance.

I wouldn't have told you I would be here in the psych ward, that's for sure. But there's nowhere else that it makes sense for me to be right now.

The thought of stepping back on campus gives me hives. Going back home would be admitting failure. And I must admit, it's simple here. No one expects much. There's a routine. Breakfast, then group. Lunch, then group. Then dinner, and sometimes group. They're big on group. And groups are easy too. Sometimes we draw or have "social time." It's all intentionally low key. A landing pad to hopefully regain your strength before attempting another launch.

After lunch (steamed vegetables, which is all they seem to think vegetarians eat), Jeri and I mosey over to group. When I say mosey, I mean mosey. Everyone moseys here. There is no hurry to get anywhere. We take up chairs in a circle. I sit next to Jeri as usual. Everyone murmurs reluctant greetings to each other, barely making eye contact. There are no cheerful people here, which is refreshing at least. No one with a perky hair band and perfect mascara and a smile that hurts to return.

Today, a new kid sits next to me. He looks about my age, and he is beautiful. I would never have described a man as beautiful before, but he is. Jeri shoots me a look, an eyebrow raise with a smile, which could be sarcastic or not. The new kid has blond hair, which slopes over his eyes, and you can tell he's buff, even in hospital clothes. He is half-slumped in his chair, looking at the floor.

"So, what brings you into this fine establishment?" I ask. The question sounds painfully dorky, even to me.

He attempts a smile. "Just passing by. You?"

"Same."

"Eli," he says, reaching out to shake hands.

"Dahlia," I answer. As he looks up at me, I notice his eyes, which are a peculiar shade of light, bright blue. Like a pool.

And they are filled with immeasurable sadness.

CHAPTER THIRTY-SEVEN

DAHLIA

D id Snyder call in tip? James texts me the next day.
Early this AM, I text back. No word back yet.

We waited to ask Snyder to call in a tip to his narco buddies until today, after we had planted more fake evidence. James sent another text from a burner phone last night. And we sent a couple more this morning from different phones. This time, we came up with the content together.

Ready to pick up, usual place?

Friend told me you could get me some blow. Text me.

Big G, awesome shit. Can I get two more oz? Hit me back.

They still sounded like a script for a bad crime sitcom, but I figure the police have arrested folks on less. And just to add fuel to the fire, James dropped off a few "Big G" bags to Natasha yesterday, while pretending to be giving her money for panhandling. She was going to trade the coke to her dealer for her own poison, simultaneously getting the "Big G" name out there. If he does make it to prison, we reasoned it couldn't hurt to have some dealers pissed off at him from the get-go for infringing on their turf.

So we have Cary G all tied up and ready to go like a pig on a spit, awaiting Step Three. But I still haven't figured out what to do about the cigar box.

"You doing anything this weekend?" Sylvia asks, rapidly touch-typing.

"Huh?" I turn to face her. I didn't even process the question.

"This weekend, you doing anything?"

I pause. "It's only Wednesday."

"Yeah, but…I like to plan." She takes out a stamper and starts thumping on papers, the rubbery smell filling our cubicle. "Beau and I are going to Newport."

"Oh, cool."

"Checking out the mansions."

"Cool," I say again and check my email for any work stuff but find nothing. Just something from Shoshana titled "Interesting?" It appears to be an ad for a prelaw summer program at Stanford for "nontraditional" (read: older, hit-some-bumps-along-the-way) applicants. Sounds interesting, in fact, but the price tag is exorbitant. With a sigh, I minimize the email.

Quitting time is still ten minutes away. I'm done with all my work, so I examine my screen again, which features a blown-up picture of the bill of the baseball cap.

Sylvia powers down her computer and starts gathering her things. "What's that?" she asks, catching a glimpse of my screen.

"Oh, it's for a case," I say, acting nonchalant.

She leans in closer for a better look. "It's a signature?"

"Yeah. Guy's saying it was a forgery. I can't even figure out whose signature it is." A work email pops up on the bottom corner of the screen, then fades off. Not from Snyder.

"Huh." Sylvia backs away, swinging her purse on her shoulder. "Beau might know. He's really into the Red Sox."

"Oh yeah? I'll email you the photo. You could show him." If this sounds desperate, it is. But so far I've gotten nowhere with it. I even cross-referenced all Red Sox merchandise on eBay, and none of the signatures matched. Though it's hard to say. The writing is shadowed and the bottom cut off, but there appears to be a loopy *J* and *R* as the first initials. Maybe.

"No problem," she says. "We still have to do that double date, anyway."

"Uh-huh," I say, well aware that will never happen.

"See you tomorrow," her voice echoes down the hall.

"See ya…" Checking my phone, I see no text from James or Snyder and decide to get going. I need to stop for cat food anyway. But as soon as I drop the phone in my purse, it rings. I grab it back out.

"Hey, gorgeous."

"Snyder," I answer.

"My buddy just called. They searched his place and you're right. He is dealing."

"Huh," I say. What good intuition I must have.

"Yeah so, they're about to arrest him at his...place of work, shall we say? I thought I might give you the heads-up. Just in case you wanted to witness it."

"I love you, Snyder."

"Yeah, yeah. That's what they all say."

He hangs up, and I text James.

Call me. It's on.

It takes us twenty minutes to get to the Dunbolt parking lot. James swears through every red light, which is very...un-James. But in the usual hurry-up-and-wait scenario, we are sitting here, waiting in the car. The clouds threaten rain, or if it's cold enough, snow.

"You think it already happened?" James asks, as disappointed as a kid missing the circus.

"I don't think so. I've been checking Twitter. There's nothing on it."

"Yeah," he says. "But there might not be."

"Let's just wait. Snyder would have called if it already happened." We stare out the windshield as a line of lightning flashes up through the clouds ahead. "Do you have the video ready?"

He drums his fingers on the dashboard. "For his girlfriend?"

"Yeah."

"Yup," he answers. "Ready to go when we are." James is sending a GIF of Cary G's vainglorious minute on the rape video to Tina Delgado's work email. He's doing it in some encrypted way that I don't understand, but he says it is supposedly "rather simple." As long as it gets there, I don't care. I just want her to see it, her beloved raping an unconscious girl. I suspect she won't find him so beloved anymore.

James checks his watch, then shifts in his seat, making the leather creak. Thunder rumbles as another lightning bolt streaks up the sky. "There's something else I wanted to bring up."

He turns to me. "Okay?"

"I talked to this other guy, Sean Gowers. You remember the one Daisy mentioned?"

James squints his eyes. "From the Phoenix or something?"

"Yes, good memory," I say. But I'm not at all surprised. James remembers everything. "He said they've been doing this for a while."

He leans his elbow on the console. I can see the fine trace of his sideburns. "Doing what for a while?"

"Raping women."

James pulls his head back with a look of shock.

"Yes, exactly. They do it every year after the new members come on. Call it a rape party."

"A rape party?" His voice is pure disgust.

"Yeah. And they keep tapes. In a cigar box, supposedly."

James shivers. "That's…awful." A couple of raindrops thud against the windshield.

"So," I say, "I'm trying to figure out if we should—"

But I don't finish my sentence, because the blare of police cars interrupts me. Four police cars come streaking into the parking lot.

"Well, hello there," I say. "Let's get the popcorn going."

"Here," James says, handing me the binoculars. A few cops stay along the front perimeter of the building. About five others rush inside. They're all wearing bulletproof vests.

"Seems like overkill," I say, my eyes pressing tight against the rubber views. The window fogs up, and James turns on the defroster. Rain is falling in sheets now. Another crack of lightning lights up the sky.

"You think he's even there today?" I ask, into the window.

"Oh, he's there all right," James says.

We wait about five minutes. It feels like forever. I lower the binoculars.

"There, there!" he calls out. "Straight ahead."

It takes just a second to train my binoculars on him. He's hard to miss. His hands are cuffed behind his back, and two burly police are at his sides. Faces peer through the window in the lobby to watch. Cary Graham looks like himself, but in a daze, his expensive haircut plastered straight down by the rain. His eyes are bloodshot and red. As he is walked to the waiting car, his face looks pale and scared. Like mine did.

The police cars exit the parking lot, and all the lookie-loos disappear from the windows. We sit there a moment in the aftermath, the rain beating against the windows in the grayed-out car. James puts his hands on the steering wheel. "How do you feel?" he asks.

I stare ahead at the Dunbolt building, a blurred mass in the rain. "I don't know. It's not a letdown exactly. It's just sort of..."

James taps his fingers on the wheel. "Sad," he says.

"Yes," I agree. "Sad. For everyone." We keep sitting there, the windows fogging as the rain lightens, changing the syncopation of the drops. "But it doesn't matter. This was decided five years ago, when he raped me. You reap what you sow. And that's that."

"Justice," James says, staring at the sun visor. "Maybe that's what my tattoo should have said."

"No," I answer, without hesitation. "Your tattoo is perfect." He gives me an *aww shucks* kind of smile, then starts up the car. "All right," I say. "Let's send the video to Tina Delgado."

"Already done."

"Good." I stash the binoculars in the console. "Because we've got three more rapists to take care of. And then we're going after that cigar box."

CHAPTER THIRTY-EIGHT

Five Years Ago

O *ver time, Eli tells me his story.*
    The medications have started helping me and maybe him too. I don't feel like a million bucks, but life has become more tolerable, manageable. The edges have softened just enough, so that walking through life doesn't tear me into pieces.

My roommate, Jeri, got discharged, so I end up spending more and more time with Eli. I get that familiar feeling of giggling when he's around, looking forward to seeing him at group and realizing with some chagrin that a little crush may be budding here.

One day in the break room, however, he does me the favor of squashing that. I am sitting on the couch with him, leaning back against a pillow and aware of how my hair might look. Eli takes a deep breath, turns fuchsia red, and says, "So the thing is, I'm gay."

"Oh." My face falls. I hope not too obviously. "Really?"

"Yeah. Really." He bites into a mini green apple left over from my lunch.

I nod with an embarrassed smile, feeling foolish at how I've been acting and feeling. Though it's just as well. I don't know if I could even kiss a man right now without feeling queasy.

"That's why I'm here. I finally told my parents." He twirls the apple by the stem. "Didn't go so well. They disowned me." As Eli takes another bite of apple, his eyes fill with tears.

"I'm so sorry."

He nods, taking a long time to swallow.

"It's okay." I rub his shoulder. "They'll come around."

"Whatever. It's not a big deal."

But obviously it is a big deal, since he's in here with Frankenstein wrists. "Give it some time," I say. "They'll understand eventually."

"Maybe." He sounds sad and unconvinced and puts the already-browning apple back on the table. "This is really a terrible apple," he says with a cry-laugh.

"I know," I say, laughing too. "That's why I gave it to you."

Then we sit there for a time, not talking. We have about fifteen minutes until group. Patients walk by us, blank-faced, some in hospital garb, some in street clothes, tossing paper cups into the trash. He doesn't ask for my story, but I know that by etiquette, it's time for me to share. I've shown you mine, now you show me yours. I haven't told anyone in here yet, except Jeri and my psychiatrist. It certainly isn't fodder for group sessions. I look around, to verify that no one is within earshot. One of the newer patients, Manju, has earbuds in with his eyes closed.

"I was attacked," I say, in a soft voice. "That's why I'm here."

He has to lean in to hear me. "Attacked?"

"Yeah, well, it happened at a party. I suppose I should just say it. I was gang-raped."

He winces at the word. "Oh." He fumbles with a wrinkle on his shirt. "Wow. That's really…wow." Eli looks down at the floor, as if he can't bear to face me. His face is flushed a deep red.

I can't deny the jolt of disappointment at his response. He's just like everyone else. He sees me differently now, like I'm tainted.

"So, this happened at Harvard?" he asks, clearly flustered.

"Yeah."

He keeps staring at the tile, hard, as if he's concentrating on something. "Did…did he have a gun or something? Were you—"

"What are you talking about?" My voice rises and a few people look over. "Are you the police now?" I whisper at him, fiercely. "Do you want to know how much I was drinking? Or what I was wearing?"

"No." His fingers are trembling. "That's not what I meant…"

I turn away from him, my heart pounding into my temples.

"Dahlia." He takes my hand, and I pull it away. "I'm sorry. I just…I don't know the right thing to say." When he grabs for it again, I let him. I'm just too damn tired to fight. "Don't be mad at me, Dahlia.

Please. I...I just couldn't bear it." He pulls my hand to his chest, so I can't help but face him. He takes a deep breath. "I'm sorry that happened to you. That's what I should have said from the beginning. So let me say it right this time. Listen to me." I am entranced by his eyes, swimming in them. "It was wrong that they hurt you. That never should have happened. It was an awful, terrible, disgusting thing. And I'm sorry. I'm so, so fucking sorry."

"It's okay," I say, breaking away from his stare. I rest my head against his shoulder. "You don't have to be sorry, Eli. It isn't your fault."

CHAPTER THIRTY-NINE

DAHLIA

After nailing Cary G, I go over to James's place for a bit of a victory dinner.

His layout is similar to mine, meaning a small box. But his box is immaculate, with everything in gray or black. Clean, austere, but not exactly cold. He picks out a slab of tofu from our Pad Thai. The delicious peanut smell fills up his little apartment.

"The tofu's good," he says, sounding surprised.

I dish out another helping. "You've never had tofu before?"

"No, I've had it," he says, drinking his water. "But usually it's too mushy. I don't like mushy things. This one has an excellent consistency."

"Mmph," I say, nodding, then swallow. "Anyway," I say. "Let's move on to Blake Roberts. Since we still don't know who the redhead is."

"You couldn't find him when you Googled the list?" he asks.

"No. His face didn't come up with any of those names." I play with the rice a little, then put down the fork. "The thing is, I can't stop thinking about that cigar box."

He spears a cube of tofu. "Okay."

"We have to do something about it," I say. "I can't just ignore it."

James stares at his plate. "That would change the plan though."

"Yes, it would. But I can't help that." Aimlessly, I mix around the rice. "I can't just go on with my personal revenge and throw all the other girls out there under the bus." I pause. "That means not helping them too, not really a bus or anything."

"No, I know that one," he says.

"Okay. So, I can't do it. I can't live with myself if I don't at least try to stop them from ever doing it again. Otherwise, I've managed to punish four people. So what? What about all the girls who came before me and will come after me?"

He pushes his plate to the side. "Okay, so what do we do then? We find this cigar box?"

"That's the most obvious answer," I say.

"Which means actually going into the club."

"Probably," I say.

"And how are we going to do that?"

"I don't know," I say. And we sit a moment with that unhelpful statement, when I suddenly feel sick of discussing revenge. "You know what?" I ask, standing up.

"What?"

"Let's not talk about the cigar box right now." I walk over to the couch, and he watches me. "We got Cary G. That's an accomplishment."

"That's true." He stands up too.

"We're supposed to be celebrating here," I say. "Right?"

"Right," he says and sits down next to me. He pauses, then moves closer so his thigh is touching mine. "So, how should we celebrate?"

It's a corny line, but I don't care one bit, and we both lean in to kiss. Not tentative or light, like before Natasha came in the other night. Deep. His lips are warm, and my tongue touches the smooth line of his teeth. His hands are rubbing my back, too lightly. I unbutton his shirt, and he lifts it off, giving me a good look at his torso, which is perfect, art museum perfect, with sculpted arm muscles and the perfectly placed black tattoo on his smooth chest. It strikes me that I have never actually seen a body like this in real life, except maybe on an exercise magazine. I touch his chest and feel his heart beating, and we start kissing again. His hands are struggling with my bra strap, so I help him and then yank off my sweater, lying back. He leans over me, his hands smoothing over my breasts, my stomach.

"Beautiful," he whispers.

"You," I whisper back. "You are beautiful."

He lays on me, my skin against his. I reach down to undo the button on his jeans, then unzip him and reach my hand into his boxers.

He moans, then gasps and jumps away. As if he's been singed.

"Sorry," he says in a strangled whisper, almost a cry. He is breathing heavily. "What?" My breath is short too, my chest tingling still. "What's wrong? Is everything okay?"

"Yeah, I just…" He swallows, then shifts a half foot away from me on the couch. He puts his elbows on his knees, hunching himself over as if he's going to be sick.

"What is it?"

"Dahlia." He bites his lip fiercely. "I don't know how to say it…"

Then I realize what's going on and throw my sweater back on in a flash. "You know what? Fuck you, James. Totally and completely fuck you."

He looks up at me, stunned. "Why?"

"You think I'm dirty or something? Is that it?" I grab my bra and try to shove it in my pocket, though it doesn't fit very well, then slip on my shoes. "Can't stop thinking about that goddamn video? Can't get it out of your head?"

He stands up quickly, towering over me. "No. It's not that at all. You've got it wrong."

"Fine. Whatever." I start looking around for my coat. "Forget it, James. I don't need you for the project anyway. I can do it myself just fine."

"Please." His voice is desperate. "It's not about the video. Honestly."

"What is it then?" I lean against the wall. "Are you gay? Is that it?"

He doesn't answer.

"It's fine if you are, but you should just tell me."

"I'm not gay." He sits back on the couch, his shoulders slumped, staring at the floor.

When he looks up at me, his eyes are rimmed with pink. "It's hard for me. I can't do things like that so easily." His fingers are interlaced, squeezing together tight. "I've got this thing…"

I sit down next to him. "Okay," I say calmly, to calm him down. "This thing…"

"Yes, this thing." He takes a deep breath. "It's called Asperger's."

"Oh." I pause a second to take this in, then a lightbulb goes off. Asperger's. Of course. "Okay," I say, almost talking to myself. "That's all right. That's not a deal breaker."

"And I've never…" He stops speaking and looks up at me expectantly.

"Never?" I ask, trying to hide my disbelief. I don't want to shame him. Never is okay. Never is just fine.

"Never," he says with an embarrassed finality.

I reach over to the arm of the couch and hand him his shirt. "Then we'll take it slow, James. We'll take it as slow as you need to."

CHAPTER FORTY

JAMES

I hit myself on the forehead three times, hard.

I'm about to do it again, when I remember how I had bruises last time that everyone asked about, so I sit down in my beanbag to calm myself. I take deep breaths, like Jamal taught me, until my head is feeling light, and I stop. When I close my eyes, I see Dahlia.

After I freaked out, she stayed for a little bit, probably to be nice. Then she left.

I'm sure it's over now since I told her, even if she was nice about it.

Obviously, she has more experience. I never doubted that. I've kissed three girls before, that's it. Emily Messey at a dance in high school. Tara Keyes at freshman orientation at MIT. And Kailey Hudson at a Dungeons & Dragons party. They all turned out bad. Emily laughed at me with her friends when I asked her out. Tara apologized that it was a mistake, and Kailey said she really liked me but was going back home for a job and wanted to focus on that.

But there's been no one like Dahlia.

Her body is perfect. This is an empiric fact. Her breasts. Her hips. My hands fit over them like we were puzzle pieces, her breath was on my neck, and when she touched me, it felt amazing.

But I fucked it up. And now she's gone, for sure.

I lean my head back to soothe my neck, which is painfully tense. Usually the crunching of the beanbag has a pleasant, calming effect, but it's not doing the job, so I reach into my drawer for a couple sand-filled stress balls. I start squeezing them, clenching and unclenching. Both the beanbag and the stress balls were Jamal's

ideas and they usually work, but not right now. The rubber bal-
loon material crinkles under my fingers, but I'm so hot-angry, and
it's not working, and I want to throw the thing against the wall.

Sand leaks through the balls, where my fingernails have torn
four slits. So I toss them into the garbage, and I'm still feeling
restless and not right, so I do what I do when all else fails. I open
the file.

I haven't told Jamal about the file. I don't know why. It's not
weird or anything, but it's mine and I don't want to share it. It's
a file full of artifacts from Ramona and Rob. A good things file in
a way, but a physical one, not just in a computer or in my brain.

Sometimes, I can look at these photos for hours. My favorite is
from when we were kids. My mom took it, of us lying down in
bed and Rob reading to me. I look enraptured. I still remember
that moment. The rough feel of the wool blanket, the book page
turning, his lulling voice. I hold the photo at the corner, which is
dented from holding it there so many times, then flip to another
picture. The postcard Ramona sent me from Milan, from the
summer before she got beat up. The blue sky reflects into the
water of the canal. The sheen of the paper is dull, the other side
tanning from age. Her writing is fading too. "I love it here. People
have been so accepting. Let's hope Mom and Dad will be too! :)"

But they weren't.

Shuffling the postcard back into the pile, I come to my favorite
piece, the one that calms me the most. It's a cross-stitch she did.
She used to say cross-stitching calmed her too. It has a deep-pink
flower border and a cursive saying in the middle in forest green.

Be Yourself

I trace the lines, feeling her presence with me and thinking how
ironic it is. That's all she wanted, to be herself. But I'm sick of
being myself. Sick to death of it.

I just want to be someone else for a change.

CHAPTER FORTY-ONE

HAWK CLUB CHAT ROOM

Bruinsblow: We got a problem here. Re: Cary Graham.

Mollysdad: What's up with Graham? He hasn't been on here in a while.

Bruinsblow: No, and he won't be on here for a while. Because he's in fucking prison.

Taxman: What???

Bruinsblow: As I said, we got a problem.

Holts: He's the one with the problem. Last time I saw him he was totally freaked out on meth or something.

PorscheD: Coke. Heard he went to rehab.

Bruinsblow: Not this time. He was selling it.

Mollysdad: No way. That's just plain stupid.

Holts: How is this our problem?

Bruinsblow: He wants us to bail him out.

Joe225: How much?

Bruinsblow: 500K

Taxman: He doesn't have that?

Bruinsblow: He emailed me. "Bit low on cashola. And the little lady's got a bun in the oven so..." Guess his parents want him to clean up his act so they're not giving him any.

Taxman: So we should? Because he's selling coke? Fuck that.

PorscheD: That's cold man. He's a brother. We should help if we can. We could all round that up pretty quick.

Holts: Roberts could. He spends that much on breakfast.

PorscheD: Yeah, where is Blake anyway?

Creoletransplant: He's never on here. Too busy.

Bruinsblow: TBH, the bailout isn't even the issue right now. We got a bigger problem. Right after he got arrested, someone sent his girlfriend a GIF of him from the Dahlia party.

Mollysdad: Oh shit. That's not good.

Holts: So what?

Bruinsblow: Don't you get it? Obviously he was targeted. The GIF was just of him. AND he's saying he was framed—he never sold drugs, just took them.

Holts: Riiiiiiight. Sounds like the cocaine talking to me.

PorscheD: PARANOID

Joe225: Cosign

Bruinsblow: Well…you may have a point there.

Creoletransplant: For sure.

Bruinsblow: So one thing at a time. First item of business, do we bail him out, or no?

PorscheD: I vote no. Let him get clean.

Holts: Agree

Bruinsblow: Not really a quorum, but anyone disagree?

PorscheD: *crickets*

Bruinsblow: Okay, so we don't bail him out. What about Dahlia? What do we do about her?

PorscheD: *crickets*

Mollysdad: Stop with the fucking crickets, man

Joe225: THANK YOU!

Bruinsblow: I repeat. What do we do about Dahlia?

Holts: I still say we sit tight. Whoever did this had their fun. Graham gets clean. All good.

Bruinsblow: Have you seen the video? You're on it, Holstein. So is Blake.

Holts: Still don't care.

Bruinsblow: Yeah, well I do care. I'm not going to jail for some shit I did to some drunk girl years ago.

Desiforever: No one's going to jail. Calm the fuck down, Drew.

Holts: Yeah, she'd never go to the police. Not in a million years.

Bruinsblow: I don't like it. This is going to come back and bite us in the ass. I just know it.

Joe225: You seriously need to chill out, man. You worry way too much.

Bruinsblow: Well jeez, I'm sorry. I just don't want to be ass-raped ten times/day in jail.

Creoletransplant: No offense to that Sawyer guy, Holstein.

PorscheD: Haha. Burn. Did that kid finally come out?

Holts: Oh yeah. He's been a rump-ranger for years.

Bruinsblow: Guys, focus here. What do we do about Dahlia?

Desiforever: Nothing.

Bruinsblow: I'm not doing nothing.

Desiforever: Oh yeah, what are you going to do then, big guy?

Bruinsblow: You'll see. Soon enough

CHAPTER FORTY-TWO

DAHLIA

The next morning, I'm exhausted.

After the adrenaline rush of watching Cary G get arrested, then the late night with James, I barely got any sleep. After James told me about the Asperger's, it was only semi-awkward. We did take it slow, meaning we lay next to each other on the couch, watching some sci-fi Netflix show. When the show ended, I told him I should go, and I think he may have been relieved.

So he has Asperger's. Honestly, not much of a bombshell if I had just opened my eyes. It all makes sense now—his shyness, his occasional quirky mannerisms. Even his hatred of idioms makes sense, after I Googled Asperger's. But when I think about last night, I hardly even think about that. I think more about James. WYSIWYG. I think about his dark eyes, vulnerable and hurt. His soft skin. The weight of his body on mine. And that special, quivery sensation spreading through me, that I'd forgotten all about.

I take a sip of fortifying coffee to focus on work.

Some hours go by. After tossing off a few work emails, I forward a new disability case to Snyder, put the finishing touches on Tabitha's cardiology case, and sign off on a realty closing for Connor. I'm shoving some papers to serve in an oversize manila envelope, when an email pops up on my screen, from an auction site specializing in baseball merchandise.

Thank you for your interest in selling your signed baseball cap. Though we are always looking for exciting new finds for our store, your "Javier Ramirez" signature is unfortunately not in high demand at the moment. Again, thank you for your—

"Javier Ramirez," I say out loud.

"Who's that?" Sylvia asks, folding some papers.

"Oh, nothing." I minimize the email. "Just that Red Sox ball cap I was telling you about. Figured out whose signature it is."

She grabs an envelope. "Oh sorry, I meant to ask Beau about that. I've been in a brain fog with all this wedding stuff." She rolls her chair toward the printer. "Was it a forgery?"

"What?" I ask.

"The signature."

"Oh, right." I'd forgotten the backstory I'd created. "Still checking."

Plugging "Javier Ramirez" into Google, I learn that he bounced between the farm team and the Red Sox for five years before retiring from the sport after a knee injury. His heyday was around thirteen years ago. Which basically narrows it down to someone living in Boston around that time, assuming the rapist didn't come into town for a childhood vacation or receive the cap as a gift.

I am puzzling over this when I get a text from Eli.

In the neighborhood. Free for lunch?

The waitress drops off the skillet of sizzling Mahi fajitas, and I dig in while Eli spoons sour cream onto his enchiladas. "So, how did the date go?" he asks. "Did you finally get to third base?"

After swallowing an oversize helping, I answer. "Fuck off."

He laughs. "Why, you still got blue balls?"

"Fuck off, yet again."

"Seriously, did you guys sleep together yet?" he asks.

"Not exactly. But we kissed. A lot."

He wipes his chin with his napkin. "Oh, you're in seventh grade now, I get it. Actually, I went further than that in seventh grade. But it doesn't count because it was with girls."

"It's not a big deal, Eli," I say, making up another fajita shell. "He wants to go slow."

"Uh-huh." He rolls his eyes and picks up his beer. "In other words, he's gay."

"No he's not. He's..." I decide whether to tell him or not. Somehow, I feel like it would be a betrayal. But at the same time, Eli doesn't have anyone to tell. And I feel like I've got to talk to someone about it. "He's got Asperger's."

Eli stops mid-drink. "Seriously?"

"Seriously."

"Huh." He lifts the beer again to finish his sip. "I don't have a witty retort for that one."

"No, me neither." I stare at my fajita. "But I like him, Eli. So don't be a jerk about it."

"Fine," he grumbles. "I'll be nice."

"So, what's up with you?" I ask, changing the subject. "Work good?"

"Fine." He saws through some cheese on his plate. "Brandon might be moving. He's looking at a new job."

"AC/DC Brandon?"

"Would you quit calling him that? He's the only Brandon I know."

"To where?"

"Colorado."

"That sucks," I answer, and he nods. We don't talk for a minute, and I debate about asking him for advice for step two on Blake Roberts. I know he isn't keen on our plan, but he might help me in spite of himself. "So, I need some advice with the revenge project." He huffs and rolls his eyes while I pull out the photocopied picture of Blake Roberts and lay it on the table.

He glances down briefly. "Am I supposed to know him?"

"Blake Roberts," I answer, moving the photocopy from a drop of soda.

"Oh yeah. Daddy Warbucks."

"Blake Roberts," I say with a shiver of disgust. "It's such a teenage movie villain name, isn't it?"

"Yeah." He shakes his head. "What a despicable human being."

"I don't know what to do about him."

I dress up my last fajita shell, though I'm already feeling full. "James thinks we should hack into his business accounts. But he said the firewall's too good."

Eli nods in thanks as the waitress delivers the beer. "Don't ask me. I'm terrible with computers. Brandon might know."

"Plus, if we did hack into his accounts, I don't even know what we would do to him. I don't know anything about banking and what's legal or not."

Eli scoffs, lifting his beer stein. "*Nothing's* illegal, apparently. I mean, think of the Recession. Those fuckers robbed the whole country and walked away with a loan. A banker would have to be funding ISIS to get arrested." He dips his fork into the mound of rice on his plate.

I drop my fork. "Eli, that's brilliant."

"What?" he asks, rice falling from his mouth.

"Funding ISIS," I say.

"Well, sure, but I doubt he actually *is* funding ISIS."

But my mind is already teeming with the possibilities. If we can get into his accounts and make it look like he's supporting terrorism, that might be our best shot at busting him. And his billion would be confiscated before you could say "off-shore account."

When the check comes by, I grab it.

"Hey," he says, making a show of reaching for it. "I invited you. That means I pay."

"You pay every time." I put my card down and keep it by my side so he can't grab it.

"That's because you're poor."

"So are you."

Eli chuckles. "Fine. I'll get it next time."

The waitress swipes it up and is off to another table, and I stir the ice cubes in my Dr Pepper. When I look up, Eli's face is flushed, and he's staring at someone in the doorway. Whipping my head around, I see a handsome man with a boyfriend. "You know him?"

"Kevin," he whispers, looking down at the table to avoid his gaze.

Kevin, the asshole with the blow, Eli's first true love, who dumped him one day out of nowhere. I squint to get a better look and notice that he appears different, more put-together. His chestnut hair is styled, not mangy like before. And he has a flannel button-down instead of a T-shirt with a tear at the neck. He's not the same creepy guy who left frenetic messages on my voicemail telling me what an evil person Eli is, which also probably means he's no longer on blow. I'm about to look away, but then he walks in, sees us, and actually winces. Taking a step back, Kevin whispers something to his boyfriend, and they leave.

"Wow," I say. "He *really* does not like you."

Eli frowns, then tosses back the last of his beer. "Fuck him. He's not worth a hair on Brandon's head."

"That's true," I say. "And besides—"

"Hi," the waitress interrupts us. "I'm so sorry," she practically whispers, bending over to me. "There's been a problem with your card."

"Really?" I'm surprised because I just deposited some money in my account.

"Yeah, maybe it's our reader or something. But it keeps saying declined."

"Oh, okay," I murmur, embarrassed after playing this up with Eli. "Here, I think I have the cash."

"No way, m'lady," he says. "This is God reestablishing the house rules. I invite, I pay."

The waitress looks at us quizzically, but Eli quickly counts out enough cash and a tip and tells her to keep the change. As she walks away, I'm already on my phone, searching through my bank accounts.

Eli takes the last sip of his beer. "You ready to get going?"

"You can," I say, furiously scrolling through the site. "I have to check something."

He grabs his gray tweed coat from the chair. "Don't worry about it, Dahl. It was probably the chip reader or something."

"No, it wasn't," I say, abruptly standing up. "I have to go call my bank."

He scoops his blond bangs out of his eyes. "Why, what's wrong?"

I stare out the window at the grim, misty cold day. "All my money's gone."

"No problem," Connor says, placing his hands on his desk. "We deal with this all the time."

"You do?" I ask.

"Sure," he says, though he doesn't sound so sure. "Dennis has started working those cases."

Dennis has barely started shaving. "How many has he done?"

"Some," he answers, again not filling me with confidence. He twirls a shiny black pen in his fingers. "So, the bank is certain about this?"

"Yeah. They said it wasn't a hack. Someone must have my social security number. Changed my password yesterday and cleared my accounts."

Connor frowns, scratching his beard. "Do you have a credit card at least?"

"No. Just the debit," I mutter. "Cut them all up a couple years ago." I exhale in frustration. "Which is obviously not helpful now."

"Well, get one." He reaches over for his phone. "I'll advance you in the meantime."

My instinctual pride kicks in. "You don't have to do that."

"Don't worry about it." He adjusts the phone on his shoulder. "Accounting does it all the time."

"Okay," I concede. I decide I'm not proud enough to fight it. Otherwise, I'll be hanging out with Natasha pretty soon. Though Eli slipped a hundred dollar bill in my pocket, probably knowing I'd never take it from him otherwise.

"Bob," Connor says. "Got a favor to ask you…"

I stand up to let him finish the call, and Connor nods at my departure. When I get back to my desk, Sylvia looks up from her computer.

"Did he help you?" she asks.

"Yeah," I say. "He's giving me an advance at least."

"Phew," she says and turns back to her monitor. "He's a good guy."

"He is," I say, but I don't expound on this, so she doesn't hint at how I should be dating him instead of James.

An email pops up on the corner of my screen, with an address I don't recognize, titled "Did you enjoy it?" My finger hesitates, but I click on it.

You like playing games, Dahlia?
    Because we like playing games too, like we did with you that night.
    And we never lose.

CHAPTER FORTY-THREE

Five Years Ago

I go back to school, but it doesn't work. Everything feels wrong.

I don't want to kill myself anymore, but I still can't concentrate. The drugs are taking the edge off life, but they are also taking the edge off my brain. I can't sit through Civ Ed anymore, and honestly, the whole thing just seems like a waste of time. The same refrain keeps running through my mind.

"Who cares?"

As the lecturer drones on about the creation of civil liberties: Who cares? *When Quinn suggests I try the hot yoga place across the square:* Who cares? *When Daisy asks which library we should hit, Winthrop or Widener:* Who cares?

I don't care.

I don't care about going for ice cream. I don't care about reading Herzog, except to wonder how such a self-involved, entitled, scatterbrained male became part of the literary canon. I don't care about going to a party because fuck that. I don't want to get high or get drunk or lose any control over anything ever again. I am not myself, or my old self anyway. I'm not even sure who she was anymore.

I see the social worker woman on the card, Rae-Ann. Her place is pretty run-down, but it's near campus. She's nice enough, offers me tea like a hundred times. I don't have much to say though. No, I'm not suicidal. But no, I'm not happy either.

I meet an old friend for coffee, a cast-off freshman roommate. She says, "You seem different somehow," her head tilted and a fake smile on her face that I want to slap. When I ask her how, she won't say. But I know what she's thinking. She won't admit that she doesn't like this new Dahlia. Dahlia 2.0, angry Dahlia. She isn't quite as airy or likable as the old Dahlia. And she's right. I am different. Pretty Girl is dead and she isn't coming back. And angry Dahlia doesn't give a fuck what you think about that.

The only one who understands me is Eli, who's back at school at BU, feeling like a "turd in a punch bowl," as he put it. We talk on the phone every night, which is my only anchor to sanity right now. I tried to call Jeri, but her mom told me she's back in the hospital.

It takes me a month before I admit that it isn't working. I am lying in my bed, staring at the ceiling, realizing that I am tempting fate. Maybe it won't happen today, or tomorrow, but soon. I'll be dreaming about pills again, searching out train routes and standing too close to the subway platform. And I don't want to go there, ever again.

So I call my mom, who answers right away.

"Hi, honey. Is everything okay?" Her voice is worried, which makes me feel awful. She is probably waiting for this call at all times. Always on high alert.

"I was thinking," I say. "I want to come home."

CHAPTER FORTY-FOUR

JAMES

I t's got to be them," Dahlia says.

As we walk out of work, I zip my coat up all the way against the cold. The wind lifts a light layer of snow off the sidewalk. "Yeah." I'd say more, but I'm trying to think about what to do.

"You're sure you couldn't find it?" she asks.

I shake my head. "Unfortunately, no. They encrypted it."

"Can we ping it or something?"

"No. That's for a cell phone." I don't mean to sound negative, like when people love to shoot down my suggestions at work. But I really don't know what else to tell her. "Maybe Snyder could help?"

"Maybe," she says, but it sounds like she's saying no.

We keep walking. I open the door to the parking garage, which always smells like urine. I'm giving her a ride home so she doesn't have to take the T. "How do you think they know?"

Her boots slap against the concrete. "I assume Cary G told them."

"Because of the video we sent to his girlfriend?"

"I'd say."

I point to the stairs, because the elevator takes forever, and she nods. "So, what do you want to do?" I ask, as we start up them. I usually like to take the stairs two at a time, but not with other people, because that's rude.

"What do you mean?" she asks.

"I mean..." I wait for her to catch up. "Do you want to keep going? Or no." She doesn't answer and our footsteps are out of rhythm. "Because we don't have to."

"Of course we do," she says. "So they played with my bank account. Big deal." Then she puts on a scary voice. "And we never lose." She lets out a laugh-snort. "Guess what, bro. You're losing this time."

"Okay," I say and don't push it. Identity theft can be a big deal, but she didn't want to hear about that. And Dahlia can be pretty stubborn. We get to the third floor, and I see my car all the way at the other end.

"It just gives me more incentive, in fact," she says, her breath a bit short. "To get that cigar box. Shut those guys down."

But her getting the cigar box worries me, because that means going to the Hawk Club, so I change the subject. "So, you were talking about something Eli said. About ISIS or something?"

"Oh yeah." Her voice cheers up some. "It was just an idea, but...if we *can* hack into his computer, maybe we can make it look like he's got connections with terrorism."

As we approach the car, I think on the surface that the concept is workable. "*If* we can get in, we could do some things. Put some jihadi searches in. Siphon off some funds. The big question is still the hack." I chirp open the door.

"Did your friend have any advice?" she asks, opening her door.

"Which friend?" I ask, climbing into my side.

"The girl from Dungeons & Dragons?"

"Oh." I hold back a beat of anger. "No help there."

"Too hard?" she asks.

"No, it's not that," I say, turning on the car. "I explained the idea behind the hack, a bit. That we were punishing him for a past wrongdoing, without getting into everything, and she said she couldn't help. On principles."

Dahlia sniffs at this. "Huh."

"Yeah, I thought that was pretty annoying too," I say.

And she looks at me with that smile. It's my favorite smile. It's soft and hard and smart. Like it was meant just for me.

"Are you doing anything for Christmas?" I ask. I don't even know why. I think that smile loosened something in my head. But truthfully, I'm hoping, just a little, that we could spend it together. Even though I'm sure she's already doing something else.

"Not sure." Dahlia leans back in the car seat, extending her neck. She has the sexiest neck. I think about kissing it all the time. "Mom wants me to go to Chicago, and Shoshana wants me to go to California."

I start backing up the car. "And what do you want?"

"I don't know." She sighs. "I'm thinking of staying in Boston. Though even Eli won't be around. He's going to some B and B with Brandon."

"Oh." We are quiet for a bit, and then I swipe my badge and the gate lifts. "Would you want to come to my house?"

She is quiet, and as I exit the parking lot, I feel myself holding my breath. I haven't checked with my mom, and Dahlia will probably freak out and run as far as possible from me. But after a few more seconds, she says, "Yes."

She curls a strand of hair around her finger. Light lavender, where it fades at the ends. I love the color of her hair on the ends.

"Yes," she repeats. "I would love to."

CHAPTER FORTY-FIVE

Five Years Ago

M y mother gasps when she sees my arm.
It is a bit shocking, but I love my tattoo.

It's the one thing I've managed to accomplish over the last couple of months in Cambridge. Ink. It was like therapy. My tattoo artist, Clare, asked why I wanted a tattoo. I told her that I wanted to take my body back. And she said "Cool" quite simply, and that was that.

We talked. Well, I talked, and she listened. It hurt, sure, but I really didn't mind. It was my idea. My pain. And while she etched *survivor* on my arm and surrounded it with darkness turning into lightness, I felt better. Tattoo therapy, maybe. It was better than that Rae-Ann woman anyway, who just drank tea the whole time.

I don't try to explain any of this to my mom.

"Your…your…" she stutters, pointing at my shoulder.

"Let's not get into it, okay?" I say, grabbing a duffel off the offending shoulder.

"Okay," she says reluctantly. She grabs a tote bag. "You can always get them removed. Dr. Altman does those all the time, he told me. Tattoo removals."

"Uh-huh," I say, thinking how that's never going to happen. I am a survivor. I've earned this fucking tattoo.

"I made your room up," she offers, as I step into it.

"Great," I say with as much enthusiasm as I can muster. I should feel relief, but I don't. More a sense of failure, defeat. The Dido poster above *my bed is cringe-worthy in its earnestness. The bedspread looks faded and childish. There's a neat stack of high school books.*

Juvenile. I feel juvenile. Like I'm regressing.

My dad steps into the room, rubbing the bald spot on the crown of his head. "Hey, honey."

"Hi, Dad."

He is looking at my desk too, like it hurts to look at me. He doesn't know how to talk to me since it happened. It seems he liked Pretty Girl better too. When he finally turns to me, he spots my tattoo and actually staggers back a step. "What is that?"

"Oh, this?" I examine it like I just noticed the ink enveloping my arm. Out of the corner of my eye, I see my mom shaking her head in warning to him.

He huffs in disgust and turns around to leave.

"So, that went well," I say when he's halfway down the stairs.

My mom purses her lips. "It's going to take adjusting, you know. It's going to take some adjustment for all of us."

"Yeah, I know." It's no picnic for them either, I'm sure. Me being home, tattooed and not exquisitely happy.

"Have you eaten?" she asks brightly.

"Not really."

"I could make you a peanut butter sandwich."

"Oh yeah." I unzip my duffel. "That would be great."

She waits a second, leaning on the doorframe. "Once you're settled, we can talk about you looking for a job, or signing up for some classes."

"Uh-huh." I open the drawer with a familiar squeak.

"I got some brochures. Northwestern has some night classes."

"Uh-huh," I repeat, balancing a pile of clothes in the crook of my arm.

"Well," she says, appearing to get that I don't want to discuss this right now. "I'll go make that sandwich."

"Great, thanks." And as she leaves, my text buzzes in my back pocket.

S'up girl?

It's Eli, thank God. I collapse onto my bed and push the button to call him. Eli, the only one who seems to understand me right now. Who never knew Pretty Girl, and probably wouldn't have liked her much anyway.

"Hi," I say.

"Hi," he answers. "How's the Windy City?"

"I don't know. We'll see. Bit of a rocky reunion."

"Yeah, sucks being home." He sighs into the phone. "Still, it's better than being in that shithole of a college."

I laugh. "Harvard is many things, but I'm not sure I'd call it a shithole."

"Hey, I've been there," he says, laughing too. "It's a shithole."

I can tell he's trying to cheer me up. "When were you there?"

"Couple times. My friend Hank goes there, from high school. Place is snobby as hell."

"I suppose." I think of Daisy, who is the picture of privilege but is not snobby. And Quinn, with her shaved hair and black clothes, who isn't snobby either. I miss them. I miss school too, but at the same time, I can't stand to be there. I don't know where I belong anymore.

"I just hope," I say, giving voice to the doubt screaming inside my head, "that coming back here wasn't a terrible mistake."

CHAPTER FORTY-SIX

HAWK CLUB CHAT ROOM

Bruinsblow: Wanted to talk about the Dahlia situation

Desiforever: None of us are worried about this, Drew

Bruinsblow: Well you should be.

Holts: Any word on Graham?

Bruinsblow: Looks like he's fucked at the moment.

Holts: Literally or figuratively?

Joe225: Hahaha

Mollysdad: Dude, that seriously isn't even funny

Bruinsblow: Turns out he got busted for possession before, a couple times. So the judge is being a hard ass. Giving him ten years.

PorscheD: Fuck me

Holts: Again, just might happen

Taxman: So, what did you do to the girl?

Bruinsblow: Stole her ID

Desiforever: What do you mean? Stole her ID?

Bruinsblow: SS #. Cleaned out ALL her accounts.

Joe225: Isn't she a paralegal or something?

PorscheD: Yeah, she's poor as fuck anyway

Creoletransplant: That doesn't seem that scary, Drew

Bruinsblow: Wait until the creditors start calling her.

Joe225: Oooh, reaaaaalllyy scaaaaaryyy...

Bruinsblow: Fuck you I don't see anyone else volunteering here.

Holts: That's because none of us actually care.

Bruinsblow: You're on that tape, asshole. You should.

Holts: And yet I don't.

Bruinsblow: Anyway. I'm turning up the heat. I'll do more if I have to.

PorscheD: Such as what? Send a bag of dogshit to her house and light it on fire?

Mollysdad: OK, *that* was funny

Bruinsblow: Ten years for Graham, guys. Think about that.

PorscheD: Yeah. That does suck.

Desiforever: You want to turn up the heat? You got to do more than steal her fucking ID

Bruinsblow: And what do you suggest, Vihaan?

Desiforever. You send her a message. A real message this time.

CHAPTER FORTY-SEVEN

DAHLIA

Y ou still smoking?" I ask.

Daisy scrunches her nose. "Trying to quit… Can you smell it?" She sniffs the sleeve of her merlot-red sweater. "Don't tell Parker," she says with a pleading look.

"I won't," I promise. Especially because I never see the man. I put my tea down at the table. I never drink tea, but I was somehow in the mood. Maybe Rae-Ann is having an effect on me. "So, any reason for our tête-à-tête?"

When she called on a Saturday morning out of the blue for coffee, I figured she'd be announcing her engagement.

She shrugs. "Not really. Just wanted to see you before the holidays hit and all that."

"What are you doing for Christmas?" I ask. I take a sip of tea, burning my tongue.

"Going to Parker's." She sips her coffee as well. "You hanging out with Eli?" she asks with a note of resignation.

"No. Going to James's house," I say.

"Oh yeah?" She lifts her eyebrows in inquiry.

"It's not like that," I say. Though I don't even know what it's like. "More as friends."

She nods, but doesn't look entirely convinced. I try another test sip of my scalding tea, and decide to take the lid off. A plume of steam moistens my hand.

"So," she says in a change-the-subject way. "How are you doing?" she asks, her focus on *you* overly intense.

"I'm okay," I answer, with my usual reserve. But then I realize it's actually true. Even despite the concern over my money situation. Despite being notified about ten credit cards that I didn't sign up for, I'm okay. I'm taking charge. I'm better than I've been in a while.

"Good," she says. "Oh, I did talk to my friend Lincoln by the way."

I blow on the tea. "Who's Lincoln?"

"My friend from work. Red Sox obsessed."

"Oh yeah."

"He never heard of Javier Ramirez, but he's going to research." She sips at her coffee as the music changes to a flamenco guitar. "He said he loves a good challenge."

"Great." We sit a minute, listening to the music. Out the window, snow is starting to fall in diagonal pellets. "There's one other guy I still can't identify though. The redhead."

"Huh," she says. "I don't remember that one." She frowns in apology. "I mean, it was hard to watch…you know."

"I know," I say. "It's okay."

She sips her drink again, thinking. "There was one redhead I knew though. A year younger than us. Henry something."

"Don't remember him." Again, Daisy knew everyone, so it's not shocking that I don't.

"I think he went to some Hillel thing with you?"

I wasn't that active in Hillel, and I don't remember any Henrys there. "*If* it's even the same redhead," I say.

"Right," she answers.

Admittedly, I hate to think the guy could be Jewish. And that would be a bit out of character for the Hawk Club. My phone rings, and I'm about to let it go to voicemail when I see it's my sister. "Sorry. I should get this."

"Of course." Daisy shoos me away.

Hurrying to the vestibule, my stomach clenches. Shoshana rarely calls. I do the math quickly. Five months along. Maybe there's something wrong. God, I hope there's nothing wrong. "Hello?"

"Hi," she says.

"Is…is everything okay?"

"Oh yeah." Her voice is light. "Don't worry. Baby's fine. I was calling about something else."

"Oh good," I say, surprised by the ferocity of both my worry and resulting relief. "What's up?"

"Just checking in about that email I sent you."

I think back to any recent communication and vaguely remember the pre-law summer program. "The Stanford thing?"

"Yeah, what did you think?"

"What did I think? Honestly, it looks great. But…way out of my price point." Especially since someone else has control of my accounts right now. Though, supposedly, Dennis is "on top of it."

"Yeah," she says. "But if you do well there, a colleague of mine said you'd have a pretty good chance of getting into the law school."

"Which doesn't help if you can't afford it in the first place."

She pauses. "That's what I wanted to talk to you about. Jordan and I were just chatting about it. And we were thinking we could definitely loan you the money for it."

"No," I shoot out. Then I soften it. "That's okay. You already loaned me some. I still have to pay you back."

"That was a gift."

"No. It wasn't." I can't help feeling piqued. I know she's trying to help, but I'm not some kind of charity case. And in the ensuing silence, I recognize this, our maladaptive pattern that Rae-Ann pointed out. Shoshana pushes and I pull back. She reaches out and I rebuff. I know she feels guilty about what happened. And I know that it's not her fault at all. But I'm not sure why I won't accept her obvious attempts at reconciliation. Except that, childishly, I'm still angry at her. For not being there for me.

But as Rae-Ann said, *you can't blame her for being young.*

"Listen," I say. "I'm with Daisy for coffee right now." I know telling her this is part bravado. See, I'm doing great. I'm normal. I have friends. I don't need your pity. "But I'll think about it, okay?"

"Okay," she says with a tinge of disappointment.

We hang up, and I walk back over to Daisy feeling guilty as usual, after talking to my sister.

"Everything okay?" Daisy asks.

"Yeah. Baby's fine. She wanted to talk about some work thing." As I give my tea another try, a text comes on the screen, which is faceup on the table. **Free tonight?**

From James.

CHAPTER FORTY-EIGHT

JAMES

When she walks in, my breath speeds up.

It always does that. I don't know why. It must be a physiological thing, but I never notice myself breathing until I see her. But I stop noticing that because she hugs me right away, and I hug her back, taking it all in. Her sweet scent, the light shining on her hair, her body against mine.

She lets go and sits down on the black couch. She drops her purse beside her with a crash. I don't know what she keeps in that thing, but it's heavy. I picked it up for her once. "So, Daisy thinks I might actually know the redhead."

"Really?" I sit next to her.

"Henry somebody. A guy from Hillel a year below us. But I couldn't find anything by Googling it."

"Henry Holstein?" I ask.

She looks at me like she just got a static shock. "You know him?"

"No," I explain. "But that's name seven on page eight. From the list."

She looks confused. "The list only had seven pages."

"No," I say. "Eight." I open my laptop to show her, but she shakes her head.

"I only got seven pages."

"I know I gave you eight," I say. I don't want to be an asshole about it, but I'm sure of it.

As sure as day, as they say.

"Well, who cares," she says. Which is another thing I like about her. She doesn't get hung up on little things like I do. "Let's just see if it's him," she urges me.

We Google the name, and an ugly face comes up. My stomach feels sick, looking at his picture. I can't even imagine how she feels.

"That's definitely him," she says, and I nod. She leans farther toward the screen, and I smell her freesia lotion. "He looks smarmy," she says.

"Yeah. I was thinking that too." Though I was going to say like a douchebag. With a pink-polka-dotted bow tie and a smile like all the brownnosers I knew in high school. Which is an idiom I totally get.

"Jesus. That is so fucking depressing."

I turn away from the computer screen, because I thought we should make eye contact, and I was right. She looks right at me.

"He's a Jew," she says.

I pause. "Okay?"

She frowns. "I don't know. It makes it worse somehow. You know? Like he's one of us."

"Oh. I see." I don't actually though. I don't get how that changes anything. Jewish guys can be assholes too. Just like Japanese guys can be.

As she shifts on the couch, the leather crinkles. "I know that shouldn't make a difference, but it's like..." She leans back, crossing her arms and staring at the ceiling. "He could be at my temple. He could be my cousin. He's supposed to know better. He's supposed to *be* better than that."

"Uh-huh," I say.

Her head falls back even farther into the cushion. "Anyway. What does he do, this Henry Holstein?"

I look up the source of the photo. "Teacher," I say. "Vermont middle school."

"Vermont's not far," she says.

"No, it's not." My D&D group went on a ski trip there once. We all ended up playing games in the ski lodge, which my mother said was not the point.

We don't say anything for a moment. And I'm thinking it's the perfect time to do it. To tell her. That's part of the reason I asked her over. Partly because I just wanted to see her. But also, because I wanted to tell her finally, about Rob and Ramona. Jamal told me that I should. That I shouldn't keep secrets anymore. I open my mouth, but the wrong thing comes out.

"So, what should we do about Henry?" I ask.

She doesn't answer though, just twists her amethyst pendant. "You know what?"

"What?" My breath goes fast again, as she sits up and moves closer to me. I decide to tell her about Rob and Ramona another time.

She leans in closer. "I don't want to talk about Henry right now."

I'm not always good at nonverbal cues, but this one is crystal clear. I lean in to her too. Her mouth is soft, her tongue sweet in my mouth. I reach under her sweater, and the skin on her back is so soft, and her hand crawls over to my thigh. It's just resting there, but then she starts rubbing me, softly but steadily, and I'm getting hard against my jeans. She loops her arms around my neck, pulling me toward her.

I want to make love to her so badly, but I can hardly breathe, and my vision turns all red, and it's too much. Suddenly, I'm gasping, standing up.

She looks at me from the couch, her eyes glassy and so, so beautiful. "I'm sorry."

"No," I say. "It's not you. It's me." I sit back down, trembling and ashamed.

"It's okay," she says and leans against me. And we sit there a while, her head resting against my shoulder, her hand laced into mine, just being, just breathing together. "Everything is okay," she says.

CHAPTER FORTY-NINE

Five Years Ago

I spend the next six months getting high.

I have a job, so my parents don't say much. If they notice the tangy scent of pot that trails me every which way I go, they don't mention it.

My job is fine. I'm a barista at a place in our little suburb that looks like Starbucks but isn't. The pay sucks but I have no real expenses, other than my ever-expanding back tattoo.

I have one pseudo-friend from high school who's still around. But we weren't that close in high school, and we're not that close now. We go to a couple artsy movies. Mostly, I get high, go to work with all the other high people, then come home and possibly get high again.

It's a pleasant enough existence. I don't think too much. I don't question too much. My mother asks if I might consider going back to school, maybe just the community college here. I pick up a brochure to shut her up.

My father asks if I'm ever going to think about getting a real job. I tell him eventually.

Eli calls every night, and we cheer each other up. He tells me about his "idiotic roommates." He wants to drop out. I tell him not to. Our conversations are meandering and pointless, full of THC-induced laughter, alternating with THC-induced paranoia.

The days spin by. The weather turns from gray and snowy to a breezy spring to bright-green summer, and Shoshana comes home from Princeton.

We hug at the airport, and it feels fake. Or maybe it doesn't, and I'm too high to know. We dance around each other at home. My parents ooh and aah over everything she does, then seem to be struck by guilt and try *to tone it down. But they can't help it. There is the golden daughter and the moody one. The one getting straight A's and studying for her LSATs, and the one spending hours in her room or coming home from work with a stained apron or with gauze pads on her back from the tattoo parlor. My father gazes at Shoshana and can barely look at me.*

One night, she goes on a blind date. My mom's friend's son from our temple. A senior from Northwestern who is applying to law school too. When they come home from the late movie, she is giggling and glowing. Jordan is his name, and he seems nerdy but nice. He's tall and skinny, and his glasses are too big. My parents ooh and aah over him like they've never met a Jewish boy before, and when he turns to shake my hand, he turns bright red and awkward, and I know then.

She told him. She fucking told him on her first fucking date, and I escape into my room and decide I'm done. I'm done with them all.

And I call Eli, who isn't home, and for the first time in the whole six months, the thought creeps in again. That it would be easier to just die.

Easier for everyone.

CHAPTER FIFTY

JAMES

t's like... I just freak out or something," I say, "when we get too close."

Jamal nods and touches the hem of his V-neck sweater. He always wears V-neck sweaters. Just like I always wear blue buttondowns because it's easy and matches everything. Maybe that's Asperger's, but I think it's just common sense. Maybe that's how Jamal feels about V-necks.

Finally, he speaks. "How does Dahlia feel about it?"

I smooth a wrinkle on his couch. "She says it's okay. I don't know... I guess she probably means it."

"Why wouldn't she mean it?"

I shrug.

"I think that's a good thing," he goes on, in his low voice. Jamal has a low, calming voice. Like a classical radio announcer. "It means she respects you."

I nod at this. I do a lot of nodding with Jamal. He doesn't make me talk too much, which is a relief. The last psychiatrist my father dragged me to wanted me to talk about everything. He kept trying to analyze my "obsession" with Dungeons & Dragons and how the wizards symbolize this and the monsters that and how it all lined up with my relationship with my mother and father, but I told him it's just a super-fun game and he was probably overthinking it.

"Are you still on for Christmas?" he asks.

"I think so." I grip my knees. "But I don't know how that will go."

"Because of…sex?"

I'm sure I turn a stupid pink color. "No. We'll be in a separate rooms, I'm sure."

Jamal writes something in his notebook. "Because of Rob?"

"Yeah," I say. "And Ramona."

He puts the pen down. "Have you told her yet?"

The couch wrinkle pops up again, and I push it down with my finger. "No."

He pauses to let me speak, but I have no more to say. "Do you think you should?" he asks.

I nod.

Again, he plucks at his V-neck. "Did you ever think that this could be the thing holding you back? Keeping this secret…won't let you get close to her?"

I think about it to be polite, but I decide he's wrong. It doesn't really fit. "I think it's just me," I say. "That's all."

Jamal doesn't seem offended that I disagree with him. He's good that way. "In any case, before you go home for Christmas… you might want to—"

"Yes," I interrupt him. "I know." I take in a deep breath. "I'll tell her."

CHAPTER FIFTY-ONE

DAHLIA

C onnor walks by and leans against the partition, creaking it. I catch a pleasant whiff of starch from his shirt. "Hi," he says shyly. "Have you had a chance to look at the Dawson file yet?"

"Just emailed it to you," I answer.

"Great," he says with enthusiasm. Unlike many at the firm, Connor actually appears to like his job. He gives me a smile, then strides off.

We work in silence for a while, then Sylvia opens her compact mirror and dots on some lipstick.

"You meeting Beau for lunch?" I ask.

She snaps her mirror shut. "Yeah. How'd you know?"

"Wild guess," I murmur.

"Huh. Well, we're picking out the flowers." This comes out as *flah-wuz* with her Maine accent.

"I'm surprised he's interested in all that."

"He's not," she returns. "But he's still coming. Since I've been doing every last fucking thing. He could show some interest in the lilies."

Clearly, I hit on a sore spot, but before I can hear any more about the lilies, I notice someone being led over to my desk. Lisa, the dowdy and unerringly efficient secretary for the floor, puts her arm out as if presenting me.

"Hi," the man says, glancing around with uncertainty. He's a fit, compact man, maybe five-four. He's got lead-gray hair and crow's-feet that sunburst around his eyes. "Dahlia?"

"Yes." I stand up to shake his hand.

He flips out a police badge. "Detective Harrison," he says.

About a hundred eyes turn our way. "What can I help you with?" I ask.

"A little issue came up at your apartment this morning."

"Okay?"

"Do you know Alethia Marrins?" he asks.

"Alethia? Sure." Alethia. The one with all the tats who's buff as hell. The one I'd be crushing on if I were gay. Who Eli calls Wonder Woman. "I mean, we're not friends really. But we're acquaintances."

"She was attacked," he says.

Sylvia looks up from her computer, then back down.

"Do you mind?" Detective Harrison asks while grabbing a chair from Sylvia's side. She shakes her head, and he shuffles it kitty-corner from me.

"I'm sorry to hear that," I say. "Is she okay?"

"She's fine," he says. "Her attacker didn't fare as well. Broken nose, four busted ribs, a concussion, and some pretty significant testicular swelling."

"Huh," I say. This story hasn't changed my leanings toward Alethia. "Sounds like he picked the wrong victim."

"Yes," he says with a nod. "In more ways than one."

I scoot my chair out an inch. "I don't get you there."

"He had your name in his wallet. And your address."

I pause to let this sink in. "But why did he go to her address?"

"He didn't. He attacked her in the stairwell. I believe it was a case of mistaken identity." The detective pulls out a printed photo of a man from an arrest record. "Do you know him?"

I peer at the picture, which shows a man with a pale, thin, birdlike face and a thin mustache. "Never seen him."

"Sergei Verchenko."

I shrug. "No clue."

"When he attacked the victim," the detective says, "he said he was here to send a message. Any idea what he might have meant by that?"

I shake my head.

"Well, I don't know either." He backs up his chair, banging

against the partition and turning at the sound. "But we did some research on ole Sergei. Looks like he got a check wired to him for five thousand dollars two days ago."

I tap my pen on the desk. "Okay?"

"From the account of…" He flips through a notebook. "Vihaan Patel," he reads out. He waits a second. "Ring a bell?"

"No. Never heard of him." I'm lying though. I do remember the name.

"Okay." He crosses his arms, as if not fully convinced. "No reason he might want to hurt you?"

"I don't think so," I say. "How do you know it's even related?"

"Sure seems suspicious. Guy gets a big payday, then goes and attacks some stranger?"

I look over at Sylvia, who is zipping up her purse and tidying her desk. "Could be a coincidence," I offer.

"Maybe." He leans toward me. "But we detectives don't really like coincidences." He pauses for a long time. "If you do know something, it would help us to say so."

"Hey." I toss my palms up. "I like Alethia. I would help if I could. But I'm as in the dark as you are." Though I have an idea. That I've stirred up a nest of dude bros. And they are not pleased.

He stares at me hard. I recognize this as some detective technique meant to unnerve me, and oddly enough, it does. He stands up, hitting the partition again. "Thank you for your time." He reaches over to hand me a card, and I take it. "If you think of anything."

"Of course."

As he walks away, I think of Vihaan Patel, the name that didn't fit in with the WASP-y ones above and below it, and where I've seen it before.

On the list of Hawk Club members.

———

"You really think they were targeting you?" James wipes some mayonnaise off his chin.

"I don't even think it's a question," I answer, scooping a potato cube from my tasteless vegetable soup. "And they weren't subtle either. This Sergei guy tried to rape her. Said he was sending a message."

James pauses. "Pretty clear what that is, huh?"

"Yeah. Cease and desist."

His face is troubled. "Seems like they upped their game a bit now."

"I'd say."

James swallows a large bite of his sub. He eats a ton of food before "swim nights." Where he swims the length of a marathon, or some such. "So, what do you want to do?" James asks.

A guy from the mail room walks by us, and we smile at him. He goes into the corner with his friends. "What do you mean?" I ask.

"Do you want to keep going with this? Or not. Because we don't have to," he stresses. "Not at all."

"Stop asking me that, James. Of course," I say. "Of course we keep going."

"But listen," he says in a low voice. "This is serious—"

"No," I say. "Listen to me. Vihaan does not win. Sergei does not win. The Hawk Club does not win. Not this time." I notice people looking over at us, and I lower my voice. My face feels overheated. "*We* win," I say more quietly. "We nail all these bastards, and we get that fucking cigar box too. We're shutting the whole thing down. It ends now. Here." I look at my hands, which are trembling. Obviously, the Alethia attack upset me more than I am admitting. "This is where it ends."

James stares at me for a second. He crumples up his sub wrapper. "Okay," he agrees, but sounds reluctant. "But we'll have to be careful."

"Yes," I say, taking a deep breath to steady myself. "I know."

"Oh, I should tell you." James glances around the room, to make sure it's empty. "I hacked into Holstein's school account."

"Of course you did," I say with a little smile.

"Yeah, well." He shrugs. "They really should have a better security system. But I can't help that."

"No, you certainly can't." I swallow a mushy pea, then push the soup to the side. "So, what should we do to him?"

James leans back in his chair, his white shirt straining at the button on his chest. From the swimming marathons, I suppose. I wonder when I'll get to see that chest again. Once more, I get that quivery feeling.

"I did have an idea," he says, "but it's kind of mean."

"Mean is okay. In this scenario."

He leans over the table for privacy, though no one else is in the room. "I was thinking," he says in a near whisper. "We could put pornography up on his work site."

I rap my fingers on the table, thinking. "Wouldn't send him to jail though. Just get him fired." A bird chirps outside, a high-pitched trill. "Let me think about it," I say, standing up. "Meanwhile, I should probably send Alethia some flowers."

James stands up too, stretching out his chest again. "Maybe you should send them to Sergei instead," he says.

And we both have a little chuckle at that one.

CHAPTER FIFTY-TWO

HAWK CLUB CHAT ROOM

Bruinsblow: WTF? He got the wrong girl?

Joe25: No, it's worse than that. He got the wrong girl, AND she beat him up.

PorscheD: Hahahahahaha

Taxman: Sergei, Sergei

Desiforever: Fuck you man, this shit isn't funny.

Holts: It is *sort of* funny.

Desiforever: Well I'm glad you're laughing. Had to pay my lawyer like 15 G to get me out of this shit. I came up with a pretend job for Sergei on one of our Boston sites.

Bruinsblow: So we're back to our original problem then

Mollysdad: Which is?

Bruinsblow: Dahlia.

Holts: Why do you got such a hard-on for this girl, bro? She's not coming after you.

Creoletransplant: We don't even know she's coming after anyone, right? Could just be Cary G.

Joe225: Or he might have actually been dealing. Maybe it had nothing to do with her.

Porsche18: Yeah, dude. I seriously think you're overreacting.

Bruinsblow: Right, well, I'm not waiting to go to jail because some bitch regrets going to a party. Watching her pick us off one by one.

Holts: And then there were none.

Desiforever: Really fucking funny

Bruinsblow: We need a plan. Sergei fucked up. And now she's probably been warned.

Desiforever: Does Blake know he's on the tape?

Bruinsblow: Yeah, he knows. He doesn't give a shit though. Said they can't touch him. Honestly, he's kind of an asshole now.

Mollysdad: He's always been an asshole

Holts: But he's right. He'll beat that shit. He's got like a billion dollars

Desiforever: Not *like* a billion dollars. An actual billion dollars

Creoletransplant: Anyway

PorscheD: He's right though. She can't touch any of us.

Bruinsblow: I wouldn't be so sure about that. I went after the tape cuts out. But who knows how much more was on that tape? She could have video of me too. All of us.

Mollysdad: Yeah, I don't want that coming back to me either. None of us do.

PorscheD: So what do we do about it? Send her another message?

Taxman: Yeah, that worked so well last time

Desiforever: Fuck you, Mike. It isn't my fault the Russian was a fucking idiot

Bruinsblow: Yo, guys. Focus here. What are we going to do?

Mollysdad: I say we wait. Let Blake deal with her. She'll be toast then.

Taxman: Not an unreasonable plan

Creoletransplant: Cosign

Joe225: So talk to Blake again. He's got the most connections.

Desiforever: Yeah. He could fuck that girl up in a million different ways.

CHAPTER FIFTY-THREE

Five Years Ago

*T*he doorbell pierces through my hazy, pot-infused dreams.

I lift my head, then let it drop again. It feels too heavy to stay up. Besides, it's probably Shoshana's boyfriend. Who else would be ringing the doorbell at this ungodly hour? I hear voices on the doorstep, my mom's fake and chipper. Which means it's someone she doesn't know very well. The sound of footsteps and more voices coming into the house.

I squint at my clock, which tells me it's almost noon. My stomach rumbles, confirming this. Wearily, I sit up, rubbing crust from my eyes.

"Dahlia?" My mom is calling.

"I'm up," I call back. We've regressed to our high school relationship of her nagging me every morning to wake up.

The door flings open. "Someone's here for you," my mom says.

I throw on pajama bottoms, which don't fit very well after my munchies-and-pot summer, wondering who the hell it could be. "Who is it? Someone from work?"

"No," she answers. She runs her hand through her hair, which I notice for the first time is flecked with gray. "It's Eli."

"Eli?" I practically leap off the bed. "Why didn't you say?" I rush past her.

"I was saying," she answers, behind me now.

I run into him and nearly bowl him over. "Eli, Eli, Eli, Eli!"

"Dahlia, Dahlia, Dahlia, Dahlia!" he yells back as we giggle and hug.

"Nice tat," he says, eyeing my arm.

"Yes," I say. "Potential employers will love it, methinks."

Out of the corner of my eye, I see my mom smile at our interaction, probably misunderstanding completely, and back away into the kitchen.

"You just came to visit? I don't see any luggage." I peek through the front window on the empty porch, though there's a car in the driveway.

"Nope, no luggage. I just came to save you."

"To save me?"

"Yup. From your dreary existence."

"Oookay," I draw out the word. "And how does this work? I was growing a bit fond of my dreary existence."

He drops his backpack on the floor and sits on the love seat, patting for me to sit next to him, which I do. "Now, listen closely," he says, "I am your intervention."

"Let me guess: you love me to death, but you don't like what the pot is doing to me."

"Something like that. I'm taking you away, m'lady. I am your knight in shining armor."

I guffaw. "Do I get to request a straight one?"

"Overrated," he says. "Now, pay attention. First, we drive to Boston."

"Boston?" My heart ticks up a beat. "What's in Boston?"

"Your new apartment and job."

I look for a sign that he's joking and find none. "I think you've been smoking too much dope."

"That may or may not be so, but let's focus here."

"Okay." I point from my eyes to his eyes, establishing my laser-like focus.

"Living at home is not good for you," he says in a low voice.

I nod in admission. "Confirmed."

Eli continues, "I have a charming—that means small—apartment near the city. Cheap. There's a room available on the fourth floor."

"Okay." I feel a touch of nerves, but also a pulse of excitement.

"I have a job as a paralegal."

I stare at him. "Really?"

"Really. They're looking for someone else, and I showed them your résumé."

"You don't even have my résumé."

"I made one up."

I snort. "This is a promising start. Did I win the Pulitzer?"

"*They want to interview you tomorrow.*"

"*Tomorrow?*" *I stand up from the couch.* "*That's impossible.*"

Right then, my dad enters the room. "*I think it sounds like a good plan,*" *he says.*

I roll my eyes, regressing yet again. "*How long have you been listening?*"

"*Long enough to know this young man has his head on his shoulders,*" *he answers. Eli gives him his best son-you-never-had smile, which my father returns in spades.* "*You don't need to stay cooped up here,*" *my father continues.* "*Go to Boston. Have some fun. Then you can go back to college.*"

In other words: "*Get your gloomy, pot-infested, ever-expanding ass out of my house.*"

But I can't say it sounds like a bad idea either.

"*Come on,*" *Eli says.* "*Let's pack.*"

CHAPTER FIFTY-FOUR

DAHLIA

I decide to take Shoshana's advice and apply for the Stanford summer program after all. Connor said he'd write a letter of recommendation. I probably won't even get in. And if I do, I can figure out how to pay for it then. I'm trying to figure out how to tell James about this, sipping from my COFFEE mug, when I am hit with an inspiration.

Got an idea for Holstein, I text James.

What?

Tell you in just a bit. Let me see what I can dig up first.

Okay

I put the phone in my drawer again. "Do you remember that case you were working on a couple years ago?" I ask Sylvia. "The trafficking one for Dicamillo?"

"Yeah. She left the firm after that. Went with the DA." Sylvia wipes her already-raw nose and drops the wadded tissue into her garbage bin, already three-quarters filled with other used tissues. "What about it?"

"I have to look it up for someone in criminal. Do you remember the defendant's name?"

"Dodson," she says with a grimace. "Could never forget it. Sick piece of shit." She wipes her nose again. "I think he's in jail now at least."

"That's good. One less pustule on the face of humanity."

She lifts an eyebrow. "I guess you could put it that way. Anyway, I don't remember the other names. I probably blocked them from my memory."

"Dodson's good enough." I stand up. "In storage, I would think. Hopefully, it's still on site."

"Who needs it, anyway?" She blows theatrically into another tissue.

"Keegan, I think?" I pick one of the shyer lawyer's names, then stand up and push my chair into the desk. "No time like the present."

"You go, girl," she says, turning back to her computer.

So I go, taking the elevator down to the creepy, musty basement, where the old files are stored. Watkins, an elderly African American security guard, sits at his post, reading a book.

"Busy, huh?" I ask, flashing my badge.

"Ghost town," he grumbles. "Where you been anyway? I haven't seen you in a dog's age."

"Yeah," I say, not really wanting to chitchat. "Just staying out of trouble."

Watkins looks down at my arm, the tattoos peeking out of my sleeve. "You get yourself a new tattoo?" he asks with a *tsk-tsk* to his voice. "Why you wanna do that? Ruin that nice arm of yours."

"You sound like my dad, Watkins," I say with a smile.

"Well, he got some sense then," he huffs. "All these kids writing all over their bodies."

"I'm looking for a file," I say. "Dodson."

"Dodson," he repeats, standing from his stool and wincing while reaching for his back. "Let me lead you to the *D*s."

I follow him through the maze of dusty shelves, and after weaving through many rows, we end up at the right spot.

"Have at it," he says, then turns to go back to his post. "Let me know if you can't find it."

"Will do."

The file drawer sticks, and I yank at it, finding the papers in the back curling up over the others. I leaf through the files for a good ten minutes before finding one with a black star sticker at the top. With some effort, I pull it out, then lean against a shelf to read through it.

The black star is appropriate.

It's beyond awful. It's vile. It's worse than my video.

With the file under my arm, I weave my way back to Watkins. "I got it," I announce. He nods and turns back to his book. So I take the file to the copy machine and make ten revolting color copies as the light flashes over and over, burning lines into my retinas.

I get back to the desk with the copies in my hand like a weight. I text James.

All set for Holstein. Meet after work?

"Did they have what you needed?" Sylvia asks, digging into a new tissue box.

"Yup," I answer as James texts me back in the affirmative. "Lucky for me, it didn't go off-site yet," I say, stashing my purse under my desk.

"I don't know about lucky," she says with a shiver. "I still have nightmares over that case."

CHAPTER FIFTY-FIVE

JAMES

Here it is," she says, handing me a manila envelope. "The whole repulsive thing."

We sit on the T for a moment, in a full train. Dry heat pours in through the heaters and my hoodie feels too hot over my shirt, but our knees are touching, so I don't even mind. Cooper's borrowing my car. I wouldn't loan it to anyone else, except maybe Dahlia. But he needed it, and he's pretty much my only friend.

"So," she says in a low voice. "What are you going to do with it?"

I lean closer to her so no one else hears. "Put it on his hard drive. Won't be hard. Should take like five minutes."

She does this twisty thing with her lips, which she does when she's unsure about something. It's actually really cute, but she'd be terrible at poker. She comes so close that I can see every eyelash. "But couldn't they trace it back to you?"

For a second, I think she's kidding, but she's not. "No. I mean…I'm not going to use my own IP, right?"

"Right," she says, doing that twisty thing again.

"I'll encrypt it definitely," I assure her.

She nods, like she doesn't totally get it, but that's fine. Not everyone gets computers, which my mom reminded me is why I have a job. Thinking of my mom makes me think about Ramona. And Rob. And what Jamal said and how I should tell her. But, of course, I can't tell her in the middle of the subway.

"Then you'll call the guy?" I ask. "The principal?"

"Yeah," she says, but she doesn't sound excited about it.

A pregnant woman in a hijab gets on. I stand up to let her sit because you're supposed to, and my father once screamed at me when I didn't. Dahlia looks at me with such an admiring look that I'm happy I did it. She stands up too and puts her hand on top of mine on the pole. We hold hands sometimes. I used to think that was a pathetic and unhygienic way to show off your mated status. But now I think it's just holding hands.

We swing back and forth, and she leans her body against me. Like she's claiming me. I remember seeing other people leaning together and wondering if I would ever do that. Which makes me smile, because now I am. The train jolts to a stop and we bang against each other a little and then get off at Harvard station. She's got her class tonight.

"I'll walk you there, okay?" I ask, as we get off the train.

"You don't have to."

"Just for company." My voice echoes in the gray, dingy station.

"Okay," she says and we climb up the stairs together. I stuff my cold hands in my hoodie pockets.

"So about the cigar box," she starts.

"Yeah?"

"Any ideas?" Her long black boots click against the cobblestone. "Besides just going in and grabbing it?"

I think hard, but no good ideas flash into my head like they sometimes do. The best coding ideas come when you don't think about them. It's probably a right-brain thing. The obvious answer would be to tell the police. But I don't say that. Because Dahlia might bite my head off, which is the perfect idiom in this case.

"Maybe Natasha could go over there and sell them drugs?" I suggest. "Then she could get the cigar box?"

A cold wind swoops against us, and Dahlia shakes her head. "They'd never let her in." We walk through the gates of the yard. An inch of snow is clumped on the edge of the grass. "And I wouldn't want her to go," she says. "I'd never put her in that position again."

I don't ask what she means by again. But I think I get it. We walk in silence a moment. Dahlia tucks her scarf in tighter. Out of nowhere, she says, "Trojan horse."

I stare at her. "Helen of Troy?" I was pretty good at history. You just memorize a bunch of dates.

"Yes," she says. "That's how I get in there."

I can see the building for her class lit up ahead. "I don't get it."

"I let them invite me in," she explains.

"How?"

"Same way I did the first time," she answers. "A party." Then she bites her lip, stretching it. Plum-colored lipstick. "I just have to figure out how to get invited." Some friend of hers jogs by, and they wave hi to each other.

We keep walking, and I think of her going in there, to the Hawk Club, and I can't stand it. "What if that Sean guy is wrong though?"

"What do you mean?" She smooths down her raspberry-colored scarf.

"I mean, what if there is no cigar box? Then, you're risking all this for nothing."

She shrugs. "No big deal. Then I'll turn around and walk out. But I have to take the chance." Dahlia stops on the pavement and turns to face me. "I couldn't live with myself otherwise. You get that, right?"

I nod. "But what if…" I brace myself for her to get upset with me. "Instead of going in there and trying to find the cigar box yourself, we could tell Snyder about it. Then *he* could bring it to the police."

Her face tightens up. "No."

"It's Snyder though," I say, feeling a little frustrated, but trying not to show it. If I say it nicely enough, maybe I can convince her. "We can trust him."

"I do trust Snyder. I don't trust the police."

I let out a little sigh. "But—"

"James," she barks. Her voice is loud in the night, and when she starts talking again, it is quieter. "You have no idea," she says, "how they treated me. No idea."

I nod. Because she's right. I don't know.

"If I tell them about the cigar box, they'll bury it; I'm telling you." A gust of wind hits us again. A flag across the street is flapping. Dahlia grabs my sleeve. "They haven't even run my fucking rape kit."

I swallow back anger. Because that won't help. But it makes me want to explode. Right then, I can feel how Dahlia feels. Like I never have before.

"No police," she says. "Never."

When I look at her, I see a glimmer of tears in her eyes, then they fade away.

"Anyway, I have to go to class."

"Okay," I say.

She leans over and kisses my cheek. And as I walk away, I feel the gloss of the lipstick on my skin. Tight and sticky. Like a magic seal from Dungeons & Dragons.

And now, I have something else for my good things file.

CHAPTER FIFTY-SIX

Five Years Ago

I sit in my semi-wrinkled suit with the top button of my pants undone. The office feels oppressively masculine, with its enormous, dark-cherry wood desk, wall full of diplomas, and rows and rows of leather law books.

I am beyond exhausted. We drove until midnight, my brain still half-addled with pot. I got there and threw my bags in Eli's place, slept on the bumpy couch in his family room, then woke up bright and early for my Miller and Stein interview.

Staring at the books in the office, I realize that in the back of my mind, I always thought I'd end up working in a place like this. But as a lawyer.

"Your course work certainly shows an interest in the law," he says. The man interviewing me, Connor O'Malley, seems nice enough. On the cute side, with sandy-brown, just-thinning hair and soft, brown eyes.

"Yes," I answer.

"And your résumé is quite impressive."

I nod. I haven't seen my résumé. "Thank you."

There is a silence as he shifts his legs behind the desk and puts my résumé down. "I have to ask you, Dahlia." His eyes turn to me. "How you ended up here?"

I clear my throat. "What do you mean?" Though I know exactly what he means.

Connor shrugs. "You're at Harvard, getting A's there, playing club field hockey, first place at Model U.N."

Most of that is true.

"And now, you're here." His voice softens. "Instead of taking your

LSATs, *graduating Phi Beta Kappa maybe, and interviewing for a job here as a lawyer."*

I swallow. *"Something happened."*

He nods. He doesn't say anything, but he doesn't look away. His gaze is warm, but probing nonetheless.

Crossing my arms, I look down at the floor. I'm not sure I even want this job. But it's something. And I can't go back home. I'll wither up and die there. *"I was raped,"* I say finally.

He inhales sharply. *"Oh."*

So, it looks like I won't get the job after all. *"Yeah,"* I say, as nonchalantly as possible. *"Kind of takes the wind out of your sails."*

His face is flushed, and he nods again. He looks down at his hands.

"I'm gathering up my resources, as it were, before I go back there again. But I will. Someday."

Connor stares out the window at the hot, muggy day outside. *"My wife is ill,"* he says. The statement comes out of nowhere.

"I'm sorry to hear that."

He grits his teeth, his jaw muscle flaring. *"Yeah, it's hard. Breast cancer."*

"Jeez," I say sympathetically. I guess since I was sharing, he decided to share too. Even the score perhaps, on my behalf. I'm not sure if this makes me like him more or less.

He pops on a smile. *"Oh well, we'll make it. She fought it before, and we'll fight it again."*

I nod again, feeling bad for him. My eyes wander to the bookshelf again, the majesty of the large, momentous books. Books full of our nation's laws. Our history. Unfortunately, I'll probably never see the likes of this room again.

"So," he says, *"when can you start?"*

CHAPTER FIFTY-SEVEN

DAHLIA

The professor is late, which is unusual. At this point, I'm rather sick of the class anyway, but it's the last class, and I need the damn thing to graduate. And if I ever want to go to law school, I'll need that piece of paper. Plus, I need it to apply to the Stanford thing, not that I'll even get in.

The door creaks open, and the students shush. But it isn't even the professor, just a late student. "False alarm," someone calls out to laughter. After twenty more minutes, the mood turns. People are turning off their laptops and grumbling to one another. The natives are getting restless.

"It's kind of rude," Whitney says, the crunchy, pretty one, the Nordic ice queen who doesn't shave her legs. "For her to just not show like that. I mean, it's not like we have nothing else to do."

"Yeah," I say. "Maybe she's got a good excuse."

"Doubt it," she complains. "They don't care. They think we just party and don't show up to class anyway. But I do show up. I'm paying money for this."

Party. Of course. Maybe Whitney can help me with my Trojan horse. "You go to college here, right?" I ask.

"Yes. But they don't have this class during the day," she says, clearly used to explaining this a lot. "Well, they do. But it's during my Russian class."

"Uh-huh. Yeah, so I have a question for you. Would you have any ins with the final clubs?"

Whitney looks at me like I've just told her I have herpes. The final clubs and Feminism in the Law are not exactly natural allies. "Um. No."

"Let me explain," I add, quickly. "I'm actually doing an exposé on them. The Hawk Club in particular."

Her expression changes completely. "You're a writer?" she asks with near adulation.

"Sort of. Actually, I'm a paralegal. But I do a blog," I say. "Well, I'm starting one," I amend, in case she asks for a name.

"An exposé on what?" she asks, her expression doubtful again.

"Rape," I say. "In final clubs."

She assesses me a second, then nods. It's the right answer. The word doesn't jar her, not in the least. "And how do you think I could help you?"

"I'm trying to get into the Hawk Club, sort of undercover. I don't know anyone on campus, though, who could get me in. To one of their parties or something."

She nods, thoughtfully, her lips pursed in concentration. "I could *possibly* help."

"Oh yeah?"

"I know a guy in there. Christian Ford."

"Okay." I grab a pen and write down the name.

"He's kind of an asshole," she continues, "and I've heard rumors about him. That he's not a good guy."

"Uh-huh." *Not a good guy* being code for rapist.

We stare at each other a second. I feel like she's trying to tell me something, but I'm not sure. Maybe she's in the unlucky club, maybe she isn't.

"Give me your number," she says. "I'll see what I can find out."

CHAPTER FIFTY-EIGHT

DAHLIA

I just don't think we should spend all that money before the wedding," Sylvia says, dropping a sheath of paper into the printer. "But Beau says we should go."

"Go where?" I ask.

"North Carolina," she says, a tad annoyed, and slams the printer door shut. "I just said that."

"Oh yeah. Sorry," I say. "Little distracted with this slip-and-fall." Which is a lie. I *should* be distracted by Tabitha's slip-and-fall but instead have been thinking about the Hawk Club and if Whitney will be able to get me in somehow. Because if not, I'll have to figure out something else. I don't really have any other connection to the undergraduate scene still, since I'm not some kind of hanger-on loser. Not to mention I didn't actually graduate.

"You're still going with James for Christmas?"

"Uh-huh," I say, opening Tabitha's file.

"Surprised you're not going somewhere with Eli," she says without any attempt at guile. Sylvia mistakenly believes that "in my heart of hearts," I have a crush on Eli. Though I have told her several times now that in my heart of hearts, I don't.

"He's still gay," I answer, "and still dating Brandon."

"Well, you don't have to get all snarky," she says, when a text comes through from James.

Pix are on his computer.

Okay, I text back. I'll make the call.

But my stomach sours. I don't want to make this call. I don't want to take down the Hillsview Teacher of the Year, one of the few who actually chose to do service instead of going directly to Wall Street and ruin his life. I don't want to put the guy from Hillel, the guy who could have been singing the V'ahavta prayer next to me, into prison for this. I don't want to live in a world where pictures like the ones now on his computer exist. And I don't want to lie and say they belong to him.

But I think of the video, of him waiting in line and stroking himself, and steel my nerves.

I don't want to do it. But I have to do it. I grab my purse, with the burner phone that I bought for this purpose.

"I'll be right back," I say.

"Hillsview Middle School. Can you hold?"

"Sure. That's fine," I answer, my voice echoing in the empty conference room. I stand there, listening to Muzak, fighting a sense of dread.

"Thank you for holding. How can I help you?"

"Um, yes." There is a lump in my throat. "Can I talk to Principal Davies?"

"May I ask who's calling?" she asks.

"I...I can't. I don't want to say that. But I do need to speak to him. It's extremely urgent."

I hear rumbling over the phone and catch the principal's surly response. "Tell her I'm sorry, but I can't—"

"Please," I insist into the phone. "It's really very important. It's a sensitive matter. Please."

A hand covers the receiver, followed by some hushed, rapid conferencing back and forth. I am sweating, the burner phone tight against my ear. The conference room is unnaturally quiet, the soft-gray walls closing in on me. They sway just an inch. I can feel a lick of the vortex in the distance. "Go home," I whisper.

"Go back from whence you came." I lean my elbow against the wall to steady myself. "Go home—"

"Hello? This is Principal Davies." His voice is baritone and sounds nonplussed.

"Hi." My breath feels short. "Thanks for speaking to me."

"Okay." His response is noncommittal.

I take a deep breath and descend into my role. "I'm so sorry to do it this way," I say, putting on a sopping, pleading tone. "I don't mean to be difficult. It's really important...but I don't want to get my child involved if I don't have to."

"Uh-huh." His tone lightens a smidgeon. "I'll hear you out at least."

I start pacing the room, the carpet crunching under my feet. "It's about Mr. Holstein. I just..." Then I pause, pretending to do an about-face. "You know what? Forget it. Maybe I shouldn't even get involved here—"

"Please," he interrupts. "Go ahead. If you have something important to say, I want to hear it."

"Oh, okay. You're...you're probably right." Bait set. Reeling in. "My child isn't in his class, but he was in his room for some kind of shared class. With Mrs. Matucci." I pick a name from the website.

"Yes."

"And what happened was..." I take a deep breath. "My child saw something on his office computer. Maybe he was wrong. He could have misunderstood."

"What was it, ma'am?"

"It was troubling, and I needed to tell someone. But I really don't want to get involved."

"Ma'am," he says more forcefully. "What was it?"

"He told me it was pictures of children...but not his kids or anything. At least, I don't think so..."

I hear the principal swallow over the phone. "Uh-huh."

"Pictures of them..." I whisper. I can barely get the words out. I am disgusted with myself. But I'm disgusted with Henry Holstein too. "It's hard to describe," I say.

"Please," Principal Davies says. "Go on."

CHAPTER FIFTY-NINE

JAMES

We're waiting in line at Subway, and Dahlia is debating her toppings. I love Subway for the opposite reason. I always get the veggie wrap, and the guy there is nice and knows just how many olives and tomato slices to put on.

We look around for a booth and find a deserted one. "Any word on Holstein?" I ask.

She shakes her head. "I keep refreshing the *Hillsview News*, but no…nothing yet."

"It'll happen," I say. "Pretty fast, I would think."

She bites into her wrap, and almost immediately, her text goes off. Reading it, she starts smiling. "Finally!"

"What?" I move my neck over to see.

"From the girl I was telling you about," she says. "Whitney from my class." She turns the screen toward me. Hawk Club party, January 10. Dahlia turns the phone off and puts it down on the table. "Some kind of after–New Year's party, she said." She starts chewing, then swallows. "And even better, I got the code word. So I can get in."

I take a bite of my sub. "What's the code word?"

"'Magna Carta,'" she says with a snort. "Talk about pretentious, huh."

I pick a fallen olive off the wrapper. "1215," I say.

She stares at me a second, then smiles. "June 15, 1215, to be exact," she adds with a wink.

There's this Police song about how everything this girl does is magic, and I never felt that way about anyone. But I feel that way a hundred percent about Dahlia.

We keep eating for a while, but I start feeling butterflies in my stomach, thinking about her going to that party. "How will that work?" I ask. "You're just going to show up and look for the cigar box?"

Some tomato juice rolls down her chin, and she wipes it off. "Sounds about right."

I put my sub down, not really hungry now. "But couldn't that be dangerous?"

She shrugs. "I don't know. It's just a party."

But I think she's lying. We both know how the last party there went. "What if they're watching for you?"

She rolls her eyes, which I would usually find annoying, but not with Dahlia. "I highly doubt they'll be looking for me."

"Who knows," I argue. "They were looking for you when they tried to get Alethia."

She doesn't argue with this, and thinking about Alethia only makes me feel sicker. "Maybe I could go in with you."

"Impossible." She sips her water. "They won't let guys in."

"Unless..." I say, as an idea comes to me. My right brain working.

"Unless what?" She narrows her eyes in a question.

"Unless you bring me in with you."

"How do I do that? Sneak you in under my trench coat?" She stretches out her arm, and I follow the ivy tattoo lacing up her arm. I touch a leaf, gently, and she smiles and puts her hand over my finger.

"No," I say. "You wear a camera."

CHAPTER SIXTY

DAHLIA

"Are you insane?" Eli asks, fully dismayed.

"Come on," I say. "It's adorable. Admit it." I'm pointing at the necklace on the computer screen, the one that James and I picked out, which also happens to be a spy camera and which should arrive at my apartment by tomorrow. All on James's credit card for now, because Dennis said there's a few more hurdles to jump, but hopefully I'll have my identity cleared soon. He wouldn't comment on how soon though.

"So let me get this straight." Eli puts his beer bottle down with a thud, and Simone lifts her head from between us, then dips it down again. "You're going straight to their little hidey-hole for some stupid box? You could be walking right into a trap here."

"Please, it's a final club. Not a Turkish prison."

"This is stupid. Ridiculous." He shakes his head. "They already tried to get you once, Dahlia."

"And failed."

"Which was just damn luck," he admonishes.

I pet Simone, who opens one eye at me, then sleepily closes it again. "That's why we have the camera. So James can keep an eye on me."

Eli snorts at this. "Excuse me for not being comforted by this." He takes a swig of his beer. "He might be James, but he's not James Bond."

"Ha, ha, ha."

"I'm not joking," he complains, getting up and heading to the refrigerator. The light gives him a ghostly glow. As the door whooshes shut, he returns with another beer. "When is this party anyway?"

I look at my phone. "January tenth. It's a Friday night."

He stares at me. "That's only a few weeks away."

I shrug. "More than enough time to prepare."

"Don't do this, Dahlia. Please." He puts his hands in a prayer position. "You don't have to prove anything to anyone."

"I'm not trying to," I insist. "This is not just about me anymore."

He rakes his hand through his hair. "Don't you get it? You've won. You don't need to do any of this." The hoppy scent of beer comes off his breath. "You've got your Harvard degree now. You can go do that Stanford thing. You know...just do it. Live your life already."

"I will," I say, patting his knee. "Once I shut them down. I promise you. I will."

The phone wakes me up at 3:30 a.m.

I grab it, not recognizing the number. "Hello?" There is a long pause, then crying. Noises in the background. People yelling and laughing. Banging, clanking sounds. "Who is this?"

A soft crying.

"Shoshana?" I ask.

"Tell them it isn't true, Dahlia." The voice is strained, husky.

"Who is this?" I repeat.

"It's Henry."

In a stuporous confusion, I try to think of any Henrys that I know. Then a chill courses through me. Henry Holstein.

"I'm sorry," he cries. "I'm sorry I did that to you."

I don't answer.

"But," he whispers, "tell them you're lying about it." I hear his rapid breathing. "They're gonna hurt me...bad...and I didn't do it. Just tell them. I'll admit to the...what happened that night. I'll admit to that. Just tell them I didn't do this," he pleads, a sort of keening desperation in his voice. "Please. You have no idea what they'll do to me."

I think about it for a movement. I can hear the fear in his voice, and I don't like to make people suffer.

But I think to minute 6:28, where Blake Roberts was sodomizing me and Henry Holstein climbed up to try to rape me vaginally at the same time. "DP!" he yelled, bowled over with laughter. "Double penetration!" His face was jubilant. "DP! DP!" There was a crying sound from the mattress, and Blake said, "Wait your own fucking turn," and pushed him on the chest. Then, Blake repositioned himself to get back to the business of anally raping me.

"I do have an idea," I say. "Of what they'll do to you. I have a very good idea."

There is soft crying again. "I'm sorry, Dahlia. I'm sorry. Please."

"Don't call me again," I say. And I hang up.

CHAPTER SIXTY-ONE

HAWK CLUB CHAT ROOM

Bruinsblow: We got a situation here.

Desiforever: No shit, Sherlock

Bruinsblow: Yeah well, nobody believed me before. Everyone was all—calm down Drew. No big deal.

PorscheD: What happened?

Creoletransplant: Holts got arrested. No bail.

Mollysdad: What for?

Bruinsblow: Kiddie porn

Mollysdad: Ew. Good then. Who gives a shit?

Bruinsblow: He was FRAMED

Taxman: How do you know that?

Bruinsblow: He told me. Someone planted porn on his work computer.

Mollysdad: Sounds suspicious though

Bruinsblow: HE WAS FRAMED

Joe225: Dude, stop shouting

Bruinsblow: Do you guys possibly see a pattern here? First Graham, now Holts?

Taxman: And you're sure it's that Dahlia girl behind this?

Bruinsblow: Who else? He said someone sent part of the video with him in it again. She's not fighting fair here. Kiddie porn? Who knows what she'll do next?

Mollysdad: Who took the fucking video anyway?

Taxman: Who knows? We don't even know who put it out there

Mollysdad: Who was filming this one though?

Joe225: No clue. Could be any of us.

Desiforever: Could be someone not active anymore. I was pretty fucked up that night. Don't remember.

Taxman: I thought it was someone new? Someone who didn't last very long?

PorscheD: Are those guys even still doing the party?

Desiforever: For now.

Joe225: How do you know?

Desiforever: I know one of the new guys. He interned over the summer with us. Christian Ford.

Creoletransplant: Maybe it's time to wrap that shit up.

Desiforever: Not for us to say

Bruinsblow: Listen. We don't have to worry about those guys right now. We have to worry about us.

Taxman: What happened with Blake R? I thought he was on top of this.

Desiforever: He said he would take care of it.

Bruinsblow: Doing what?

Desiforever: He said he was going to do something personal. "Very personal." That's all he said.

Bruinsblow: Yeah, well tell him about Holts. Maybe that'll light a fire under his ass. He needs to get very personal soon here.

CHAPTER SIXTY-TWO

JAMES

For the whole summer?" I hope the question didn't sound as panicked as I feel. But it probably did. I'm not good at hiding things like that. I feel like someone just sent a shock wave through my motherboard.

"I *may* be going there for the summer," Dahlia says evenly. "Meaning, I applied. I probably won't even get in. But I wanted you to know."

I think about it for a half second. "You're smart. You probably got good grades." She half shrugs, which means yes. "You probably *will* get in."

"Who knows?"

I feel my heart going faster, so that it almost hurts. "And then you'll get into the law school, and then you'll be there forever."

"Whoa, whoa there," she says, lifting her hand in a stop pantomime. "Let's see if I even get into the summer program first. And if I do, I'm not even sure I can afford it, so…"

I can feel myself calming down, because I have a great idea how law school could work out just fine. "There are probably a lot of places in Boston you could get into also. Maybe you should apply to a summer program here."

"Maybe," she says, and I can't tell if she means it.

"Let's see," I say and type *Boston law schools* into Google. "Suffolk Law School. That one would work." I tilt my screen to show her. "That's got a crazy-high acceptance rate. So even you should get in."

She chuckles. "Thanks for the vote of confidence."

"No, I didn't mean it like *that*." I move down the list. "Boston

University, where Eli went. They've got a summer program too. But, oh no. That's really expensive."

"It's okay, James. I'll figure it out," she says, brushing my shoulder with her arm, which is her way of brushing me off too but nicely. Rob once told me, "Sometimes you don't know when to give it a rest." Since then, I've always tried to give it a rest when need be.

"So," she says, standing up abruptly from the couch. Simone opens one eye in response. "Are we going to do this thing or what?"

She's referring to the reason I came over, to set up the necklace and the computer. "All right," I say. "Let's get it going." As I start setting up the program, she fingers the necklace, which looks incredible on her.

"So, how does this work?" she asks. "The camera feeds into the computer?"

"Eventually. The camera transmits to it."

She is leaning in toward me, and I catch a faded scent of freesia. "How far can it go and still transmit?"

"About 150 feet. Give or take. I don't know. I figure we'll test it."

She leans her elbow on the table, even closer to me. "That doesn't seem very far." She reaches down to pet Simone, whose tail lashes against my leg.

"Yeah, the high-powered ones will get you two thousand feet. But they probably wouldn't have fit in the necklace. And we don't need that anyway. Because I'll be right across the street, parked in the car with my laptop."

"True. You're too smart," she says and tickles me under my chin like I'm the cat. And I absolutely don't mind. The computer sounds, signaling the download is complete, and she looks up from the screen. "It's ready?"

"Yup. So we have to turn on the camera." I look down at the black, beady eye with the fake diamond in the middle.

"Oh yeah." She fumbles with the necklace. "It's somewhere on the back of it…"

"Here, let me see."

She lifts her head, exposing her delicate, pale neck, and I turn the evil eye over. My fingers are awkward, too big on the little pendant, but I find the button finally. A crunch of feedback sounds over the speaker, then an image of my jaw looms up embarrassingly close on the screen, showing my birthmark and a trace of stubble and the stupid cleft that I hate, but which Dahlia told me makes me look like a superhero.

"How about that?" She glances at the screen. "It actually works." She twirls around, whirring the room on the computer. Then she stops and the image stills.

"Pretty crisp picture," I say, and we both stand there, admiring the computer. "Go into another room. Let's check the audio."

Her footsteps pad into the bedroom, and I see the corner of a soft, purple comforter. A desk stacked with books. "Testing, one two three," she says.

The audio comes in a bit fuzzy but definitely audible. "I can hear you," I call to her. "Just one more thing. I want to check out the range."

"Yeah, but I'm starved," she says, walking back into the room.

"Me too. It won't take long though—"

"How about this?" She shrugs on her coat. "I'll go down the street to pick up the Thai, and you let me know when you lose me."

"Okay. That should work." I look around the room. "I'll flick off the lights when I can't see you anymore."

She nods and grabs her purse. The screen dips to the floor a minute, then pops back up.

And the necklace works. Perfectly. All the way down the stairs and the street. The night looks soft and pretty on the screen, the streetlights and the storefronts. And as she keeps up a running commentary, I can hear every word. At about three hundred feet, the screen starts to stutter, fading in and out of a grainy, dotted picture, then goes black. And I flick the light on and off, then keep it off. Three hundred feet. Not bad. Even better than I expected. We probably won't even need that much distance.

Then it hits me like a ton of bricks. Which is another stupid idiom, as no one would survive such a thought. But anyway, I think of it, right then, and realize I'm an idiot not to have thought of it before.

A transmitter. Of course.

And I know how we can hack into Blake Roberts's computer.

CHAPTER SIXTY-THREE

DAHLIA

S o, explain it again," I say.

We are finishing breakfast at a secluded table in the basement cafeteria. James has already tried to explain the hacking technique multiple times, and it still won't sink in. He was so excited about the idea last night that he went right home after our Thai food to research it. And since it was a work night, I supposed it was just as well.

"Okay," he says with a tincture of impatience. "We get the cell phone."

"Uh-huh." I am peeling an orange, getting skin in my fingernails. "But how does that get into the computer?"

"That's what I'm saying. It doesn't." He unwraps another portion of his protein bar. "We're just using it as a receiver. The computer lets off EMF emissions, right?"

"Um, right," I answer, though I never knew this was a fact.

"So, we can capture data from that. But we just need a receiver. And your basic cell phone is…" He waits for my response.

"A receiver?"

"Yes!" His face is puppy-dog excited with my good guess.

I swallow an orange section, which is slightly bitter. "But how are you going to get a cell phone into his office?"

"That's the beauty of it," he says. "It's like the transmitter in your necklace. If the signal is strong enough, it doesn't have to be in the same room. A hundred, two hundred feet away is fine." He tosses the yogurt container in a nearby garbage. "Turns out the Israelis have been doing this for years."

"Of course they have." I wrap the orange peel up in my napkin. "Why do you say that?"

"Because Jews are smart."

James tilts his head. "Isn't that racist or something?"

I smile. "Not if I say it."

He smiles back. "Right." At that, we both stand up and he tosses his protein bar wrapper into the garbage and me my decimated orange peel. "There's one minor thing though," James says as we enter the stale-smelling stairwell. "We still have to get the malware on his computer."

I start climbing up and let out an audible sigh. "Then we're back to square one, right? How are we going to do that?"

Our footsteps clang together on the stairs. "That's the thing," he says. "It doesn't have to be a big virus or anything. Just a couple of lines of code. We can slip that through in an email."

"We can?" I am breathing a bit heavily keeping up with him, which tells me I have to get back to kickboxing.

"Definitely," he answers as we get to his floor. Mine is one more up. "But we just have to figure out who's going to email him."

"What do you mean?"

He leans his elbow against the gray concrete wall. "It has to be from someone he trusts. Or at least someone tempting enough for him to open it without thinking."

"Uh-huh," I say, and at once think of who it has to be, of course. Who would tempt him so mightily, he couldn't help but open it.

———

After Sylvia goes to lunch, I make the call.

"Of course I'll do it," Daisy answers. "But I can't guarantee he'll open it."

I shift the phone on my ear. "He gave you his frigging hotel key. He'll open it."

She sighs into the phone. "Most men do think with their penises."

"Uh-huh," I say.

"So, what should it say?" she asks. "Hard sell? Soft sell? What are we thinking here?"

I have to admire her business school approach to the problem. "The subject line is key," I say. "Maybe 'get-together this weekend?' That would definitely pique his attention."

"Yes, it would."

"Then just put in some bullshit about how you're not getting along with your fiancé and wanted a mindless, fun trip and he came to mind."

"You think he'll buy that?" she asks, sounding unconvinced.

"It doesn't really matter. From what James told me, all he has to do is open the damn thing."

"Good point."

"And James will send you the code for the virus to include in the email."

"Okay." She pauses then. "But, Dahlia…"

"What?" I sense the misgiving in her voice.

"I don't know how to put this exactly, but this one. Blake Roberts. He's a big fish. He's not some cokehead or teacher or whatever. He's got lawyers, spokespeople, all that crap."

I tap my pen on my legal pad. "Okay?"

"I'm just saying, you come at him, and he could really hurt you. I don't have to tell you how the game is played. He'll get you for defamation. He'll countersue. He'll bankrupt you in, like, ten seconds."

"No problem," I say with a chortle. "They've already done that."

"Just think about it," she says. "Be sure you really want to do this. It might not be worth it in the end."

I twirl the pen between my fingers. "Believe me, it'll be worth it."

———

At the end of the day, I'm getting ready to leave when my phone vibrates, rattling in the drawer as if it's alive. I yank it open with a squeak.

It's from Daisy. Emailed the message James sent me.

With the code?

Yup. BR emailed me right back. Wants to get together. She sends an emoji of a snake, and I laugh and send her a picture of a snake and a gun.

She sends a smiley and xxxooo.

And I xxxooo her back. Because I really xxxooo her right now. Then I get on my office phone and call James. "He took the bait."

"Good," he says. "So now we have to get someone near the office for a few minutes at least. Less than a hundred feet away would be best." Deep-throated laughter rings out in the background, and he muffles the phone. "We don't need much time to pick some stuff off his computer. A few snippets, passwords."

Sylvia starts powering off her computer and deposits all her blue pens in her mug, like she does every day.

"I have his work address," I say. "Should we try for tomorrow?"

"Yeah, we should get it done soon. Before someone catches it." He pauses. The laughter rises up again. "I was thinking, maybe it shouldn't be you though, who does it."

"Why not?" I ask. Sylvia throws on her coat and whips on her scarf like she's in a race. "Cake appointment," she half whispers, pointing to her wristwatch.

I give her a smile and a thumbs-up. "I can do it, James. I'll be fine."

"I don't know," he demurs. "Vihaan Patel already sent one guy after you. Blake Roberts might be on the lookout too."

This gives me pause. "That's true." I lean back in my chair, as secretaries and paralegals are abandoning their posts all around me.

"Okay." I hear something slam in the background, then coworkers swearing. "Got to go. I'll call you later."

As we hang up, I realize the perfect person to hang out near Blake's office and not attract any attention in New York. I dial the number, though I doubt she'll answer. She never answers her phone. But if worse comes to worst, I figure I can hit her up at her usual spot after work.

This time, she does answer, and her smoky, hoarse voice has never been more welcome. "Hello?"

"Hey, it's Dahlia."

"Dahlia!" Natasha's voice lightens. "What's up, babe?"

"Not much. I was just wondering…" I unbend a paper clip on the desk. "You feel like making some money?"

CHAPTER SIXTY-FOUR

Five Years Ago

I am living out of boxes, but I'm happy. Happy enough, anyway.

Eli quit the job after two weeks, and some new girl's starting. Sylvia something. She seems nice. Overall, I don't mind being back in Boston. The work is just challenging enough, and it's something to do every day. Somewhere to go, instead of hanging out in my pajamas and fighting with my family.

I ran out of my medication, but I don't think I need it right now anyway. I haven't thought about suicide once this whole month. That might not seem like a real accomplishment, but for me, it is. It's something. Life is something I can get along with, for now.

Cash is low, but Eli brings leftovers from his new job at the restaurant. It scares me sometimes though, what I would do without him. He's not just my anchor; he's my everything. I know it's not healthy, but I try not to beat myself up too much. He's all I have right now. Maybe someday that will change. I'll make friends from work, go back to school. Baby steps, Eli says. And he's right. So again I'm quoting Eli, but that's okay. He can be my everything for now.

The days are fine, right up until bedtime.

The evenings are bearable. I go out with Eli sometimes, but he mostly wants to drink and pick up men, and I have no interest in either right now. So I stay up reading or watching crappy TV, but I can only drag that out for so long. Then it's time to go to bed.

Bed is the problem.

Usually, I lie there, trying to turn off my brain. My brain turns against me at night. It wants to replay the night, over and over. What I could have done differently. How I should have just said no to Daisy and stayed home. How I'm never going to graduate. My brain doesn't want to count sheep. It wants to count all the ways in which I am a loser.

Then when I finally do sleep, I always wake up there.

A stale mattress is all I remember. Every time, I hear laughing, some kind of bird noise, then the smell of the mattress, and I wake up drenched in sweat. When I try to analyze it, the image slips away. I tried to write it all down, but it didn't help. I can dream about it all night, but I still don't know what happened. A mattress tells me nothing.

Last night was the same, more nightmares. And this morning, I am feeling tired and a bit raw, but it's okay. I have somewhere to go and something to do. And that is something.

Baby steps.

I do my ablutions. I put on my clothes, my makeup, and get ready to start my day. It's chilly in my little box this morning. They said on the radio that the day would be unseasonably cold. So I grab my spring pea coat, which I haven't worn since I was back in college.

And in the pocket is a glossy business card.

RAE-ANN RHIMES

CHAPTER SIXTY-FIVE

DAHLIA

It turns out Natasha did indeed feel like making some money. As soon as possible.

So the next day she's in New York City, at the base of Blake Roberts's building.

"I'm getting hungry here," Natasha whines into the phone. "What's going on?"

We've spent nearly an hour moving her back and forth to get the best reception for the cell phone in her other hand. "Okay, that's good," I say. "You're in a good spot. James says we need at least ten minutes."

She grumbles.

"It won't be too long," I say, as if I'm talking down a toddler. She huffs into the phone in response, and it strikes me that she's jonesing for something besides food. "So," I say, to distract her. "Have you been to S.O.R. lately?"

"Got kicked out again."

"Oh. That's too bad," I say, as Sylvia erases something on a document, making a scratching noise.

"Yeah. They *say* I stole from some girl. Which I didn't." She sighs heavily into the phone again. "Dude, I am really getting tired of standing here."

How are we doing? I text James.

It's working. Want to get a bit more info though.

"So, what else is new?" I ask. I would like to make small talk, but our lives have very little in common right now. Except that we were both raped, and she likes taking my money.

"Friend OD'd the other day," she says rather matter-of-factly. "Which is pretty sad. But you almost come to expect it by now, in a way."

"Wow," I say, which is inadequate, but it's hard to backtrack that far with her. "Sorry."

"Yeah, it sucks, but whatcha gonna do? Live by the game, die by the game."

We're good. Got three different passwords. Should be enough.

"Okay," I say brightly. "You are released. James will give you the other hundred at your usual spot."

"All righty then. Pleasure doing business with you."

As I put down my phone, Sylvia takes a loud sip of coffee. "James will give you the last hundred in the usual spot," she echoes, her voice a question. "Sounds very mysterious."

"Yeah. We're a regular pair of gangsters," I joke, to deflect the question. "It's actually a loan for a friend," I add, for good measure.

"Hmm," she answers, probably not believing me but also not caring enough to challenge it. She leans down to grab some paper for the printer. "So, what do you think of bubbles instead of birds?"

I stare at her. "Bubbles instead of birds?"

"You know, instead of rice, for coming out of the church?" She takes her seat again. "We were going to go with birds. But that's just a logistical nightmare and you have to get a permit and everything."

"Oh yeah. Well, bubbles are nice," I say distractedly, trying to catch up on the work I missed while babysitting Natasha.

"Don't you think bubbles could get messy though? My mom said they might stain the dresses."

"Oh, I don't know. Maybe," I say. She answers, but I don't hear a word. Because there's a new text on my phone from a number that I don't recognize.

I guess you didn't learn your lesson the first time, bitch.

Who is this? I type back.

One of the people who fucked you so good, you couldn't walk for days.

My face feels hot, as if I've been scalded.

Now you want to complain about what a whore you were. So, it's time to teach you another lesson.

When I swallow, it is painfully dry. Fuck off, I text back, but the bravado rings false to me.

Oh, we will. Lesson #1. You might want to watch out for Simone.

Sylvia's phone rings, and I jump. "Miller and Stein. Can I help you?"

A picture pops up of me holding Simone as a kitty. An old Instagram photo from an account I never use anymore and clearly need to close. Then, another photo comes on the screen. It takes a second to recognize the lump of gray as a dead cat, its neck twisted and paws bloody, with one glazed eye staring, the other an empty eye socket.

Gagging, I put the phone down.

———

"You okay?" Sylvia asks with concern. "You don't look so hot."

"I'm fine," I lie. "Just getting a migraine."

"Oh. Those suck." She bangs the stapler with the heel of her hand. "My cousin gets migraines."

I can't even answer. My brain is stuttering, picturing Simone meowing softly, hurt somewhere. At once, I call Eli and wait out too many rings. But just as the phone should go to voicemail, he picks up.

"Hey."

"Hey," I say. "Are you home?"

"Yeah, why?"

"Phew." I realize my hand is in a fist and loosen it. "Can you check on Simone?"

There is a pause on the phone. "Check on Simone? Why, is she supposed to be doing homework or something?"

"Just…check on her for me. Please."

"Fine, fine," he says with a sigh of exasperation. "I'll call you back."

"No," I say. "I'll stay on the phone. Just go ahead."

"This minute."

"This minute," I confirm.

He heaves another sigh, and I hear him walking and the door open. "Never mind what I was doing. That's not important. Just need to check on the cat right this minute for some reason." I hear his shoes clomp down the stairs, then the key scraping in the slot and the click of the dead-bolt lock. "And I'm here. And I'm looking for a cat."

I'm holding my breath.

"Simone," he calls out. "Simone." His footsteps sound out as he wanders through the apartment.

"Is she—"

"Aw, who's that good girl with the crazy mommy?" he coos. "Who's the good kitty?"

"She's okay?" Relief floods through me.

"Yes, she's okay. What's wrong? Did you have some kind of premonition about her or something? Choking on a hair ball?"

"Never mind," I say, breathing normally again. "Could you do me a favor though?"

"Anything, my dear."

The stapler slams again, and I grip the phone tighter. "Could you keep an eye on her today?"

CHAPTER SIXTY-SIX

DAHLIA

A few days later, we're on our way to Maine for Christmas Eve. James twists the gas cap back on and climbs back into the Prius, the fresh scent of gas hanging off him. The evening is crisp and cold, a fine dusting of snow on the ground.

We're three hours into the ride, deep into the country now. Towering trees, with bare branches weaving into black. And I don't have to worry about Simone at least. Daisy has agreed to keep her not just for the visit, but as long as I need.

"Hey," James says. "Did you see the article on Henry Holstein?"

"No." I adjust the seat back.

"Check it out. From their local newspaper."

Googling the name and newspaper brings me quickly to a huge article, which makes sense. Child pornography would be a big deal for a schoolteacher. Accompanying the article is a photo of his house, an old white farmhouse with the words *pedophile* and *pig* in fuzzy, red spray paint. I think of his maniacal laughter on the video. *Pig*. I don't bother to read the article.

"Has he called you again?" James asks.

"No. Blocked the number."

"Good."

As I close the article, a text appears on the screen—a cute picture of Simone in the sun, taken by Daisy. It's a blissful improvement over the last cat picture. After this, she sends another text.

Got info from my friend about the Red Sox hat.

What??

Special version of hat as charity for St. Jude's in 1999 with Javier Ramirez signature. Only five hundred in circulation.

Wow. Thanks!

"Who was that?" James asks through a yawn.

"Daisy. She got more information about the Red Sox hat." I tell him her news.

"That definitely narrows it down." He folds the wrapper over a half-eaten protein bar and sticks it in the cup holder.

"So, 1999," I say, doing the math. "We were only six years old then."

"I was four," he says with a Cheshire grin.

"Yeah, I know. Stop reminding me. I'm a cradle-robber." I take a sip of coffee. "Probably someone who grew up in Boston then."

"Yeah," he says. "Unless they bought it off the internet or something." He checks his speed, then slows by about five miles per hour. Other than our getaway adventure with Cary G, James is an exceedingly careful driver.

He clears his throat, like he's about to say something, and I look over.

"About Ramona," he says but then falters, tapping his fingers on the steering wheel.

"Yes?"

"I wanted to tell you something…" His lips purse, his fingers still tapping.

"Okay?" I encourage him.

He takes a quick breath and gets off at an exit. "Forget it. I'll tell you later. It's not important."

"All right," I say, wondering what he was about to say as we drive past an intersection with the usual chain stores. Within minutes, we are transported to a rustic, picture-perfect town with open fields skirted by pine trees. A few stores dot the landscape. An old bar, a diner, a gas station.

We turn down his street and finally up to his driveway.

"You ready?" he asks.

As we walk in, the smell of a ham cooking pervades the house.

"Dahlia," his mom says with genuine warmth. She reaches out, and we hug. His mother is pretty and petite. I can feel all her bones through her thin sweater. "We are so happy to have you," she says with a strong accent.

"Me too." My voice comes out too high-pitched. "Thanks so much for having us." I am gripping the neck of the red-wine bottle we brought.

James comes up behind me with our luggage, and he swallows her up with his hug. When they pull away, her eyes are misty.

"I'm going to throw our stuff upstairs," he says.

"Dahlia takes the guest room," she says, pointing her head up the stairs.

"Yeah, I'll sleep in the den," James says.

"Hello!" a voice booms out behind us.

"Dad," James answers, his voice more restrained.

"John Gardner," he says to me with a handshake and smile. He and James exchange a perfunctory hug. They are both tall men, though James is maybe an inch taller. "How was traffic?"

"Not bad," James says.

We start taking off our boots while his father whisks our coats away to the front closet.

"Come in," his mother says, motioning toward the kitchen. "I made the tofu for you. No ham," she says. James must have told them I was a vegetarian.

"Can I help with anything, Ms.—"

"Asuka. You call me Asuka. Please."

"Okay." I walk into the kitchen, which is the same tasteful design as the foyer. Dark-cherry wood and the jade-green granite countertops. I put the wine bottle down.

"So, how long you know James?" She lays out crackers on a cheese plate.

"Well, we've worked together a while. But I only really got to know him in September."

"I see," she says and sprinkles some croutons on a huge salad in a light-brown wooden bowl. Through the doorway, I catch a glimpse of the family room. Multicolor lights from a tall, fake tree reflect on the leather chair. A sparse smattering of gifts surround the base. Upstairs, we hear James rumbling around.

I'm turning back to the kitchen when a large family portrait on the wall catches my eye. A formal, family oil painting with James and his parents. There's also a boy who looks like James, maybe a couple of years older.

But no Ramona.

"James?" Asuka calls up, and we wait for him to come down.

CHAPTER SIXTY-SEVEN

JAMES

They changed her room.

Everything is tan and mauve, like a hotel. Not at all like Ramona's room, which used to be Rob's room. No trace of either of them in there now.

I open the closet to put Dahlia's bag in there, feeling like I'm snooping somehow. But it's empty too. No clothes carrying her scent. No rolled-up posters of bands she outgrew, no sandals mounded on the floor. Stuffed in the back of the top shelf, something catches my eye. Blindly reaching in, I pull out a bedraggled teddy bear. Holding the stubby, soft leg, I am hit with a flash of a memory. Rob was playing with the bear one day when we were little. He was maybe eight, too old to be playing with teddy bears. He was trying to put my mom's underwear on it and my dad found him and smacked him. I still remember his heavy breathing as he towered over us, Rob crying, four pink finger blotches across his cheek.

I hear my mom call again, and I shut the closet door. When I come down, Dahlia is standing there, her arms crossed and looking awkward. Relief fills her face as I join them. "Ready to eat?" I ask.

"We have been," my dad answers, which is his way of being an asshole as usual.

"It's fine," my mom says, which is her way of trying to defend me as usual. We all sit around the formal dining room table. I told Mom not to make a big dinner or anything, but she did anyway and said we'd have leftovers tomorrow for Christmas.

"Mmm," Dahlia says, scooping out her tofu dish and green beans and helping herself to salad. "I was starved."

"Me too," I say, laying a shiny slice of ham on my plate. It's almost eight o'clock already. We had to leave a bit late, because we did a big reboot while none of the lawyers were there to complain. I take a first delicious, warm bite and feel at home again. It's quiet while everyone ladles dishes and starts eating.

"So, James says you're a paralegal?" my dad asks, a thin rectangle of ham on his fork.

"Yes," she says. "That's right."

"How did you get into that line of work?" he asks, swallowing.

"Well, I hope to be a lawyer. Eventually."

"Oh," he says, approval in his voice. "Where did you go to college?"

"Dad," I say to the third degree he seems to need to give all my friends. And I don't have very many of them.

"Harvard," she says.

His head shoots up from his plate at the response, and I almost have to laugh. A month ago, before she got her degree, he wouldn't have given her the time of day. She wouldn't have been worth speaking to. They say I see things too black-and-white, but really, it's my father who doesn't have time for gray areas.

"Well, that's very impressive," my father says.

"Thanks." Dahlia spreads out some green beans on her plate. I wonder if she even likes green beans. "Took me a little while, but I finally did it."

"Our son applied there," my mom says. I can see my father squirm in his seat.

"Oh, I didn't know that." Dahlia turns at me with surprise. "Well, anyway, MIT's just as good."

"No, not me," I mutter.

"Robert," my father says. "Not James."

Dahlia takes a big drink of water, looking totally confused, and I know now how stupid it was to bring her here. To think we could act normal and it would all be okay. I should have told her. Jamal was right. I should have told her for sure.

"I haven't heard about Robert," Dahlia says carefully.

My father flicks me a look of disgust.

"He passed away," my mom says. She tries to say it sort of matter-of-factly so no one feels bad, but I can see her chin tremble just a little.

"Oh, I'm so sorry." Dahlia puts her water glass down. "And Ramona too. How awful."

There is a terrible silence then.

"Excuse me?" my father asks, bewildered.

"Oh." She turns bright red. I've never seen her blush like that. "I'm sorry," she says, almost like a question. Like she isn't sure what she's sorry for. She checks with me in desperation, but like a mute idiot, I can't speak.

Again, there is silence, followed by little clinks of silverware as my mom stares at her plate, but then she brings her hand up to her mouth so she doesn't cry. Finally, she stands up and races out of the room.

My dad glares at me. "Are you happy now?"

"I'm sorry," Dahlia says. "I didn't—"

My father stands up, throwing his napkin down. "I told you, James." He points a trembling finger at me, ignoring Dahlia entirely. "I do not want to hear that name in the house. Ever."

"But that's not right," I say, shaking my head.

"It's the rule, James," he states like he is the maker of all rules. Like he is some kind of D&D wizard. For some reason, this makes me furious. I'm tired of accepting everything he says. I'm tired of my mom sticking up for him because he's a big bully. He does not make the rules. He does not make the laws of the universe.

"No," I say, louder now. "It's not the rule. You're wrong."

He pounds his fist on the table, making the silverware jump. "I said it is, and it—"

"No!" I yell, standing up too. It feels good, yelling at him. My voice is unbelievably loud. And I realize right then that I am taller than him. Bigger than him. I don't get how I never noticed this before. He isn't towering over me anymore, and I'm not a little boy. "You are wrong," I say again, slowly. "You can't erase her, Dad. She is not null. She is not void. She had a value."

"There is no her."

"She loved you, Dad," I say. "And you loved her. That has a value, an absolute value. It is not correct to call that zero."

"No." He shakes his head.

"Love," I say. "That has a value."

My dad sits back down and clears his throat. He takes in a long breath. "I have told you before that we do not say that name in this house. Whether you like it or not, that is the rule. And as long as you stay in this house, you will live by my rules."

I look over to see Dahlia staring at the table, and I feel terrible because this is all my fault, so I make a decision. The only way I can make things sort of right.

"You don't have to worry about it," I say. "We're not staying in your house."

CHAPTER SIXTY-EIGHT

Five Years Ago

I remember her by the tea.

Seeing her office now, I realize what a fog I must have been in back then. I barely remember the side street, the rickety stairs, the stuffy waiting room. But I remember the tea.

And she remembers me.

"I wondered if you'd be back," she says with pleasure, as if I were a long-lost friend.

"I am," I answer, a touch embarrassed at her exuberance. I tell her about going home. I tell her about my new job. Eli. And I tell her about the dreams.

"Classic PTSD," she says.

"I know," I say. I've done my fair share of reading on it. "But it's more than that. It's like the dreams stay with me all day."

She nods, as if this is not news to her.

"Then I'm left with this nagging feeling that if I could just remember, then everything would be okay. And I try. But the more I try, the more I can't."

She nods again. "It's tough."

"Yeah."

In the pause, she takes a sip of tea. "How about the suicidal thoughts?"

"At bay," I answer, honestly. "For now."

"You know, there's a good group in the area on this. S.O.S." Rae-Ann rifles through a drawer, then pulls out a stack of flyers and hands me one.

S.O.S. SURVIVORS OF SUICIDE. The cover is glossy with a cartoonish picture of a sad person. "Yeah, maybe," *I say. I've never been one for support groups.*

"Check it out," *she says.* "It might help."

The flyer makes me think of Jeri, and I wonder how she's doing. Maybe she would want to go with me. Or Eli. "So, what can I do about the dreams?" *I ask.*

She sighs. "We can talk about some methods to help. I don't have a magic cure for you, unfortunately. Though there are some medications out there."

"Which means seeing a psychiatrist."

"Yes," *she answers.* "Which wouldn't be the worst thing."

"No, I suppose not." *I turn over the flyer.*

Gathering the stack of pamphlets, she puts them back in the drawer and shuts it with a squeak. "Have you considered self-defense at all?"

This is an unexpected question. "No, why?"

"I'm not saying that would have helped in the situation," *she assures me.* "But sometimes it can help give you a sense of control back. I've found that can help in PTSD."

I shift on the couch. "Judo? Karate?"

She motions to her own zaftig body. "As you can see, I'm not one to talk about it."

I smile. "You look…good." *Which is true. She is overweight and fits perfectly in her body.*

"Thank you, Dahlia." *She smiles.* "Do some research. Try a few classes. See if something sticks."

I nod, glancing at the clock. Our session is almost done, and I must say, I am feeling a bit better. I definitely need to get in touch with Jeri. The positive feeling sticks with me all the way home. A sense of possibility. Wrenching control of my life back. As I get off the subway, I pass a shop that I see nearly every day. I've wondered about it, but never ventured in. The blinking, tuna-orange neon sign, the dark interior. I decide to take a chance.

The bell rings as I walk in, glancing around. A man stands at the counter, middle-aged with a white goatee and some faded tattoos on his arms. "Hi. Can I help you with something?"

"I don't know," I say, uncertain, staring at the rows and rows of guns laid out on the wall behind him. A staggering array.

"Did you have any particular one in mind?"

"Not really," I say, dazed. Then, I see one, shining out at me like a beacon. It's oddly beautiful, like it's calling out to me.

"Have you ever—"

"That one," I say, pointing.

He turns around to look, and his face lights up. "Oh, yes. She's a beauty, all right. The Beretta Px4. Compact, tons of power. Can't go wrong with that one." He takes it off the shelf and hands it to me gently, like a gift. It feels perfect in my hand. "No bullets in there," he says. "So you can get a feel for the trigger."

I lift the gun with two hands, point at the wall, and squeeze hard, with a satisfying click.

"Nice, huh?" he asks with a knowing smile.

"Very nice," I say, smiling right back. "I'll take it."

"Great," he says. "I'll just have to do a quick background check. Make sure you weren't in a loony bin or something," he adds with a grin.

"Ha," I croak out. And as I tap my fingers on the glass case, I make a quick decision. Worst case, I can always walk away. "Here's the thing," I say. "I was planning on paying cash...just so you know."

"Cash, huh?" He stares at me. His tongue dabs his lips. Carefully, he says, "That would be five hundred dollars even then." Though the sign below the gun clearly shows $259.99 in a bright-red sign in a black-markered starburst.

"That'll be fine," I answer without dropping eye contact.

I happen to have lots of cash on me, in fact. My dad just sent an influx from his "anything-to-keep-you-out-of-my-house" fund and I was going to start paying Eli back. But I can certainly give him some money tomorrow instead.

"Let me go check on that," he says.

"I'll be waiting," I answer, trying for a light tone.

He's gone for nearly a minute, probably for show. When he swings over from the back room, he's all smiles again. "Looks good from my end."

"Perfect," I say, and he waits while I count out five one-hundred-dollar bills and lay them on the counter.

CHAPTER SIXTY-NINE

DAHLIA

James throws our bags in the trunk and slams it. Among our stuff is something I didn't notice before, an old teddy bear with loose stitching.

"Please, James," his mother pleads. "Your father is sorry. You stay."

"I can't, Mom." He gives her a brief hug, and she stands there. Her face is terrible, a rictus of sorrow. "I have to go," he says. "I'm sorry." He goes back to the car as I stand by my door, huddling in my coat. The night is cold and foggy.

"Sorry," I say before stepping in the car. It seems gratuitous after all my previous sorries. Though I don't even know what I'm apologizing for. I climb into the car.

"I'll call you," he yells out to her, then shuts the window. She waves at us, desperately, like a lover waving her sailor off to sea. And just like that, we're driving again.

"Do you mind telling me what's going on?" I ask, as we start down his street.

James grits his teeth, his jaw clenching. "I fucking hate my father."

"Yeah, I got that," I say. "I meant about the other stuff. The fact that you had a brother?"

"Robert," he answers.

"Yes, Robert. And for some reason, we're not allowed to talk about your sister?"

It takes him a while to answer. "It's hard to explain."

I turn down the heater, which is blasting lukewarm air. "Try me."

He grips the steering wheel tight, his knuckles a row of knobs. "I want to tell you."

"Okay?" I give him some time, but he doesn't say any more. "I'm here. Maybe I can help."

His jaw starts gnawing again. "I can't do this right now."

After a bit, he turns on the radio, and I reach over and turn it back off.

"Please, Dahlia," he says, his voice desperate. "Don't do this."

I put my hand on his arm, the fold of his black leather jacket. "What happened?"

Slowly, he pulls his arm away. "I can't."

The heater is flowing warmer, suffusing the car. "I told you," I say. "I told you everything." I don't like the petulant note in my voice, but there it is. And it's true. I've shared everything with him.

"This is different," he says but without conviction.

I shake my head. "Secrets will kill you. They're like a…" I search for a metaphor he might understand. "They're like a black hole. They'll suck you up and spit you out."

His breathing goes ragged, and his eyes fill with tears.

"Tell me," I say gently. Fog slides across the road in front of us while I wait for his answer.

But he wipes the tears away fiercely. "I'm sorry. I can't. I just can't."

———

It's nearly 1:00 a.m. when I get home.

Shoving my suitcase against the wall, I look around for Simone and remember she's still with Daisy or some weird psycho might try to kill her. I sort through the mail, which isn't much: a few bills I forgot to put on auto pay, the newest issue of *The Economist* (though I haven't read the last one yet). Nothing from Stanford.

Putting the mail down, I'm about to head to bed, when my phone rings with Eli's number. "Hey, what's up?"

"Hey."

"What's going on?" I can tell something's wrong by the tone of his "hey."

"Nothing. We broke up. I'm on my way home."

"Why? What happened?"

I hear a whistle in the background and realize he's on a train. "It's the Colorado thing. He never asked me to come with him."

I pause. "Do you *want* to go to Colorado?"

"That's not the point," he whines.

"Right. Okay," I say, realizing this is not the best moment to logically assess that. "Anyway, I came home early too."

"You did?" The whistle sounds again. "Why?"

"Long story. But we didn't break up. We're just... I don't know what we are. I'm going to bed. Call me tomorrow, okay?"

"Love ya," he says, which he hasn't said in a while.

"Love ya too." We hang up, and I get ready for bed, then lie down. My body is dead-tired, but my brain has other plans. I turn over in the bed, check on my Beretta, and close my eyes again, but my mind keeps spinning through the same questions.

Why didn't he tell me about his brother?

Why won't his father talk about Ramona?

Finally, I sit up and grab my phone. Plugging *Robert Gardner* and *Maine* into the search box, I get some immediate hits. It's mostly high school stuff: he was on the track team, he played violin in a semiprofessional group, he was the president of the French Club. These accomplishments seem to speed sadly into his death announcement, which provides directions about flowers and the funeral hours, the next of kin. But no why, no how.

Next, I Google Ramona Gardner. But I'm stymied.

I sit up straighter in bed. The only person I can dig up is a middle-age African American woman. So, I shoot through some social media sites, everywhere I can think of: Facebook, Instagram, Twitter. For a second, I consider calling James for help searching, but then I realize that I can't. I am trying all the places and search engines I can think of. Ramona Gardner, Ramona Gardner Maine, Ramona Gardner Forest High School, Ramona Gardner Cornell University.

Finally, I put the phone down and settle myself back to bed. I have to get some sleep; the secrets will have to wait.

Because I'm starting to realize that maybe there is no Ramona Gardner.

CHAPTER SEVENTY

DAHLIA

The day after Christmas, the place is like a ghost town.

Still, it's almost a relief to be back at work. Sylvia is tapping on the keyboard with hot-pink nails, while I finish Tabitha's scaffolding case.

Time to talk? It's Eli.

I haven't taken lunch yet, so I decide to take a break. 5 min, I text back.

After grabbing some Cheetos and a Dr Pepper from the vending machine, I sit down at a table and call him. "What's up?" I ask.

"Nothing," he answers. "Just depressed."

"Yeah," I say. "I get that." I pop a Cheeto in my mouth. "You want to talk about how much Brandon sucks?"

"No," he says with a sigh. "I don't even want to do that."

"That bad?"

"Yup," he says. He doesn't talk for a bit and we sit in a comfortable silence, while I munch on my Cheetos. "So," Eli says, breaking the silence. "Tell me what's new with you?"

"Not much. Just the Ramona thing I was telling you about."

"Oh yeah, right."

"It's weird, isn't it?" I ask, wiping orange powder off my hands. "That she's not anywhere on the internet?"

"It is," he agrees.

"And not only did he never say a word about his brother, but you should have seen the reaction when I brought up Ramona. It's like she's verboten or something."

A loud yawn sounds out over the phone. "Did you ask him about it?"

"I tried." I say, crumpling the empty bag. "He got too upset."

"I'm sure he'll tell you eventually," Eli says, sounding a bit bored.

"Well," I say with nothing more to offer, "I'll let you go."

"Okay," he answers. He sounds as dejected and depressed as when the conversation started.

"Hang in there, okay?"

"Okay," he repeats.

I bring my Dr Pepper back to my desk, and Snyder is there, making stilted small talk with Sylvia. His face brightens to see me. "Hey, gorgeous."

"Snyder." I pitch my phone in the drawer. "What are you up to? Just lurking around?"

"Yup, that's me. I'm a PI. I lurk." He sits on the edge of my desk. "Got that contact from the FBI you wanted. The terrorism guy?"

"Oh yes. Perfect," I say. "Connor will be thrilled."

"Uh-huh," he says, his tone dubious. "Detective Omar Mahmoud." As he hands me a scrap of paper with the name, the phone in the drawer buzzes loudly. I ignore it, and then it happens again. Snyder stares at me with amusement. "You need to get that?"

"Not really... I mean..."

He motions his head toward it, and I pull the drawer open and peek in.

Surfed some Jihadi websites, sent inquiring emails. No alarms going off yet.

I shut the drawer again.

"What does Connor need Omar for anyway?" His eyes pop up from the closed drawer. "He's taking on an anti-terrorism case?"

"He *may* be accepting one," I lie. "I think he's just doing some initial research."

"Right." He stands up to leave, but leans in toward me first, lowering his voice. "I don't know what you're up to, gorgeous.

But be careful. You're a good kid." He gives me a lopsided grin. "But you won't look good in orange."

With that, he walks away, and I quickly text James. Omar Mahmoud. Snyder's connection.

Great, will call soon.

I'm putting the phone away when it vibrates another text in my hand. Ready for another lesson?

My breath catches, and I stare at the screen. This time, I decide not to answer, figuring engaging this sick fuck is probably turning him on. And Simone is safe with Daisy anyway.

Then a picture pops up of my sister, smiling, her hand over a large baby bump.

What do you want? I type. I can't help myself.

We want you to stop. If you don't, we'll kill her and her little baby. But first we'll fuck her good, just like we fucked you.

The phone seems to ring forever.

My eyes wander over to Simone's usual spot, then I remember she isn't there.

"Hello?" Her voice is short of breath, as if she ran to the phone.

"Shoshana," I say with relief. "You're okay."

She giggles. "Of course I'm okay." Her voice is teasing. "Are you drunk or something?"

"No," I say. I consider grumpily reminding her that I don't drink anymore when I remember why I'm calling her. "It's—"

"It's about Stanford? Did you get in?"

"No, it's not." I stand and check out the window. There's a silver sedan out front that I haven't noticed before. I peek out behind the curtain. "I mean, yes, I'm applying. But I didn't hear from them yet."

"Oh, well, I'm sure you'll get in."

The silver car takes off, and I let out a sigh. "Yeah, um…that's not what I'm calling about. I… There's a little problem."

"Okay?" Her tone is warm and immediately helpful as usual.

"It's about…what happened that night."

There's a heavy pause.

"The guys involved…well, who raped me. I should just say it. They seem to be coming after me again."

She breathes in sharply. "Oh no. Why? What do you mean?"

I walk away from the window. Then, I explain about the video, though I don't tell her about James, or our revenge plan, positing it instead as more of a preemptive strike on their part. "But here's the thing," I continue. "As part of the threat, they're talking about you."

"Me?" she asks in shock. "But how did I get involved?"

"To scare me," I say, "into not saying anything."

"Jesus," she whispers.

"I'm going to send you the text that they sent me. Because I think you should know. But I'm warning you, it's upsetting."

"Okay," she says, sounding suddenly weary. "Did…did you call the police?"

I don't answer, because I can't bear to lie to her about that. Not when she may be at risk.

"No," she answers for me. "Because you don't like the police." There's a tinge of bitterness in the statement, and I can't blame her.

"But you can," I urge her. "You should."

"All right," Shoshana says with a sigh. "Send it to me."

CHAPTER SEVENTY-ONE

JAMES

Faneuil Hall isn't too busy, which is perfect.

I walk over to the pier, watching the waves slap against the cement. The night is cold, and the water must be freezing. I imagine Ramona hitting the cold water and make my brain stop. Like Jamal said, I have to change the neural circuitry, put a stop code in the if-then loop somehow.

A couple walks by holding gloved hands; they whisper something to each other and then laugh. I cross my arms and just stare out, hoping I don't look too obvious. I wore all black and picked somewhere a lot of people might go. The noise of the water should wash over any other easily identifiable sounds.

In the distance, someone is walking a dog, coming my way. The cold is stinging my fingers, and I want to get this over, so I type the number in the phone and wait out the rings until the answering machine comes on.

"This is Omar Mahmoud from the Federal Bureau of Investigation. I am not available right now, but…"

"Hi. I'm calling about someone from work. I…I think he's giving money to terrorists. I saw something really weird when I walked by his computer." An ambulance wails out in the distance, which the phone is probably picking up. But so what—there are a lot of ambulances out there. "I don't want to get involved. But Blake Roberts is his name. 617-554-9292. I'm afraid he's planning something bad." I hang up.

The dog walker is about twenty feet closer.

Some freezing droplets fly up from the pier onto my face, and I turn away and start walking. As I walk by an Irish bar, some people file out, laughing and yelling. Pulling my hoodie up against the wind, I move on.

The money transfers have gone through, and I have a few more lined up for tomorrow. Then that's it. It's too fast. It's not at all realistic. They might not believe our scenario, but maybe they will. And as Dahlia said, if we can't send him to jail, we can at least ruin his reputation. And I don't want to take the time and chance someone connecting the dots back to us.

Unexpectedly, my phone rings, and for a weird, scary moment, I think it's Omar Mahmoud calling to say he caught me out. But then I remember that's the burner phone, not mine. I look down at the screen and see it's my mom. I put it back in my pocket. I'll talk to her, but not now. I'm not ready yet.

Sidestepping a puddle, I take the phone out again and text Dahlia.

Called OM

I wait for a response, but it only says delivered, not read, and I put the phone away again.

I have to tell Dahlia the truth. I know that. Texting her isn't enough. She's right to be upset with me after that dinner. In fact, I'm surprised she's even communicating with me. Especially after everything she's told me.

Maybe after the project is done.

It almost is anyway. She still wants to go to the New Year's party for the cigar box. I don't think that's such a good idea, especially with them threatening her sister. And her cat. But Dahlia does, and sometimes there's no talking to Dahlia.

And when it's all over, I'll tell her. I'll tell her everything. And hopefully she'll still love me. Or if she doesn't yet, maybe she will eventually. Because it took some time, but I figured something out, and there's nothing I can do about it.

I love her no matter what.

CHAPTER SEVENTY-TWO

HAWK CLUB CHAT ROOM

Mollysdad: So, what's the word?

Desiforever: Blake took care of it

PorscheD: What did he do?

Desiforever: Threatened her. He doesn't think she'll be a problem anymore

Bruinsblow: Well, that's good for him. I'm not so sure about that. Bitch is like a dog after a bone.

Creoletransplant: Well she is a dog. And she did get boned. So…

Desiforever: He said it's over. I trust him. Blake knows what he's doing.

Mollysdad: I suppose

Desiforever: I also told the guys in the club. Just in case she tries anything.

Mollysdad: Doubt she'd do that.

Desiforever: See above. Dog. Boned. Etc.

PorscheD: How did you warn them?

Desiforever: Sent them her picture. Total skank. She's got like a million fucking tattoos and purple hair. It would be hard to miss her.

Bruinsblow: Who's the point man on that then?

Desiforever: Christian Ford. If she ever comes there, they'll be prepared. But as I said, Blake is all over it. He said she's done.

CHAPTER SEVENTY-THREE

Five Years Ago

J eri texted me that she'd be at S.O.S., but she wasn't.

Eli had work so he couldn't come, but he said he'd be there the next time. And overall, it went well. The leader was a bit odd, but earnest. Lots of crying in the room. I told a bit of my story, and that was enough. There was a feeling of community, of sharing something sacred, but taboo. Something no one else wants to talk about.

And when I left, I felt better. Which is the point, I suppose.

As I stand on the platform of the station, I can literally and figuratively see a light at the end of the tunnel, and I feel semi-hopeful the whole ride home. Emerging from the stairs to the street, I get a text from Eli.

Got you a present

Tell me tell me tell me

It's a surprise

Be home in 10 min

Meet at your place, *he texts.*

When I open the door, he has a devilish grin.

"What?" *I ask.*

"You'll see," *he says.*

I drop my purse and sit on my new couch. "What is it?"

"It's around," he answers, mysteriously.

I jump up from the couch. *"Should we play hot and cold?"*

"That might not be so easy," he says. *"Kind of a moving target."*

Then I see it. A tiny gray kitty, slinking in a shadow. *"Oh my God."* I tiptoe over to the cat, who takes hesitant steps backward.

Eli is beaming. *"It's a she."*

"She's adorable," I say. *"Look at that beautiful face."* I creep closer and slowly reach out my hand to pet her neck. As if she can't help it, she leans in toward my hand.

Eli is on his hands and knees next to me. *"You like her?"*

"I love her!" She ventures closer to my palm.

"What are you going to name her?" he asks, schoolboy excitement in his voice.

"I don't know. I'll have to think about it."

Eli offers the kitten his hand as well, but she moves closer to me. He got me the whole kit and caboodle—the litter box, some food, toys, and a kitty bed. We play with her forever. Finally, the kitty starts to totter on her feet, and her eyes close.

"I think someone's tired," I whisper.

Eli nods, smiling at her. He squeezes my shoulder, then stands up. *"I should be going anyway. Interview tomorrow."*

"For what?"

"A job I won't get." He gives me an air kiss and leaves.

I slump down in the couch, watching the little bundle breathing, her ribs rising and falling. Grabbing my phone, I text Jeri again.

You jerk! I add a wink emoji. You didn't show! Next time, you better be there, girl. Now a smile emoji. I put the phone by my side and stroke the kitten, thinking about possible names. But I can't think of a good one right now, and watching her sleep makes me drowsy. So I lie down next to her and, soon enough, find myself dozing off.

Sometime later, the sound of a text ding wakes me up. The kitten opens one eye, then lazily closes it again, and I wipe some drool off my mouth. Yawning, I sit up to check the phone.

This is Jeri's mother. I'm sorry to tell you, but Jeri passed away suddenly last night.

An involuntary gasp escapes my lips.

She truly appreciated your friendship. Thank you.

I'm sorry, I text back. And wait a while, but there is no further response.

I pull up Eli's number to tell him, but stop. I don't have it in me right now. A wall of sorrow falls on me. Almost buries me. S.O.S. couldn't save her. The hospital couldn't save her. I couldn't save her.

And I sit there on the couch, crying again, that hopeful feeling evaporating. I am so, so sick of crying. Right then, I feel as low as I've been in a long time. A black hopeless feeling. And the familiar thought snakes into my head. How easy it would be to just let go.

To let it all go, like Jeri.

But I wipe my eyes and try to push through it. The blackness. The useless, useless feeling. Because there's a tiny kitten breathing at my feet.

And she needs me.

CHAPTER SEVENTY-FOUR

DAHLIA

The week blurred by, hurtling toward the day I circled in red on my calendar. And it's finally here. D-day. The after–New Year's party. And after the texts, it couldn't come a day too soon.

But at the same time, I face the night with a mixture of excitement and dread. My nerves are jangling and I feel weirdly high, though I'm not. Like my brain is in overdrive, so hyper-alert, it's almost disengaged. Like my brain is rebelling against me, telling me not to do this. Just like Eli told me.

But I have no choice. I have to.

"You're absolutely sure now?" James asks, his jaw set as if he's about to face the guillotine. "Positive?"

"A hundred percent," I lie. "I'll be fine. You'll be right there, watching me."

"True," he says, but he sounds unsettled still.

Earlier tonight, James and I tested the necklace again. We have a semi-plan. I'm using the name Sarah. And we've come up with a code in case I'm in trouble. I'll say "Red Sox," then he'll call 911.

I adjust my sweater in the mirror. It's cream-colored, with a little frill around the V-neck, which calls attention to the shiny, black evil eye. And I've got on my fitted black skirt. But no heels this time, just long, black leather boots with my beautiful Beretta tucked inside.

Digging through my purse, I uncap my lipstick, dab on another bloodred coat, then take one last look at myself. The evil eye glistens in the light. Frilly top. Black skirt.

I have an odd urge to touch the mirror. And I realize, with some tenderness, that I am trying to reach out to her. Pretty Girl. And tell her everything is okay now. That it gets better, a lot better. But I don't touch the mirror. I stand up straight.

Because I'm not really Pretty Girl anymore. I'm not even Angry Girl. I'm just Dahlia. And I'm finding your fucking cigar box.

"Hey," he says, and I turn to him. "About Ramona." He chews on his lip.

"Yes?"

He takes a breath, looking more nervous than I've ever seen him. "I'll explain everything," he says. "After tonight. Okay?"

I smile at him. "Okay."

He smiles back with an air of relief and starts packing up the computer. "All righty then. Are you ready?" he asks.

"Yes." I lean down and trace the leather of my boot for the familiar bulge. "Let's do this."

I don't remember a thing about the place.

I would have walked right by it had Google Maps not told us to stop there. The building is a nondescript gray brick with a black door and gold, flaking numbers and a patina on the copper knocker. It could be any random office building.

A cold wind slices through my scarf. I wrap it tighter and hit the buzzer on the doorpost.

"Yo" comes out over the speaker. A flash of girlish laugher inside.

"Magna Carta," I say.

"All right, come on up." The door buzzes again, and when I push the knob, it releases. The hallway is also nondescript, a concrete gray, claustrophobic tunnel. I climb the steps, butterflies swarming in my stomach. Halfway up, the sound of voices builds around me, and warmth bubbles down from the party, offsetting the chill of the stairs. When I reach the top step, I am short of breath. I walk in the room, forcing a smile on my face.

Nobody notices me.

The party is already in full blast, raucous and loud. It strikes me that James may not be able to hear anything, let alone *Red Sox* in the event of an emergency.

"Hey." A young man sidles up by my side. My coat and scarf are dangling in my hand while I figure out where to put them. He snags them both. "Tom Burns," he says. "Let me take care of that for you."

"Thanks," I say, actually appreciative, wondering if the place has changed. Though, a man can politely take your coat and still rape you.

When I turn around, Tom Burns is at my side again, ruddy-faced with orange-red hair and a face splattered with freckles. He has a purple bow tie. "Do I know you?"

"Not yet," I say in what I hope is a sexy voice. Or a sexy shout anyway, because I can barely hear myself think. "You might know Whitney," I add.

"Ah, Whitney," he says, his eyes lighting up. "I do remember Whitney."

"*Everyone* remembers Whitney," I say, playing the jealous, always-the-bridesmaid friend.

"But frankly"—he looks me up and down in an appreciative way—"I'm surprised I didn't remember you."

"Sarah," I say. I was worried someone might recognize me, but it certainly doesn't appear that way. I hold out my hand for a shake.

Instead, he kisses it with mock gallantry. "Drink?"

"By all means." Since I'm going to plant my lips on the rim and lose the thing whenever possible anyway.

"Be right back."

I smile and look around the place. Again, nothing familiar. Though I'm not sure what I expected—a sudden burst of a memory dam perhaps. If so, it isn't happening. The decor is pleasant enough. Walls painted pale gold with antique, cherry wood furniture, and a forest-green oriental rug over a scuffed but rich-looking wooden floor. Holly abounds, along with mistletoe conveniently in every doorway and silver ornaments laid around the table with an enormous bowl of rose-pink punch.

Punch bowl.

My brain stutters a second.

"Hey, this stuff's killer," Tom says. "Don't go too crazy with it."

"I won't," I say, taking the sweating glass from his hand. He throws back half of his, not taking his own advice. "Hear, hear," I say and pretend to sip.

Looking around the room, my eyes soar up to an empty spot by the wall. I can see a pinpoint of an old nail hole. "Where's the cuckoo clock?" I ask.

Tom scrunches his face in puzzlement. "How much punch did you have?" he jokes, peering into my full glass. "We've never had a cuckoo clock. Not since I've been here anyway."

"Oh." I can feel myself flushing. "Must have been a different place."

"Yeah, must have been."

And maybe there was something else up there. An old picture. The room doesn't look at all like the one in the video anyway. There is an awkward silence as a Frank Sinatra Christmas song comes on and we both gaze around the room. "Hey, I'll be right back, okay?"

I nod lightly, and he jets off to bear hug someone who just came in. I put my drink down on a corner table, figuring it's as good a time as any to start investigating.

Up ahead, I spy a winding staircase.

CHAPTER SEVENTY-FIVE

JAMES

The room whirs as she makes a sudden turn, as the computer speaker *whomps* with the music pulsing in the room.

This time, Dahlia moves more slowly, and I get a panning shot of the room. The car is hot and stuffy, and I feel an odd mix of nervous and bored. The scene is totally depressing. Well-dressed college students, drunk and laughing. Not a part of college life that I ever experienced, thankfully. The only time I ever came close was a D&D party where we decided to drink for whenever anyone had to use a saving throw. Everyone got totally sick and hungover the next day, and we never did that again.

"Okay," Dahlia says. Her voice threads through the blaring music. "I'm going in." Her voice is half-joking, and the screen bobs as she ascends a dark, winding stairway. The kind like in the *The Wizard of Oz* that you don't see much anymore. A door squeaks on the computer screen, then a light flicks on, revealing a pile of coats stacked up on someone's bed. Loud scratchy noises come over the speaker as she bends down to look under the bed. Then a creaking as she swings open a closet door, stuffed with hung-up coats. "Nothing," she whispers, and the light turns off. I get a view of the hallway again, then another room opens and she flicks on the light.

"Hey!" a voice complains.

On the screen is the outline of a half-clothed couple on the bed. "What are you doing?" the female asks, annoyed and covering herself up.

"Sorry," Dahlia says, then swooshes the door shut. Angry murmurs follow as she leaves.

CHAPTER SEVENTY-SIX

DAHLIA

After that close call, which appeared consensual at least, I tiptoe back into the dark hallway. The music is pounding downstairs, and people start drunkenly singing to some song, which means they probably can't hear me at least. I open a door to a damp-smelling room, which appears to be a storeroom, with boxes and rolled-up posters tossed everywhere. I turn on the light, which flickers and then settles into gray overhead. A light, whining buzz.

As quietly as I can, I start rifling through boxes. They're chock-full of all sorts of crap, one with gory Halloween decorations, rubber masks with protruding eyeballs, bloody stumps of fingers. The next box holds Hawk Club steins and a huge, folded felt banner in crimson with the navy-blue HC shield in the center. Dispirited, I glance at the dozens of boxes left. This could take forever, and Tom might start wondering about me. Though he's probably getting some other girl drunk by now anyway.

In the corner is a tall, narrow closet door. I open it to find yet another box, this one overflowing with tinsel and ornaments. On my tiptoes, I reach for the top shelf to feel for a cigar box, but my fingers barely graze the wooden slat.

"Here goes nothing," I mutter, more for James than me, and drag a somewhat sturdy box over to stand on. Finally, precariously balanced on the wilting box, I peek onto the top shelf, which is completely empty.

I'm turning back around when the box crumbles and I fall down, smacking my tailbone right against the floor. Something clatters off to my side. "Fuck."

Suddenly, a shadow looms in the doorway. "Hello?"

I look up at the shaded figure, my heart slamming into my chest. "Hey," I say, slowly standing up, my tailbone bleating out in pain.

The young man assesses me. He's wearing a pale-blue shirt and has blond hair that falls into his eyes. He's handsome in the self-assured way of those who have always been handsome. "You lost?"

"Guess so," I say with a fake smile, painfully speed-walking to the door. "I was looking for Tom."

"Well, he isn't in here." He stands in the doorway so I'm forced to rub against him. "Who did you say you were?"

"Sarah," I say, trying to calm my breathing.

"Christian," he says with a smile that is close to a sneer. "Christian Ford."

"Well, Christian Ford," I say, tugging his arm and throwing a slur in my words. "Let's go back to the party and *dance*."

"Sure, Sarah," he says, putting his arm heavily around me to slow me down. "After you tell me what you were looking for."

I guide us toward the faint light down the hall, wishing I hadn't gotten so far away from the party. Patting my skirt pocket back for my phone, I find it missing and realize what the sound of the clattering was. Shit. "I told you," I say, trying to sound jokey and casual. "I was looking for Tom. I lost him somewhere."

"See, now, I don't believe you."

"Oh no?" I ask, light and flirty. I try to shrug off his arm, but it isn't easily removable.

"I think you were looking for something else." There is menace in his words.

I stop suddenly to throw him off stride, but it doesn't work. "Okay, you got me," I say. "I *was* looking for something else."

He stares at me.

"A skull."

His look turns skeptical. "A skull?"

"The hundred-year skull."

He narrows his eyes, still smiling. "What are you talking about?"

I start walking again. "So here's the thing. I write for the

Crimson, right? So when I was invited to the party, I just had to check it out for myself."

"Okay?" He stays right with me.

"And you know the rumor about the Hawk Club and the hundred-year-old skull." I am talking too fast.

"No, I didn't know that one." Then he grabs my wrist, not lightly.

"What?"

"You missed a room," he says. We are standing in front of a wooden door. I'm not sure if I tried this one or not. "Maybe the skull's in here," he says, leaning in toward me, almost pinning me against the wall. I'm not certain if he's trying to be sexy or aggressive. And sometimes it's a fine line. My options race before me. I could flatten him outright, but I wouldn't gain anything. I don't have the cigar box yet, if there even is one. And I can't exactly shoot him.

"So, you're admitting there's a skull after all?" I ask, figuring it's a good a play as any.

"No," he says and opens the door. "I thought you might be looking for something else." He fixes his cold, blue eyes on me. "Dahlia."

CHAPTER SEVENTY-SEVEN

JAMES

Something went wrong after she was in the closet. She fell or something and the screen shook, then went blank. And she's not answering her phone. I stare at the black screen, my neck sweating. I have a bad feeling. A bad, bad feeling.

Think, James. I smack my forehead. *Don't panic,* I am commanding myself.

Think, think, think.

This can't happen again. I won't let it. God wouldn't do that. Twice in a row would be too coincidental. Lazy coding. Maybe she's fine, she's probably fine. She might be pissed if I call the police and ruin her chances to get the stupid, fucking cigar box. She might be fine, but what if she's not. What if she's not?

I smack my face again, hard. *Fuck.*

Leaving the computer on in case the camera starts working, I jump out of the car into the frigid air. I slam the door shut and the sound echoes into the night. I've parked a bit away from the club and I start running, looking for the right door. My breath is too fast, and panicking won't help, but I can't help it. All I know is I won't forgive myself if something happens to her. If something happens, and I don't save her this time.

Finally, I find the right building and start smacking the door, slamming it as hard as I can. The cold wood stings my palm.

"Hey," a voice cracks out over the intercom.

"My friend's in there," I say to the speaker. "Sarah. I need to talk to her." Then, I remember. "Magna Carta."

"That's not for dudes, man. Get lost."

"I need to talk to my friend," I insist. My brain flicks through the best scenario to get ahold of someone quickly, no questions asked. "Her mom just died."

"Oh." There is a pause. "Jesus. Okay. One sec."

I stand there on the sidewalk, watching the crack turn into a Y shape and considering the angle it makes, and the night is too quiet, and I smack on the door again.

"Chill, dude," the voice bursts out through the speaker. "You got the wrong place. There's no Sarah here."

"She's in there," I yell, my voice squeaking. "You've got to get her."

"Dude. Go away. There's no girl by that name here." The crackling noise of the speaker cuts off, leaving silence again. I stare at the door. I call Dahlia again and hear her chirpy voice—"Hi, sorry I'm not here to get your call"—on the voicemail for the hundredth time.

"Please call me," I plead into the phone. "Please call me back. Please."

CHAPTER SEVENTY-EIGHT

DAHLIA

The word echoes in my ears. *Dahlia.*

How does he know my name?

"Red Sox," I say as loudly as I can, though it sounds like a whimper. "Red Sox."

Christian shoves me into the room, and there are four other men in there. A sound makes my breath catch, and I look up to the noise. A little, yellow cuckoo bird, tipping out of the clock, dipping its beak down. On the mantel, there is a large, rectangular, mahogany cigar box with a shiny brass clasp.

And in the corner, a bare mattress.

"Yo, Christian, what up?"

"Got the girl."

"Who dat?" asks a skinny white kid trying to talk gangster.

"The girl they talked about. Dahlia."

"Oh yeah?" The skinny kid observes me with interest, like I'm a healthy-sized pig at a county fair. "You sure it's her?"

"It's definitely her," he says, insulted. "She's got the tattoos and the hair and everything."

Another young man strides forward, his belly straining his black leather belt, which is cinched on a screwdriver-made hole. "What are we going to do with her?"

Christian shrugs. "What should we do with her?"

Another man, his hair buzzed into a faux-hawk, turns to me. He is light-skinned something, maybe Italian. "Let her go. It's not even the right party."

My eyes glimpse the cigar box again, then back down at the gaggle of men. Christian's grip is tight on my bicep.

"I say we do her," the skinny kid says, and his pants are obviously bulging at the thought.

"Whatever," the one by the corner says, trying to play it cool.

"Just you," I say to Christian, deciding this is my best shot. If the others leave, I can beat the crap out of Christian and make off with the box. Otherwise, I have to use the Beretta, which I didn't want to do. I hold on to his arm. "Just you, okay?"

"You don't make the rules, bitch," the skinny kid says.

A man with a ponytail approaches from the corner. "I'm up for it," the fat kid says, looping a finger around his belt.

Faux-Hawk sighs, as if I were a nuisance. "Fine, let's just do it."

Pretending to itch my leg, I reach down toward my boot, but the backhand catches me clean, out of nowhere.

The room tilts and then goes black.

CHAPTER SEVENTY-NINE

JAMES

I stare at the door, willing it to open. A cold wind waters my eyes.

I could call 911.

But what if she's okay? What if the necklace isn't working and I ruin her chance?

I start pacing up and down the sidewalk when a man comes out of a convenience store a few houses down and starts walking towards me. He is in some kind of black uniform, a plastic bag swinging in his hand. And as he walks by me, I see the large, silver reflective letters on the back of his coat.

CAMPUS POLICE.

I don't believe in God, but God has answered. "Sir," I call out to him. "Can you help me?"

He turns to me. He's African American, overweight but not obese, with chipmunk cheeks. "What is it, son?"

"My...my girlfriend."

He steps toward me. "Your girlfriend what?" His coat has a huge fur hood that smells like a million cigarettes.

"She's in there," I choke out. I can barely breathe. I point at the unassuming black door.

"What about her?"

I swallow. "I'm afraid they might hurt her."

He squints like he doesn't quite believe me. "Who might hurt her?"

"The men in there. In the Hawk Club. We need to get her out."

He looks at the door, then back at me. "How do you know she's getting hurt?"

I decide that this is useless. I can't waste another second of time and start wailing on the door again. "Hey!" I am yelling at it, but my voice echoes uselessly into the night. "Hey!"

"Hold up," the campus police says. "This is private property. You can't go barging—"

"They're going to rape her," I say, quietly but forcefully. "Please. Help me."

CHAPTER EIGHTY

DAHLIA

When my vision clears, I'm on a mattress.

"Bitch," a voice says. The sound is warped. I can hear out of only one ear.

Rough hands against my shoulders, holding me down. I start fighting, reaching for my boot when a half punch catches my chin and lip. I can feel my lip starting to swell, and I struggle to catch my breath. "Red Sox," I moan.

My head feels heavy, woozy. I strain to reach my boot, but someone is sitting on my arm, the elbow joint hyperextended. A knee jams into my crotch, making me gasp. "Red Sox," I am shrieking. "Red Sox, James. Red Sox!"

The skinny kid starts giggling. "Why the fuck does she keep saying that?"

Hands are prying my legs open.

"Who knows," Christian says. "Just grab her other arm."

Someone is licking my thigh. I will myself to be present. I am not drugged. I am not drunk. I don't need to panic. I will remember this. I will remember everything, and I will stop it this time. I slam my leg against the licker's face, which is answered with a solid punch to my hip.

"Jesus Christ, this cunt is on steroids," Christian complains. Sweat runs down his sideburns. "Somebody grab her fucking leg."

A hand tightens around my ankle like a clamp, and my leg is whipped back unnaturally, wrenching my hip socket. I can hear it clicking as I struggle to keep my leg closed.

"Fuck it," Christian says. "She's gonna blow me. That should take some of the fight out of her." He straddles me and scoots up to my face. Pinning my shoulders with his knees, he unzips his fly, releasing a smell of sweat and musk, and yanks my head viciously toward him.

Out of the corner of my eyes, I see the others like an audience. Watching with fascination, like I'm some animal in a zoo. They have lightened their grip on me in the meantime for the show.

"Lick 'em, bitch," Christian says, dangling his testicles in my face. His weight is heavy on my chest, and I pause an instant and bite down hard on him. His screech is shattering. Before the others can react, I shoot my legs up over his shoulders and throw him backward. I hear his head smack against the floor.

This is followed by stunned silence.

"Fuck. Dude." The ponytailed one stares at Christian's body. "I think she killed him." The others are glaring at me, the audience not so friendly anymore as they start to close in on me.

"What the fuck did you do, bitch?" the skinny kid says.

I reach down into my boot and pull the gun out. Slowly standing off the mattress, I move the gun from side to side, and the men scuttle backward. The Beretta trembles in my hand, clicking against my ring. I steal a glance at Christian, whose head is awkwardly cocked to the side but appears to still be breathing. "Okay," I say. "Who's up next?"

No one answers. They all stare at the gun, which apparently wasn't in the script. "No one?" I ask. "Come on, you were all hot and bothered a minute ago. Who's the big stud here? Who's going to rape me first?"

Again, no one answers, but someone bursts through the door behind me. A pop goes off, so loud that it hurts my ears, and only then do I realize that my finger has pulled the trigger.

CHAPTER EIGHTY-ONE

JAMES

The sound snaps through the air. A pop like fireworks, then glass breaking.

Our heads swivel toward the upstairs window.

"Holy lord." The officer leans down into his walkie-talkie. "Backup needed. Shots fired at the Hawk Club. 99 Lowell." He pounds a leather-gloved fist against the door, which looks like a bear paw. "Police! Open the door. I repeat, open the door." We wait four long seconds, and he slams it with his shoulder. "Damn it." He slams it again, and it doesn't budge.

"Here," I say, backing up a few steps and wallop myself against the door, as hard I as have ever hit anything in my entire life, and my shoulder feels like it got dislodged, but the thing opens.

The officer flashes an appreciative look and starts up the stairs. "Stay down there," he calls to me, but I ignore him. The place is wild. People are running around in a panic, and the officer is screaming, "Police! Get down! Everyone get down!"

Some people get down and others run past us. A girl in a black, poofy cocktail dress says, "Upstairs. Someone's shooting up there."

Again, he runs and I follow, and when we open the door, Dahlia is sitting on a bare mattress, cradling something in her arms. One of her eyes is puffy and her lip is bleeding. Her cream-colored sweater is ripped and lopsided. "They're gone," she says, her voice hoarse.

The officer stares at her. "Who?"

She stares back at him, through him, and doesn't answer. I don't see a gun anywhere, so it's probably back in her boot. The officer puts his gun back in the holster without taking his eyes off her. The sirens blare, closer and closer outside.

"What have you got there?" the officer asks, motioning to the square in her arms. Car doors slam outside. Red and pink flash in streaks against the windows.

She doesn't answer, though I already know what it is. She just sits there, her arms wrapped around the box, like she's guarding it with her life.

CHAPTER EIGHTY-TWO

DAHLIA

At the police station, they unlock the cigar box.

Opening it, I am reminded of the scene in *Pulp Fiction*, where some glowing angelic or demonic being emerges from the briefcase. In this case, it is a rainbow of underwear.

Blazing red, pale pink, plain white and black. Lace, satin, cotton. Zebra stripes, cougar spots, hearts. Briefs, thong. The year is written in black sharpie. Including mine. Crumpled, dark purple flowers.

"Lots of underwear in there," I say, dumbly, putting my pair back down in the box with latex-gloved hands.

"Yeah, I'd say they've been in this business for a while," Detective Harrison says with disgust. He's the same man who investigated Alethia's attack and said he took the call when he heard my name on the dispatch.

Underneath the jumble of underwear are tapes. They show the march of technology. A smattering of mini camcorder tapes, then DVDs, and now, of course, you just take out your phone and plaster it on a website. Which is probably why there's no tape with my name on it. I've searched through it twice now. Which also means no way to find the guy with the Red Sox hat, unless there's a longer clip out there somewhere.

"Pretty stupid to film yourself though," he adds.

"I suppose," I say, shifting the bag of ice from my lip onto my eyebrow. "Unless, of course, you know there's a ninety-eight percent chance you won't go to jail anyway."

The detective's expression darkens, but he doesn't debate the point. "It doesn't help when you don't press charges though, does it?"

"Why press charges when no one ever goes to jail?" I return.

We stare at each other in a stalemate. He knows I'm right too. Victims get torn apart on the stand, then nothing ever comes of it. The guy walks. This is not a script I'm willing to follow.

Detective Harrison mulls over his notebook. "So, let me ask you something."

"Go ahead." I take the ice off, because it's stinging.

"Why does a woman who's not even in college anymore go to a college party, tell everyone her name is Sarah, wander around the place talking about skulls, and happen to be carrying a handgun in her boot?"

"How'd you hear about the skulls?" I ask, knowing I told just one person. "I take it Christian is okay?"

He shrugs. "Bit of a headache."

I smile, feeling my bottom lip cracking. "Uh-huh."

"Much like the other guy. Sergei."

"Funny that is," I say as a text comes over my phone from James.

Called Connor. He said he's getting a lawyer for you and don't say anything.

I won't, I text back. Where are you?

Waiting in the car.

"Funny, yes," the detective says. "That's one way to put it. You just always seem to be in the wrong place at the wrong time."

I reposition the ice again. "Guess I attract that kind of thing."

"Or you're looking for it."

I look him in the eye. "Sort of like asking for it, you mean?"

"No, I didn't say that," he says carefully. He plays with a pen on his desk, moving it back and forth like a rolling pin. "It's just the coincidence thing again. I don't like coincidences." He stops rolling the pen and looks at me. "Let me float a theory out there for you."

"Float away."

"Here it is. You were raped at that place when you were in college, and now you're trying to get revenge on the folks in the club. And they don't like it."

I shrug. "It's a theory."

Detective Harrison leans forward, placing his elbows on his knees. "I don't know what happened in the past. I don't know how the police treated you. I'm guessing not well. But listen. I'm not the enemy. I can help you. But we do it my way. Not the vigilante way."

"If you want to help me, give me the cigar box," I say, turning the tables.

He frowns. "Unfortunately, I can't do that. It's evidence. And I suspect you know that."

But it strikes me what he can do for me. There's no use hiding it anymore. The secret's out. I have nothing left to lose. "Okay. I've been getting threatening texts."

His eyes widen. "Oh yeah?"

"Yeah," I say. I take my phone out to show him. "That's my sister," I say.

Reading the threat, he winces. "Have you told anyone about this?"

"I'm telling you."

He nods and smiles, deepening his crow's-feet. "Let me grab some information from your phone on this."

I hesitate just a second, then hand it to him. Fuck it. If he can help Shoshana, let him.

"And your sister's phone number?"

I give it to him, and he disappears into another office. After fifteen long minutes, he's back. "We're putting a trace on the number, and I've already contacted campus police, the Boston station, and your sister's precinct in California."

"Thank you," I say. The feeling is unfamiliar, gratitude to the police. But it's not entirely unwelcome. And I do feel a tiny bit better.

A text sound interrupts us, from James again. How are you?

Good, I answer. Coming soon. A yawn escapes, which stretches my lips. "I'm sorry. I really need to get going. I'm really tired." I stand up, a bit stiffly, and the detective stands up too.

"We'll be in touch," he says.

I nod, gingerly putting on my coat. My face hurts and my shoulder is sore, but all in all, I'm okay. To be honest, I've gotten as much after a tough judo workout. "Oh, can I have my gun back?"

The detective crosses his arms. "You have an LTC?"

I give him a blank look.

"License to carry," he answers, and I don't respond.

"I didn't think so," he says and starts sorting some papers on his desk. "The gun is evidence for now. I'll let you know if and when you can have it back."

As I push the heavy metal door, a cold wind sweeps over me. Across the way, I see a car waiting at the curb, a soft snow falling in its headlights. James lowers the window as I get closer.

"Hey," he says. Snowflakes tilt toward the window. A few cling to his hair.

"Hey," I answer back, then walk around to the other side to climb into the warm, inviting inside. He revs off, and I lean back in the seat, finally relaxed.

"The detective give you a hard time?" he asks, checking his rearview mirror.

"No, not really. You?"

"No, I didn't say much." He slows down at a red light.

"Good idea to call Connor."

"Yeah," he answers, waiting out the light. "I wasn't sure."

"Definitely," I answer, to squash any doubt on the matter. "He's on our side." We keep driving in a comfortable silence, and I can feel my eyes closing. When my phone buzzes with a text, I pop awake. I rub my eyes, but then remember that hurts and drop my hand.

Call me back. You are an idiot.

Eli, of course. He's left five messages by now.

You are an idiot, I write back. Call you tomorrow.

"I assume you told Eli?" I ask.

James shifts in his seat. "Yeah. After we found you. Thought he should know."

"Fair enough," I say, through yet another yawn. Headlights from an oncoming car flash across his face, lighting up his eyes. I notice that they are watery. And his jaw muscle is popping.

"Hey," I say, touching his stiff sleeve. "Are you okay?"

Lightly, he sniffs then clears his throat. "I'm fine."

"You're not fine."

"You should never have done that." He turns to me with a burst of anger. "I should never have let you."

"Let me?" I ask, annoyed. "I don't need your permission to do anything, James. I don't need anyone's permission."

"I know that." His voice is raspy. "I was so scared though. I thought I was going to lose you."

"Like you lost her," I say.

He nods.

"Ramona," I say, and he nods again. "Maybe..." I start. "Maybe it would be a good time to talk about her."

"Okay," he says, sighing with resignation.

The snow dances in the headlights, dots jumping and swaying before dying on the windshield. "Because I don't think there is a Ramona," I say.

He shakes his head. "There was a Ramona." Tears spill from his eyes.

"I looked her up," I say softly, touching his arm again. "I found your brother. I didn't find her."

"You don't understand."

"Then tell me," I whisper.

But he starts crying harder. His hands are gripping the wheel as he sobs silently, his chest shaking.

"Pull over, James," I say.

And he does. Slowly, carefully, like he does everything, he pulls over to the side of the road and turns on the hazard lights. The noise clicks rhythmically as he sits there, hiccupping in the seat and wiping his eyes. The headlights flash through the trees in the copse by the road.

Finally, his breathing steadies, and he turns to me.

"I had a brother," he says, "named Robert."

CHAPTER EIGHTY-THREE

JAMES

He was my big brother," I say, "and he was everything to me."
I sit a minute to let my thoughts settle. The blinking noise
of the hazards soothes me. "He never judged me. Not like other
people, other kids...even my parents. Everyone thought I was
weird." I tap on the steering wheel to the rhythm of the hazards,
then stop. "I *am* weird, but he didn't care."

I sniffle and Dahlia digs through her purse and pulls out a
crinkly, clean tissue. It smells nice, like lilacs. I would never use
anyone else's tissue, even a clean tissue, with all the germs from
sitting around there. But I take Dahlia's without a second thought.

"Over time, I got it though, why he was so nice to me. Not
just because we were brothers, because I've seen a lot of brothers
hate each other, like crazy. But Robert understood me, because he
felt weird too." I wipe my nose again, using up the tissue and she
hands me another one. A deer trots through the forest, turning to
us, eyes turning white in the lights. Then he disappears.

Dahlia pats my arm to continue.

"I should have figured it out, if I were paying attention. The
clues were all there." I smooth the soft, clean tissue against my
fingers. "Like when he got in trouble for dressing up in my mom's
clothes. And how he always wanted to play with girl things."
Balling up the tissue, I put it in the empty coffee cup. "People
called him a faggot, but that wasn't right. Because the summer
before he was going to college, he told me the truth. I remember,
because he was trembling so hard I thought he was sick or dying.
But he told me that wasn't it. He just felt like he was really a

woman. Inside. That he'd always felt that way and wanted to become one." Dahlia nods, her eyes understanding. She doesn't seem weirded out at all.

"He asked me to call him Ramona and keep it a secret from Dad."

She frowns. "That's a big secret to have to keep."

"Yeah. It was." Dahlia was right. So was Jamal. Secrets are like a black hole. They suck you right up. "But she told my mom. I think she kind of already knew anyway." I touch the rim of the paper coffee cup. "It went really fast. She was taking the medication, the hormones or whatever. And she really looked like a girl, if you didn't know her."

"Yeah," Dahlia says. "She looked pretty in the picture."

I think of her picture in my wallet. I never had one of Rob, never needed to. "She was so happy that summer. The happiest I've ever seen her. She went to Italy and met this group of kids who were really cool to her." I think back to her coming home. Tanned and smiling, with lip gloss. "Then, she told my father."

Fog lifts off the street ahead of us, cold pavement, warm air. A car whirs by us, then it is silent again.

"He didn't take it well," she guesses.

I shake my head. "Wouldn't accept it at all. Called her Rob. Told her to take all that shit off her face. She went back to Cornell early."

Dahlia bites her lip. "That's too bad."

"I've always wondered if...maybe he had just..." But I let the thought go. As Jamal told me, the what-ifs aren't helpful. The endless loop again. "Anyway, she went back. And before classes began, she went out to a bar with a friend."

Dahlia looks down at the car floor. I feel nauseated going on, but I do. "She had too much to drink and her friend ended up leaving. And some guys figured out that she wasn't really a girl."

Dahlia takes a breath, and her face looks both angry and sad. "And they didn't like it."

"No," I say. "They didn't. And they beat her up. Bad." I start crying again, tears running down my face, but I don't wipe them this time. It feels kind of good, just to let them go. "She was never the same. She wasn't sure of herself anymore. She stayed in her dorm all the time. She didn't even go to class."

Dahlia swallows, and her eyes fill up too.

"She left me a note though, before she did it. She said she was sorry, and she'd always love me." I take a deep, steadying breath. "And the note said, 'I know you think you're weird, but you're not. You're you. Always be yourself,' it said. 'Don't forget that.'"

Dahlia holds my hand, hers warm and strong. "I'm sorry."

"Yeah," I say, taking another deep breath. "And what's so sad is that she tried to be herself. And it killed her."

CHAPTER EIGHTY-FOUR

DAHLIA

Finally, we get to my street and walk through the velour-soft snow up to my apartment. The place seems empty without Simone, but hopefully I'll get her back soon. I drop my keys on the kitchen table, and James sits on the edge of the couch. I reach into the refrigerator, uncap a half-full glass bottle of Dr Pepper and take a long, wonderful sip. I shut the door to the refrigerator.

"About your parents…" I say as I think of it. "Have you talked to them yet? Made up with them?"

He shakes his head, staring at the floor.

"You should," I say.

"Yeah, I know. I will. Eventually."

He leans against the arm of my couch, then looks up at me. "Do you want me to stay with you tonight? Or…"

In response, I walk over and sit next to him on the arm of the couch, with barely enough room for us both. Leaning against him, I feel the warmth of his chest, the soapy smell of his T-shirt.

"I want you to stay over," I say. "If you want to."

"Stay over…as in…?"

I answer by kissing his neck. His warm skin, the softness of the groove in his neck. His pulse pounding under my lips. I answer by taking off his shirt. And he holds me, gentle but strong against his chest. And we go to my room.

He is shy, undressing the rest of him, against the soft light of the little, white work lamp in the corner of my room. The same lamp I've had since college days. I watch him. I admire him, that long arm span, sturdy shoulders, the symmetry of lines cutting through his abdomen. His boxers stretching across his hip bones.

Sitting on the corner of the bed, the pale-purple comforter balloons under me. I shrug off my clothes. He watches me, his eyes serious. I watch him as he lifts the comforter, softly, carefully, and climbs into bed.

I climb in beside him, and we put our arms around each other, lying and breathing.

We hold each other.

CHAPTER EIGHTY-FIVE

JAMES

When we kiss, I feel like I'm breathing her in. Not air anymore, but her.

Dahlia.

She takes up so much room in my head, but now she's in the room with me, so I don't have to imagine her. I don't have to dream about her. She's here.

There is dried blood on her lip, but her tongue is delicious and tastes like Dr Pepper, and I probably smell damp and sweaty, but she doesn't. She smells like lotion, like sweetness, like Dahlia. Her hair is purple silk in my fingers and soon we are kissing so much we are gasping.

Her fingers loop on my chest, over my tattoo. She kisses it. From top to bottom. Her lips are so light, they feel like magic.

Her skin is warm and smooth, and I kiss the notch in her clavicle. I lean in to kiss her beautiful breasts. Her beautiful body. She lies back in the bed, rubbing the back of my neck.

"As slow as you want," she says.

I nod, but I'm not thinking about that. I'm thinking of the softness of her. The swell of hips over her bones. My hands run over them, and she closes her eyes, murmuring something. Her skin is so pale white and lovely in the bed. I trace one hand down her stomach and she shivers. "Do you want to?" I ask. After everything that happened tonight, I don't want to pressure her. At all.

"Yes. But only if you're ready."

"I'm ready." And I am. We kiss some more and then she's breathing heavily, almost panting and she guides me into her and

I push softly at first and ask if she's okay, if I'm hurting her. She shakes her head no and holds on to my hips and I push in all the way. And we fit together perfectly. Like one body, we are rocking together, slow then faster and I have never felt anything so good in my life. And her hands run up and down my back and it's not too much. I don't panic. I just breathe her in and I can't stop pushing, and she tells me not to stop anyway, and then it happens.

Everything stops. The world freezes and aligns.

Solidifies into perfection.

Her breath slows down, and her fingers are still rubbing my back but slowly now, lazy wide circles. I am wonderfully, perfectly tired. Like after a great swim, but better. Much better. When I open my eyes, I see a little earlobe. Her black-purple hair fanning across the pillow. I want to say I love you. I mean to say I love you. But she half opens her eyes and closes them, then smiles a sleepy smile.

And by the time I am ready to say the words, she is already asleep.

CHAPTER EIGHTY-SIX

HAWK CLUB CHAT ROOM

Desiforever: Did you guys hear?

Bruinsblow: No, what?

Desiforever: She came

Joe25: Who came? What are we talking about?

Desiforever: Dahlia. She went to the after–New Year's party

Taxman: And?

Desiforever: She shot up the place. Girl's crazy. The police came

PorscheD: No fucking way

Desiforever: Supposedly she took the cigar box

Creoletransplant: WHAT???

Bruinsblow: How do you know this?

PorscheD: If this is some kind of joke I'll fucking kill you, dude

Desiforever: It's not. Christian Ford told me. The guy who I was telling you about. Current member. He was in the hospital for a concussion, I guess.

Taxman: A concussion?

Desiforever: Yeah, he said the bitch sucker punched him.

Joe25: Oh shit

Connorsdad: So who's got the cigar box now?

Desiforever: I assume she does

Bruinsblow: Or the police do

PorscheD: Fuck

Bruinsblow: I told you. I told you guys this would happen

Taxman: 'I told you so' isn't very helpful right now, Drew

Desiforever: Not time to blame each other folks. Time to figure out a plan

Bruinsblow: A plan? She gave the cigar box to the fucking police! GAME OVER

PorscheD: Calm down, man

Connorsdad: What does Blake say?

Desiforever: Not sure if he knows. Can't get a hold of him. Off the grid.

Bruinsblow: So what the fuck do we do now?

Desiforever: We chill. Can't even use it in court, I bet.

Taxman: Oh, what, you're a lawyer now?

Joe25: We could call Stevie-O. He might know.

Bruinsblow: You guys do what you want. Chill. Call Stevie-O. Call Blake. Whatever the fuck you want.

Desiforever: Yeah? And what are you going to do?

Bruinsblow: I'm doing what I suggest all of you do. Getting the hell out of town.

CHAPTER EIGHTY-SEVEN

DAHLIA

Eli comes by with bagels later in the morning, after James has left.
"I'm not even hungry," I say.

"Yeah, me neither." In silence, we stare at the brown bag. "You look like shit by the way,"

"What a coincidence, I *feel* like shit too!" Now that the adrenaline has worn off, I am definitively sore. My lip is swollen, my eye cut, and I've got a bear of a headache. But none of this diminishes the sweetness of my night with James.

Not in the least.

"But you got your damn cigar box," he mutters. "So it was worth it."

"It was actually. Those Hawk boys aren't going near me ever again."

Eli glances around. "Where's Simone?"

"Still with Daisy…until…"

He grimaces, then taps his fingers together. "So, did you see all the guys then? Could you identify everyone?"

"No." I rub my forehead, still waiting for the Motrin to kick in. "There were tapes in there, just not mine. But I got the evidence for the other girls at least. I'm going to talk to Connor about it, figure out what we can do for everyone."

He exhales, then shakes his head. "You scared me you know." Then, he frowns. "James too. He was a basket case. And honestly, Dahlia, I hate to admit it. But he actually seems like a decent guy."

I smile, cracking my lip. "He is a decent guy. And I'm sorry about scaring you. But I had to do it. That's all. There was no other way."

He sits up in the kitchen chair. "It's just… I won't be here to protect you forever."

"For the hundredth time," I grumble, digging into the brown bag finally. "I don't need your protection." I pick out a poppy seed bagel, and as I break off a piece, something about what he said nags at me. "What do you mean anyway, you won't be here to protect me forever… You planning on going somewhere?"

Eli scratches the back of his hairline, looking uncomfortable. "I was going to talk to you about it, but obviously now is not such a good time."

"Talk to me about what?" I rip off another piece of bagel, and he still doesn't answer. "Come on, now you've *got* to tell me."

"Okay." He rifles through the brown bag and also comes up with a poppy seed bagel. "I got back together with Brandon."

"That's good, right?" A piece of bagel gets stuck in my throat as I swallow.

"And he asked me to come with him. To Colorado."

"Oh." I take a sip of water to hide my wobbling frown. "That's…that's great. Terrific."

"Anyway," he says after smearing cream cheese on his bagel. "I thought about it for about two seconds…" He gives a wry smile. "I decided I might as well go. I mean, nothing's really keeping me here." He looks up from his plate. "Besides you."

I don't want to, but I start crying. And I'm too damn exhausted to even try to stop it.

"Oh, Dahlia." Eli looks miserable.

"It's okay," I say. "Don't mind me. It was a crazy night."

His gaze darts around the room, then he pops up when he sees the tissue box. Kneeling by my side, he gives me a handful. "I'm sorry."

"Don't…don't be sorry," I say with an embarrassing sniffle. I ruffle his hair, hard, and he lifts his face to me. "Of course you should go, Eli. Of course. I'm just going to miss you, dummy."

His expression scrunches in a funny way for a second, and I

realize he's trying to keep himself from crying too. "I'm gonna miss you too, dummy." He reaches over, pats my head, then stands up. "And now, I've got to start packing."

"You do that," I say. "I'm going to drown my sorrows in a bagel."

"Ha." Then he reaches into his coat pocket. "I almost forgot. I grabbed the mail for you."

After he leaves, I look through the mail at the kitchen table. It's at least something to take my mind off things for the moment. Eli is leaving. And of course he should. The end of a chapter for us. And hopefully a new, better one for Eli. I knew it would happen eventually, I just didn't think eventually would come so soon.

Taking a deep breath, I sort through the mail. Bills, more bills, an office supply catalog that should have gone to work, a glossy shoe postcard, some coupons. And then I see it. I hold it between my thumb and index finger tightly, like it might fly away.

An envelope. From Stanford.

CHAPTER EIGHTY-EIGHT

JAMES

My arms are slow, like I'm swimming through molasses. (That idiom I do like, because it completely makes sense.)

I hate these days, when my strokes go like this. Sometimes, I can't figure out why. It's just some kink in the machine. The mitochondria not working right. But today, the reason is obvious. Last night was exhausting. Wonderful, but exhausting. I've never had a day that was so low, and then so high.

My feet push off against the wall and the water shoots past me. My breath is stacked up in my chest, and I start working my arms again and letting my thoughts flow wherever they want.

Men are evil. That's the sum of it. Maybe because we have all the power or it's a testosterone thing, but it's hard to argue about who starts all the wars, who shoots up schools, who beats up women and rapes them. Men. Not all men maybe. Not me for instance, but enough men. Men who would corner a girl in a room on a mattress. Year after year after year. And videotape it.

I threw up after I saw the cigar box. Detective Harrison leafed through the underwear with confusion on his face, disgusted like he might throw up too, with sweat beading on his forehead. I felt my stomach lurch like someone punched me straight in the gut, and I got to the bathroom just in time. When I came out of the stall, some other police guy was in there but didn't say anything. Maybe it's not so odd in this line of work. Evil does that to you, makes you want to vomit sometimes.

Grabbing the rough concrete wall, I steal another deep breath, then jet off again. My arms are cutting through the water better now. Not so slow and leaden. More like my usual rhythm. I love her. I know that now, with absolute certainty. Not a hypothesis… a theorem. But I'm not sure if she loves me too. She should probably be with someone easier, like Connor. Someone normal who could say funny things and make her laugh all the time. Like Eli, but not gay.

But she's not with them. She's with me.

This thought lifts me for another twenty laps. And then my number is done, and I get out, shower off, and get dressed. As I zip up my coat, my hand finds my phone. There's a missed call from my mom. I sit down on the metal bench, staring at it, deciding. I think back to what Dahlia said. I should talk to them, I know. And I will, just not right now. Later.

I put the phone back in my pocket.

CHAPTER EIGHTY-NINE

DAHLIA

I take a couple of sick days to heal, then I'm back at work, sorting through a hundred unread emails. Sylvia's out today, which is just as well. I'm not sure if I could withstand her wedding soliloquy anymore. And anyway, I'm just going through the motions today.

It's odd. I feel like I'm stuck in a sort of liminal state.

We're done with the project, and yet nothing's done. Blake Roberts is stuck in step two. I got the cigar box, but it's in police custody and my video wasn't in there to see the guy filming anyway. And those assholes are still out there threatening my family. Though I haven't gotten any more texts, I also haven't heard back from Detective Harrison.

But I have an appointment with Connor at 2:00 p.m., which should go a long way toward ending this thing, once and for all. I turn back to my interminable emails when I hear someone whistling, and then Snyder is at my desk. For the life of me, I'll never figure out how he appears like that.

"Hi, gorgeous." He's got a rolled-up newspaper under his armpit.

"Hi, Snyder."

"Got something for you." He sweeps the newspaper from under his arm and unfurls it. "Turns out my friend at the FBI caught a big one."

"Oh yeah?" I take a peek at the paper.

"Yeah, Omar got a hot anonymous tip. Found some banker funneling money into terrorist cells."

"Is that so?" Laying the newspaper out, I see another picture of the wunderkind Blake Roberts. But he doesn't look quite so self-satisfied in this one, and there's no adoring wife looking on. "What's happening to him?" I ask, scanning the article as fast as my eyes can manage.

"U.S. District Court," he says. "In Boston."

"Hmm," I say. "Sounds serious."

He raises an eyebrow. "If he's a terrorist? Yeah, I'd say that's serious. He won't be getting out of prison anytime soon. If ever."

I almost feel bad. Almost. Then I think of the other women that he gang-raped in his time at Harvard. And I don't feel so bad anymore. He should be enjoying step three for quite a while.

"Funny," Snyder says, "how I gave you Omar's name, and not a month later he makes a big bust."

"Funny indeed," I say, and go to hand him the paper.

"Keep it," he says. "In case you want to frame it."

I smooth the paper out, over his expression that looks more angry than afraid. But that will change I expect. And then I fold the paper up. Because I don't need to see his face anymore.

The finality of this act gives me a certain satisfaction. All of the rapists on the video are in jail, except of course for the one filming. Rapists #1 through #3 are finished off at least.

Now, only five more hours until my appointment with Connor. Then, it will be really over.

———

The sky is gray, with curdled clouds.

I am waiting in the little corner chair in Connor's office, when he finally comes in.

He's wearing a powder-blue shirt and a navy pin-stripe that suits his coloring. He pulls the door not all the way shut. "Claire said you wanted to talk to me about something?"

"Yes."

He chuckles. "You didn't have to make a formal appointment, you know. You could have just grabbed me. I even know where you sit."

"Yeah, I know." I chuckle too. I feel weirdly nervous, considering this is the same man I've seen most days for the last five years.

But he looks nervous too. "Is it about the party thing? I talked to them. They're not pressing any charges about the gun or anything—"

"No," I interrupt him. "It's not about that. Well, not directly..." Right then, someone sticks their head in the door, notes our meeting, then backs out again. One of the new lawyers, whom I don't recognize. "It's about the evidence they found there."

Revulsion streaks across his face. "The cigar box."

"Yes."

He nods slowly, his eyes on the desk. "What about it?"

"Can we use it?" I ask.

He looks up at me. "What do you mean?"

"Against them?"

His eyes narrow in thought. "Yeah, we should be able to. Why wouldn't we?"

"Even if the police have it?"

He wipes a chalk mark off his suit sleeve. "Yes, especially since the police have it. That's actually a very good thing. It means it's not tainted."

"You think it's admissible?" I ask. "Even if I was in there under false pretenses with a gun?"

He shrugs. "The police were investigating the commission of a crime in the act and found the evidence. That's the much better argument."

I nod at this, heartened. "So, can we do it then?"

"Of course we can do it. We can prosecute them... Well, I can call the DA," he amends. "I can't be the lead man, but I can help out—"

"A civil suit," I say. "That's what I want. I want to sue them."

"Them." He pauses. "The Hawk Club?"

"Yes," I say. "The other women can decide if they want to prosecute their attackers. I'll leave that up to them as soon as we reach them all. But I don't want that myself. I want to sue. Sue the whole club."

"Okay." He relaxes in his chair, as we're back in his comfort zone. "Civil suit. That'd be an easy one." Now he grins. "With those tapes, we could even file a mass action."

"Yes," I agree. "If that's what the other women want."

He starts jotting down something on his canary-yellow legal pad with a studious expression.

I lean over the rounded corner of the desk. "How much money are we talking here?" I ask. "Do you have any idea?"

He looks up from the pad. "I hate talking numbers when I don't have the basics of the case put together yet, but—"

"I'm not looking to get rich," I explain. "I mean, not that I mind profiting off their suffering. I don't. But I just want it to hurt. Bad. Put-them-out-of-business bad."

He pauses, stares at me a second, then gives me a smile that is almost rueful. "We can do that, Dahlia. That's my job. And I'm good at it." He looks at the window then. "Sometimes I feel bad about that fact. When you're bankrupting some poor bastard who doesn't even see it coming. But not today," he says. "Not that place. I'll take every single goddamn cent they have, and then some."

I pat the desk. "Good," I say. "Just let me know what you need from me." I stand up to leave.

"Oh," he says. "Before you go. Dennis called me. You're all set. All the paperwork has been filed."

"So?"

"So, you are you again," he says with a grin.

"I am me," I echo, with relief.

"Yes," he says. "And you are a goddamned force to be reck-oned with."

CHAPTER NINETY

DAHLIA

I get the call on the way up to Eli's apartment.

"Hello?"

"Hello, Detective Harrison here," he says.

"Yes?" I stop by the wall in the stairwell, nervous. "I know how these things go. Attempted rape and I'll be the one busted for having a gun."

"I wanted to get back to you. About the texts you were getting."

"Oh." With relief, I start walking the stairs again. "Yes?"

"I don't think that'll be a problem anymore."

I can hear the smile in his voice and find myself smiling too. "Oh no? Why's that?"

"We tracked down the phone. I figured the guy would be smart enough to use a burner, but he didn't. So, the phone was registered to BR Funds. And the only person we could track down with a connection to the Hawk Club was BR himself." He pauses theatrically. "Mr. Blake Roberts."

"I've heard of him," I say, playing it coy.

"Yeah, no doubt," he says with obvious pride at his catch. "He's some millionaire big shot in New York. But get this," he continues, "it turns out he was just busted, for terrorism of all things."

"Really?" I say. "That's shocking."

"Yeah, so anyway. The phone has been taken into custody. But...no offense, that's small potatoes to them. They're going after him for some pretty heavy stuff here."

"So it seems," I say, and start walking up the stairs again.

"Anyway, just wanted to tell you. Let your sister know too. All is good."

"Thanks," I say with a new bounce in my step. Because after I help out Eli with his packing, I'm going to pick up my gorgeous and wonderful Simone.

———

Standing in the doorway, I gaze around Eli's destroyed apartment. It looks like somebody robbed the place.

"Hmm," I say.

"Yeah," he agrees. "Hmm."

"Where does one even start?" I ask.

"One doesn't even know." He points to some stacked boxes in the tiny foyer. "I've got the kitchen practically done." He grabs a garbage bag from a roll. "I'll start tossing away junk. You pack up some books?"

"Deal."

I get to work on the bookcase, and Eli starts filling the crinkling bag. Most of the books are oversize paperback textbooks from college. "*Mao Tse-Tung and the Gang of Four*," I read out loud. "Do you even look at this stuff anymore?"

He examines a tchotchke and tosses it. "A house should have books."

"Yeah, but books you actually might read," I say, stacking the box. "Doesn't Brandon have books?"

"Not really. Just boring tech stuff." Eli drags his bag to the corner. "Speaking of books, did you tell James about Stanford yet?"

"Not yet."

He stops filling the bag and looks at me.

"I will. I will," I say, fitting in one more book, then folding the box top shut. "I'm excited though. I could use a change of scene." I close up the next box, and we work in silence for a while. The bookcase is empty except for stripes of dust, and the family room is finally taking on a similitude of order. I walk over to the little front closet and open it. "Pack up the coats?"

He glances over. "Sounds good."

Dragging a longer, rectangular box over, I begin unhanging coats. "So, I told you about Blake Roberts, right?"

"Ten times." He tosses a navy sweater onto a pile on the floor.

"Can you believe that he used a fucking phone from his office?"

Eli tosses some old papers into a recycling bin. "He's probably cheap."

"Yeah, probably." Pushing the hangers to the side with a high-pitched squeak, I spy a set of plastic drawers in the back of the closet. "Dump all this stuff in too?"

"That's fine," he says, not looking.

The first of the three plastic drawers has a bunch of old ski stuff, bulky, rolled-up socks, and threadbare long johns. I toss those into the box and move on to drawer number two, filled with a jumble of old electronics and cords. I remove the whole drawer and slide it down the floor, figuring he'll toss the whole thing. Bending over, I yank on the last drawer, which sticks on something. Finally, with one strong pull, I open it and see an old BU sweatshirt, a couple BU mugs, and a ball cap, which is still stuck between the two drawers. It takes a couple tries, but I finally pull it free.

Then, I hold it in my hand, staring at it blindly, without comprehension.

I expected a BU hat, but it's not a BU hat. Staggering backward, I feel the room spin. A tidal wave sweeping in. The vortex swirling.

It's not a BU hat. It's a Red Sox baseball cap.

With a Javier Ramirez signature on the bill.

———

"You okay?" Eli is at my side.

"Yeah," I say, though my mouth has turned to shoe leather. I point to the hat. "Where'd you get that?"

"This thing?" He leans down and turns it in his hands, like he's trying to remember. "I think I won it off some kid on a bet." There is a flicker of a twitch in his lips.

My legs feel loose, and I slip onto the arm of his sofa chair. "What kind of bet?"

He shrugs. "I don't know. I was probably blotto at the time. I just remember that if he won... I don't even remember the kid's name, Colin something. Anyway, if he won, I had to give him my Yankee cap, and if I won, he had to give me his Red Sox one." He looks at the bill. "It's probably worth something. It's signed and everything."

"Yeah." I sit on my hands, because they are shaking.

"Why, do you want it?"

I shake my head because I cannot speak.

I don't believe him.

I don't know why. But I don't believe him. Maybe it was the twitch of his lips. Maybe it was all the details in the story. I can't say why exactly, except that I know Eli better than I know myself. And I think he's lying.

"You can see how much I cared about it. It ended up in the bottom of my closet."

My head feels like it's floating. "I have to go."

He looks surprised. "Oh, okay." Walking closer, he puts a hand on my shoulder. "You sure you're all right?"

"Just." I lick my lips. "I have some things to get done."

"Sure, sure. Thanks for helping anyway. I'll call you later, okay?"

"Yeah, sure." My voice sounds odd, not like my voice. A dead voice, a stranger's voice. I feel as if I float out of the room, and I grip the metal railing in the stairway to pull myself back down.

It couldn't be him. It's impossible.

My mind churns through the possibilities. There are five hundred signed hats. Only a 0.02 percent chance it would be him. And he didn't even go to Harvard. It couldn't be him. It couldn't be. And yet, I can't shake the feeling that he was lying.

I barely make it to my couch, and then lie there a while, gathering my strength. I feel like I've been oddly stricken. I grab my phone, and feel like I barely have the strength to lift up my arms. "It can't be," I say out loud to no one.

Then I call James.

He listens to the whole story, then pauses. "You're right. It's unlikely," he says. "But not impossible."

We sit in ponderous silence on the phone.

"Are you sure he even went to BU?" James asks.

"I don't know, but I think so. He's got BU stuff everywhere. And a yearbook."

"Could he have transferred there from Harvard?"

"I…I guess it's possible. He wasn't in our face book though."

"But he would have been two years younger."

I lie there, immobilized. I can hardly even think.

"I could try to find out," James says. "Maybe get into their records."

I pause over this one. I could probably go to the Registrar, but they probably wouldn't give me the information. "Daisy," I say, thinking of it then. "She's on the reunion committee. She might be able to find out for us."

CHAPTER NINETY-ONE

DAHLIA

The night is endless, but somehow I get through it.

James offered to come over, but I was too unsettled and agitated for company, even his calming company. Even my Beretta was gone. But at least I had Simone back, delivered safely from Daisy's excellent care. I finally fell asleep to her soft breathing, her fur against my head, but my sleep was light and disjointed, riddled with images of Eli wearing the Red Sox hat, laughing and laughing.

At work, I can barely sit in my seat.

"You okay?" Sylvia asks.

"Fine, why?" I busy myself by organizing a binder.

"You seem off or something."

I force a laugh. "Too much coffee." My phone rings, and I jump, then grab it. "Yeah?"

"He didn't go to Harvard," Daisy says. "No record at all. He didn't transfer in either and wasn't enrolled in any final clubs. Nowhere in the registrar."

"Okay," I say, nodding. "Okay."

"You don't sound completely convinced," she observes.

"I don't know what I am," I admit. "Probably just in shock."

She lowers her voice. "You know I don't love the guy, Dahlia. I never made that a secret. But I never said he was a rapist."

"I know you're right. I'm obviously going crazy with all this."

"All right, dear," she says in her high-pitched voice, which means she's kindly dismissing me. "Hang in there. I got to get going."

I throw myself into work, but I'm still edgy. Maybe because I came close to accusing my best friend of the worst thing possible. Maybe because I still have a feeling that something isn't right. I don't know, but my mind was still only half engaged in work, if that. Finally, I text James.

Break room?

Sure

When I get there, he's standing by the window staring at the falling snow. His body throws a gray shadow on the wall. He joins me at a table, and when I tell him Daisy's info, he seems relieved.

"That's good news, right?" he asks.

"Right." But there's a niggling part of me that won't settle. What did Detective Harrison say about coincidences? "I don't know. My gut's telling me something isn't right."

He nods, folding his fingers on the table.

"What's your gut saying?" I ask.

James shrugs. "I don't have a good gut. My brain always overrides it."

"Huh." So we sit in silence a few minutes as people file in and out, pouring coffee and talking about the weather. *A storm coming. Maybe a nor'easter.*

"He didn't seem weird about the hat at all?" he asks when the room empties again.

"No." My hand tattoos a rhythm on the table. "Not at all. Just more concerned at how I was acting."

As James concentrates, he rocks back and forth just the slightest bit in his chair. "Would he have told anyone? His parents?"

"I doubt it," I say. "They're not really close."

"A friend then?" he asks. "A boyfriend, maybe?"

The name hits me as soon as he says this. "Kevin."

James slows his rocking. "Who's Kevin?"

"This guy he used to date," I say, my mind reeling with the memory. "I wonder if that was it," I muse aloud. "If that's why Kevin broke up with him."

James gives me a quizzical look. "There are lots of reasons to break up with somebody."

"Yeah, but this was different," I say. "One day they were totally in love, and the next, Kevin dumped him. He left me this voicemail about how awful Eli was. Which was really bizarre... I mean, I hardly knew the guy."

Maybe it wasn't the cocaine talking after all. Maybe he just wanted to tell me the truth.

I think back to the Mexican restaurant, when Kevin could hardly bear to look at us. "Eli said he revealed his true self, and Kevin dumped him." I replay the words in my head. "I just figured Eli was being dramatic. But maybe that's what he revealed."

Outside, the snow is falling harder, thick flakes dotting the window.

"Could you call this Kevin guy?" James asks.

"Maybe. But I don't even know his last name. I always called him 'the asshole with blow.' Rutgers? Rogers? Rizzo? Something like that. With an *R*." I tap my fingers, thinking. "And I can't exactly ask Eli because he'll definitely know what's up."

James turns from the window. "Didn't you say he left a message for you before though?"

"Yeah, but that was years ago. Those messages would be long gone."

He scrunches his eyebrows. "Perhaps. Different IOS. But it's still worth a try." He lays out his palm. "Want me to give it a go?"

———

Back at my desk, I am trying to get some work done to take my mind off Eli.

"Gonna be a bad one tonight." Sylvia frets, glancing at the window down the hall.

"Yeah." I am trying to focus on a scaffolding case for Tabitha but end up highlighting all the wrong stuff. My brain can hardly process words right now.

"Beau's lucky. He's in North Carolina. No snow there." She

pauses, then rapid typing starts up again. "He wants to move there eventually, but I don't know... I'm not sure if I could do that."

"Uh-huh." I highlight a few more lines, then automatically reach for my phone to look at the time, when I realize James has it, and I don't wear a watch. "What time is it?"

Sylvia gives me an odd look and checks her phone. "Three forty-four."

"Okay, thanks." It's been two hours. He probably won't be able to get the number. I could call that Mexican restaurant, but Kevin never even sat down, so they wouldn't have the receipt. He might still be in Eli's contacts, but that means getting a hold of his phone, which is practically surgically attached to him.

I put Tabitha's document down just as Connor is walking by.

"Hey, guys. It's going to get pretty bad out there if you want to leave early."

Sylvia leans forward to observe the window. The sky is a mottled gray. "That might not be such a bad idea," she says as he walks away. "It really is getting bad."

For show, I look outside too. "Yeah, it is." Sitting back in my chair, I do a quick check of my email for an update. A couple new things from work, nothing from James. With an inward groan, I force myself to read a few more unbearable paragraphs of Tabitha's case.

Sylvia leans over to look outside yet again. "You know, I think I will head home early. Before it gets really bad." She stands up and starts gathering her things.

"I will soon," I say, and then see the welcome form of James walking through the doorway. I can't read his expression right away, but he gives me a thumbs-up, and I feel a sense of relief followed by immediate panic. Now I'm going to have to call him. Now I'm going to have to find out, one way or the other.

"I fixed your phone," James says for Sylvia's benefit.

But she's trussed up in her winter gear and barely notices. "See you, guys." Sylvia gives a gloved wave and marches off. Once she leaves, James sits in her chair.

"I saved him in your contacts under Kevin Blow."

Chuckling at this gallows humor, I open up my phone and get to his number. "Should I do it?"

"Might as well," he says, then half stands. "Do you want me to leave or—"

"No," I say. "Stay, please."

Nodding, he settles back into the chair. I touch the contact number then wait. As it keeps ringing, I feel my heart tapping against my sternum. James leans forward, his chin held up by his fists.

"Hi, this is Kevin Riley. I'm not here right now. But if you leave your number…"

I inhale, realizing I'd stopped breathing. "Hi, you might not remember me, but I'm Dahlia. Eli's friend. You had left me a message a while ago. Well, a few years ago, but…if you wanted to talk about that…I want to listen. Um. I don't even know what I'm saying here. Anyway, call me, if you can." I leave my number, while James watches me intently.

Then I put the phone down, the glaze of my sweaty handprint still on the case.

CHAPTER NINETY-TWO

DAHLIA

The evening is dreadful.

After some convincing, James agreed to go straight home from work, while I went back to my little apartment. Eli called a few times, leaving messages with a hint of uneasiness, a slight quiver to his tone. Unless, of course, I'm imagining that. He called about the logistics of the move, when Brandon is coming by, doing breakfast this week…things he could have easily texted me, or even run down two flights of stairs to say.

When my text rings, I jump up from the couch and Simone stares at me.

Did he call yet? It's James.

Not yet. I will definitely tell you when he does.

Hopefully, he'll take the hint. It's the third time he's texted me. I turn on the television, but after a few minutes decide there's nothing worth watching, and the commercials are blaring and annoying. As I click it off, there is silence, followed by the sound of wind beating against the pane. Warily, Simone watches me.

With a sigh, I reach down on the coffee table for my issue of *The Economist* and flip through an article, glossing over the words. Why our trade policies are failing in China. Blah, blah, blah. I drop the magazine and lean back in the couch.

A weird part of me wants to call Eli and simply ask him. *Were you there? Did you rape me?* Just to hear him say *of course not*, angry for even asking him, then I can go on with my life. I can be okay knowing three out of four of the rapists. I can be fine with that if I knew, at least, it wasn't him.

The phone wails out from the coffee table, and I lean over to see *Kevin Blow* on the screen. My hand trembles when I pick it up. "Hello?"

"Hi. Is this…Dahlia?" His voice is low and sounds nervous.

"This is she."

"It's Kevin Riley." There is a pause then. "You called me? About Eli?"

"Yes." I take a second, figuring out how to ask the question. "Did—"

"He—"

We both speak at the same time, then laugh nervously. "Okay," he says. "You first."

I swallow. "I know you don't know me very well, at all even. But when you broke up with Eli… I don't know if you even remember this. Or if you were just upset or on drugs or something…" I can hear myself rambling. "But you said that Eli was evil. I think that's the word you used."

"Yes," he confirms. "Evil. That's what I said."

"Right, so you said he was evil, and I should call you if I wanted to find out why."

There is a long pause.

"So, I guess that's what I'm doing. Calling…to find out why."

I hear him take in a breath. "Dahlia." The word is pained.

"Just…tell me. You can tell me. It's all right."

"This is so hard." He sighs, and then waits so long that I'm not sure if he will speak again, but he does. "It was years ago now. Do you even…"

"Could you just tell me what it was?" I know I sound desperate. I don't care. My hand is squeezing the phone. "Just tell me, please."

"You deserve to know, if you want to. It's just—"

"Did he?" I ask. Tears are falling down my face. "Did he… Was he there that night? Did he…"

"He was there, Dahlia," he says, almost breathing out the words. "He told me he was there at the party."

"Okay." The word is choked, barely intelligible. "Okay."

"He said he didn't want to do it. But someone made him. Though I don't understand how someone can make you do that."

I nod. I don't try to speak. I am swallowing tears.

"And I don't want to excuse him for what he did, at all. But to be honest with you, I think he's been pretty much tortured by it." His voice is soft, as if trying to soothe me. "It might even be a relief to him that you know."

I try to sniff softly, so he can't hear me crying.

"We couldn't get past it. Well, obviously, I couldn't anyway. But it was like he couldn't either. He was just kind of stuck."

"Right," I say, my voice cracking. "I could see that."

We don't speak for a while. Finally, he says, "I'm sorry, Dahlia. I have to go, but…are you safe? Will you be okay?"

"Yeah," I lie. "I'll be okay." But I feel like I will never, ever be okay.

"Do…do…" he says, struggling. "Do you want me to call you back later?"

"No, that's okay." I inhale deeply to calm my breathing. I appreciate his honesty, but I don't need his pity. "Thank you, Kevin, for telling me."

We hang up, and I put the phone down on the table. I stand up because I have to move. As if this would change something, erase the ugly truth in my head. The truth that I knew as soon as I saw the ball cap in his drawer. I am pacing, trying to outrun this new reality, but I can't do that. It chases me down.

The vortex, the tidal wave, sucking me in.

"No," I say out loud. The room is tottering under my feet.

"Go back from whence you came. Go home." I hold on to the table by the wall. Simone appears next to me, her tail straight up. "Go back from whence you came," I repeat, stronger now. "Go home."

I hear her mewing as the roar of the vortex dies down, recedes. Carefully, I sit back down on the couch, and Simone leaps right next to me. The phone beeps, faceup on the coffee table.

Sorry to bother you. Just want to make sure everything is all right.

It's James again, and I text him back.

It was him.

CHAPTER NINETY-THREE

DAHLIA

Moments later, I climb the interminable two flights of stairs and open the door to his apartment. Eli is sitting on the sofa in the bare room, drinking a beer. He looks me up and down. "What's up?"

Plodding over, I sit down on the lone wooden table left in the room. I can hardly even look at him.

"What's up?" he asks again, a jitter in his voice.

"I know, Eli. I know everything."

He doesn't answer for a minute. "You...you know what?"

"Don't," I say. "Just don't. I talked to Kevin."

When I finally look at him, his face has gone deathly white. His gaze skitters about the room. "Did he... What did..."

"I know, Eli." I take a deep breath. "I know."

He looks down at his hands, his expression shattered. The silence is overwhelming. Finally, a small, tired voice breaks it. "I suppose I'm sorry doesn't mean much right now."

I shake my head. "Why didn't you tell me?"

He doesn't answer, just stares straight ahead, licking his lips.

"Has this been some kind of sick game for you all along?" I ask.

"No." He clasps his hands together. "I've been wanting to tell you. For years." The heat register clicks on beside him, then starts humming. He leans forward in the couch. "I didn't want to do it, you know... I *didn't* even do it."

"What do you mean?" I ask.

"He told me I had to. But I couldn't. I just pretended to..."

"To rape me?"

"Yes." He starts wringing his hands. "I told him I was gay. He was the first person I came out to." The heater clicks off again to utter silence. "He said I wasn't. That he knew I wasn't. And he was going to show me. Take me to a party for some 'good old-fashioned fun.'"

I shift on the hard table, my stomach clenching.

"And if I didn't go along with it, he'd tell everyone I was a faggot."

"Who?" I ask. "Who did all this?"

"Hank Holstein. My best friend from high school. I was up there visiting him."

"And you couldn't say no? You couldn't say…" Then it wallops me. "Wait, is that Henry Holstein? The one on the tape?"

He nods, looking ill.

"And you just pretended you didn't even know him?"

"I couldn't… I didn't know how…" Eli slinks down farther in the couch and for a moment, we don't speak. "How did you find out?" he asks finally. He chews on his lip, his teeth stretching the skin. "I mean, what made you ask Kevin?"

"The Red Sox cap," I say. "The fourth guy was wearing it in the video." Then I remember—not the fourth guy. Not Rapist #4, the guy in the ball cap, the one filming. Just Eli Sawyer, my best friend. "You," I say. "You were wearing it."

"It was Hank's," he says, his voice strangled. "It wasn't even mine." A single tear drips down his face.

I shake my head. "Why on earth did you keep it?"

Quickly, he wipes his eyes. "I don't know… I tried to throw it out. More than once. But I couldn't do it." He shrugs, helplessly. "I guess I wanted to keep it as evidence of what I'd done. So I wouldn't forgive myself. And maybe in some sick way, I was hoping you would find it." He looks up at me with those haunted, ponderous eyes. "So I wouldn't have to tell you."

"But why, Eli? Why couldn't you just say something?"

"How could I?" he asks, his voice a plea.

"Easy. You say, Dahlia, I have something to tell you. You're going to hate me, but I have to tell you anyway."

"Oh my God," he moans. "I've been wanting to, for years. Every single fucking day. Don't you think I've been wanting to do that? Dying to do that?"

I smooth my fingers against the grain of the wood. "When did you figure it out? At McLean?"

He nods. "Talk about a fucking awful coincidence." His jaw clenches. "And I couldn't say anything then. I wasn't in the state to. You weren't in the state to." Sitting there in his empty apartment, snow clogging the air outside, I feel like I'm in an alternate universe. This isn't Eli. This is an imposter. A stranger. This couldn't be Eli.

"When the video came out…it was awful, of course. But I thought maybe it was a good thing. You could get over it finally. Move on." He is wringing his hands again. "You were always so tortured over not remembering it. I was afraid you'd find out about me, of course. But I also hoped it might help. Give you the time back so you could go on with your life." He stares glumly at the floor. "I didn't know you'd go all *Kill Bill* on everyone."

"We didn't…" I shake my head in anger. "We didn't hurt anyone. Not a single hair."

"You know what I mean. Those guys are screwed." Then he seems to remember which side he is supposed to be on. "Which is fair, I mean. Totally fair."

"Eli," I say, exhausted. "You are one of those guys."

He blinks. "Not really. I didn't mean to be. I didn't want to be."

Tears prick my eyes, but I won't let myself cry. I won't let him see that. No more crying to Eli. He is not my shoulder anymore. The truth of this guts me. We are no longer friends. I straighten myself off the table. "I'll tell you what you're going to do."

"Okay?" He sounds eager to follow any command, any action to start earning his forgiveness.

"You're going to turn yourself in."

He pauses as if he didn't hear the words right, then his expression turns shocked. "What do you mean?"

"You can go to Detective Harrison if you want. Or whoever

the fuck you like. But you're going to the police, and you're going to turn yourself in."

"Don't," he says. "Don't do this, Dahlia. I beg of you. I'm moving in with Brandon. I'm going to be out of your life. You can hate me. You should hate me. But it's time for both of us to move on."

"You can turn yourself in," I say, "or wait for something worse to happen."

He stares at me, then lets out a laugh of disbelief. "Is that a threat?"

"It is what it is."

Eli glares at me. "You and your freak of a boyfriend? You're going to come up with some fucking revenge for me?"

For the first time ever, I feel a stab of hatred for this man.

"I'm sorry," he says, frowning. "I shouldn't have said that." He searches my face for softening perhaps, or some forgiveness, but finds none. "No, you're right. I know you're right. That's what I have to do. That's what I should have done five years ago. If I were brave enough."

I nod, and then move away from the table, feeling like I've aged a thousand years.

"Can I wait until tomorrow though?" he asks in a small voice, like a little boy. "I just want to talk to Brandon first."

"You know what, Eli?" I start walking toward the door because I need to get out of there. I need him out of my sight, now. "I don't give a fuck what you do."

———

We are lying together in the dark.

Just being with him helps. Simple, healing. I appreciate his as-is nature more than ever tonight. WYSIWYG. James is James, kind, smart, loving. No false advertising, no games.

I realize then that it's time to tell him, and let the chips fall where they may. No more secrets. No more black holes. "I have to tell you something," I say.

He turns to me, his face half shadowed by the pillow. "Okay?"

"I got into the Stanford program."

A long pause follows this. His face is hard to read in the dark. "Uh-huh," he says finally. "Are… Do you think you'll come back then? After?"

I move an inch closer to him, feeling the warmth radiate off him. "I don't know," I say honestly. "Connor said he'd save my job. But I don't know. I think it might be time for me to move on."

He nods, the motion scratching the pillow. "It's a good school." His voice is husky.

"Shoshana's there. And…she might give me a loan. I might let her."

"Yeah." He is staring at the wall, not at me.

"But I was thinking…" I reach out to touch his hand. "Maybe you could come too."

He turns his whole body to me. "To Stanford?"

"Yeah, why not?" I scoot even closer, our knees touching. "I'm sure you could find something out there in IT. It's California, after all."

"Right, but…" He lets this trail off. He turns his body again, staring at the ceiling. I can't see his expression at all. "It wouldn't work."

"It could work," I argue. "Why not? I mean, I know you don't love Miller and Stein, that you're too smart for what you're doing. Why not come?" I put my hand on his chest. "What do you have to lose?"

When he turns to me, there is hurt in his eyes. "Everything."

His voice vibrates on my hand through his chest. "I know it would be an adjustment but—"

"No," he says. "You don't. You have no idea."

"You're in tech, James. There's a ton of jobs out there for people like you."

He pauses and takes my hand off. "What does that mean, people like me?"

I shake my head. "Not what you think it means."

At once, he sits up. The sheet yanks away from me. He is rumbling around, bouncing the bed, throwing on his jeans, his shirt.

"James," I say. "Come on. Don't leave like this. Let's talk about it."

"There's nothing to talk about."

I sit up on my elbow. "I don't mean to pressure you to move. You can visit at least. It's only a plane ride away." I am speaking to his back, his beautiful broad back. "It's only the summer anyway. Who knows what will happen after that."

He turns and looks at me in the darkness. "I have to go."

CHAPTER NINETY-FOUR

JAMES

For people like you.
   The words bounce in my head painfully like rocks. Like sticks and stones from that saying. I can't believe she would say that. I can't believe she would do this to me.
   Leave.
   I run down the street to my car, the snow above my ankles, soaking my shoes. Yanking open the door, I slide into the frigid leather seat.
   I can't go there. Of course, I can't. I don't know anyone there. I don't have my place, my routines. My parents would be too far away. Though, the thought sickens me. My parents. I haven't even talked to my parents. My fucking father. Who always loved Rob more than me.
   People like you.
   Losers like you, with Asperger's. She feels sorry for me is all. She feels fucking sorry for me. The heater shoots cold air straight at me, and I drive too fast through a yellow light.
   And what if I did leave? Leave everything I know here, and she didn't need me anymore? What if she met some other guy, some guy who talks all the time and wears the right clothes…someone who's actually in her league? What then?
   No, I can't do it. It's impossible.
   My phone rings in my pocket, and when I take it out, I see it's Dahlia. I turn the ringer off and put it on the seat. The light shines as the phone buzzes on the leather.
   No. I can't do it.

She knows I can't do it, and she's leaving anyway. What an idiot I was, to think someone like Dahlia could love me. That she would want to stay with me.

When I park and walk from the ramp to my apartment, I understand how Ramona felt. Maybe for the first time, I get it completely. The deepest sadness. Sadness that hurts your bones and your heart.

I get to my apartment, flick on the light, and looking around the gray-lit room realize fully how awful this is going to be. How totally, awfully lonely. It would have been better to never have met her. So I wouldn't feel like this right now. A text tone rings from Dahlia.

Call me. Please.

I type her back a message.

Please don't call me anymore. Don't text. I can't do this. It's over. I'm sorry.

CHAPTER NINETY-FIVE

DAHLIA

After his text last night, my fingers were on the phone to call Eli. I got halfway through his number, when I realized that I couldn't call him. And I couldn't call Shoshana or my parents, since I haven't even told them about James. So I called Daisy, who recommended "giving him time to come around."

Since I've been at work, it's been about an hour. One hour that I've given him to come around. I orange highlight Tabitha's newest railroad case.

"Did I tell you about the song?" Sylvia asks.

"No," I say, my hand getting tired from highlighting. "What song?"

"For the rehearsal dinner. They're putting together a song for me and Beau. Like a parody. Doesn't that sound hilarious?"

"Yeah, sure," I say, thinking that it sounds dreadful.

We get back to work and another hour drags by. "Beau's friend from Hawaii is coming," Sylvia says as though we were still talking about the wedding.

"That's nice," I say and text James. Daisy said give it some time. Maybe two hours would do. Break room?

"I have a friend coming from Jackson Hole, which is far away too. But Hawaii. That's, like, eight hours."

I wait an unbearably long time for no answer. "Fuck it," I say without meaning to and stand up.

"What?" Sylvia asks.

"Nothing. It's...not about you. Sorry. It's something else." I grab my phone and start walking. "Give him time." Daisy means well, but that's not how Dahlia works. Or James, for that matter. I walk down two flights of stairs and over to his cubicle. His chubby friend, I forget his name, glances up at me with a look of shock that's almost comical.

"Hi," I say.

James turns to me and blushes. "Hi," he mumbles.

"I need help with my computer," I announce. His boss glances over at us and tugs on his ridiculous mustache.

James doesn't look up from his computer. "Cooper, can you help her?"

"Sure, dude."

"No," I say. "I need you. You already know what's going on."

He refuses to look at me. "I'm sure I can fill Cooper in."

"James," his boss barks. "Go help her."

"Oh. Okay." He stands up with clear reluctance and we start walking off together.

"Let's take the stairs," I say, loud enough for them to hear, and we go into the stairwell. I stop and lean against the wall. "Don't do this."

He bites his lower lip, staring at the glossy cement floor. "I don't know any other way."

"I don't leave until August," I say. "We've got five months together in the meantime."

He moves a step away from me, shaking his head.

"Maybe you're not ready to move, okay. Maybe we're not ready for that anyway. Let's see where we are in a few months. Let's just see how it goes."

"Dahlia." His face is pained.

"Or let's just stay friends at least. If you don't want to keep dating, that's fine. But don't stop talking to me. Let's just be friends, like we were."

He stares down at his black shoes, then puts his hand on the doorknob. "I'm sorry. I can't. It hurts too much." He turns the knob with a click. "Don't do this again, okay? I just… I can't. That's all."

As he walks away, I don't call after him. It would be useless anyway. Obviously, it's over.

And I'm not going to beg.

CHAPTER NINETY-SIX

HAWK CLUB CHAT ROOM

Desiforever: Did you guys hear?

Joe25: Hear what?

Desiforever: Blake, he's in the ICU.

PorscheD: Seriously?

Desiforever: Seriously. Some guys beat him up really bad

Creoletransplant: Wow, that's terrible

Mollysdad: Yeah, is he okay?

Desiforever: He's in the fucking ICU. How okay could he be?

Mollysdad: No, I mean, is he going to die or something?

Desiforever: I talked to his wife. It was touch and go for a while. But they think he'll come out.

Joe25: That's too bad, man

Desiforever: Yeah, she said they had to reconstruct his face

Taxman: Shit. That's fucked up

Desiforever: Yeah, I know.

Mollysdad: Anyone know how the others are doing? Cary? Holts?

Desiforever: Still in prison, as far as I know. And Drew took the fuck off to Mexico.

PorscheD: Maybe we should all be thinking about that.

Desiforever: Maybe. Stevie-O said he wouldn't sweat it. But he also said we should stop talking to each other. Online anyway.

Mollysdad: For real?

Joe25: He's probably right

Creoletransplant: Drew kept this thing together anyway.

Desiforever: Yeah, so I wanted to let everyone know. I'm shutting down the server.

PorscheD: Okay, see you guys in jail, I guess.

Taxman: That isn't even funny, dude

PorscheD: Sorry, poor attempt at humor. I can't deal with goodbyes. *sob sob*

Joe25: Catch you at the next reunion

Creoletransplant: Yup.

Desiforever: Okay, pulling the plug guys

Mollysdad: One more thing. About reunion, did you guys ever—

Oops! Something went wrong. Please try again later or contact your administrator. Thanks!

CHAPTER NINETY-SEVEN

JAMES

Five Months Later
September

I thought about her today, because it's her anniversary next week.

That's a lie, really, because I think about her every day, anniversary or not. But I thought about her more today, if possible. Jamal said it's natural, being hurt and upset after a breakup. But I haven't told him the whole truth, that Dahlia didn't even want to break up. When she got to Stanford, she texted me. Not a pleading text, more matter-of-fact, here's my address, etc. Just opening the line of communication. But I never texted back.

Jezebel, my SPCA cat, leaps on my lap. Stroking her, I notice my arms are sore. I've been swimming a ton lately to feel better. It's not working.

Jezzie looks up at me with her adorable alien eyes, when the phone rings. I have this weird hope that it will be Dahlia, but it isn't. It's my mom. We haven't spoken in a while, just a brief, weird conversation on the Fourth of July. Usually, I automatically let it go to voicemail. But maybe because I'm feeling so down, I answer.

"Hi, Mom."

"Oh, I am so happy you answer the phone." Her words rush together. "It's about your father."

"What? Is he okay?" Jezebel must hear the worry in my voice because she jumps off me.

"Here, wait a second," she says.

There is a bit of a clamor on the other end, then my father's stern voice. "James?"

My grip tightens on the phone. "Yeah?"

"I wanted to tell you something." He sounds serious, like he's announcing that he's ill. "You were right," he says. "That's what I wanted to say." He clears his throat. "She wasn't null. At all. She wasn't."

I swallow. "Okay?"

"They both had a value." He pauses, and I hear his breathing. "It's just hard, James…because I miss them."

My grip lightens. "Yeah, I know."

"It's worse than null, they're not being here."

"I know," I say. "More like a negative value."

"Yeah, maybe," he answers.

I pause for a second. "I miss them too."

We don't say anything for a bit, then he starts again. "It's hard, but I shouldn't have taken it out on you. I love you, son, more than you will ever even know. So, that's all I wanted to say. That I'm sorry."

I swallow again and my throat is tight. "Thanks, Dad. I'm sorry too."

He lets out a breath. "You say hi to that nice girl of yours, okay?" He sounds relieved, happy to be finished with his task. He doesn't like to talk on the phone either, just like me.

"Yeah, um. Could you put Mom back on? Just for a second?"

He calls out her name, and I hear a scramble again as she gets on. "You guys make up?"

"Yeah. We're good."

"Good," she says. "Oh, I am so happy."

"I had one more question though…about Dahlia."

"Oh, Dahlia." Her voice brightens with the name. "Very nice girl."

"Yeah, I know," I mutter. "I kind of screwed things up…maybe."

"What happened?" She asks warily, like when I told her there was a little problem with the car when I was learning to park and took off the side mirror.

"It's kind of a long story." I lean my elbows on the desk and tell her the long story. I tell her everything, including the last time I saw her in the stairwell. After a while, she says, "Hmm." The *m* sound goes on for a long time. My mom always "hmms" when she's thinking.

"Do you love her?" she asks finally.

"Yes," I answer. "No doubt."

"Then you tell her." She waits another beat. "But you write her a real letter. No email."

"Email's fine, Mom."

"A letter, James. You write her a letter."

So I agree to do it, figuring she's probably right. She knows more about this kind of thing. After we hang up, I pull out my desk drawer and find the box of fancy stationery, a college graduation present that I never even opened. I pick out my favorite black pen that has just the right roller and dispenses just the right amount of ink. But then I'm stuck.

"Dear Dahlia" is easy enough. But then there are so many possibilities, an almost infinite number after that, and a very bright, white piece of stationery. Just saying *I love you* sounds too easy. Fake almost. I stare out the window for a bit at the leaves turning red down the block, and then I think of what I can say.

What I should have said in the first place, before she even left.

CHAPTER NINETY-EIGHT

DAHLIA

Another year, another anniversary.

This one wasn't too bad, all things considered. No seizures at least. It's amazing how much has changed in a year. Last September, I was going to S.O.S. with Eli.

Last year I met James.

Turning that thought off, I move on to the next page. The text on Civil Law is so dry, I can barely keep my eyes open. But, dry or not, I still have a test in two weeks. So, onward I plow.

I called Rae-Ann this morning, for some bolstering, and it helped. I told her everything going on in my life. The good and the bad.

The good: After the summer program, I got into Stanford Law School. And I don't have to worry about paying for it, because Connor is settling the case for nine million dollars.

The bad: Eli turned himself in and got six months. Six months' probation, that is, not jail. "Because he showed such remarkable remorse for the act," as per the judge. I think his remarkable remorse was more for being caught, but I wouldn't know for sure. Maybe he's with Brandon. Maybe he's still bartending. I couldn't say for sure, as I don't talk to him. And I don't plan on talking to him ever again.

But I do miss him, which is the deepest cut of all. He not only hurt me, he took away my best friend. I miss him, almost like a brother. Maybe the way James misses Ramona, but it's not the same. Because I can't think about Eli and smile anymore. All the good memories are tinged with bad now. And that will never change.

So I gave Rae-Ann the update, and she gave me kind words in return and sent me on my way. I haven't found a new therapist yet, though I'm going to need one eventually.

Most days I'm fine. More than fine even.

Classes are invigorating, fertilizer to my brain, which has been stultifying for the last five years. My study group is enlivening and accepting. It's California, I'm not the only one with tattoos and nose rings.

My phone signals a text, and a few annoyed stares fly my way. I mouth *Sorry* and check the phone.

Dinner later? Pizza? Sadie misses Aunt Dada.

It's Shoshana. I chuckle, picturing Sadie with her blond, curly, Shirley Temple hair who can't pronounce Dahlia yet. I answer yes with a pizza emoji. We are moving toward something, she and I. Now that I've gotten my own act together, I don't resent her so much. Maybe we'll be better friends someday, or at least better sisters.

Besides, it was never her fault anyway. It was never anyone's fault. Except the boys from the Hawk Club, including Steve from Miller and Stein, who was outed on one of the tapes and who fell precipitously from partnership track to defendant. Daisy told me the case was on the *Globe* front page for like a month. I even saw it on CNN right before we settled. And they are definitely closing up shop. That was part of the settlement. So there will be no more rape parties ever again.

My eyes droop at the next page. I decide it's time for a change of scene and shut the book. Packing up my things, I leave the library to a sunny but breezy day.

A bird loops from one tree to a next, chirping away, and I zip my windbreaker. The weather is a touch cool for September in Stanford, so I'm told. High sixties and breezy. It feels altogether different from Boston, where it's freezing one day and muggy the next this time of year. I'm starting to get used to it though. The first month, I felt unmoored, like when you walk outside and forget what season it is for a minute. I kept feeling like I'd been shuttled off to the wrong place.

But now I realize it's the right place.

And as I open the door to my apartment, that unfamiliar feeling weaves its way through me again: happiness. Simply put, I feel happy. Even on my anniversary, I can still feel this sensation.

And I'm beginning to understand that this could be a normal feeling, not such a surprising one. I've been living on high alert for so long, almost afraid of happiness. Because happiness is transient and can be snatched away too easily. Only fools would believe in that fairy-tale nonsense. Pretty girls.

But Pretty Girl is gone. And Dahlia is in law school, and she's doing just fine.

Opening the mail slot, I see the usual mess of bright-colored, attention-grabbing flyers. Neon green for the Stanford Environmental Law Club, pale blue for the Stanford Law Chess Club, and deep purple for the fourth year Domestic Violence Clinic. It seems I have traded support groups for clubs, which, all in all, seems like a healthy change.

Standing out from the mix is a bright-white envelope, printed with my address in boxy letters with a fireworks Forever Stamp, which is perfectly, squarely placed in the corner. No return address.

I carry the stack of mail upstairs, wave hello to my nice-but-boring married classmates/neighbors, and head into my apartment, undoing only one lock.

Simone slips through my legs, nearly tripping me, as I deposit the mail on the little kitchen table. She's still not quite used to her new abode and deviously lets me know by trying to kill me every once in a while. Sitting down at the table, I tear the envelope open to reveal a white stock card. On it is a carefully printed poem.

I love you.
I love everything about you.
I love your black eyebrows. I love the notch in your clavicle.
I love the way your voice is soft and brave at the same time.

I love the way you made me breathe differently, when we were together.
The way you made me scared and brave at the same time.
I'm sorry if I hurt you, because I would never want to hurt you.
I miss you.

James

Unexpectedly, tears are streaming down my face. Simone jumps on my lap and starts nosing the card, so I pull it away. Then she rubs her velvety, little head against my neck, trying her best to comfort me. I pet between her ears the way she likes, before wiping my eyes and putting down the card.

Then I pick up my phone, and I call him.

READING GROUP GUIDE

1. Do you think Dahlia was right to take revenge on her attackers? Did you feel bad for any of them? Do you think it helped her in the end?

2. Why do you think Dahlia's relationship with her sister was troubled? Her parents? Were you upset with her parents' reactions to what happened to her?

3. What was the impact of Dahlia's rape, not just on her, but on others? Do you think it had long-ranging effects?

4. Dahlia describes her depression during college in detail. Did you get a feel for what she was going through? Is this something you've had any personal experience with?

5. Could you relate to James and his view on the world? Did his voice ring true to you? Do you have any personal experience with autism?

6. Were you surprised by James's secret? Did it explain his motivation for helping Dahlia?

7. Did you empathize with James and his struggles? Could you see why he did not feel he could follow Dahlia to California?

8. Do you think Dahlia and James will end up together? Why or why not?

9. Did you relate to Dahlia and Eli's friendship? In the end, do you see Eli as a net positive influence on her life, or do his other actions negate that?

10. Did you empathize with Eli at all?

11. Does this book change the way you view the societal problem of sexual violence?

A CONVERSATION
WITH THE AUTHOR

This may be kind of a funny question, but is the novel based on a true story?

I'm sure many people may wonder about that, so I'll put it this way. Yes, it is based on a true story—just not *my* true story. Unfortunately, rape and sexual assault are all too common on college campuses. (*The Hunting Ground* is an excellent documentary on this.) Every time I thought my subject matter might become outdated or impertinent, sadly, another story would crop up in the news. And, this doesn't account for the untold number of cases that go unreported. I just felt this was a story that needed to be told.

Would you say *What Happened That Night* is a feminist book?

Absolutely, and I don't shy away from that term. It wasn't like I set out to write a feminist manifesto or something, but this idea has been rattling around in my head for some time. And the subject is not original. We've seen revenge stories about rape before but usually scripted by men as the vanquishers (i.e. *Deathwish*) or with women as vehicles for fancifully violent revenge (i.e. *Kill Bill*). I wanted this to be fully a woman's story instead.

Some might wonder why Dahlia didn't just go to the police as soon as she saw the video. What would you say to that?

It's a valid question, but I wonder how many people in her shoes would actually do that. Women know the justice system is flawed. From statute of limitations to victim blaming to overly light sentences for perpetrators, the system not only fails rape victims, but also often retraumatizes them. All Dahlia wants is justice, to put the men "in prison, where they belong," and feels she must work outside of the system to achieve this. Yet, she still maintains a code of conduct—to avoid physically harming anyone—so she doesn't lose her humanity in the process.

So, we've established that this is a revenge story. But it's also a love story, is it not?

Indeed! In fact, I pitched this as a "revenge-love story." There's a yin and yang at play throughout between the destructive force of the rape and her revenge, but also the positive, formative power of the love between her and James.

Speaking of the love story, let's move on to James's character. Obviously, we can all agree that he's handsome. Is there a reason that he's half-Japanese? Or that he has Asperger's? Were these conscious choices?

In terms of his race, he just came to me that way. That's how I pictured him from the beginning. But, his identity as a person of color (and mixed ethnicity) also made him feel like an outsider or "other," which is how Dahlia views herself.

As for the Asperger's, that aspect came later in the writing. At first, the book was only in Dahlia's voice. But, this felt too constrictive and "one-note" to me. So, I let James start talking and found his voice to be almost contradictory, with simple, even stilted verbiage and yet a brilliant complexity to his worldview. It made sense then that he had Asperger's.

We all know Dahlia's story right away. But James's story unfolds more slowly. Was there a reason for this, or for why you gave him that heavy secret to carry?

On one level, his secret is meant to be a "reveal" within the plotline, but it also informs his motivation to help Dahlia in her mission for justice, beyond just having a crush on her. His desire to get revenge for Dahlia stems from his guilt over not doing the same for his sister. But in the end, they save each other. They both have wounds, and both need each other to heal them.

As a reader, there were times that I almost empathized with the rapists and felt bad for what they were going through. Did you feel that way about the characters? Did you draw them that way intentionally?

That was intentional. First off, Dahlia is not a cold-blooded warrior. She struggles with what she is doing but still feels the need to do it. As she points out, these men are not monsters. They were all in the upper echelon of schooling and now society. The idea that all rapists are sociopaths is not only inaccurate, but also not helpful in solving the issue of sexual violence. This is a societal problem that isn't always black-and-white. People we love can do awful things. That's part of the reason for the final twist at the end, to drive that point home. Heroes can be villains too.

This story also revolves around the secrets of multiple characters. Would you agree?

Yes, secrets are an integral part of the book. Dahlia is the only one who is unflinchingly honest about what happened to her. She chooses whether to divulge her past based on the situation but is not ruled by fear of exposure. As Dahlia says, secrets are "like a black hole. They'll suck you up and spit you out." And she's right—Eli and James both hold secrets that nearly tear them apart.

Depression is a theme woven throughout Dahlia's flashbacks. At one point, she describes life as "quicksand," which she wants to escape. Your descriptions ring very true. Is this something you've personally dealt with?

I do have depression, and I'm very open about that because I think it's hugely important to remove the stigma of mental illness. Depression colored my college experience, and my roommates were an enormous source of support through that.

As doctors, we see patients with depression all the time. Unfortunately, this is also a case of "physician, heal thyself." We lose four hundred doctors (one medical school) yearly to suicide. And again, part of the problem is that doctors do not seek help due to the stigma.

ACKNOWLEDGMENTS

To Rachel Ekstrom. Thank you for being my endless cheerleader and champion.

To Shana Drehs, thank you for seeing something special in Dahlia and James, and helping me tell their story.

To the whole team at Sourcebooks: Margaret Johnston (who managed to make me giggle with her edits), Heather Hall, Bret Kehoe, Lathea Williams, Valerie Pierce, and Adrienne Krogh (what a cover!).

To the Tall Poppies, my band of sisters. May we continue to lift each other up.

To my PMG ladies (my other band of sisters): you are all, literally, the best.

To the women from Response, who helped me through so much.

To Lisa Scottoline, thank you for your beautiful, evergreen quote.

To Jim, Alla, Lexi, Jordie, Aunt Karen, and Uncle Sid—love you guys!

To Charlotte, we love you. May you thrive in college and beyond!

To Owen, you make us so proud...

To Grandma, thank you for helping us and being there for us. We couldn't do it without you!

Thank you to my parents. I cherish you and your unwavering support. Always.

To Patrick, who remains the best decision I ever made.

And last but not least, to my beautiful roomies (Maye, Becca, Kath, Nell, and Allison—in order of appearance). Thank you for always being there for me. I love you guys.

ABOUT THE AUTHOR

Photo © Brian Block

Sandra Block is an International Thriller Award finalist and the author of *Little Black Lies*, *The Girl Without a Name*, and *The Secret Room*. She graduated from Harvard, then returned to her native land of Buffalo, New York, for medical training and never left. She is a practicing neurologist and proud Sabres fan and lives at home with her husband, two children, and her cute but untrainable yellow lab, Delilah. Visit her at sandraablock.com.